THE CRITICS HAIL

The Innkeeper's Song

"A multifaceted fantasy told . . . in elegant yet simple prose."
—*Publishers Weekly*

"A gentle, romantic, lyrical tale . . . drawn so skillfully that Tolkien and C. S. Lewis come to mind."
—*Booklist*

"A finely crafted piece as well as a rich, evocative fantasy."
—*Library Journal*

"Admirable . . . stylish."
—*Kirkus Reviews*

"A rare and welcome event . . . a very satisfying journey."
—*Denver Post*

"Beagle surpasses [*The Last Unicorn*] with his new novel . . . a superbly crafted tale . . . a lyrical marvel."
—*South Bend Tribune*

"A tour de force . . . among the most memorable worlds in recent fantasy . . . the novel we've all been hoping Beagle would write."
—*Locus*

The Innkeeper's Song

a novel by

Peter S. Beagle

A ROC BOOK

ROC
Published by the Penguin Group
Penguin Books USA Inc., 375 Hudson Street, New York, New York 10014, U.S.A.
Penguin Books Ltd, 27 Wrights Lane, London W8 5TZ, England
Penguin Books Australia Ltd, Ringwood, Victoria, Australia
Penguin Books Canada Ltd, 10 Alcorn Avenue, Toronto, Ontario, Canada M4V 3B2
Penguin Books (N.Z.) Ltd, 182–190 Wairau Road, Auckland 10, New Zealand

Penguin Books Ltd, Registered Offices: Harmondsworth, Middlesex, England

First published by ROC, an imprint of Dutton Signet,
a division of Penguin Books USA Inc.
Previously published in a ROC hardcover edition.

First Mass Market Printing, October, 1994
10 9 8 7 6 5 4 3 2 1

The Library of Congress has cataloged the hardcover edition as follows:
Beagle, Peter S.
The innkeeper's song : a novel / by Peter S. Beagle,
p. cm.
ISBN 0-451-45288-7 [hc] — ISBN 0-451-45414-6 [pbk]
I. Title.
PS3552.E13I55 1993
813'.54—dc20 93–3800
CIP

Printed in the United States of America
Original hardcover design by Leonard Telesca

FOR PADMA HEJMADI
at last, and for always.

If we were simply friends,
colleagues sharing an art, a language,
a country sketched on restaurant tablecloths,
dayenu—it would have been enough—*dayenu*
But that we are truly married
is all I know of grace.

"There came three ladies at sundown:
one was as brown as bread is brown,
one was black, with a sailor's sway,
and one was pale as the moon by day.

The white one wore an emerald ring,
the brown led a fox on a silver string,
and the black one carried a rosewood cane
with a sword inside, for I saw it plain.

They took my own room, they barred the door,
they sang songs I never had heard before.
My cheese and mutton they did destroy,
and they called for wine, and the stable boy.

And once they quarreled and twice they cried—
Their laughter blazed through the countryside,
The ceiling shook and the plaster flew,
and the fox ate my pigeons, all but two.

They rode away with the morning sun,
the white like a queen, the black like a nun,
and the brown one singing with scarlet joy,
and I'll have to get a new stable boy."

The Innkeeper's Song

PROLOGUE

Once there was a village on a river in a southern country. The people who lived there grew corn and potatoes and a kind of blue-green cabbage, and a tawny climbing fruit that tasted better than it looked. All the roofs leaked in the rainy season—some more than others—and most of the children were lean, though the cows and pigs were not, but no one went very hungry in that village. There was a baker as well as a miller, which was a convenience, and just enough leisure time to inspire enough disagreement to produce two separate churches. And the bark of a certain tree, which grew only in that region, broke fevers when steeped into tea, and could be shaved and pounded to make a dye like green shadows.

In the village there were two children, a boy and a girl, born just hours apart, who grew up loving each other and were promised to marry in the spring of their eighteenth year. But the rains were long that year, and the spring was late in coming, and there was even ice on the river, which was a thing that only grandparents could recall. So when the warm weather came at last, the two lovers walked out on the little bridge below the mill, where they had not gone for almost half a year. The afternoon sun made them blink and shiver, and they talked about weaving, which was the boy's trade, and about who would not be invited to their wedding.

The girl fell into the river that day. The winter rains had rotted a long stretch of the railing where she leaned, laughing, and it crumpled under her weight and the water lunged up to her. She had time to catch her breath, but no time to scream.

Few in the village could swim, but the boy could. He was in the water before her head came to the surface, and for one moment her arm was around him, his face one last time pressed breathlessly against hers. Then a tumbling log took him away from her, and when he gained the shore she was gone. The river had swallowed her as easily as it had the little stones they had been skipping from the bridge, a life ago.

Every soul in the village turned out to hunt for her. The men took their dugouts and coracles and poled slowly back and forth across the river all that day, like sad dragonflies. The women toiled along both banks with fish nets, and all but the youngest children splashed in the shallows, chanting the rhymes all of them knew to make a drowned body float to shore. But they never found her, and when the night came they went back to their homes.

The boy stayed by the river, too numb with grieving to notice the cold, too blind with tears to know that it was too dark to see. He wept until there was nothing left of him but whimpers and twitches and a tiny, questioning sound that continued even after he finally fell asleep in the rough embrace of tree roots. He wanted to die, and indeed, weak and wet as a newborn in the night breeze, he might have had his wish before morning. But then the moon rose, and the singing began.

To this day in that village, old men and women whose greatest grandparents were warm in their cradles on that night will speak of that singing as though they themselves had wakened to the song. There was no one in the village who did not wake, no one who did not come wondering to the door—though few dared step beyond—but it is always said that each heard different music from a different quarter. The cobbler's son was the first to wake, by all accounts, dreamily certain that the hides of two marsh-goats his father had hung and scraped the day before were singing bitterly beautiful lullabies in the tanning shed. He shook the old man, who leaped up swearing that he heard the voices of his dead wife and his brother cursing him by turns like soldiers under his own window. On a hillside above the town, a shepherd roused, not to the roar of a charging *sheknath,* but to mocking airs of rebellion among his flock; the baker woke, not to a sound at all, but with a sweet aroma, such as his earthen ovens had never known, in his nostrils. The blacksmith, who never slept, thought he heard the terrible Moon Hunters coming for him on their pig-snouted horses, crying his name in the voices of hungry babies; while the weaver who was the young man's teacher dreamed a pattern she had never imagined before and walked, still sleeping, to her loom, where she wove until dawn, smiling with her eyes closed. It is also said that children too young to speak sat up in their cradles, crying out longingly in unknown tongues; that milkmaids and goosegirls hurried to meet the lovers they believed were calling them in the grape arbors, and that the silent marketplace was crowded with clumsy, grizzled badgers dancing round and round on their hind legs. Stars were seen on that night that have never been seen again, as everyone who was not there remembers.

And the boy? What about the boy, crying in his cold sleep by the river? Why, he came awake with his dead love's laughter teasing and soothing him, so near that his cheek was still warm with her breath when he sat up. And what he saw, as no one else was fool enough to see, was a black woman on a horse. The horse was standing in the river, up to its hocks in racing snow-water and not pleased about it, but the black woman held it motionless without effort. The boy was close enough to see that she was dressed as the fierce men of the southwestern hill country do, in shirt and leggings of rough leather, meant to surprise a sword with its stiff resistance. Yet she carried no weapon herself, save for a walking stick slung at her saddlebow. Her face was wide and high at the cheekbones, narrow at the chin, and her eyes were as golden as the moonlight on the water, and she was singing all by herself. That much is told of her; but what she truly sang, and what her true voice sounded like, even the folk of that village will never quite venture to say. Not the grown ones, at any rate; the children at their games still chant what they call *The Black Woman's Rhyme*, but they get smacked if their parents hear them. It runs so—

Dark to daylight, stone to sky,
caterpillar, butterfly,
sleeping, waking, buried, blind,
come and seek me, come and find . . .

Nonsense now, of course, but perhaps not nonsense then, for the boy watching saw the water where her horse stood grow flat and still as a midsummer frog-pond, with the moon floating like a great calm lily pad in that churning river. And presently out of that second moon his love rose up, dead and drowned and standing before the black woman with her hair dripping thickly and her wide blind eyes full of the river's darkness. The black woman never stopped singing, but she leaned down from the saddle, taking a ring from her forefinger and setting it on that of his dead love. And when she did that, the drowned girl's eyes came wondering awake, and the boy knew her and called to her. She never heeded, but held up her arms to the black woman, who lifted her up behind her onto the horse. The boy called and called—there is today, in that part of the country, a small brown-and-green bird with his name and a desperate nighttime cry that sounds almost like *"Lukassa! Lukassa!"*—but all that won him was a single long look from the black woman's golden eyes before she wheeled her horse toward the far side of the river. The boy tried to follow, but there was no strength in his body, and he fell before he even reached the water. When he could stand again, all that remained for him was a single green spark from the ring on his love's finger, and the distant voices of two women singing together. He fell a second time then, and lay so until dawn.

But he was not asleep, nor, after some while, weeping, and when the sun began to rise, bringing a little warmth back to his arms and legs, he sat up to wipe his muddy face and consider. If he was a child still, with a child's taste for hopeless, unbearable sorrow, yet he had also the stubborn cunning of a child in the teeth of hopelessness. Presently he rose and walked very slowly back to the village, and straight to the hut of the aunt and uncle with whom he had lived since the death of his parents and younger brother seven years before, when the plague-wind came. No one was awake; he bundled what belonged to him—a blanket, a best shirt, a second pair of shoes and a knife for cutting the little bread and cheese that he judged it fair to take. He was an honest boy, and a proud one as well, and he had never in his life taken more than his barest needs from anyone. His girl had teased him about it, called him stiff-necked, stubborn, even unkind—which he could never understand—but so he was made, and so, at eighteen years, he was.

Which made it all the more painful for him to steal the blacksmith's little chestnut mare, the best horse in the village. He left every coin he had been saving for his wedding in her stall, and a note, and walked her softly to the river road. He looked back once, in time to see smoke rising from the chimney under which the village's two priests lived in furious harmony. They always rose early, to have more time for quarreling, and their fire was always the first lighted. It was the last sight that boy on the stolen horse—his name was Tikat, by the way—ever had of his home.

The Stable Boy

I was the first to see them—perhaps the very first in this country. Marinesha would have been first, but she ran off into the woods while I was still trying to apologize. I never knew the right way to be with Marinesha. Perhaps there was none. I wonder if I would ever have learned.

Of course, I had no business on the road at that hour. It was late, past sunset, and time to bed down the horses. In justice to old Karsh, no one will ever be able to say that he treated an animal unkindly. I would leave the finest, most high-strung horse with him at any time, or a blind, useless, beloved dog, but not a child. My name, as far as I know, is Rosseth, which in our tongue means something not quite worthless, something thrown in to sweeten a bad bargain. Karsh named me.

Marinesha, now. Marinesha means *scent of the morning,* and I had followed that scent through both our chores all day, teasing and plaguing her—I admit it—until somehow she had half-agreed to meet me after milking by the bee tree. There are no bees there now—they all swarmed long ago—but Marinesha still calls it that. I found this as maddeningly touching as the way her hair goes back from her forehead.

Well, then. I swear I had no more than stroked that hair, not even uttered my first fumbling lie (in honesty, I had never expected her to come—she had never kept her word before) when she was gone again, skittering away through the trees like a moth, leaving nothing but her tears in my hands. I was angry at first, and then alarmed: there would be no way of slipping back to the inn before Karsh had noticed my absence, and while that fat man misses with most of his blows, the few that land land hard. So it was that I was still standing in the middle of the road, trying with all my weary wits to think of a story that, in the right mood, Karsh just might choose to believe, when I heard the three horses.

They came around the bend beyond the little spring where no one drinks, three women riding close together. One black, one brown like Marinesha (though not nearly as pretty) and one so pale that to call her "white" has no meaning. Lilies, corpses, ghosts—if these are white, then there must be another word for that woman's skin. It seemed to me, gaping in the road, that her color was the color of something inside her, some bright, fierce life thumping and burning away with no thought at all for her body, no care or pity for it at all. Her horse was afraid of her.

The black one was a little way in the lead. She drew rein in front of me and sat silent for a moment, considering me out of long, wide eyes. If you could make gold out of smoke, you would have something like the color of those eyes. For my part, I stood like a fool, unable even to close my slack jaws. I know now how different it is elsewhere, but in the country of my birth women do not ride out unescorted, however many they be. And Lal—I learned her full name later, though never how to say it properly—Lal was the first black woman I had ever seen. Black men, yes, often, as traveling merchants and now and than a poet, rhyming for bread in the marketplace, but never a woman. I believed, with most, that there were none.

"Sunlight on your road," I managed to greet her at last. My voice had changed some years before, but you could never have told it then.

"And on yours," the black woman answered. I say it in shame and honesty that my mouth fell open again to hear her speak my language. I would have been less astonished if she had barked or flapped her arms and screamed like a hawk. She said, "Boy, is there such a thing as an inn or a tavern in these parts?" Her own voice was low and rough, but even so the words rose and fell with the sound of small waves breaking.

"An inn," I mumbled, "oh, aye, you mean an inn." Lal said later that she was certain their prankish luck had brought them upon a natural, a wandering carrot. I said, "Aye, there's a such—I mean, there's an inn. I mean, I work there. Stable hand, Rosseth. My name." My tongue felt like a horse-blanket in my mouth, and I bit it twice getting all those words out.

"There would be a place? For us?" She pointed at her companions and then herself, still talking carefully to an idiot.

"Yes," I said, "oh, yes, certainly. Plenty of rooms, business is a little slow just now"—Karsh would have killed me—"plenty of empty stalls, hot mash." Then I saw the brown woman's saddlebag ripple and lurch and twitch open at one corner, exactly like my poor idiot mouth, and I said *hot mash* again, several times.

The sharp, grinning muzzle first, black nose reading the wind; then the red-brown mask and the crisp arrowhead ears. Throat and chest white gold, shoulders—for he came out of the bag no further just then—darker than the mask, the play of muscles casting small shadows all through his fur. I have seen many foxes, most of them dead in snares, or about to be, but never a fox that rode in a saddlebag like a gamecock or a hunting *shukri*; and certainly never a fox that looked back at me as though it knew my name, my real name, the one I don't know. I said, "Karsh. The patron. My master. Karsh won't."

"We will see how slow business is," the black woman said. She gestured for me to mount behind one or the other of her companions, then smiled to see me stand flat-footed, frightened now for the first time and hot with shame to be so. But I was not sharing any saddle with any fox, and it was beyond me to take the least step toward that white, burning woman. Lal's smile widened, making the corners of her eyes tilt up. "With me, then," she said, and I scrambled to join her, clinging as though I had never been on a horse before. Her leather garments smelled of weariness and the sea, but under that smell was Lal's own. I said, "Three miles to the crossroad and a mile west," and I forgot Marinesha for the rest of that day.

THE INNKEEPER

My name is Karsh. I am not a bad man.

I am not a particularly good one, either, though honest enough in my trade. Nor am I at all brave—if I were, I would be some kind of soldier or sailor. And if I could write even such a song as that nonsense about those three women which someone has put my name to, why, then I would *be* a songwriter, a bard, since I would certainly be fit for nothing else. But what I am fit for is what I am, everything I am. Karsh the innkeeper. Fat Karsh.

They talk foolishness about me now, since those women were here. Since that song. Now I am all mystery, a man from nowhere; now I am indeed supposed to have been a soldier, to have traveled the world, seen terrible things, done terrible things, changed my name and my life to hide from my past. Foolishness. I am Karsh the innkeeper, like my father, like his father, and the only other country I have ever seen is the farmland around Sharan-Zek, where I was born. But I have lived here for almost forty years, and run The Gaff and Slasher for thirty, and they know that, every one of them. Foolishness.

The boy brought those women here to devil me, of course, or else simply to make me overlook his slipping off after that butterfly-brained Marinesha. He can smell strangeness—has that from me, at least—he knew those three were not what they seemed, and that I want no part of any such folk, no matter how well they pay. Mischief enough with the usual lot of drunken farmers on their way to Limsatty Fair. All he had to do was direct them to the convent seven or eight miles east: the Shadowsisters, as we call them. But no, no, he must needs bring them to *my* door, fox and all. Fox and all. That bloody fox is in the song, too.

When they rode into my courtyard, I came out—I'd been polishing glass and crockery myself, since there's no one else to trust with it around this place—took one good look at them and said, "We're full up, stables, everything, sorry." As I told you, I am neither brave nor greedy, merely a man who has kept house for strangers all his life.

The black one smiled at me. She said, "I an told otherwise." I have heard such an accent before, very long ago, and there are two oceans between my door and the country where people speak like that. The boy slid down from her saddle, keeping the horse between us, as well he might. The black woman said, "We need only one room. We have money."

I did not doubt that, journey-fouled and frayed as all three of them looked—any innkeeper worth his living knows such things without thinking, as he knows trouble when it comes asking to sleep under his roof and eat his mutton. Besides, the boy had made a liar of me, and I am a stubborn man. I said, "We have some empty rooms, yes, but they are unfit for you, the rains got into the walls last winter. Try the convent, or go on into town, you'll have your choice of a dozen inns." Whatever you think of me, hearing this, I was right to lie, and I would do it again.

But I would do it better a second time. The black woman still smiled, but her hands, as though twitching nervously, fidgeted at the long cane she carried across her saddle. Rosewood, very handsome, we make nothing like that in this country. The curved handle twisted a quarter-turn, and a quarter-inch of steel winked cheerfully at me. She never glanced down, saying only, "We will take whatever you have."

Aye, and didn't that prove true enough, though? The swordcane was the end of the matter, of course, but I tried once again; to save my honesty, in a way, though you won't understand that. "The stables wouldn't suit a *sheknath*," I told her. "Leaky roof, damp straw. I'd be ashamed to put horses as fine as yours in those stalls."

I cannot recall her answer—not that it makes the least difference—first, because I was looking hard at that boy, daring him to say other and second, because in the next moment the fox had wriggled out of the brown woman's saddlebag, leaped to the ground and was on his way due north with a setting hen by the neck. I roared, imbecile dogs and servants came running, the boy gave chase as hotly as if he hadn't personally brought that animal here to kill my chicken, and for the next few moments there was a great deal of useless dust and clamor raised in the courtyard. The white woman's horse almost threw her, I remember that.

The boy had the stomach to come sneaking back, I'll say that much for him. The brown woman said, "I am sorry about the hen. I will pay you." Her voice was lighter than the black woman's, smoother, with a glide and a sidestep to it. South-country, but not born there. I said, "You're right about that. That was a young hen, worth twenty coppers in any market." Too much by a third, but you have to do that, or they won't respect a thing you own. Besides, I thought I saw a way out of this whole stupid business. I told her, "If I see that fox again, I'll kill it. I don't care if it's a pet, so was my hen." Well, Marinesha was fond of it, at least. They suited each other nicely, those two.

The brown woman looked flustered and angry, and I was hopeful that they might just throw those twenty coppers in my face and ride on, taking their dangers with them. But the black one said, still toying with that sword-cane without once looking at it, "You will not see it again, I promise you that. Now we would like to see our room."

So there was nothing for it, after all. The boy led their horses away, and Gatti Jinni—Gatti Milk-Eye, the children call him that—my porter, he took in what baggage they had, and I led them to the second-floor room that I mainly keep for tanners and fur traders. I already knew I wouldn't get away with it, and as soon as the black one raised an eyebrow I took them on to the room where what's-her-name from Tazinara practiced her trade for a season. Contrast, you see; most people jump at it after that other one. Swear on your gods that *you* practice no such sleights, and that dinner's a gift, fair enough?

Well, the black woman and the brown looked around the room and then looked at me, but what they had it in mind to say, I never knew, because by then the white one was at me—and I mean *at* me, you understand, like that fox after the broody hen. She hadn't said a word since the three of them arrived, except to quiet that jumpy horse of hers. Up until then, I could have told you nothing about her but that she wore an emerald ring and sat her saddle as though she were far more used to riding bareback on a plowhorse. But now, *quicker* than that fox—at least I saw the fox move—she was a foot away from me, whispering like fire, saying, "There is death in this room, death and madness and death again. How dare you bring us here to sleep?" Her eyes were earth-brown, plain peasant eyes like my mother's, like most of the eyes I ever saw. Very strange they always looked to me, that pale, pale face burning around them.

Mad as a *durli* in the whistling time, of course. I won't say that I was frightened of her, exactly, but I certainly *was* afraid of what she knew and how she knew it. The Gaff and Slasher had a bad name before I bought it, just because of a killing in that same room—and another in the wine cellar, for the matter of that. And yes, there was some bad business when the woman from Tazinara had the room. One of her customers, a young soldier it was, went lunatic—came there lunatic, if you ask me—and tried to murder her with a crossbow. Missed her at point-blank range, jumped out the window and broke his idiot neck. Yes, of course, you know the story, like everyone else in three districts—how else could fat Karsh have bought the place so cheaply?—but this pale child's voice came from the south, maybe Grannach Harbor, maybe not, and in any case she could not possibly have known which room it was. She could not have known the room.

"That was long ago," I said back to her, "and the entire inn has been shriven and cleansed and shriven again since then." Nor did I say it as obsequiously as I might have, thinking about the cost of those whining, shrilling priests. Took me a good two years to get the stink of all their rackety little gods out of the drapes and bedsheets. And if I had had the sense of a bedbug, I could likely have gotten rid of those women then, standing on my indignation and injury—but no, I said I was a stubborn man and it takes me in strange ways sometimes. I told them, "You can have my own room, if it pleases you. I can see that you are ladies accustomed to the best any lodging-house has to offer, and will not mind the higher price. I will sleep here, as I have often done before."

Silly spite, that last—I dislike the room myself, and would sooner sleep with the potatoes or the firewood. But there, that is what I said. The white one might have spoken again, but the brown woman touched her arm gently, and the black woman said, "That will do, I am sure." When I looked past her, I saw the boy in the doorway, gaping like a baby bird. I threw a candlestick at him—caught him, too—and chased him down the stairs.

TIKAT

On the ninth day, I began to starve.

I had taken far too little food with me. How could I not have, sure as I was of catching up by first sunset and making that black woman give me back my Lukassa? Amazed I am to this day that I even thought to bring a blanket for the chill when we would be riding so happily home together. *As long as she lay in the water, she will be frozen to her poor heart.* That is all I was thinking, all, for nine days.

And of course I know now that it would have made no difference if I had stopped to steal a dozen horses—as though there were that many in the village—and load them to backbreak with food and water and clothing. For I never caught up with those two women, never drew within half a day's ride, though my mare broke her own brave heart in trying. They were never closer than the horizon, never larger than my thumb, never any more solid than the chimney smoke from the towns they skirted. Now and then I crossed the remains of a campfire—carefully scattered—so they must have slept sometimes; but whether I rested or galloped all night, they were always far beyond my sight come dawn, and not before midday would I catch the least movement on the side of the furthest hill, the twitch of a shadow among stones so distant that they looked like water across the road. I have never been so lonely.

There's this about starving, though, it takes your mind off things like loneliness and sorrow. It hurts very much at first, but soon you start to dream, and those are kind dreams, perhaps the sweetest I ever had. They weren't always about food and drink, either, as you'd suppose: most often I was old and home with my girl, children close and my arm so tight around her when the bridge railing broke that she still bore the mark, all those years later. I dreamed about my father, too, and my teacher, who was *his* teacher, and I dreamed I was little, sitting in a pile of sawdust and wood shavings, playing with a dead mouse. They were very dear dreams, all of them, and I tried harder and harder not to wake.

I don't remember when I first noticed the tracks of the second horse. The ground was hard and stony, and growing worse, and I often went a day or longer finding nothing but a hoofscratch or two on a displaced pebble. But it must have been some little time after the dreams began, because I laughed and cried with pleasure to think that Lukassa would at last have a horse of her own to ride. When we were children, she made me promise one day to buy her a real lady's horse, none of your plough-beasts that might as well be oxen, but some dainty, dancy creature, as far beyond my reach then as now, and likely as useless in our life together as bangles on a hog. But I swore my word to her—so small a request it seemed, when she could have had my eyes for the asking. Seven we were, or eight, and I loved her even then.

If I had been in my right mind, surely I would have wondered where that second horse had come from in this empty country, and whether it truly bore Lukassa or another. A woman who had sung my girl up from the river bottom could summon a horse as easily, like enough; but why now, as far as they had come on the one, and tireless as he plainly was? But by then I was walking as much as riding, hanging on my mare's sagging neck, pleading with her not to die, to live only a little longer, half a day, half a mile. You couldn't have told which of us was dragging the other, and I couldn't have told you, for I was swimming in the air, laughing at jokes the stones told me. Sometimes there were animals—great pale snakes, children with birds' faces—sometimes not. Sometimes, when the black woman was not looking, Lukassa rode on my shoulders.

On the eleventh day, or the twelfth, or perhaps the fifteenth, my mare died under me. I felt her die, and managed to sprawl clear to keep from being crushed by her bones. If I had been strong enough to bury her, I would have done it; as it was, I tried to eat her, but I lacked even the strength to cut through her hide. So I thanked her, and asked her forgiveness, and the first bird that laid claw on her I fell on and strangled. It tasted like bloody dust, but I sat there beside her, chewing and growling in full sight of the other birds. They left her alone for a while, even after I walked away.

The bird sustained me for two more days, and cleared my mind enough at least to realize where I must be. The Northern Barrens, no desert, but almost as bad. As far as you can see, the land is broken to pieces, everything smashed or split or standing on edge. Here's a toss of boulders blocking the way, the smallest bulking higher than a man on horseback; here's a riverbed so long dry there are wrinkled little trees growing up out of it; there, all that tumble and ruin might have been a mountain once, before great claws ripped it down. No road, never so much as a cart track—if you have all your wits about you, you pick your way across this country, praying to the gods' gods not to break a leg or fall in a hole forever. Starving mad like me, you stagger along singing, peaceful and fearless. I dreamed my death, and it kept me safe.

There was an old man in one of those dreams. He had bright gray eyes and a white mustache, curling into his mouth at the corners, and he wore a faded scarlet coat that might have been a soldier's. In my dream he came galloping on a black horse, crouched so far forward that his cheek lay almost against the horse's cheek, and I could hear him whispering to it. For a moment, as they flashed by me, the old man looked straight into my face. In his eyes I saw such laughter as I never expect to see again while I live. It woke me, that laughter, it brought me back to the pain of being about to die alone in the Barrens, without Lukassa, and I fell down weeping and screaming after that old man until I slept again, truly slept, on all fours like a baby. I dreamed that other horses passed, with great hounds riding them.

When I wakened, the sun was dropping low, the sky turning thick and soft, and the least breeze rising. The sleep and the hope of rain made me feel stronger, and I went on until I came to a place where the ground sloped down and in on all sides: not a valley, just a stony dimple with a stagnant pool at the bottom. They were down there, the hounds, and they had taken prey.

There were four of them, Mildasis by their daggers and their short hair. I had only seen Mildasis twice before—they come south but seldom, which is good. They had the old man in the scarlet coat between them and were buffeting him round and round, knocking him savagely from one to the other until his eyes rolled up in his head and he could not stand. Then they kicked him back and forth, like the ragged ball he rolled himself into, all the while cursing him and telling him there were worse pains waiting for a man insanely foolish enough to steal a Mildasi horse. Not that I know two words of Mildasi, but their gestures made things quite clear. The horse in question stood loose nearby, reins hanging, pawing for thistles among the stones. It was a shaggy little black, almost a pony, the kind the Mildasis say they have been breeding for a thousand years. They eat whatever grows, and keep running.

The Mildasis did not see me. I stood behind a rock, bracing myself against it, trying to think. I was sorry for the old man, but my pity seemed as quiet and faraway as all the rest of my feelings, even the hunger, even the understanding that I was dying. But my horse was already dead, and there were the four other Mildasi horses, waiting untethered like the black, and I did know that I needed one of those, because there was a place I had to go. I could not remember the place, or why I had to be there, but it was very important, more important than starving. So I made the best plan I could, watching the Mildasis and the old man and the setting sun.

I know about the Mildasis what everybody knows—that they roam and raid out of the barren lands, never surrender, and value their horses more than themselves—and perhaps one thing more, which my uncle Vyan told me. He had traveled with caravans when he was young, and he said that the Mildasis were a religious people in their way. They believe that the sun is a god, and they do not trust him to return every morning without a bribe of blood. Usually they sacrifice one of the beasts they raise for that purpose, but the god likes human blood much better, and they give it to him when they can. If my uncle was right, they would kill the old man just as the sun touched the furthest hills. I moved around the rock slowly, like a shadow stretching in the sun.

The horses watched me, but they made no sound, even when I was very close to them. I am not wise with horses, like some—I think it was my madness that made them take me for a friend, a cousin. Uncle Vyan said that Mildasi horses were more like dogs, loyal and sometimes fierce, not easy to frighten. I wanted to pray that he was wrong about that, but I had no room for prayer. The Mildasis had their backs to me, making ready for the sacrifice. They were not beating the old man anymore, or even mocking him—they seemed as serious as either of the priests in our village when they blessed a baby or begged for rain. First they smeared his cheeks with something yellow, then made marks in it with their fingers, so carefully. They made his mouth black with something else.

He stood quite still, not speaking, not struggling. One of the Mildasis was singing, a high, scraping song that quavered as though he were the one about to be killed. The same few notes, over and over. When he stopped singing, there was no more than a breath of wind between the sun and the hilltops.

The Mildasi who sang took a long knife from another one. He showed it to the old man, making him study it, pointing at the blade, handle, the blade again, like my teacher trying to make me understand the real life of a pattern. I would know that knife if I ever saw it again.

The horse I had chosen hours, days ago was gray, like a rabbit. He let me touch him. The Mildasi began to sing again, and I was up on the gray horse, shouting and waving my arms to terrify the others. They looked surprised, a little disappointed in me; they danced on their hind legs and glanced toward their masters, who were only now turning, gaping, as silently astonished as the horses, but two with their throwing axes already out. The Mildasis can bring down nightbirds with those, my uncle Vyan says.

It was the black horse who suddenly decided to be frightened, to rear and scream and bolt, knocking down the singing Mildasi and trampling the knife-man, who rushed in to help him. The two others jumped for the reins, but the black dashed past them, heading for the comfort of its friends. But now they caught the panic themselves, as though it were a torch bound to the black, setting their tails afire. My gray—the Rabbit, as I called him from that day—went up in the air, all four feet off the ground, and came down out of my control, running straight back toward the two Mildasis who barred the way, axes whirling red in their hands. I flattened myself along the Rabbit's back, clutching him as I had held Lukassa in the river. I could not see the old man.

One axe sighed past my nose, taking nothing with it but a hank of gray mane. The second I never saw at all, but the poor Rabbit yelled to break your heart and shot away in a different course, as rabbits will do. The tip of his right ear was gone, blood spraying back on my hands.

I looked back once, in time to see all four Mildasis—two of them limping—scrambling madly after their horses, and those in no hurry at all to be sane and obedient ever again. Then, with my head still turned, a hand on the saddle, a hand in my belt, a grunt and a wheeze and me almost spilled to the ground, and the old man was up behind me, laughing like the wind. "Ride, boy," he barked in my ear, "ride now!" and I felt him turn to shout back at the Mildasis, "Fools, imbecile children, to think you could kill *me*! Because I chose to play with you a while, to think you had me—" The Rabbit flew over a narrow ravine then, and the old man yelped and clung to me, never finished his brag, which suited me just as well. If he would only be silent, perhaps I could pretend that he was not really there.

But he would not hush, not for five minutes together. When he was not prattling about the stupidity of the Mildasis and praising himself for escaping them, he was urging me to press the Rabbit harder, to put more distance between ourselves and our pursuers. I did not want to talk to him. I muttered that it was dark, that we had to go carefully, but he scoffed shrilly, "They have eyes in their feet, these Mildasi beasts, he will travel all night without stumbling once. As will *they*." His voice hurt my head, and whatever his talk, he smelled of fear.

The Mildasis never caught us. I cannot say if they even followed, since I was paying no attention at all to signs, nor to the old man's yapping, nor to anything but the trick of staying in the saddle and the harder trick of remembering the reason for it. We might be still on the track of Lukassa and the black woman; we might as likely have been circling back the way I had come. I was at the end of sense, the end of everything but hanging on. There was nothing to think about past hanging on.

The old man saved me, no arguing that. It was he who held me when I slept and toppled sideways, and it was he who guided the Rabbit across those smashed lands all night, surely chattering in my ear the whole time, not caring if I heard or no. I remember nothing of that night, no dreams, nothing, until I woke on a hard hillside, wrapped in the old man's scarlet coat, with the high sun blinding me and the Rabbit nudging to get at some prickly sprigs under my arm. The old man was gone.

There was a waterskin slung to the Rabbit's neck, and I drank from it, not too much. I was very weak, but I think not mad anymore. The morning sky was pale, almost white, and the air smelled of distant snow, a breath from beyond the mountains. I leaned against the Rabbit, looking far across the Barrens where birds like the one I had eaten were circling, sliding downwind, and I said to my little gray horse, "I will not die. There is water in this land, and I will find it—there is game to hunt and roots to dig, or the Mildasis could not live here. I will not die. I will follow Lukassa over the mountains and wherever more I have to go, until I speak with her and touch her again. And if she will not come home with me—well, *then* I will die, but not till then." The Rabbit nibbled on my ragged sleeve.

He winded the fox before I did; not until he whinnied and shook his head to make his ears snap did I see it trotting boldly up the hillside toward us, a bird half its size dangling limp in his jaws. A small fox, but burly and handsome, with bright, bright eyes. It waited deliberately for me to make sure of it before it changed.

A sway in the air, no more, the way you can see it shiver above a flame, and it was the old man there, holding out the bird as he came up to me. The Rabbit stamped and snorted and ran off a little way, but I was too tired to be frightened. I said, "A man who can turn into a fox. A fox that can turn into a man. Which are you?"

His thick white mustache softened the fox's pointed grin. "The bird can turn into us. That's what matters." As jaunty as though he had never been helpless in the hands of the Mildasis, beaten bloody, listening to his death song, he dropped down beside me and began plucking feathers. The sacrifice paint on his face was gone, and the bruises on his pink cheekbones were already fading. He kept on smiling at me as he worked, and I kept on staring at him.

"If you're expecting me to drip my tongue out and pant," he said gently enough, "I don't do that. Nor will I eat this bird whole and raw, crunching the bones. In this shape, I am a man like you."

I laughed then, though the effort almost put me on my back. I told him, "A man like me has opened as many bellies with his teeth as any fox." Which was not true, but I felt it so then. The old man answered me, "Well, then perhaps you might be pleased to start a fire for us, since men cook their food when they can." He took flint and steel out of a leather scrip at his waist and handed them to me.

There was dead wood—an armload, no more—within easy reach, or I could never have gathered even that much. Merely breaking up the kindling twigs took me so long that the old man had the bird cleaned, neat as you please, by the time I had the fire going. Hardly enough heat to cook it through, but we managed, and we dined together like men, though the very last of my strength went to keep me from gobbling my half-bird half-cooked, and after that his, too. For his part, he chatted along blithely, getting my name from me—though never offering his own—and telling me that he was companion to a great lady from a far shore. I asked if she were black, but he shook his head. "Brown, if you will, but certainly not black. She is called Nyateneri, and she is very wise."

"And you stole the Mildasi horse for her," I said. "My soul, I wish I had such a loyal and valiant servant."

That provoked him, as I thought it might. "We are comrades, equals, make good note of that. My lady sends me on no errands—I come and go on my own affairs, exactly as I choose." For a moment he was truly angry, gray eyes gone almost yellow with it. "I do not serve."

"What need of a horse, then, for one who can travel on

four feet as he chooses?" I hoped to make him careless in his anger, but he was already on guard again, laughing at me, lolling tongue between teeth on purpose. "That was only my sport with the stupid Mildasis. Should it surprise you that my idea of play is not yours?"

"They beat you half to death," I said, "and would have cut your throat, but for me. What kind of sport is that?"

"I was never in danger," he answered me, haughty as a man may be with his mouth full and greasy. "Your diversion was well enough, but completely unnecessary. It was my play."

I said, "They would have killed you. I saved your life." For once he did not speak, but only turned his head, watching me out of the sides of his eyes. "Man or fox, you are in my debt," I said. "You know you are in my debt."

His mustache truly bristled, and he licked it down again. "Why, so are you in mine, boy, with my food and water in your belly. If you saved me indeed, you did it by chance—and well *you* know *that*—but I chose to help you, when I could have left you to get on about your business of dying. I hunt for no one, but I hunted for you, and so we are well quits in your world and mine." And he would say nothing further until we had finished the bird and buried the scraps, to leave no trace for the Mildasis.

"If you want to wash your face and paws," I said then, "I could look away." I yawned as I spoke, because the good meal made me want to sleep immediately. The old man sat back with his arms around his knees, considering me long and long after that, not moving at all. Kind and cozy as a grandfather he looked, but I felt the way that bird must have felt in the last seconds, seeing him too late.

"You'll never catch them, you know. Not on a Mildasi horse, not on any other. And if you did, you would dearly wish you hadn't."

I did not ask whom he meant, or how he knew. I said,

"The black woman is a great wizard, surely, for my Lukassa was drowned and she brought her back to life. And whatever terrible things she can do to me, she will have to do, and do them all twice over to make sure of me. For I will find her, and I will bring Lukassa home again."

"Boys' talk," he answered contemptuously. "The woman's no more magical than you are, but what she does not know about flight and following, about tracking and covering tracks, about sending the hounds howling off after their own smell, even I do not know. And now my lady Nyateneri has joined her—yes, as you guessed—and between the pair of them, a poor fox can only chew his paws and pray not to be too corrupted by their subtlety. Give over, boy, go home."

"Fox talk," I said in my turn, praying myself not to be convinced. "Tell your mistress, tell them both that Lukassa's man is coming after her." I swung myself up on the Rabbit's back and sat still, glaring down at the old man as fiercely as I could, though I could hardly see him for the sudden giddiness that took me. "You tell them," I said.

The old man never moved. He licked his mustache and licked it, and each time his smile slid a little wider. He said, "What will you give me if I leave you a trail to follow?"

The yellow-gray eyes and barking voice were so mocking that I could not believe what I had heard. "What will you give me? You're still too near death for vanity—you *know* you've lost their track forever unless I help you. Give me that locket you wear on your neck. It's cheap, it's no loss to you, but I help no one without pay. The locket will do."

"Lukassa gave it to me," I said. "For my name-day, when I was thirteen."

The old man's teeth glittered in his mouth like ice. "Do you hear, Lukassa? Your swineherd sweetheart prefers your bauble to you. Joy of it, then, boy, and good luck." He was on his feet, turning away.

I threw the locket at him then, and he whisked it out of the air without looking back at me. He said, "Get down, you are in no case to travel yet. Sleep out the day there"—he pointed, still not turning, to a rocky overhang where I could lie shadowed—"and start north at moonrise, keeping those hills on your left. There is no road. There will be a trail."

"A trail to where?" I demanded. "Where are they bound, and why are they taking Lukassa with them?" The old man began to walk away down the slope, leaving me infuriated. I slipped from the Rabbit's saddle and ran after him, reaching for his shoulder, but he wheeled swiftly, and I did not touch him. I said, "What about yourself, tell me that at least. That's not north, the way you're going."

Pink cheeks, white mustache, hair as wicked-white as the water that took my girl, he grinned until his eyes stretched shut to see me afraid of him. Even his whisper was harsh. "Why, I'm off after that black horse, where else?" And he was the fox again, loping off without a glance or farewell, brushy tail swaggering high as a housecat's until he thought himself out of my sight. But I watched him a long way, and I knew when that tail came down.

LAL

The dreams began again as soon as I gave my ring to that girl. I knew they would, but there was nothing for it, because of the other dream, the one *my friend* sent. Drowned white, crying out with all the unused strength of her unlived life, calling so desperately from the riverbed that even my skin hurt with it, miles distant, even the soles of my feet. She was still alive when that dream came to me, three nights before.

But that was not one of the bad dreams, that is only the way *my friend* talks to me, as he has done for all the years since I first knew him. The bad dreams are older, far older and come from another place; the bad dreams are the way I bleed—I, Lal, Lalkhamsin-khamsolal, sleek and lean and fearless, Sailor Lal, Swordcane Lal, Lal-Alone, prowling the seas and alleys of the world for her own mysterious delight. Lal who wept and screamed in the night, every night from the time she was twelve years old, until *my friend* gave her that emerald ring that a dead queen gave him.

"You have dreamed enough," he told me, the smile hiding in his braided beard like a small wild animal. "There will be no more dreams, no dreams, I promise, not unless I send them, as I may. Keep the ring until you meet one whose need is greater than your own. You will know that one when the time comes, and after that you will need my ring no longer. I promise you this, *chamata*." That was always his name for me, from the first, and I still have not the least idea of its meaning.

Well, he was wrong, wise as he is, wrong about me, not the ring. Every one of those old terrors had been laired up in wait for the moment when I handed it on; every last one of them came hopping and hissing and grinning to crouch on my heart, even before I closed my eyes when I finally had to sleep. Jaejian, with his mouth like a hot mudhole, Jaejian and his nameless friend, and me not three hours stolen from my home. Shavak. Daradara, who killed him, and what she did to me in his blood. Loum, that little boy, I could not have helped him, I could not have helped, I was little too. Unavavia, with his striped nightgowns and his knives. Edkilos, who pretended to be kind.

Bismaya, who sold me.

I am not a queen, nor ever claimed to be one, though the story follows me. I was raised from birth to be somewhat less and something much more than a queen: a storyteller, a chronicler, a rememberer. The word we use is *inbarati*, and in my family the oldest daughter has been the Inbarati of Khaidun since the word and the city have existed. By the time I was nine years old, I could sing the history of every family in Khaidun, both in the formal language I was taught and in the market speech my teachers whipped me for using. I could still—if I ever spoke either tongue anymore—along with every battle song, every beast-tale, every version of the founding of our city and the floods and droughts and plagues we survived. Not to mention every legend imaginable of great loves and magical, terrible lovers, forever testing each other's faithfulness. My people are extremely romantic.

Bismaya. Cousin, playmate, dearest friend. Dead in childbirth before I could kill her, not for arranging to have me stolen and sold, but because she did it out of a child's boredom. If we had loved the same boy, quarreled once too often over my bullying ways (and I *did* bully Bismaya, it was impossible not to), if it had even been that she wanted to be Inbarati in my stead—well, I doubt I could yet forgive her, but at least there would be something to forgive. But she betrayed me out of a vague need for excitement, and for enough money to buy a pet bird. I dream of Bismaya more than any of the others.

But I know a way of dealing with dreams, a way that I taught myself before ever I met *my friend*, because, though I wanted so to die, I refused to go mad. There is a story that I tell myself in the night, an old Khaidun waterfront tale of a boatwoman who knew the talk of fish and could call them where she chose or, with a word, empty the harbor of everything but children diving for coins. This gift made her much courted, though not popular, and her many adventures will usually see me from moonrise to moonset in something like peace. If I am yet awake, I know an endless praise-song for a king, full of heroes, victories, and feasts enough to guard me until dawn. The ring was better, the ring let me sleep truly, but this other is an old friend, too.

The girl slept like the dead she was those first nights, while I lay watching the low, prowling stars of this country and listening with all of myself for *my friend* to call a third time. The first dream had wrenched me out of a lover's bed—which, in this case, was probably just as well—but the second woke me in sick convulsions, vomiting with another's pain, feverish with another's fear. There was a rage of despair in it such as I—who thought I understood helplessness as well as any—have never known. Nor could I imagine a magus powerful enough to crumble great ships of war into the sea like biscuits in soup (and kind enough to send dolphins to bear the sailors home) so desperate as to cry out for the aid of an escaped never-mind-what whom he found hiding naked under a fish-basket on the wharf at Lameddin. But he *had* called, and I was in the saddle within half an hour and on my unprepared way into an alien land. There are those to whom I owe my life, as others owe me theirs—this one gave me back my soul.

The third dream came to me in the Barrens, on the night that we ran out of road. Lukassa—I had her name from that boy's crying after her—was as much herself as she could be by then: a pretty, gentle, ignorant village girl who had never been anywhere in her life, except dead. She had no memory of that, nor of much else before—neither name, family nor friends, nor that idiot boy still blundering after us, stupid as a rock tumbling downhill. Everything began for her with my voice and the moon.

That night, like a child begging to hear a favorite story again and again in the same words, she asked me to tell her once more how I sang over her and raised her from the river. I said, weary and impatient, "Lukassa, it was only a song an old man taught me long ago. He generally used it in his vegetable garden."

"I want to know it," she insisted. "It is my song now, I have a right to know it." With shy peasant guile she looked sideways at me and added, "I could never be a great wizard like you, but maybe I can learn just a few things."

"That's all I know," I said, "a few things, a few tricks, and it has taken me all my life to learn that much. Be still, I'll tell you another tale about Zivinaki, who was the king of liars." I wanted her to sleep quickly and leave me to think what I must do if no third dream came. But it was a long time before she gave up asking me to teach her that song. Stubborn as that boy, really, in her way. It must be a remarkable village.

I did not sleep at all that night, but *my friend* came to me even so. He rose from the fire as I knelt to feed it: a trembling old man, as scarred and naked as he had first found me. The jewels were gone from his ears—*four in the left, three in the right, I remember everything, my friend*—the color from his eyes, the braids and the silly little ribbons from his beard. No rings, no robes, no staff; and, most terrible of all, he cast no shadow, neither in the moon nor the firelight. In my country—in what was my country—it is believed that to see a man or woman without a shadow is a sure sign that you will die soon, alone, in a bad place. I believe it myself, though it is nonsense.

But I went to him with joy, trying to put my cloak around him. It fell to the ground, of course, and my arms passed through the shivering image of his body; wherever he was cold, it was not here. I spoke to him then, saying, "Tell me what to do," and he saw me, but he could not answer. Instead he pointed to where the stars were graying over the blunt, broken-nosed hills of the Northern Barrens. A ribbon of light, green as his eyes had been, leaped from his finger: it fled away across the Barrens, straight on into mountains too far to see clearly even by day. When he lowered his arm and looked at me again, I had to turn away from the pale terror in his face, because it was wrong for me to see even his ghost so. I said, "I will find you. Lal is coming to find you."

If he heard, it was no comfort to him. He vanished with the words, but the smell of his anguish burned in my throat long past dawn, as that glowing green trail lingered on the hills even after Lukassa and I were on our way once again. I pointed it out to her, but she could not see it. I thought then that *my friend* had just enough strength left to call to me, no one else.

That day, I remember, I told Lukassa a little of myself and more of where we were bound, and why. For all her persistence, she asked no real questions yet but only, in different ways, *"Am I alive, am I alive?"* Beyond that, she seemed perfectly content to ride behind me, day after day, across a land so bitter and desolate that she might well have wished herself drowned again, safe in the sweet, rushing waters of her own country. I told her that a friend of mine was in great danger and need, and that I was journeying to aid him. That was when she smiled for the first time, and I saw what that village boy was following. She said, "It's your lover."

"Of course not," I said. I was actually shocked at the idea. "He is my teacher, he helped me when there was no help for me in all the world. I would be more truly dead than you ever were, but for him."

"The old man who sang to his vegetables," she said, and I nodded. Lukassa was quiet for a while; then she asked, "Why am I with you? Do I belong to you now, the way that song belongs to me?"

"The dead belong to no one. I could not leave you, neither could I stay to tend you. What else could I do?" I spoke flatly and harshly, because she was making me uneasy. "As for lovers, yours has been hot after us from the night I took you away. Perhaps you would like to stop and wait for him. He certainly must care dearly for you, and I am not used to company." Whatever power was besieging *my friend* so terribly, she could be no help against it. I had no business bringing her any further, for all of our sakes. "Go home with him," I said. "Life is back that way, not where we are going."

But she cried that one road was as foreign to her as the other, that in a world of strangers she knew only death and me. So we went on together, and her boy after us, losing and losing ground, but still coming on. As frantic for speed as I was, we began to walk by turns, to spare my horse; and there came days in that ugly land when we both walked. As for food, I can live on very little when I have to—not forever, but for a while—which was fortunate, because Lukassa ate, not merely like the healthy child she was, but as though only by eating almost to sickness could she remind herself that she was truly alive in her own body. I have been just so myself, over food and more.

Water. I have never known country where I could not find water—where I was born, a two-year-old can smell it as easily as dinner. It is not nearly as hard as most people think, but most people only think about finding water when they are already in a panic of thirst and not thinking well about anything. But those Barrens came as close as ever I saw to being completely dry, and if it had not been that the green trail, glimmering more faintly every night, sometimes crossed the course of an underground trickle, Lukassa and I might have been in serious trouble. As it was, most times we had enough to keep the horse going and our mouths and throats from closing against the burning air. How that boy following managed, I have no idea.

When we began climbing, the country improved, though not by much. There was more water, there were birds and rabbits to snare, and a small, small wind began to pity us just a bit. But from our first night, I could no longer make out the green trail, and I wept with rage when Lukassa was asleep, because I knew that it was still there, still trying to lead me to where *my friend* waited, but grown too weak now for even my eyes. The road, such as it was, forked and frayed and split constantly, going off in every possible direction: up box canyons, treacherous with tumbled stones; down and away into thinly wooded gullies; around and around through endless foothills, half of them sheared away by old landslides, and any or all of them the right path to take, for all I knew. I trusted to my luck, and to the fact that a wizard's desires have body in the world: what one of those people wants to tell you *exists,* like a stone or an apple, whether or not the wizard has the strength to make you see it plainly. I could only hope that the reality of *my friend*'s road would call me by day, as the reality of his pain did by night.

Nyateneri came out of the twilight of our fourth day in the hills. She made no attempt at stealth—I heard the hoofbeats before we had our cooking fire built, and Lukassa was burying the remains by the time she came in sight—but for all that, she surprised me: not there one minute, there the next, like a star. I cannot afford to be surprised, and I was angry with myself until I felt the prickle of magic on my skin, and saw the air tremble between us as I stared at her, very slightly. Live long enough with a magician, and you cannot help acquiring that sense, exactly as you'd feel just where a stranger's shoe pinched if you lived with a cobbler. It wasn't her own magic—she was no wizard, whatever else she was—but there was surely some sort of spell on her, though what it might be I could not say. I am no wizard either.

She was brown-skinned, the shade of strong tea, and her narrow eyes, turned slightly down at the corners, were the color of the twilight itself. Taller than I, long-boned, left-handed; a lot of leverage in those shoulders, probably a powerful shot with that bow she carries, but not necessarily accurate—when you have lived as I have, those are the things you notice first. For the rest, she wore riders' clothes distinguished only by a drabness that seemed deliberate: boots, trews, over-tunic, a Cape Dylee *sidrin* cloak—common west-country stuff, nothing quite matching. The hood of the *sidrin* covered her hair, and she seemed in no hurry to push it back. She rode a roan as gangling and strong-looking as herself, and behind her there followed a shaggy little black horse, not much bigger than a pony, and with the faraway yellow eyes of a carnivore. I have never seen a horse like that one.

She did not speak at first, but only sat her horse and regarded us. There was no friendliness in her bearing, nor menace exactly: nothing but that least spell-shimmer and a sense of dangerous exhaustion. Lukassa came quickly to stand beside me. I said, "What you see is yours," which is a greeting from home. I cannot break myself entirely of using it, perhaps because it says something important about the people to whom I was born. Generous they are with the physical—known for it—but they keep a close watch on the invisible. One day I will just stop saying it.

"*Siri te mistanye,*" she answered me, and the back of my neck sparked coldly. That I did not take her meaning is not the point; there is a civilized understanding that a greeting is to be answered in the tongue of the greeter. Her tone was courteous enough, and she bent her head properly when she spoke, but what she had done she had surely done deliberately, and I would have been within my rights to challenge her or bid her ride on. But I was too curious for that, whatever my neck thought, so I compromised, asking merely for her name and adding that we could speak in Banli if common speech was too difficult. Banli is trade-talk, a pidgin for peddlers in markets far from home. She smiled at me then, taking the insult as it was meant.

"I am Nyateneri," she said. "Daughter of Lomadis, daughter of Tyrrin." Then I thought that she must be from the South Islands, clothes or no, because only there do the women take their descent through the mother's line. Her voice suited this, being lighter than mine and slower, moving from side to side where mine goes up and down. She said, "And you are Sailor Lal, Lal-after-dark. This other I do not know."

"Nor do you know me," I said. There are two names I use when I journey, and I gave her one of them. "Why do you take me for this Lal?"

"What other woman would be traveling in this heartless country? Let alone a black woman with a swordcane at her saddle? And why here, in the blind hills, with no road to guide her—unless she were following a green night trail to the aid of a great wizard in greater trouble?" She laughed outright as I gaped, waving me to hush. "And it is better known than you may think that Lal-khamsin-khamsolal"—she almost had it correctly—"was once the adopted companion and student of the magician—"

"The magician whose name is not spoken," I said, and that time she was silent. I said, "Some call him the Teacher; some, the Hidden One; some, just the Old Man. I call him—what I call him." I stopped myself, angry because I had almost told her my own name for him, though what harm it would have done, I could not be sure. One corner of her mouth twitched slightly.

"And I have always called him the *Man Who Laughs*. One who knows him as you do may understand." The back of my neck prickled once more, and I could not speak for a moment. He laughs quietly, that magician, and not often, but I never found a way to keep from laughing with him. It is a child's laughter, loud and unseemly, and utterly innocent of its own power; it is the true heart of what he is. It was that laughter that held me and kept me safer than swords and dragons could have done when they found out where I was and came for me. Anyone who knew that knew him. Nyateneri swung a leg over the saddle and waited, raising her eyebrows.

"Get down," I said. "You are welcome." Her hood fell back as she alighted, and Lukassa gave a small gasp to see her thick, graying brown hair chopped into random patterns of tufts and whorls and spearpoint strips: it looked like mud churned up by armies. I said nothing before Lukassa—that could wait—but I know a convent cut when I see it. I even know a particular handful by sight, but not this one. Not this one.

We were helping her rub down and feed both horses, when the fox followed his nose out of the saddlebag. Nyateneri had a thin silver cord around his neck on the instant and introduced him to us as her familiar friend, her traveling partner of many years. Lukassa made much of him, begging to carry him everywhere, feeding him scraps and singing sad little lullabies to him as he lolled grinning in her arms. For myself, I studied that grim haircut and wondered what convent allowed its sisters to keep pet foxes in their cells. Nyateneri watched me wondering, while Lukassa asked and asked for him to sleep by her this one night. That granted, she carried him off in triumph to her blanket: he blinked back at us over her shoulder, and Nyateneri called to him in her own language, something sharp and warning. He yawned, letting us see his white teeth and wound-red tongue, and closed his eyes.

"He will not harm her," Nyateneri said. She stood looking at me out of her strange eyes, mist-gray a moment before, shading into near-lavender as the twilight faded. She said, "And now?"

"How do you know him? And from where?" This time she smiled truly, her teeth just a little like the fox's teeth. "From as far away and long ago as you do. The only difference is that I know where he is."

She leaned against a boulder, waiting for me to propose gratefully that we join forces. I said, "There is at least one other difference between us. *I* am not in flight from some fanatic convent, with a bounty waiting for whoever returns me to my vows. You could be a highly inconvenient companion, as well as an irritating one." It was a wild shot, but for just an instant her superior air trailed away, leaving behind the look of a woman on a rack one turn away from madness. I know that look. I saw it in a puddle of muddy water, the first time.

Her face recovered before her voice did. "There is no bounty on me, I promise you that. No one wants me back, anywhere in the world." That long body, made for wars and winters, had not so much as twitched against the stone. She said, "The girl can ride my packhorse—we'll all make better speed that way. And I will tell you the road, this very night, so that you will have no further need of me. After that, the choice is yours."

We looked at each other for some time, standing so quietly that I heard her breathing, as she did mine, and both of us heard Lukassa still singing sleepily to the fox. At last I said, "I have never called him anything but *my friend.*"

The Fox

Yesyesyesyes, and if I want I can steal all their horses, all, all at once, out from under their stupid, ragged, hairy backsides. That boy has no notion, no one has any notion of what I can do if I want. When I want. No idea who I am, what pleases me, why, when. Mildasis, that boy, black woman, white woman, fat innkeeper, no difference. Only Nyateneri.

Hoho, and what I know about Nyateneri, no one but me. Nyateneri knows what makes me laugh to myself, I know what makes Nyateneri afraid. Why Nyateneri sleeps on the floor, not in bed, and not for long, not ever for long. *I* sleep in the bed, sweet as mice, but if I twitch one ear where Lukassa's arm crushes it, if I flick my tail across Lal's breast, yes, then see Nyateneri up that moment, quicker than me, back to the wall and dagger out, shining in the moon, waiting. Sometimes I do that for fun all night, scratch myself, stretch, make little, little sniffs, and each time there is Nyateneri up and ready, ready. Ready for what?

Ready for those two men, following for so long? Not the boy, who cares about that boy? Two men, small, light, running softly, mile after mile forever. No spears, no big swords, only teeth, like me. Nyateneri knows they follow, but never sees. But I see, smell, know what they eat, when they rest, what they think, what they will do. I know everything I want to know.

It makes me laugh, so much hunting and chasing all scattering after us, all that way. That boy catches his girl, what then? *I* know him, she not a bit. Those running men catch Nyateneri—ho, what *then*? Best killers, all three, two dead anyway. Nicer if Nyateneri kills, otherwise no more riding in saddlebag, no more fire in cold night. Better with Nyateneri.

Here at the inn, too many people crashing and tramping, nobody likes foxes. Sweet pigeons upstairs, on the roof, and chickens, little nice chickens tumbling everywhere under all the feet. Nyateneri says to me, "You eat my food, stay with us, never go near fat innkeeper's birds, never let anyone see the tip of a whisker." So I hide, sleep, wait, let Lukassa feed me yams and melons. And sometimes I sit so still, very, very still, and run far away inside, wind and blood and silence, day this way, night that way, listen for who follows, smell what comes. Roll in the dust, in the wild lands, laughing, sitting so still.

"There will be a trail," man-shape tells that boy, and so there is a trail, but *I* leave it, not man-shape. Hoho, see me slipping away from Nyateneri as we travel to squat on the hot stones, see me cock a leg, scratch, leap, squat again, leaving my mark for him through the rocks and the hills, straight to fat innkeeper's front door. So I keep man-shape's word, and that boy, sniffing after me he is still, and a long journey yet, looking down all the time. But he comes here soon, he keeps his word too. Yes.

Two times now, I take the man-shape when Nyateneri does not see. Nice old man, such whiskers, sits in big room downstairs, talks to everybody, *such* a nice old man, visiting his grandson in the town. Marinesha brings the good ale after fat innkeeper goes away. Innkeeper does not like man-shape. Marinesha likes. Boy Rosseth, porter Gatti, they like red cheeks, bright old eyes. Sit and bring man-shape ale, ask questions, tell things. Tell about players sleeping in the stables, horsetrader come to buy and sell, shipbuilder on his way to Cape Dylee. Both times Rosseth talks, talks about three women in fat innkeeper's own room. So pretty, all three, such wonder, why here, what for? Both times Marinesha walks away.

Boy Rosseth never notices. Says, "Lal is nicest. Moves like water, smells like sea and spice together." Laugh. Drink. Say nothing.

Porter Gatti—little man, one white eye in angry little face—he says, "Nyateneri. Nyateneri. All woman, that one, no swagger, no swordcane, nothing but grace, modesty. She invades my dreams."

Not laugh, but ale runs down. Man-shape says, "Stay awake, stay awake, lucky Milk-Eye. Women from that country, they love short, strong men like you. Stay awake, one night she carry you off into woods, same way you carry strangers' chests upstairs." Gatti stare then, stare all the time at Nyateneri now. Waiting.

Makes Nyateneri nervous. Asks fat innkeeper where comes Gatti Milk-Eye, how long here? Innkeeper answers, whose business? Nyateneri stares at *him*. Innkeeper says, eighteen years, walks away. Nyateneri goes outside, kicks over a rain barrel.

Twelve days now, gone every day, Lal and Nyateneri, not a thought for poor fox, never a thought for Lukassa alone. She sits, waits, walks outside, talks to players, talks to Marinesha, talks to me. Cries once. Twelfth night, those two come back so late Rosseth already asleep, they stable horses themselves. In the room, I drowse on pillow like kitten, very decorative. Lukassa lies by me, not sleeping.

They come in, walk tired, smell angry. Lal says, "You said you knew."

Nyateneri says, "He is here."

Lal sits hard on the bed, pulls off her boots. "He is not in the town. We know this. So what is *here*?"

Nyateneri only says, "Tomorrow. Every farm. Every hut. Every cave, every byre, every blanket stretched across a ditch. He is here."

Lal says, "If he could speak to us. If he could come to us in one more dream, one more." Throws boots into corner.

"Too weak," says Nyateneri. "When there is too much pain, too much struggle, what strength is left for dreams, messages?" Open one eye through Lukassa's fingers, see Nyateneri trimming feathers on arrow. Stops. I close eye. Nyateneri's voice, all different. "Magicians die."

Bed bounces. Lal is up, turning back and forth, to door, to window where tree branches go *crick-sish*. "Not this one. Not this way. Magicians die sometimes because they grow greedy, because they become frightened, but this one wants nothing, fears nothing, laughs at everything. No power has any hold on him."

Nyateneri, sharp now. "You don't know that. You know nothing about him, and no more do I. Tell me how old he is, tell me where he came from, tell me about his family, his own teacher, his real home." Arrow breaks, goes after Lal's boots. Nyateneri says, "Tell me whom he loves."

Lal draws breath, lets out again. Lukassa sits up, watches, smooths my fur. Nyateneri. "No. Not us. He was kind, he protected us—saved us, yes—he taught us much, and we love him, we two. We are here, as we should be, because we love him. But he does not love us." Smiles then, teeth white, lips tight. "That you know."

No sound, just me breathing, so sleepy, so good. Lal looks out window, watches pretty chickens roosting in bush. Lal says, "He loves somebody. Somebody knows his name."

Nyateneri starts on another arrow. Lal's voice so quiet. "You saw him. No one could have done from a distance what has been done to him. Whoever has broken his magic was deeply trusted, greatly loved. It must be so."

They say names. Men, women, even something that is neither, lives in fire, in mud, who cares? But always Lal shakes head, Nyateneri says, "No, I suppose." One time, they laugh even, and Lukassa looking one to the other, forgetting to scratch my ears. But at last, no more names. Lal says, "It is no one I ever knew."

Knock on door. Nyateneri curling around and up like smoke, no sound, big bow ready. Voice. "Me, Rosseth, please." Bow comes down, Lal goes to door. Boy stands there, looks all unlicked, holding wooden platter. I smell cold meat, nice cheese, bad wine. He says, "I woke up, I heard your voices, you came back late, I thought you might not have had any dinner." Eyes big as grapes, figs.

Lal makes in-between sound, almost sigh, almost laugh. Lal says, "Thank you, Rosseth. You are very thoughtful."

Pushes platter into her hands. Says, "The wine is a little sour, Karsh keeps the best locked away. But the meat is fresh yesterday, I promise."

Nyateneri comes up, says, "Thank you, Rosseth. Go back to your bed now." Smiles at him. Boy can't breathe. Legs take one step to go away, rest of him takes two steps into room. Sees me on Lukassa's pillow, tail over nose, little, little sweet snores. Eyes get big as plums, he says, "Karsh," like ghost of a sneeze.

Lukassa swifts me up, backs away. Nyateneri. "Karsh wants not to see a fox. He has not."

Lal. "Neither have you." She touches boy's cheek, pushes him out with her fingertips, closes the door. He stands there, I smell him, a long time. Lal turns, sets platter down. "A good child. He is full of wonder, and he really does work very hard." Stops then and laughs, shakes her head. Says, "I suppose my—I suppose our friend has said exactly the same thing about us, many times. To whomever he loved." Nyateneri goes back to arrows.

All this time Lukassa is silent. Watches, holds me, not a word, but something down her arms, hands, into me, fur jumps with it, bones too. Now she says, "Today."

They look at her. Nyateneri. "Today. What?"

Lukassa. "Not tomorrow. You found him today." Stands there, looking right back, stubborn, *certain*. In her arms I turn, yawn, stretch out legs. Lal, gentle, careful. "Lukassa, no, we have not found him. The trail he left us ended in this country, but we have been hunting everywhere for twelve days, and we are good hunters, Nyateneri and I. No one even remembers having seen him—there is no sign, no slightest trace—"

Lukassa interrupts her. "You've been where he was, then—you've been where something happened, something bad." Now they look at each other. Nyateneri raises eyebrow just a little, Lal not. Lukassa sees, voice gets louder. "It's on you, I can smell it. Somewhere today, a place of death, you were there, it's all over you." Trembling harder, might drop me. Says, "Death."

Nyateneri turns a little to Lal. "In that room, the day we came. Now again. Doesn't she know any other tricks?"

Lal. "It is no trick." Very soft, golden eyes darken to shadowy bronze. Lal is angry. Says, "She knows death as we do not, she can tell where it has passed. And you will have to take my word for this."

Slow, Nyateneri. "So I shall." Quiet then, everybody quiet. Lal tastes wine, makes a face, keeps drinking. Lukassa takes slices of cold meat, one for me, one for her, one for me. Nyateneri says, "The tower."

Lal blinks. "Tower." Then, "Oh, that. A pile of red rocks, we saw nothing but spiders, owls, centuries of dust. Why there?"

Nyateneri. "Why centuries? Nothing else in this country is old enough to be that ruinous. Why only one tower, and everything else—*everything*—squat as a horse-pile?" Shrugs. "We have to start somewhere." Looks at Lukassa. "She comes with us. Our very own little deathstalker."

Lukassa tosses me on the bed, me, just like that, like a pillow. Walks straight up to Nyateneri, stands almost on tiptoe to meet her eyes. Says, "I belong to no one. Lal told me. I am not a hat, not a pet fox, not somebody who does a trick. I am your companion, and Lal's, or I am not, and if I am, then from tomorrow I go where you go, and there's an end to that." Mouths open, even I. Lukassa. "For I have come a longer journey than you have."

Lal is smiling, turns away. Nyateneri. Years, years, not

friends, not not-friends, each one other's secret, coming, going, saying nothing, knowing what we know. Hoho, Nyateneri. Only one time before so still, so amazed, long ago, both of us nearly die that time. Shakes head slowly, sits down, picks up the big bow. Says, "Well, companions. I am now going to put a new string on my bow. If *this* doesn't bite me too, it should take me about five minutes. Then I am going to sleep, as we should all do, because tomorrow will be a hard day." No more than that.

In bed, Lukassa whispers to me, like every night, "Fox, fox, what is your name?" I lick inside wrist, she makes little tired sigh. Whisper. "They call me Lukassa, but I don't know." Like every night.

Sleeps. Lal sleeps. Nyateneri leans over bed, speaks in the other talk, ours. Says, "Hear me. Old man drinks no more ale downstairs." I keep eyes tight shut. Nyateneri. "Hear me."

Early, early morning, they go out, all three together. Lukassa kisses nose, says, "Be good." Nyateneri looks at me. Boots on stairs, gone. I eat rest of the meat and cheese, go under bed when Marinesha comes in to sweep. Very safe place. Marinesha opens window a little, goes away. Tree makes *crick-sish, crick-sish* against window.

People don't know foxes can climb trees if they really want. Squirrels know.

MARINESHA

What happened was, I was running after the fox in the tree—I mean, the fox wasn't actually *in* the tree anymore, because it had already jumped down to the ground, given me one quick look, and then flashed out of sight between the stable and my vegetable garden. I was carrying a basket of new-washed clothes to hang in the sun, but I just dropped them where I stood and went after that animal. It had killed my hen—she wasn't really mine, exactly, but I was the one who named her, Sona was what I called her, and she always followed me everywhere, even when I didn't have any grain for her. And that fox killed her, and I would have killed it if I could. I would have.

But it was gone when I came around the stable—just completely vanished; it must have turned on its track, shot right under the bathhouse and slipped away through the wild berry-brambles beyond. Rosseth has been told and told and *told* to block up that place—the frogs pop up and frighten the guests, and once or twice there's been a *tharakki*. Rosseth can be quite pleasant, in his way, but he is simply an irresponsible boy.

Anyway, I stood there for a moment—so angry all over again about Sona, she was such a *nice* hen—and then I remembered the wet clothes, and I hurried back, hoping I hadn't spilled any out of the basket. And I hadn't, thank goodness, at least nothing that would be any the worse off for one more grass-stain, and I was just turning toward the *naril* tree where I like to hang wash this time of year because everything picks up the smell of the blossoms—and suddenly there they were, two men coming up out of the orchard, as though they'd cut right across the fields, not staying to the road at all. I didn't trust them right away. I don't trust people who don't walk the road.

They were small, thin, brown men, both of them, dressed in brown, and they looked almost exactly alike to me, except that one of them had something wrong with his mouth—only half of his upper lip moved when he spoke. The other had blue eyes. I was frightened of his eyes. I can't tell you why.

I stood very, very still, pretending I hadn't seen them. That's what Sona used to do, my hen, when a hawk was circling overhead. The other chickens would be running in all directions, screaming and cackling, and Sona would just stand right where she was, so still, never once looking at the hawk, not even at its shadow sweeping over the ground. It always worked for her, poor Sona, so she thought it always would.

Well, it didn't work any better for me. They came up to me—they really were small, no taller than I am, and they made no sound. Their feet didn't, I mean. The one with the blue eyes stood right in front of me, facing me, and the one with the funny mouth stood just behind my shoulder—I couldn't see him without turning my head, but I could feel him there.

They were very polite, I'll say that for them. The blue-eyed one said, "Please excuse us, good young lady, we are looking for a friend? A tall woman? With a bow and a pet fox? Her name will be Nyateneri?" That was how he talked, everything a question, in a soft, slidey kind of voice. Foreign accents like that make me nervous, anyway.

I know they shouldn't, working around inns most of my life, but they always do.

Just the kind of friends that hulking creature would have, that's what I thought. I didn't have any reason to do her any favors, strutting around in her ugly boots and letting her fox kill my Sona. "There's no one like that staying here," I told them. "The only women we have right now are with the players, sleeping in the stable. But they don't have any bows." Let her miss her stupid message, I thought—maybe she'll learn to say *Good morning, Marinesha* once in a while.

The blue-eyed man asked me, "Perhaps she only stayed here a night or two, and then went on? It would be recent, quite recent?" I just shook my head. I said, "We had some dancers here last month, and a horse-coper, she cured Rosseth's donkey of the staggers, but she was small, tiny. That's all, honestly." Once you start lying, it's amazing how you go on, how it catches you up. I made up all that part about the horse-coper.

The other one said, at my shoulder, "Perhaps we should talk to the landlord? You could take us to him?" The same sort of voice, you couldn't have told them apart with your eyes shut. I looked around for Rosseth, but of course he wasn't anywhere in sight.

Blue Eyes nodded. He said, "That would be best? If we spoke to the landlord?" He put his hand on my shoulder, and I actually cried out with the heat of it—I *did,* and I felt that heat for a week afterward, what's more. I can feel it now, if I think about it. Blue Eyes said, "We will follow you? Please?"

So I walked back to the inn, with my arms still full of washing, and those two right behind me. They didn't touch me again, and they didn't say anything to frighten me—they didn't say anything at all, and that was the most frightening thing, because I couldn't see them, you see, and they were so silent I wouldn't have known they were there. And when we got to the door, I just jumped aside, and I said, "In there, just wait, you wait for Karsh," and

I *ran* back to the *naril* tree and began hanging those clothes over the branches as though my life depended on it, and I never once looked back over to see if they had gone inside. I just hung those clothes and hung them, and I didn't even know I was crying until I was done.

Rosseth

I hadn't slept very well, because of the players. They were supposed to give a performance in two days for the Mercers' Guild in town, and they had been rehearsing almost all night every night for a week. It wasn't that they didn't know the play well—there can't be a traveling troupe in the land that doesn't give some version of *The Marriage of the Wicked Lord Hassidanya* twenty or thirty times a year—but I think this must have been the largest and most knowledgeable audience they were ever likely to face, and none of them could sleep for nervousness anyway. So they kept going over and over their parts, two and three at a time or all together, running the whole thing through just once more: there in the straw by lantern-light, with the horses looking on solemnly over their stall doors and nodding at the good parts. Finally I came down from the loft, wished them all disaster for luck, and went outside to walk and think until sunrise, as I do sometimes.

The women rode out just before dawn, all three together for the first time. They didn't see me. Usually I waved at them when I saw them setting off each day—and Lal, at least, always waved back—but this once I stepped aside, into the hollow of a burned-out tree, and watched them pass by in silence. It might have been a different air about them, literally, a new smell of purpose, for I was already as tuned, as pitched to their scent as to no other in my life, except that of Karsh, because of the way he likes to slip up and catch you not working. Or perhaps it was simply the way they looked in the red and silver morning: sudden strangers beyond my conception of foreignness, alien as I had never imagined them, although I should have. I was too young then to see past my own skin, and my skin was in love with them, all three. Yet I never saw them more truly than I did that morning.

They troubled my sleep terribly, as they do now sometimes, even now, even knowing what I know. I don't want you to think that I was an utter innocent—I had already been with a woman, in a sort of a way (no, not Marinesha, not ever Marinesha)—but Lal and Nyateneri and Lukassa were shadows of the future, though I didn't know it, and what I feared and adored and hungered for in them was myself-to-be, you might say. But I didn't know that either, of course: only that I had never in my life been hurt so by the sound of women laughing in a little rented room upstairs.

What? Forgive me. I had tasks to do, and I did them as always, mucking out stalls and filling mangers, laying down new straw, combing burrs out of manes and tails—even trimming a few hooves, depending on what the beasts' owners had required of me. Karsh set me to work in The Gaff and Slasher's stables when I was five, and I am good with horses. I can't even say whether I actually like them or not, to this day. I am just good with them.

Karsh had gone to town, to the market, not long after the women left. Gatti Jinni usually runs things in his absence, but Gatti Jinni gets drunk one night in the month, without any particular pattern or regularity to it. One night in the month, and last night had been it—I know, because I helped him to his room, cleaned his face of tears and slobber, and put him to bed. So I was keeping an eye on the inn as I worked, and I saw those two men follow Marinesha to the door. Nothing out of the way there, but when they went in alone and she came flying back to her laundry-basket, trembling so hard that I could see it from where I was, then I dropped my spade and went to her. I did turn back and pick the spade up again, after a few steps—even a dungheap warrior needs his lance, after all.

She could not speak, which had nothing to do with the fact that she had not *been* speaking to me for two days, or whenever it was that I'd said something admiring about Lukassa in the taproom. When I touched her, she clung to me and whimpered, which frightened me in turn. Marinesha is an orphan, like me: we may adopt obsequiousness as a condition of survival, but we have never been able to afford terror, any more than we can certain kinds of courage. So I patted her back and mumbled, "It's all right, just stay here," and I hoisted my trusty spade and went inside.

They were on the second floor, just coming out of the little room where Karsh had put two old pilgrims from Darafshiyan. I don't know if they'd been in the women's room or not. Small men and slender, graceful in their movements, almost dainty, their plain brown clothes fitting them like fur. They reminded me of *shukris,* those hot, rippling little animals that follow the smell of blood down holes, up trees, anywhere, endlessly. I said, "May I be of service, gentlemen? My name is Rosseth."

At times it's an advantage not to know your true name, since you should never tell it to strangers anyway. The two men looked at me without answering for what seemed a very long time. I felt myself trembling, exactly like Marinesha—the difference between us was only that my fear made me angry. "The patron is not here," I said to them. "If you want a room, you will have to wait until he returns. Downstairs." I made my tone as insulting as I could, because my voice was so unsteady.

The blue-eyed man smiled at me, and I wet myself. It is the truth, no more: his lips stretched and thinned and a sudden wash of absolute terror sluiced over me like the blast from an open furnace. I fell against the wall. If it had not been for my spade, bracing myself with it, I would have collapsed completely. But I didn't; and I have just enough of Karsh's idiot-stubbornness to behave like him, like an idiot, like a rock, when my bowels are falling to the floor. I said again, gasping, I'm sure, "You will have to wait downstairs."

They looked at each other then, and I suppose it was kind of them not to burst out laughing. The one whose mouth broke upwards on one side said, "We do not wish a room? We seek a woman?" Later it seemed to me that I almost knew the accent—all I thought at the time was that fire would speak like that if it could make human words.

The blue-eyed man—and I should tell you that in this country blue is the color of death—came to me in two strides and lifted me by my throat. He did it so daintily and tidily that I barely had time to realize that I was strangling before I was. He hummed into my ear, "A tall woman with gray eyes? We have tracked her here? Please?" I heard an irritating sound, somewhere very far away, and somebody realized that it was my heels kicking at the wall.

I would have told them. Nyateneri said afterward that it was brave of me to keep silent, but truly I would have told them anything if they had only let me. I saw the other man's lips move, though I couldn't hear anything anymore except the howl of blood in my ears and that thin, caressing voice saying, "Please? Yes?" Then Karsh came. I think that's what happened, anyway.

THE INNKEEPER

I should have married when I had the chance—then at least there would have been someone instead of me to do the marketing. Now and then I take on someone just for that purpose, and I always regret it. No one who wasn't born to it can deal with those old thieves in the Corcorua stalls; anyone else comes home with a cartload of rotting vegetables, maggoty meat, and salt fish you can smell before you hear the wagon wheels on the road. I manage well enough, but I don't like it, never have, even when my father used to take me with him to teach me the trade. He loved it as much as they did, the butchers, the fishmongers, and the rest of them—he loved the yelling and haggling as much as finding the first fresh melons off the ship from Stimeszt, and he would have died of contempt instead of drink if people had stopped trying to swindle him out of his shirt. I am not like that.

So I came home that day as I do every market day, tired and disgusted, breakfast going rancid in the back of my throat. There have been times when I wouldn't have minded walking into The Gaff and Slasher to look up the stairs and see that fool of a boy pinned to the wall with his neck half-wrung, but all I wanted to deal with then was a gallon of my own red ale, and this was one plaguey annoyance too many. Especially from outlanders.

I roared, "Put him down!" in a voice to rattle crockery—how else would *you* make yourself heard across taprooms for forty years?—and the one who had the boy said, "Ah? Certainly?" and dropped him. They turned toward me, smiling as though nothing in any way unusual were going on, smiles to scrape your bones. "At last the patron? The master of the house?"

"My name's Karsh," I said, "and no one but me lays a hand on the help. Come down here and talk to me if you want a room."

They did not move, so I climbed the stairs to them. Pride is not my problem. Close to, they were older than I'd thought, though you had to stare to be sure of it. Long necks, triangular faces, light brown skin so tight over the bones that the lines were no more than tiny pale grooves. I felt their faces would rattle like kites if I touched them. The one who'd been choking the boy—yes, yes, he was already on his feet, coughing a bit, no harm done—told me that they were looking for a woman, a friend of theirs. "A good, *good* friend? It is most, most urgent?"

A southern voice, like hers, but with something else to it, a kind of restless twitch that isn't southern at all. I knew whom they meant, of course, and saw no reason not to tell them she was staying here. No, I didn't care much for their manner, nor for their way of taking liberties in my house without so much as paying for a bottle; but I'd put up uglier sorts many a night, and besides, I had no worries on Miss Nyateneri's account. She would have made two of them, and she'd likely enough teethed on that dagger and that bow of hers. I said to the boy, "Is she here?"

I can read his mind sometimes, more often than he likes, but never his face, not for years. The way he looked at me, I couldn't have told you if he was grateful for my showing up when I did, angry because I didn't pay his squeezed windpipe enough mind, or alarmed—or jealous, for that matter—because these dubious customers were claiming intimacy with Miss Nyateneri. He shook his head. "They went out this morning. I don't know when they'll be back." Voice just a bit hoarse, but not bad at all—air flowing up and down his neck like anyone else's. I put up with worse, from worse, at his age, and here I am.

Half-Mouth said, "We will wait? In the room?" No question about it, as far as that pair were concerned—they were halfway down the hall by the time he was done speaking. I said, "You will *not* wait in the room," and though I didn't shout, that time, they heard me and they turned. My father taught me that, how to catch a guest's ear without losing either the guest or your own ears. "The rooms are private," I told them. "As yours would be, if you were staying here. You may wait downstairs, in the taproom, and I will stand you each a pint of ale."

I added that last because of the way they were looking at me. As I have told you, I am not brave, but doing what I do for so long has taught me that a joke and a free drink take care of most misunderstandings. Few people come to a crossroads inn like this chasing trouble—not with trouble so handy in town, less than five miles away. There's a *dika*-wood cudgel behind the bar that's come in useful once or twice, but these days I'd have to dig for it under dishrags and aprons and the tablecloth I keep for private meals. The last time any eyes made me as uneasy as this pair's, they belonged to a whole roomful of wild Arameshti bargemen with ideas about the barmaid who worked here before Marinesha. Half-Mouth shook his head and half-smiled. He said, "We thank you? We would prefer?"

I shook *my* head. Their shoulders went loose and easy, and the boy moved up alongside me—as though he would have been any more use than a hangnail. But Gatti Jinni came in just then, with a couple of those actors, trying to cozen them into a game of *bast*. I never let stable-guests into the house before nightfall, but I greeted this lot like royalty, calling down that their rooms were ready and dinner already on the hob. They were still gaping at me when I turned back to my precious little southerners and beckoned to them. No, I jerked a finger—there's a difference.

Well, they looked at each other, and then they looked down at Gatti Jinni and his new pair of marks (I cuff his head at least once a month over this, but he still regards it as his legal, sovereign right to skin my guests at cards); and then they looked back, sizing up the boy and me again. I hadn't yet seen a weapon on either of them, mind you, but there wasn't a doubt in my belly that they could have killed us all and barely raised a sweat. But it clearly wasn't worth the sweat to them, nor the clamor. They came toward us, and I pushed the boy aside—him waving that spade of his to scatter muck all over the hall—and they passed by without a sound or a glance. Down the stairs, across the taproom, and on out into the road. The door never even creaked behind them. When I went myself to look outside, so as to be sure they weren't bothering Marinesha, they were already gone.

The boy said, "I'll go after her." He was red and pale by turns, sweating, and shaking, the way it happens when you're either going to soil your breeches or kill people. He said, "I'll warn her, I'll tell her they're waiting." I almost didn't catch him at the door, and me with the slopjars not even emptied.

NYATENERI

The boy was watching us from hiding as we rode out that morning. I found that odd, I remember. There was never anything in the least furtive about Rosseth when it came to us: he wore his worship as a bird wears its feathers, and it gave him color and flight, as feathers will. The other two did not see him. I would have said something about it, but Lal was riding ahead, singing one of those long, long, incredibly tuneless songs of hers to herself; and as for Lukassa, there is no way to tell you how her presence changed even my smell and set the hairs of my body at war with each other. I know why now, of course, but then all I could imagine was that I had been far too long away from ordinary human company.

Corcorua is the nearest to a proper town that I ever saw in that wild north country. City folk would think it hardly more than an overgrown fruitstall, a bright spatter of round wooden houses all along the dry ravines that pass for streets and roads. There are more of those houses than you first think: more horses than oxen, more orchards and vineyards than plowed fields, and more taverns than anything else. The wine they serve tells you how tired the soil is, but they make an interesting sort of brandy from their pale, tiny apples. One could come to like it in time, I think.

The townspeople are a low-built lot in general, dwarfed by the wild generosity of their own mountains and sky, but they have something of that same honest wildness about them, which at times restores me. I was born in country like this—though taken south young—and I know that most northerners keep the doors of their souls barred and plastered round, turning their natural heat inward against a constant winter. These folk are no more to be trusted than any other—and less than some—but I could like them as well as their brandy.

The marketplace doesn't fit the town, and yet it *is* the town, really, as it must be the trading center of the entire province. According to Rosseth, it is open all year round, which is rare even in kinder climates; and it is certainly the only market where I ever saw the woven-copper fabric they make only in western Gakary on sale next to crate on crate of *limbri,* that awful tooth-melting candied fruit from Sharan-Zek. They even sell the best Camlann swords and mail, and half the time there's no finding such work in Camlann itself, so great is the demand. I bought a dagger there myself, at a price that was shameful but almost fair.

I rode up beside Lal as we trotted straight through (skirting the town to pick up the main road takes you the better part of two hours, which no one had bothered to tell us the first time). I said to her, "Northerners can't abide *limbri*. I've never seen it north of the Siritangana, until now."

Before I came to know Lal, I most often took her laugh for a grunt of surprise, or a sigh. She said, "He always did have a revolting passion for the stuff. And he likes places like this, plain dust-and-mud farming country. Did you ever know him to live for long in a real city?"

"When he first took me up, we lived in the back of a fishmonger's in Tork-na'Otch." Lal made a face—Tork-na'Otch is known for its smoked fish, and nothing else. I said, "He may be gone, but he *was* here, and not long ago, everything says it. He may have sent you dreams because they could find you most easily in your wanderings, but I was in one place for many years, and to me he wrote letters. I have them still. They came from here, from Corcorua—he described the market and the look of the people, and he even told me what his house was like. About this, I cannot be mistaken. I cannot."

My voice must have risen, for Lukassa turned in her saddle and stared back at me with those light eyes of hers that were always wide and always seemed to see, not me now but me then, me peering over my own shoulder in time. Lal said, "I take your word, but you can't find the house, and we have been everywhere twice between the market and the summer pastures. Now I follow Lukassa's fancy back to the old red tower, as you suggested, because I do not know what else to do. If we find no trace of him there, then I will return to the inn and get drunk. It takes me a very long time to get drunk, so I need to start early."

I had nothing to say to that. A young merchant caught my stirrup, holding up a cageful of singing birds; another, a woman, was plucking at Lukassa's bridle, crying a bargain in silken petticoats. "Two for hardly more than the price of one, my lass—a sweet snowdrift of ruffles for a lover to wade through!" Lukassa never looked at her. We followed Lal down the lines of vegetable barrows, wove single-file between the wine vendors and the stalls drifted high themselves with sheepskins and carded wool—our horses held motionless at times by the crush of trade and the fear of treading down one of the market brats who squalled and scrambled between their legs—until a narrow cobbled alley opened to our left, and there were orchards, and the white road away to the yellow hills. We let the horses run for a while then. It was a pleasant day, and I hummed to myself a little.

When Lal drew rein, we were almost to the hills, within sight of houses we had already searched twice over, more or less with the consent of their inhabitants. These are larger than the dwellings below in town, mostly of wood still, save for the occasional stone or brick mansion. They keep to the round design, though, with painted, high-arched roofs that make them look just a bit like muffins beginning to rise. Dull as muffins, too, to my taste: an afternoon of all that snug rotundity, let alone a week, and you begin to pine for eaves, gables, crests, ridges, *angles*. Of course, the mountains beyond must provide as much edge, even to contentment, as anyone could use. They eat too much of the sky, even at this distance, and snow does not soften them: it is ice that shines like saliva down their lean sides. They look like great wild boars.

Lal touched Lukassa's shoulder and said, "Today you are not only our companion but our leader. Go forward and we will follow." She said it with careful lightness, but there came such a look of terror and revulsion into Lukassa's eyes that both Lal and I turned quickly to see what danger might be slinking upon us. When we turned again Lukassa was already away, and we were well into the hills, far past the first houses, before we caught up with her.

I had been tired and irritable the night before, and suggesting that we return to the red tower had been as much an angry joke as anything else. Lal had given Lukassa neither orders nor directions, but she turned off the road at the only path that could have led her there, as though she knew the way of old. Nearing the place, she drew her horse to as slow a walk as it had been held to in the Corcorua market. Her eyes were empty, and her mouth loose—I have seen diviners look so, in realms where the art is honored, tracking the scent or sense of water to a place where water cannot be. Behind me Lal's breath, quick and shallow.

The red tower was as much a ruin as a building can be without falling down, but it would have stood out as absurdly among these bitter gray mountains if there hadn't been a single brick out of place. This country runs to endurance, to keeping your head down and well swaddled:

a grand manor here is just a crusty muffin; a fortress just a stale, stone-hard one. A tower—a tower with an outside stair, windows at every turning and what must have been an observatory of some kind at the top—belongs strictly to southern fairy tales, to nights and lands where you can actually see the stars long enough to make up stories about them. It was just the sort of thing he would have set up for himself, that impudent, impossible old man. I should have realized it yesterday, before Lukassa, before anyone.

She dismounted in the tower's shadow, and we crept after her—at least, it felt like creeping, somehow, still as the day was and slowly as she passed through the great shambly entranceway. The gate was flat, with ground vines lacing over it, but we had already proved the place safe enough to enter, else we would never have let her go ahead of us. She paid no heed to the stair but went straight to an inner wall, opened an all-but-invisible door that neither of us had ever mentioned to her, and unhesitatingly began to climb the steps within, never speaking, never looking back.

We followed silently, Lal swatting spiderwebs aside and I covering my face against the owl and bat droppings that Lukassa's progress dislodged, and which made the shallow steps treacherous. It was just as long, tiring, and smelly an ascent as it had been the first time. I thought often of the look in the boy Rosseth's dark hazel eyes as he watched us pass that morning, so clearly imagining us on our way to the wonderful adventures with which he so busily endowed our lives. Too much going on in his head, and no idea of his own worldly beauty—no combination more attractive. As though I needed more trouble than I had.

Dark as it was, both Lal and I knocked our heads—as we had before—on the sudden low ceiling that ended the steps. Lukassa did not. Moving easily, despite having to bend almost double, she slipped away to the left, so quickly that we lost her in the darkness for a few moments. When I had caught my breath, I whispered to Lal, "Whether or not we ever find our friend, sooner or later you will have to tell me how she knew. You owe me that much."

The tower was double-built, of course: a hard secret core at the heart of all that crumbling frippery. The outer stair would never have brought us to the landing where we stood, nor ever to the little room where we knew Lukassa had gone. Lal and I had spent all yesterday afternoon tapping, prowling, discussing, reasoning—and, at the last, cursing and guessing—our way to this chamber, and that *blank* child had gone straight to it as though she were strolling home. Lal said softly back, "It is not mine to tell. You must ask her." But it was not in me then to ask Lukassa to pass the cheese, to help me with a harness buckle. Lal knew that.

The room is very cold. Magic does not have a smell, as some believe, but it leaves a chill behind it that my laughing old friend said so often was the breath of the other side, that place from which magic visits us—"like a neighbor's cat, whom we coax over the fence with bits of chicken to hunt our mice." There was a cooking-tripod and its stewpot, overturned on a straw mat; a deep-blue silk tapestry, hanging by one corner on a far wall; there were a few retorts, a long table, a high wooden stool; a single wineglass, broken; and a number of patterns chalked and charcoaled on the floor, which neither Lal nor I could interpret. They had been trampled over and badly smudged.

Lukassa was standing in the middle of a black-and-red scrawl that looked like nothing but a baby's play with colored inks. When she looked at us, her face was terrifying: a sibyl's face, crawling with furious prophecy, wrinkling like water to unhuman rhythms and commands. She screamed at us, our pale companion who never raised her voice, even when challenging me head-on, "Can you see nothing, can you feel nothing? It was here—it was here!" I will swear that the stone room *jumped* when she cried out, as a good lute will sigh and stir in your arms when someone speaks close by.

Lal said gently, "Lukassa. Truly, we cannot see. What happened in this room, Lukassa?"

For no good reason but personal vanity, I wish to set down here a moment's defense of my own vision, and Lal's as well. Neither of us would have been alive to stand in the doorway of that cold little room, had we read the air and recent history of certain others as poorly as we had that one. Either some sorcerous residue slowed our senses when we came there first without Lukassa; or, as I would prefer to believe, it was her presence that summoned onto the table the little dry red-brown stain, brought the clawmarks on the floor out of hiding, and made the silk tapestry give up a hidden design in green and gold, showing a man with dragon's wings locked in battle with something like a glittering shadow. Whatever had dragged the tapestry almost down from the wall had ripped a raw gash almost from top to bottom, and the woven blood of the fighters seemed about to spill into our hands as we stood dumbly before it. I said a word of blessing, for my own comfort, not meaning it to be heard, and Lal breathed what must have been an *amen,* though in no language I know.

Lukassa's rage of knowledge seemed to ebb somewhat; when she spoke again, saying, "Here and here," she sounded more like a child driven to exasperation by the sluggishness and stupidity of adults. "Here stood your friend, and here stood *his* friend—and here"—casually nodding to a near corner—"this was where the Others came from." It was all so truly obvious to her.

In that corner, which is stone and slate and mortar like the rest, there is no air, only cold. If the tower is gone today, as it may well be, that corner is still there. Lal and I looked at each other, and I know that we were thinking the same thing: *This is not a corner, not a wall—this is a door, an open door.* Behind us, Lukassa said impatiently, "There, where you stand—look, look," and she hurried to join us, pointing into an emptiness so fierce that I had to struggle with an impulse to snatch her hand back before that ancient, murderous absence bit it off. Instead, I turned and spoke to her as soothingly as I could. "What other, Lukassa? What did he look like?"

She actually stamped her foot. "Not *he*—the Others, the *Others*! The two men fought, they were so angry, and then the Others came." She peered back and forth at us, only beginning to wonder now: a child first discovering fear in the faces of adults. She whispered, "You don't. You don't."

"Nothing comes uninvited from this kind of darkness," I said to Lal, over Lukassa's head. "There has to be a call." Lal nodded. I asked the girl, "Who summoned the—the Others? Which man was it?" But she took hold of Lal's hand and would not look at me.

I repeated the question, and so did Lal—to no avail, for all her petting and coaxing. At last she gestured, *let it be,* and, to Lukassa, "The men fought, you say. Why did they fight, and how? Which of them won?" Lukassa remained silent, and I wished that I had brought the fox with us. She murmurs to him constantly; by now he surely knows far more about her than either of us does. And will continue to—I know *him* that well, at least.

"Magic," Lal said. "They fought with magic." Lukassa pulled away from her, less by intent than because she was trembling so violently. Lal's voice became sharper. "Lukassa, one of those two was the man we have sought so long, the old man who sang over his vegetable garden. If it were not for him—" She glanced quickly at me, hesitated, then turned Lukassa to face her again, pressing both of the girl's hands together between her own. She said, clearly and deliberately, "No one but you can help us to find him, and you would be dead at the bottom of a river but for him. What happens from this moment is your choice." The words rang like hoofbeats on the cold stones.

Unless you are a long-practiced wizard (and sometimes even then), it isn't good to spend more time than you have to within walls as encrusted with old wizardry as those. It causes mirages inside you, in your heart—I don't know a better way to put it. In that moment, it seemed to me—no, it *was*—as though Lal were holding all of Lukassa in her two cupped palms like water, and that if she brimmed over them, or slid through Lal's fingers, she would spill away into every dark corner forever. But she did not. She bent her head, and raised it again, and looked steadily into both our faces with those backward-searching eyes of hers. I will not say that she was Lukassa once more, because by then I had begun to know a bit better than that. Whoever she truly was, it was no one she had been born.

"He fought so bravely," she said to no one in the world. "He was so clever. His friend was clever, too, but too sure of himself, and frightened as well. They stood here, face to face, and they turned this room to the sun's belly, to the ocean floor, to the frozen mouth of a demon. These walls boiled around them, the air cracked into knives, so many little, little knives—all there was to breathe was the little knives. And there was never any sound, not for a thousand years, because all the air had turned to knives. And the old one grew weary and sad, and he said *Arshadin, Arshadin.*" Even in that clear, quiet voice, the cry made me close my eyes.

Lukassa went on. "But his friend would not heed, but only pressed him closer about with night and flame, and with such visions as made him feel his soul rotting away from him, poisoning the pale things that devoured it as he looked on. And then the old one became terrible with fear and sorrow and loneliness, and he struck back in such bitter thunder that his friend lost power over him for that moment, and was more frightened than he, and called upon the Others for aid. It is all here, in the stones, written everywhere."

I looked at the clawmarks, waiting for Lal to ask the question that came now. But she said nothing, and when I saw her face I saw the hope that I would be the one to speak. I also saw that she was immensely weary. It matters much to Lal to seem tireless, and never before had she let me see the legend frayed this thin. She cannot be that much older than I; yet I was young still when I heard my first tale of Lal-Alone. When did she last ask a favor of anyone, I wonder?

"Last night you spoke to us of death," I said. "Who died here, then, the old man or that one you call his friend?" Lukassa stared at me, shaking her head very slightly, as though my blindness had finally worn out her entire store of disbelief, anger, and pity, leaving her nothing but a kind of numb tolerance. The man we were seeking had often looked at me like that.

"Oh, the friend died," she said casually and wearily. "But he rose again." It was I who gasped, I admit it—Lal made no sound, but leaned against the table for just a moment. Lukassa said, "The friend summoned the Others to help him, and they killed him, but he did not die. The old man—the old man fled away. His friend pursued him. I don't know where." She sat down very suddenly and put her head on her knees, and went to sleep.

LISONJE

Well, if you'd just mentioned the legs straight off. I told you, love, I never remember names, only my lines. *And* the odd historical event, like that child's legs—such sweet long legs, practically touching the ground on either side of that funny little gray horse he rode into my life. It was one of those moments that you know right then, on the spot, will keep you company forever: me scrubbing yesterday's makeup off my poor old face (well, I *do* thank you, most kind) at the rain barrel that stands near the woodshed—and suddenly those *legs*, just at the bottom edge of my washtowel. I kept raising the towel—like this, slowly, you see—and those dear legs just kept going on and on, all the way up to his shoulders. Nothing but bone and gristle, poor mite, as shaggy as his little horse, and not a handful of spare flesh between them. My own life, it seems to me so often, has been nothing but endless traveling in an endless circle, as far back as I can remember—which means practically the beginning of the world—but I took one good look at *him* and I knew that not all my silly miles together would amount to a fraction of the journey that boy had come. I do understand a *few* things besides playing, if I may say so, whatever you may have heard.

Well, we looked at each other, *and* we looked at each other, and we might be standing there to this day if I hadn't spoken. What I think is that they had just come to a stop in that inn-yard, the two of them, that neither he nor his horse had a step or a thought or a hope left in them—they were completely out of *momentum,* do you see, and that is quite the worst thing you can be short of, you may believe me. His eyes were alive, but they had no idea why—there was nothing in them but life, nothing at all. I've seen animals look like that, but never people. A sheltered existence, I daresay.

What did I say? Oh, something completely absurd; I'd be ashamed to remember it. Something on the order of, "Know me next time, hey?" or, "Where I come from, staring at a person that long means you'll have to get married." Something that stupid, or worse—it doesn't matter, because I wasn't finished saying it when he simply toppled right off his horse's back. Just began listing, as you might say, listing quietly to one side, and kept on listing and listing until he was on the ground. I managed to break his fall and to brace him up against the rain barrel and splash some water on his face. Nothing unusual about *that*—such of my time as hasn't been spent on some road or other, rehearsing some play or other, has gone on getting some man or other to sit up and wipe his mouth. Disgusting waste, when you let yourself think about it.

Not that this one wasn't a nice enough mouth, and a nice face, too. A country face, or it had been once—I was born on a farm myself, somewhere near Cape Dylee, they used to tell me. We moved on the next day, so I can't be sure, of course. He opened dark country eyes after a bit, looking right into mine, and said, "Lukassa." Perfectly calmly, quite as though he hadn't just fainted from hunger and exhaustion. Real people are too much for me sometimes.

Well, by now that was *one* name I knew as well as my own, and a good deal better than I wanted to, let me tell you. I am quite old enough to have no shame in saying that I have spent as many nights as the next fool listening to someone mumbling and crying someone else's name until morning. But the choice was my own, ridiculous or not, and that is considerably different from being wakened every night, without exception, for almost two weeks, by that boy Rosseth tossing in the stall next to mine, crooning, "Nyateneri . . . Lukassa, sweet Lukassa . . . oh, Lal . . . oh, *Lal* . . . !" Discussing the matter with him had no more effect than kicking him awake—he still bounced up singing in the morning, while the rest of us came to look more and more as though we'd spent all night doing what he was dreaming about. There was talk of murder. I was opposed, but wavering.

"Lukassa has ridden out with her friends," I said. "They may return tonight, tomorrow, I have no idea. Sit there and I'll bring you something to eat. Don't move, stay right where you are—do you understand me?" Because I couldn't be sure, do you see? I couldn't be sure whether those unbearable dark eyes saw me at all. "*Stay* there," I said, and then I ran to find Rosseth.

He isn't a bad lad, you know, apart from that obsession of his, which I'm sure he's grown out of by now, if he's alive. He went straightaway to filch some scraps of last night's dinner (which was to be *our* dinner tonight—the Karsh system of feeding his stable guests), and even managed a cup of rather flat red ale. Meanwhile I appropriated some grain for the horse and a tunic from our wardrobe trunk: the one I wear myself in *Lady Vigga's Two Daughters,* where I'm disguised as a man for half the play. We don't do that one much anymore, unless someone requests it, so the front was practically clean, for a wonder.

When I returned, Rosseth was already spooning soup into our long-legged waif, and a few of the company were lounging about asking questions. He paid none of them any heed, but spoke to me as soon as he saw me, saying, "Friends. How many?"

"As many as you have," I said, a bit shortly. I *must* be

getting old, when an ordinary "thank you" begins to matter more to me than epic quests after some mislaid princess or other, even when the hero *does* have the most charming pair of legs for twenty years in any direction. "A black woman"—he was nodding impatiently—"and a tall brown creature, a warrior sort." Petty of me, I suppose, but there was Rosseth already turning puppy-eyed at the mere thought of them, and now *this* one, and it was all suddenly *irritating*. Comes of playing this same story far too many times, doubtless. I said, "My name is Lisonje, and the person feeding you is Rosseth. Can you tell us your name?"

"Tikat," he said, and went to sleep again. Trygvalin, our juvenile, began giving him brandy, but I made him stop. He makes the stuff himself, and there are towns and entire provinces we can't return to because of his openhandedness. I said to Rosseth, "He can stay in the loft with you. The landlord won't know."

Rosseth just looked at me. He said, "Karsh always knows." Tikat woke up and announced, "I am from—" and he named a place I couldn't repeat to save myself. "I have come for Lukassa," simple as that. All the time we were getting him into the stable, easing his clothes off—there were deep scratches and open sores all over his poor body, and some of those rags were stuck to him by his own caked blood—and washing him as well as we could, he kept saying it, "Tell Lukassa I have come for her." He'd certainly come the long way around, that country child.

Rosseth said, "We will have to tell Karsh."

"The boy has no money," I said. "He hasn't got anything but his horse and a bit of flesh. Do you think that will be enough for your master?" Time out of mind, we've played Corcorua and lodged in this same stable, and I still despise that slouching fat man. He's no thief—which is absolutely the only reason we stay here—but his virtues end right there, as far as I know. There's no imagination in him, no generosity, and certainly no charity. He'd give his best room to a family of scorpions—if they could pay—before he lodged one penniless wanderer under his leakiest outhouse roof. Everybody knows Karsh.

"He needs another pair of hands just now," Rosseth said. "We've three separate parties coming to market and likely to be with us for a week, maybe two. It will be more than Marinesha can handle alone, and I'll be too busy myself to help her. If he can work, even a bit, I think I could talk to Karsh."

Tikat said, "I can work." He tried to stand up, and very nearly made it. "But only until Lukassa comes back, because then we will go home together." Simple and clear as that.

Dardis came up to me then to grunt, "Run-through in five minutes," and away out of range before I could get in amongst his ribs and tell him what I thought of *that*. Twenty years leading the company, playing the Wicked Lord Hassidanya at every crossroads between Grannach Harbor and the Durli Hills, and he's still terrified of drying up in the last act, the way it happened that one time in Limsatty. Which means that *we* are condemned, if you please, to rehearse and rehearse that wretched old masque at every free moment, probably for the rest of our lives. Still, it did give me a decent excuse to stop sleeping with him—better Rosseth's dreams, better horses breaking wind, than those lines in my ear in the middle of the night—and we've been much better friends ever since, I do believe. Odd, the way these matters work out.

Rosseth pulled the tunic over Tikat's head and nodded me away, saying, "Go on, it's all right—I'll let him rest awhile, and then we'll go and see Karsh. It's all right." When I looked back from the stable door, the boy was sitting up, trying again to stand and getting tangled up in those blessed legs, like a newborn marsh-goat that already knows it *has* to walk right now or die. In my own experience, there's not a soul in the world, male or female, worth that kind of devotion—but there, as I told you, all *I* know is my lines, so there you are.

TIKAT

When I woke I asked about the Rabbit, and the stable boy said that he had already bitten two horses and one actor, so I went back to sleep.

The second time I woke alone to twilight and silence, except for the occasional stamp and whuffle below. The players, or whatever they were, had gone, and the boy, Rosseth, was whistling somewhere outside. I climbed down from the loft, going slowly, noticing in a far-off way that I was wearing a tunic too small for me, stiff with other peoples' dried sweat. There was a dog, I remember—my head seemed to become huge as a cathedral, and then slowly small again, every time he barked. I saw the Rabbit in a stall near the door; he whinnied at me, but it was such a long way, and I could not reach him. I leaned against the door and said, "Good Rabbit. Good Rabbit."

From the stable door, the inn bulked larger than any building I had ever seen. Two chimneys, lights in every window, laughter and cooking smoke blowing down the night breeze that cooled my face and made my legs feel a little stronger. I started toward the inn because I thought Lukassa might be there.

Rosseth found me under a tree next to the hog pen. I had been sick, I think, but I had *not* fainted again—I knew as well who and where I was as I understood that it would be better for me to stay on all fours for a little while longer. He crouched beside me, saying, "Tikat. I've been past this place twice, looking for you. Why didn't you call out?"

When I did not answer, he put his hands under me and began trying to lift me to my feet. I pushed him away, harder than I meant to, perhaps, and he sat back on his heels and stared at me without speaking for a long time. He was a year or two younger than I, and built very much like the Rabbit: short-legged and thick through the chest, with shaggy red-gold hair, a wide mouth, and quick dark eyes. A kind, curious, irritating face, I thought it then. I said, "I don't need any help."

Rosseth grinned at me, unoffended, unmalicious. "Then you and Karsh should get along wonderfully well. He doesn't give it. Come," and he held out his hand.

"I don't need your Karsh," I said. "I need Lukassa and my horse, nothing more." I got to my knees then, and we faced each other like that, while the hogs grunted in the deepening dark, muzzles pushing between the raw fence posts, trying to reach the place where I had vomited.

"Lukassa has not returned," Rosseth answered, "nor have her friends. As for what you need and don't need, believe me, the only thing that matters right now is Karsh's permission to sleep here and eat here while you recover. Come *on,* Tikat." Suddenly he looked his age, and very anxious with it.

I stood up without his aid, but my legs buckled under me at the third step. Rosseth caught me, but I was growing very tired of being picked up and patted and set down somewhere else, like a baby, and I shook him away again. "I can crawl," I said. "I have crawled before."

Rosseth blew out his breath, exactly the way the Rabbit does when he is displeased with me. Then he took hold of me and dragged me upright once more, would I or would I not. Stronger than they looked, those small, broken-nailed hands. He said in my ear, "I am not doing this for you, but for Lukassa. You are her friend, so I must help you until she comes back. After that, you can put your bloody pride where it belongs. Come on. You can either lean on me or I'll just keep picking you up. Come on." I felt him chuckle, setting his shoulder under mine. "You and Karsh," he said. "I can hardly wait."

The inn was somehow smaller within than it had seemed from outside. We entered through the kitchen—a woman came pushing past us in the greasy smoke, and then a man, but I never really saw them, my eyes were watering so. Someone was chopping meat so furiously that the racket drowned out whatever he was screaming. Rosseth led me like a blind man into the dining hall, where the smoke thinned out enough for me to see a good dozen or more people seated at their dinners. The chairs and tables were rough, splintery work, legs all uneven—I remember that especially, remember thinking, *Oh, we do much better than that back home.* The hall felt cold to me after the kitchen, in spite of the flames booming in the fireplace. It had a low ceiling of soot-blackened half-logs, held up by huge posts with the bark still on them. There were three lamps hanging from the crossbeams, swinging slowly in a draft and sending long, slow shadows twisting over the plaster walls. Rushes rattled underfoot.

No one took any notice of us. The guests looked little different from the ones who used to stop the night with Grandmother Taiwari, who alone in our village kept a room or two for travellers. A few merchants, a long table full of drunken drovers, a sailor, a holy man and woman making a pilgrimage to the hills—and off in a far corner, watching everything, a fat, pale man in a dirty apron. Rosseth led me toward him, saying out of the smiling side of his mouth, "Remember this. He detests people who contradict him, but he despises people who don't. Bear it in mind." The fat man watched us approach.

Close to, he was bigger than I had thought, exactly as his inn seemed smaller. Raw dough, nothing but dough, a gingerbread man who had magically escaped the oven.

His face was bread pudding, with moles and blemishes for the occasional raisin or berry; but the eyes stuck into it were round and blue and surprised, a little boy's eyes under the creased, pouchy lids of a grum old man. I do not know if they would have seemed ordinary eyes in a gentler face. What I know is that I have never again in my life seen eyes like the eyes of fat Karsh the innkeeper.

Rosseth spoke rapidly. "Sir, this is Tikat. He comes from the south, looking for work." The sweet blue eyes considered me, the thin mouth hardly parted; the fat man's voice rasped its way through the dinner noise. "Another of your midden-heap strays? This one doesn't look as though it could empty a chamberpot." The blue eyes forgot me.

Rosseth patted my arm, winked, and moved quickly to put himself back into Karsh's line of sight. "He's weary, sir, travel-worn, I'm not denying that. But give him a meal and a night's sleep, and he'll be ready for any task you set him, in or out of doors. I promise you this, sir."

"You promise." The voice was heavy with dismissal, but he did look at me again, longer and more thoughtfully, finally shrugging. "Well, let him get his meal and his sleep where he likes and see me tomorrow. There might be something for him, I can't say."

"He can sleep in the loft with me—" Rosseth began, but Karsh's head turned toward him and his voice cracked and dried. Karsh said, "A day's work for a night's lodging. I said, let him come back tomorrow." The thick, wrinkled eyelids almost hid the little boy's eyes.

Rosseth started to say something further, but I put him aside. My head was still swinging in and out, vast and clanging one minute, a withered pignut the next. I said, "Fat man, fat man, listen carefully to me. I have not come as far and hard and lonely as I have come to sleep and eat in your sty. I will work well for you, better than anyone you have, until my Lukassa returns, and then we will go home together. And while I work for you, beginning this night, I will sleep in your stable and eat as good a meal as you serve anyone." Rosseth was desperately converting his grin into a coughing fit, muffling it in his sleeve. "If you do not agree to this, say so and be damned—I could find better quarters with no money than the best this midden-heap can offer. But I will be back for Lukassa tomorrow, and the next day, and the day after that, so you might as well get some use out of me, don't you think?" There was more I said, but the echoes in my head drowned out the words. Rosseth's hands were under my shoulders again, easing me down into a chair.

When I could open my eyes, the innkeeper was still studying me, his sagging white face as blank as the meal-sack it resembled. I heard Rosseth saying earnestly, "Sir, we do need the extra help just now, with the two new parties staying as long as they'll be—" and then the slow reply, like a keel grating over stones, "I had no need to be reminded. Be quiet and let me think." Doubtless it was only my exhaustion, but it seemed to me that the clamor of the dining hall softened slightly at his words. I had disliked Karsh the innkeeper on sight—I still do—but there was more to him than bread pudding.

"Take him away with you," he said to Rosseth after a time. "Feed him in the kitchen, let him sleep where he will, and in the morning set him to cleaning the bathhouse and stopping those holes you haven't yet touched, where the frogs get in. After that, Shadry should have some use for him in the kitchen." He opened his eyes wide for a moment and peered at me with some kind of wonder that I was too weary to understand, drawing a breath as though to say something further, important, something to do with Lukassa, with me. But instead he looked at Rosseth again, mumbling, "Those two, those men, anywhere about, have you seen them?" Rosseth shook his head, and Karsh turned without another word and disappeared into a back room. He moved gracefully, the way a wave swells and rolls from shore to shore, never quite breaking. My mother, who was also fat, moved that way.

Rosseth said, very quietly, "My," and began to laugh.

He said, "I know what I told you, but I can't believe—" and his voice trailed away a second time. "Come on," he said, "you've earned as much dinner as you can eat. What is it, what's the matter, Tikat?" At the drovers' table they had begun singing a dirty song that every child in my village knows. It made me think of Lukassa, and I was ashamed. Rosseth said, "Come on, Tikat, we'll go and have our dinner."

Rosseth

They came back just as Tikat and I were finishing our meal, which we ate outside, sitting under the tree where Marinesha liked to hang her washing. I heard them first—three plodding horses and the unmistakable squeak of Lal's saddle, which no amount of soaping and oiling could get rid of. Tikat knew it too: he dropped his bowl and wheeled to see them passing in the dusk, turning into the courtyard, Nyateneri's eyes and cheekbones catching the light as she leaned to say something to Lal. Lukassa rode some way behind them, reins slack, looking down. None of them noticed us as they went by.

In honesty, I forgot about Tikat for the moment. His concern with Lukassa was his concern; mine was to warn Nyateneri about the two smiling little men who had come seeking her. I jumped up and ran calling, and Lal as well as Nyateneri reined in to wait for me. Behind me I heard Tikat crying, "Lukassa!" and the sorrow and the overwhelming joy and thankfulness in that one word were more than I could understand then, or ever forget now. I did not look back.

Clinging to Nyateneri's stirrup, I panted out everything: what the men had done and said, how they had looked, sounded, what it had felt like to be breathing the air they breathed—very nearly as terrible as strangling in their hands. I remember how vastly pleasant it was, when I got to that part, to hear Lal miss a breath and feel Nyateneri's hand tighten on my shoulder for just a moment. She seemed neither frightened nor surprised, I noticed; when Lal asked her, "Who are they?" she made no reply beyond the tiniest shrug. Lal did not ask again, but from that point she watched Nyateneri, not me, as I spoke.

I was telling them how Karsh had gotten the men to leave the inn when there came a sudden wordless shout from Tikat, a rattling flurry of hooves, and Lukassa exploded into our midst as we all turned, her horse's shoulder almost knocking Lal out of the saddle. Lukassa made no apology: it took Nyateneri and me to calm all three horses, while she gasped, over and over, "Make him stop *saying* that, make him stop! He must not say that to me, make him not say it!" Her eyes were so wild with terror that they seemed to have changed shape, because of the way the skin was stretched around them.

Tikat came up after her, moving very slowly, exactly as you do when you're trying not to frighten a wild creature. His face, his whole long body, all of him was plainly numb with bewilderment. He said—so carefully, so gently—"Lukassa, it's me, it's Tikat. It's *Tikat*." Each time he said his name, she shuddered further away from him, keeping Lal's horse between them.

Nyateneri raised an eyebrow, saying nothing. Lal said, "The boy is her betrothed. He has followed us a very long and valiant way." She saluted Tikat with a strange, flowing gesture of both hands at her breast—I was never able to copy it, though I tried often, and I have never seen it made again. "Well done," she said to him. "I thought we had lost you a dozen times over. You know how to track almost as well as you know how to love."

Tikat turned on her, his eyes as mad as Lukassa's, not with fear but with despair. "What have you done to her?" he shouted. "She has known me all her life, what have you done? Witch, wizard, where is my Lukassa? Who is this you have raised from the dead? Where is my Lukassa?" Three hours I'd known him, proud and stubborn and cranky, and my heart could have broken for him.

"Well, well, well, well, *well,*" Nyateneri said softly to nobody. Lal reached out and took hold of Lukassa's hands, saying, "Child, listen, it's your man, surely you remember." But Lukassa jerked back from her as well, scrambling frantically down from her horse and rushing toward the inn. On the threshold she collided with Gatti Jinni, who went over on his back like a beetle. Lukassa fell to one knee—Tikat cried out again, but did not follow—then struggled up and stumbled through the door. The noise of the drovers' singing swallowed her up.

In the silence, Nyateneri murmured, "Secrets everywhere."

"Yes," Lal said. "So there are." She swung down from her saddle, and after a moment Nyateneri joined her. Lal handed me the three horses' reins, saying only, "Thank you, Rosseth," before she hurried toward the inn herself. Nyateneri winked slowly at me and strolled after her. Gatti Jinni continued rolling and squalling on the doorstep.

I did what I could. I took all the reins in one hand, and I put my free arm around Tikat's shoulders, and I brought everybody back to the stable. The horses crowded me, eager for their stalls, but Tikat came along as docilely as though he were on a rope himself, or a chain: head low, arms hanging open-palmed, feet tripping over weed-clumps. He said no word more, not even when I helped him up the ladder to the loft, raked some straw together, gave him my extra horse-blanket, and wished him good-night. While I was rubbing the horses down, I thought I heard him stirring and muttering, but when I climbed up again to bring him some water, he was deeply asleep. I was glad for him.

With the horses taken care of, I thought I had better go up to the inn and help Marinesha clear away dinner. I was halfway there when a figure seemed to leap out of the bare ground just in front of me. I almost dropped to the ground myself—those two hunters were somewhere very near, I knew that in my belly—but the shape hailed me, and I recognized that curious sharp voice immediately. It was the old man with the grandson in Cucuroa, the one who wandered into the inn now and again to sit long over his ale and chat with anyone he could find. As handsome a grandsir as ever I'd seen by far, with his bright cheeks, white mustache, and marvelously long, delicate hands. Every time I watched him turning one of our earthenware mugs round and round between them, talking of strange beasts and old wars, I would think, *I wish I had hands like that, and a life that such hands could tell and frame.* Although I had never seen him with Lal, Nyateneri, or Lukassa, I thought of him in the same way: a southwest wind blowing across my common days, smelling of such stories, such dreams, as all my soul could not contain, let alone understand. His voice made me nervous and irritable if I listened to it for very long, but that seemed right too, then, in those days.

"And there you are," he said, "and where else should I have expected to find you but journeying between one chore and the next?" He patted my arm and smiled at me out of eyes as blue as Karsh's eyes, but completely different, eyes like snow in shadow, almost as edged and painful to look at as his voice was to hear. He said, "Tireless child, I am sent bearing yet another task for you. The lady Nyateneri has gone to the bathhouse this quarter of an hour past, and wishes you to attend her there. I volunteered to bring you the message if I met you on my way home. Now you have it and I will be gone, and a very good evening, young Rosseth." He was already by me with those last words, already easing into darkness.

The summons did not strike me as unusual. The bathhouse at The Gaff and Slasher was a grand one for the time and the region, with two rooms: one for a tub and the other divided by a long trench filled with great stones.

By now Nyateneri would have lighted the fire laid under the stones and some would be starting to glow red. Steam-baths are popular enough in other northern parts, but never much so around Corcorua—Nyateneri was one of the few guests I had ever seen make use of Karsh's odd and only extravagance, which he loudly regretted building every day that I ever knew him. I never thought to turn and look after the old man, but hurried on the rest of the way to the inn.

At the kitchen pump, I drew two buckets of water and started for the bathhouse. The path was treacherous in the darkness, being cross-laced with thick old tree-roots—even knowing it as well as I did, I could have broken an ankle almost as easily as spilling a bucket—and I went slowly for that reason, and for another as well, which I admit with some shame even now. To raise steam within the bathhouse, I never went inside, but gradually poured the cold water over the hot stones through a channel set low down between the logs. But there was another space, a bit below eye level, a slit as long as my hand and wide as my thumb, through which I had great hopes of glimpsing Nyateneri before the steam hid her nakedness. I offer no defense of this behavior, except perhaps what came of it.

The night was so still that I could easily hear Nyateneri's soft footsteps, so close. I wished the rising half-moon out of the sky behind me, since I feared that one as quick as she might well notice the golden glint suddenly vanishing when my head blocked the light. Setting down one bucket, I began carefully tilting the other, stooping at the same time to peer through the tiny gap in the bathhouse wall.

For a moment I saw nothing but bark and my own eyelashes. Then something bright flashed across my vision and instantly back—*left, right*—followed by a swift double thump of feet, as though one dancer had mimicked the step or leap of another. I pressed my face closer against the logs, squinting for all I was worth, and at once caught my longed-for, impossible, mouth-drying view of Nyateneri's left breast. For just a moment, it filled my vision: golden-brown as summer hills, round as the *piniak* gourds that spill over the market stalls a bit later in the year, with just their sudden upward lilt at the tips. I heard her voice, speaking in a language that I had never heard, and then a reply in the same tongue. The answering voice was a man's, and I knew it from the first word.

Nyateneri moved away from the wall, giving me a better perspective on the steam-room. She stood with her back to me now, long legs wide apart and slightly bent at the knees, a dagger in her left hand and a bathtowel wound loosely around her right arm. Beyond her I could see the fire-trench and smell the heat of the huge dark stones. She spoke again, her voice amused and inviting, beckoning with the dagger. Another man replied, and a moment later Half-Mouth moved into my view on the far side of the trench, grinning like a snake as he approached Nyateneri, barely lifting his feet, yet somehow *dancing*. He carried no weapon at all.

When he was close enough that I could hear his light, unhurried breathing, Nyateneri suddenly flicked the towel in his face and leaped easily across the fire-trench to land half-crouched on the other side. Blue Eyes was waiting for her there, sliding in to come under her guard before she regained her balance. But she had never lost it: the dagger flickered too fast for my one eye at the crack to follow, and she was past him as he drew back and heading for the door. Behind her, Blue Eyes licked at his left wrist and chuckled quietly, not bothering to turn.

I could not see the door, nor Half-Mouth either—I could only listen for the thud of his feet and Nyateneri's, and judge from Blue Eyes' placidity that she had not made her escape. An instant later, she was back in my range of vision and on his side of the fire-trench, literally whirling toward him, spinning so fast that her one dagger looked like a dozen. Blue Eyes got out of the way only by springing high into the air and somersaulting over the slash that passed within two inches of his belly. As he came down, he slashed out himself—it seemed only with three fingers, and I never saw the blow land. But Nyateneri tumbled sideways, against the wall, and the two of them were at her, laughing in their awful voices. I heard my own voice then, crying out in despair, as she never did. I think they heard me, too.

It would be nice to think that my useless wail distracted them even in the least, but I doubt it very much. What is important is that Nyateneri doubled herself, kicked out and rolled in a way I can't describe, and was back across the fire-trench while Half-Mouth and Blue Eyes were still getting to their feet. Half-Mouth was breathing differently now, and what he called to her had no laughter in it, in any language. Nyateneri did a quick little saunter of triumph, flourishing her dagger and slapping her rump in derision. May I be forgiven for finding her beautiful and myself as disgracefully randy as any dog, in the midst of my terror for her.

So it began, and so it went on, that dance of hunters and quarry that I can still see in its every pace to this day. Nyateneri plainly had no desire to come to close quarters with Blue Eyes and Half-Mouth, unarmed or no: her goal was the door and the night beyond. For their part, they wanted nothing but to get past her dagger, and room to use their long, thin hands. One on each side of the fire-trench, they pressed and harried her, trusting themselves to wear her down, content to let her whirl and jeer and flurry out of their grasp, knowing that sooner or later she *must* stumble, *must* misjudge, *must* need one breath too many. They had her both ways: she could not kill them; and, elude them as she might, as long as she might, she could not get out of the bathhouse. The end was certain—I knew it as well as they.

Ah, but Nyateneri! She assumed nothing, conceded nothing. There was a third element, the fire-trench itself, and she built every foray, every sortie around it, springing back and forth to safety only when one or another pair of hands were closing upon her, trying constantly to lure her pursuers into fiery space, right down onto the burning stones. Twice she almost managed it: one time Half-Mouth was actually in the air, actually flailing his arms and legs in silent, gaping horror, when Blue Eyes snatched him to safety with one arm, cheerfully saluting Nyateneri with the other. Her dagger danced its own butterfly dance, even when she was in full leap or mid-roll, and she left her mark on those two, each time so swiftly that it might be minutes before they noticed themselves bleeding in two new places. She was the first warrior I had ever seen.

But she could not reach the door. Finally, nothing mattered but the fact that she could not reach the door. Scratches or no scratches, Blue Eyes and Half-Mouth's endurance was yet greater than hers, and one of them could allow the other time to rest, as she dared not allow it to herself. Even now she was slipping most of their blows; but when one or another fingertip or palm-edge or elbow as much as grazed her, the shock clearly roared through her whole body, and each time she was slower to recover, slower to escape to another momentary sanctuary on the other side of the fire-trench. Half the time I could only go by sound even to guess what was happening, but one moment is with me now, telling it: she has gathered herself, gathered in all her *hakai*—oh, you don't have that word, do you? let's say her deepest strength, it's the best I can do—and flies straight across the trench, out of the corner into which Blue Eyes has driven her, straight at Half-Mouth's throat. A gallant gamble, but a rash one—Half-Mouth takes two steps back, one to the left, and smashes her down with a two-handed blow that knocks the dagger from her hands and sends it skidding back toward the fire. Lunging dazedly, desperately after it, she goes partway over the edge herself, and completely out of my range of vision. The dagger spins away on its side: red, silver, red.

And still she makes no sound. All I can hear is Blue

Eyes and Half-Mouth's soft, joyous giggling; all I can see is the aching happiness in their faces as they rush past my spy-hole, closing on Nyateneri. Then nothing. Nothing for how long? Five seconds? ten? half a minute? I have turned from the wall, my eyes closed, too numb for grief—like Tikat, perhaps—vaguely conscious that I should run, run, get to the inn, the stable, anywhere, before those two come out and find me. But I cannot move, not to help Nyateneri then, not to save myself now—*and it has been like this before. Fire, blood, laughing men, and me aware, aware but unable: lost and alone and terrified past thought, past breath. It has been like this before. There was a huge man who smelled like bread and milk.*

No sense in any of that for you, is there? No. I only opened my eyes when I heard Half-Mouth's snarl of incredulous outrage, for all the world like a *shukri* who has suddenly discovered that mice can fly. How she had saved herself from the burning stones, I have no idea to this day, but as I stooped to the spy-hole again, Nyateneri backflipped across my sight and stood there for a moment, the dagger in her right hand now, and the left hanging oddly crooked. Oh, but I do remember her—as I shouldn't, for any number of reasons—with her ragged, graying hair sticking out on all sides, her mouth glorious with mockery and her body wearing blood-flecked sweat as a queen wears velvet. Want her? Did I still *want* her? I wanted to *be* her, with all my soul, do you understand me? Do you understand?

It was the end, you see, and even I knew it. When she challenged them once more in their own tongue, there was a shadowy wheeze in her voice; when she crouched, arms open, coaxing them into her embrace, one knee trembled—only a very little, but if I noticed it, you can imagine what Blue Eyes and Half-Mouth saw. Her left hand was plainly useless, and she kept shaking her head slightly, as though to clear it of doubt or a lingering dream. There was no fear in her, and no resignation either. Blue Eyes moved into view, smiling, touching his brow with a forefinger in a way that was no salute this time but a farewell. Nyateneri laughed at him.

And suddenly I was there. No, I don't mean to brag that at last I sprang into decisive, heroic action, for I don't believe that I could have looked a second time into those two men's faces for anyone's sake. I mean only that I knew I was *Rosseth,* which was, for good or ill, something more than a pair of eyes peering through a crack in a wall. I could think again, and I could move, and feel anger as well as terror and dull loss; and what else I could do was what I had come there to do in the first place. I lifted the bucket that I had absurdly never set down, bent, and carefully poured the water into the channel at the base of the wall.

You have to do it slowly; it always takes less water than you think to fill the bathhouse with steam. I heard one of them shout, then another, and then a wild surge of laughter from Nyateneri which—I will swear—made the log wall pulse like warm, living flesh against my cheek. I emptied the bucket, straightened, and set my eye to the crack in time to see Half-Mouth backing toward me, seemingly setting himself to chop billowing nothingness to pieces with his deadly hands and feet. Nyateneri's dagger, glinting demurely, slipped through the steam as gently as it did through the skin just below his ribs. The first thrust probably killed him, though I think there was another. He folded silently forward into clouds.

I dropped the bucket and crept to the door. Blue Eyes had to be stopped there if he tried to flee, somehow impeded long enough for Nyateneri to catch up with him. I had no plans: I knew that whatever I did might likely mean my death, and I was frightened but not paralyzed, no more of that. I have done a great many foolish things in all the years between that night and this, but never, never again through inaction, and I never will until I do die. Nyateneri taught me.

Crouching by the door, I cursed myself for abandoning the bucket; perhaps I could have hit Blue Eyes with it, or thrown it in his way when he bolted from the bathhouse. It didn't cross my mind for a minute that he might *not* bolt, but he might still be more than a match on his own for an exhausted Nyateneri. There was no sound from beyond the door. I imagined Blue Eyes and Nyateneri circling invisibly in the steam, all bearings lost except for the sense of the enemy inches away: reaching for each other with their skins and their hair. Something cracked against the logs from inside—a solid, unyielding thud that could easily have been a skull—and I promptly began my new life of active stupidity by pushing the door open.

What happened next happened so quickly that it isn't clear to me even now. There was the steam, of course, blinding me immediately—then a body banged into me, hard, utterly shocking, as though I had blundered straight into a wall. I went down flat on my back. The body came down with me, because our legs were tangled up together. Something hot and silent clawed at me, and I kicked out in wild panic, trying to free my legs. One foot found softness; there was a gasping whistle, and then another weight crushed the air out of my lungs in turn. Blue Eyes and Nyateneri were raging over me like storm winds, pinning me to earth, battering me so that I struggled in a helpless fury of my own, wanting in that moment to kill them both because they were hurting me. Somebody's elbow caught my nose, and I thought it was broken.

Then it all stopped. I heard—I *felt*—a dry little sound, like someone unobtrusively clearing his throat. A body slid slowly off me when I pushed at it; a head wobbled in the dirt next to mine. Nyateneri's quiet, tired voice said, "Thank you, Rosseth."

I couldn't stand up at first; she had to help me, which she did quite gently and carefully, even with one hand as limp as Blue Eyes' neck. He lay so still, half-curled on his side, looking small and surprised. The blood from my nose was dripping all over him. I asked Nyateneri, "Is he dead?"

"If he isn't, we are," Nyateneri said. "You only get one chance at people like those." Then she laughed very softly and added, "As a rule." She reached inside the door to pick up her dagger where it lay, turning it a bit awkwardly in her right hand. "I have never been able to throw a knife properly," she said, almost to herself, "not once. I don't know what possessed me to try it this time. Until you opened that door, I was finished. Thank you."

The pain in my nose made me feel sick, and the blood wouldn't stop coming. Nyateneri had me lie down again, my head in her lap, while she held my nose with a soaked cloth in a particularly unpleasant way. When I honked, "Who were those men?" she pretended to mishear me, replying, "I know, we'll have to tell Karsh—I don't see any way out of it. I am just too weary to bury anybody right now." She stroked my hair absently, and I gave myself up to the smell of her quieting body and my first understanding that nothing ever happens the way you imagined it. Here I was at last, lying with Nyateneri's damp skin under my cheek, the breasts I had so earnestly spied on sighing in and out above me as she breathed, and all I had strength or ambition to do was wait for my nose to stop bleeding. Yes, you can laugh, it's all right. I thought it was funny even then.

After a time, I was able to sit up, and Nyateneri went back into the bathhouse to find her robe. I said through the doorway, "They came looking for you, they meant to kill you. Why? What had you ever done to them?"

She did not answer until she came out again. I sat there in the calm dark, with a dead man at my feet, and *lirilith*—what you'd call a nightcryer—already mourning for him away down in the orchard. I don't understand how they can know death so instantly, but they always do; at least, that's what I grew up believing in that country. Nyateneri leaned in the doorway, gingerly trying her left hand with her right. She asked me, abruptly but without expression, "How did you happen to be bringing the water and not Marinesha? I had asked for her."

"I never saw her," I said. "I met that old man—you know the one? with the white mustache?—and he told me that you had given him the message for me. Perhaps he got it mixed up. He's really quite old."

"Ah," Nyateneri said, and nothing more until I asked her a third time about Blue Eyes and Half-Mouth. Then she came to crouch beside me again, looking into my eyes and putting her injured hand lightly on the side of my neck. She said, "Rosseth, if one thing goes against my nature more than another, it is lying to a person who has just saved my life. Please don't make me do it." Her own ever-changing eyes were silver half-moons in the moonlight.

"Secrets everywhere," I answered, emboldened to mimic her. But I felt honored, like a child cozened with just the least fragment of an adult confidence, the least suggestion of a world beyond the nursery. "I won't, then," I said, "if you'll tell me about them sometime." She nodded very seriously, saying, "I promise." Her hand was hot on me, hot as Blue Eyes' hands had been when he held me up by my throat, so long ago. I asked her if it was much hurt, and she replied, "Badly enough, but not as badly as it could be. Like your nose," and she kissed me there; and then, quickly, on the mouth. "Come," she said, "we'll have to help each other back to the inn. I feel really quite old."

I went around the bathhouse to pick up my buckets. When I returned, she was standing with the dagger out again, holding it by the point and thoughtfully tossing it up high enough to let it turn one slow circle in the air before she caught it. "It's not very well balanced, of course," she said softly, not to me. "It wasn't ever meant for throwing." She turned and smiled at me, and I thought she might kiss me again, but no.

The Innkeeper

There is a queen in this country still, in her black castle down in Fors na'Shachim. Or perhaps it's a king by now, or the army back again, no matter. The tax collectors stay the same, whoever rules. But king, queen, or jumped-up captain, one day I mean to travel there and seek audience. It will be a hard and tiresome journey, and any highwaymen will have to wait in line for whatever the coachmen and hostellers leave me; and *then* it will take the last coins hidden in my shoe-soles to bribe my way into line to make my complaint. But I will be heard. If it costs me my head, believe that I will be heard.

"Your Majesty," I will say, "where in all your royal scrolls and parchments of law is it decreed that Karsh the innkeeper is to be forever denied a single moment of simple peace? Where have your noble ministers set it down that when I am not being racked by the daily balks and foils of running my poor establishment, I am to be plagued by an endless succession of zanies, frauds, incompetents, and maniacs? And please, just to satisfy an old man's curiosity, sire, where do you get them? Where could even so great a monarch as yourself procure, all at the same time, three madwomen—none of whom is even remotely what she claims to be—an impossible bumpkin who claims to be betrothed to the maddest of the lot, a stable full of penniless actors who keep my guests' horses awake with their goings-on, and a stableboy who was never worth much to begin with and lately shows real promise of becoming a complete liability? And that final touch of true genius, those two chuckling little assassins who ended up dead in my bathhouse—Your Majesty, my peasant palate isn't sensitive enough to appreciate such brilliance. To me it's all equal, all blankly vexatious; why waste such jewels of aggravation on fat, weary Karsh? Show me only where this is written, and I will trudge the long way back to The Gaff and Slasher and trouble you never again." I will say all that to someone on a throne before I die.

Not that it will change a thing—I have no illusions about *that*. My lot is my bloody lot, whoever inscribed it wherever, and if I were to doubt it for a moment, all I have to do is remember that evening when I stood looking dumbly down at two sprawled bodies by lantern-light, while that brown soldier-nun Nyateneri had the face to demand whether I sent such attendants to wait on everybody who bathed at my inn. The boy was standing as close to her as her skin would let him, glaring at me, defying me to send him about his proper business. And so I would have done, but for the way—no, let it go, it's nothing to do with anyone, and besides, I had other affairs to think about. Dead men had put The Gaff and Slasher into my hands thirty years ago, long enough for me to have learned just how easily two more dead men could snatch it away again. And I am too old to start over as some other innkeeper's Gatti Jinni.

Miss Nyateneri carried on for some while about murder, irresponsibility and the law, but that was all for show. I am also too old not to know that sort of thing when I see it. I did marvel at it though: two ragged little heaps of laundry stiffening there, as her muscles and nerves and heart must surely have been freezing and stiffening in her, in the wind that always seems to come after *that* sort of thing; and she still able to rant briskly away at me just as though her own wash had come back dirty. I let her run down—that was fair enough—and then I said, "We have no sheriff or queensman in Corcorua, but there is a county magistrate who rides through every two months or so. By good fortune, he is due here in another four or five days. We can turn this matter over to him then, as you please."

Well, *that* quieted Miss Nyateneri in a hurry. I don't mind saying that it was a pleasure to watch her lower her eyes, hug her elbows tight, and mumble about her and her companions' need for haste and privacy. I don't take any particular joy in someone else's discomfiture—what good is that to me, after all?—but of those three women who had imposed themselves on my custom two very long weeks ago, this one had been a special nuisance on her own account, from the moment that fox of hers ran off with my hen. So I folded my own arms and enjoyed myself while she fumbled on and the boy glowered as though I were menacing his darling, a head and more taller than he. Her left hand was hurt in some way; he kept touching it very gently, very shyly. Two long weeks for both of us, truly.

At last I interrupted, saying, "In that case, I think what's wanted here is a shovel and silence. Do you agree?" She stared at me. I went on. "We landlords deal in forgetfulness as much as in food and wine. All that interests me about these men you killed is that they were no strangers to you. They followed you to my inn, as that mad carl from the south followed your friend, as worse trouble will follow you all here—do not even bother to lie to me about that. I can do nothing, you stay against my will, by force of arms, but do me at least the small honor of not asking me to be *concerned*. The boy and I will bury your dead. No one else will know."

She smiled then: only the quickest, leanest sort of fox-grin, but real enough even so, and the first such courtesy she had ever offered to her host at The Gaff and Slasher. "Do other guests misprize you as much as I have?" she wanted to know. "Say yes, please, of your kindness."

"How can I tell?" I asked her in my turn. The boy was goggling past me, but I never looked over my shoulder. "I deal in forgetfulness," I said. "I ask only whether people wish a warming pan, an extra quilt, or perhaps a stuffed goose at dinner. The goose is Shadry's specialty, and requires a day's advance notice." I heard the black woman, Lal, chuckle at my side, and the white one's breath in the darkness beyond.

"Much else requires notice," Lal murmured, "and doesn't get it." Miss Nyateneri's face slammed shut—you could *hear* it, and I am not an imaginative man. Lal said, "Go back to your guests, good Master Karsh. My friends and I will deal with this foolish business. You may take Rosseth with you."

A notably arbitrary tone she always had, that one, but just then I could yield to it happily enough. I was a good ten strides gone before it occurred to me that the boy was not following. When I turned he was standing with his back to me, facing the three of them, saying, "I will bring you a spade. At least let me do that, let me get the spade." Hands on his hips, head shaking stubbornly. He was doing just that in the hayloft, in the potato patch, when he was five.

"Rosseth, we do not need you." Lal's voice was sharp, even harsh, almost as much so as I could have wished. "Go with your master, Rosseth." He turned away from her and flung toward me, marching so blindly that he would have blundered right into me if I hadn't stepped aside. I looked back at the women—they were not looking at us, but drawing together over those dead bodies like so many ravens—and then I walked behind the boy back to the inn. For the first time in a very long while, I followed him.

LAL

Good or ill, it might all have been avoided if I hadn't already been drinking. I drink very seldom—it is one of the many pleasant habits that my life has never been able to afford—but then I drink with a purpose. You will say that I should have been rejoicing: that this day had not only set Nyateneri and me squarely back on the track of the one I called *my friend* and she *the Man Who Laughs,* but also offered us at least some part of a vision of some part of his fate. True enough, and a meaningless, useless kind of truth it seemed, that evening long ago in a little low room smelling of Karsh's life, Nyateneri's fox, and the dozen pigeons Karsh kept in the attic directly above. What good to know that our dear magician had lived near Corcorua in a ridiculous pastry tower, and had been betrayed by a beloved companion—himself in turn slain by demons of some sort—when there was no imagining how long ago this had all happened, or where in this world he might have fled? Lukassa could tell us no more than that terrible chamber had told her; for the rest, the trail was even colder than it had been when we set out in the morning. *My friend* would have to come to us now—there was truly no going to him.

For my part, I was weary from my skin inwards, angry with everything from my skin on out, and capable neither of thought nor of sleep. So I had Karsh send up what he complained were his last three bottles of Dragon's Daughter—the southernmost wine in his cellar, so red that it is almost black—and I was decently into the second when word came that I was wanted at the bathhouse. I brought the bottle with me, for company's sake. Lukassa followed.

When I drink too much—and I *only* drink too much, as I have said—I most often become sullen, brooding and resentful. Perhaps this is my true nature, and all else of me a mask, who knows? I said no word to Nyateneri—no questions, no reproaches, nothing—while the three of us were burying the two bodies in a wild tickberry patch, a tedious distance from the bathhouse. It was work we both knew, and best done mum in any case. I finished the second bottle then, without offering it round. Nyateneri said something in her own tongue over the graves, and we walked back to the inn with her looking sideways at me on my left and Lukassa sneaking glances on my right. And I said nothing at all until we were in our room with the last wine bottle open before me. I am like that, to this day. It is why I prefer to travel alone.

Then, finally, I rounded on her, on Nyateneri. I am not proud of much that I said, and there is no reason to recount every word. The main of it was that she had deceived Lukassa and me: she had endangered our lives from the moment we met, saying that no one pursued her and all the while knowing that those two killers were drawing nearer as she lied to us. When she defended herself, pointing out that she had said only that no one anywhere wanted her *back*, never that she was not wanted *dead*—oh, then I lost language completely and came around the table reaching for her. Which was certainly foolish—hurt and tired or not, she was still stronger than I—but she swiftly put the bed between us, holding up her hands for peace. In the attic the pigeons woke up and began gurgling and flapping, making chilly dust filter down between the rafters.

"What does it matter? They came to kill me, and I killed them—you never even saw them until they were dead. What danger, what smallest inconvenience for you? what night's sleep did it all ever cost you? It was my business, mine to deal with, and I did, and it is done. It is done, finished, no harm to anyone but me. Tell me differently, Lal-after-dark."

"Is it?" I screamed at her. "Two little deaths and all well—is it always finished so easily for you, with no—" I was still dribbling words—"no *echoes*? Tell Rosseth, whom they almost strangled—tell *her*." Between the tower, and the encounter with Tikat, and then helping to bury Nyateneri's victims, poor Lukassa had endured the hardest day of us all; small blame to her if she had now gone to huddle in a corner, whining wordlessly to the fox and twisting an end of her hair. I'd have done likewise, but for the wine.

Nyateneri turned to look long and thoughtfully at Lukassa, who looked back quickly, and then away. "Indeed I will," she said. "And then perhaps she will tell me what it is like to be dead, and then to be raised into life again, and even possibly why it was never mentioned to me that I was traveling with a wizard and a walking corpse, who were in turn being followed by a mad farmboy. The matter might have been brought up, surely? At some well-chosen point?" Her voice remained as pleasantly ironic as ever, but it shook very slightly as she stared at me. Furious as I was, I would not have charged her again.

"That was *our* business," I answered. "None of it put you in peril, as your secrets did us. I would have told you if it were otherwise."

Nyateneri's laugh was high and contemptuous. "There was only one wizard whose word I ever took for anything." Her left hand was swelling badly: she had used it without complaint as we dug the graves, but the slightest gesture obviously hurt her now. She went on loudly:

"And even he never tried to raise the dead. He said there was no way of doing that that was not wrong in its nature, and the greatest of mages could not make it right. So there's no need to tax yourself persuading me that you learned the art from *him*. I knew him better than that."

"The devil you do!" I shouted, and it was not until I saw her blink uncomprehendingly that I realized I had fallen—and a long, long fall it was—back into my oldest childhood tongue, the secret speech of an *inbarati* of Khaidun. That may not tell you how angry I was, and how drunk, but it tells me. I was trembling myself, from the shock of that sound, as I repeated the words in common speech, carefully. I said, "If you knew him as well as you say, then you ought to remember how much he loved gardening, and how dreadful he was at it. His melons were like fists, his greens crackled like parchment—his corn came up withered, and his beans never came up at all. He couldn't have grown so much as a potato without the aid of magic."

Nyateneri was staring at me, shaking her head, looking half-drunk herself with weariness and amazement. *"That?"* she said. *"That?* You did it with that old garden rhyme of his? I don't believe it." But she was beginning to laugh, in a different way this time, a kind of deep, boiling giggle. "Oh, I don't believe it, I don't believe it. You raised her like a squash, like a—" but the giggle took over then, and she collapsed onto the bed beside Lukassa, pounding her thigh with her unhurt hand and hooting helplessly. The fox's cold laughter joined hers.

Lukassa looked offended at first, but Nyateneri's laughter swept everything before it until we were all three rocking and yapping like the fox, who bounced between us, nipping painfully at chins and noses. I slapped him off the bed, and he promptly sprang to the table and stood there listening to the pigeons overhead, plainly counting them with his pricked ears. Why did Karsh keep those birds, I still wonder, and to whom in this world would Karsh send messages? I certainly never found out.

The laughter dissolved the clawing ball of fury that had been turning in my stomach all that day—longer, perhaps. Lukassa in particular clung to her mirth like a child to the last moments of a holiday; as well she might, who hadn't laughed twice since her return to this life. Nyateneri kept asking her about that, still chuckling but without mockery: "What was it like to be a squash, a head of cabbage? What did it *feel* like?" Lukassa finally answered her, speaking in a voice that I would give more than I can tell you to forget.

"I was never that," she said, quite gently. "A vegetable has no notion of what is happening to it, but I always knew. When I was in the river, I was Lukassa dying, and when I was dead I was still Lukassa, still, still." And so she had been, for no reason I understand yet: crying her death with such hunger, such outrage, that it changed my road, and next my journey, and at last my life. She continued, "And when I rose to moonlight through the water and stood before Lal, I was Lukassa there, too, only"—the voice faltered then—"only not so much. Different. Some Lukassa was left among the stones of the river, and I cannot go back to find her. And if I could, she would not come to me, because she has no name now, so no one can call her." She stopped then, and not even the fox could meet her eyes.

When I felt the tears begin, I did not know what they were. It had been that long since the last time I wept. I thought first that I was sick from the wine, and then that I might be having a taking, a fit, for the muscles of my face and throat and stomach took themselves away from me, though I fought them so hard that I could not breathe. *My own body, turned treacherous as Bismaya, effortlessly cruel as men.* I heard a strange, light voice, a child's voice, saying something very far away, and then the tears came in full and I gave in, gave in, I who never gave in, not to any of them, not in my heart, never, and they all knew it, every one, always. Until that moment, no one living had seen me cry, except for *my friend,* if he indeed lived.

I have cried since, but only once, and that time for joy, and it has no place in this tale.

How they gaped at me, Nyateneri and Lukassa as well. I was doubled over, almost retching with sorrow—and, yes, some of that was undoubtedly the wine, but there was more. You see, absolutely all that I have of my beginnings is my name, *Lalkhamsin-khamsolal,* and to have lost that, to have your soul not answer to its name—oh, do you see, I could just imagine that, but for me even the imagining was beyond dealing with, beyond fighting or enduring or turning into a story. And there she was, that village goose, staring down at me in vague wonder while I wept and wept for her loss and her courage, and for myself, for *my friend,* for Khaidun where I was born. It had been that long.

Nyateneri finally put her arms around me, which quieted me immediately. She was stiff at it; and, in honesty, I am not easy being held, not by most people. I moved a little from her, wiping my face and eyes. Nyateneri turned away then, and busied herself refilling my winemug. She sipped, gasped, shivered slightly, and said, "I think we are going to need some more of this appalling swill."

"No more left," I snuffled. "Karsh said." I cried a little more at the thought.

"Karsh misunderstood," Nyateneri said. She swung herself off the bed and was gone in what seemed the same movement, already calling for the innkeeper as she clattered down the stair. Lukassa and I sat silent, shyer than strangers, while I cleaned myself up as well as I might. When I could speak again, I said finally, "Lukassa, there is only one person who can call back Lukassa, the one there in the river, under the stones. That person is Tikat."

Lukassa shuddered. I could feel it where we sat, as though the earth had shuddered beneath both of us. She would not look at me. I said, "There is no other. If you want her back, that part of yourself, you must go to him."

"I will not. I will not." I could barely hear her, so low

she spoke. She clenched her hands on the bedframe, looking down at her knees pressed tightly together. "Let me alone. I will not."

"He loves you," I said. "Little as I know of love, I know that much past doubting." But she shook her head so that I heard the very gristle of her neck crack, crying to me, "Lal, no, let be, I cannot bear this." She called me by my name rarely, and Nyateneri not at all. I touched her to comfort her—as clumsily as Nyateneri had me—but she pushed my hand away and sat still until we heard booted feet on the stair again. Then she turned to face me, paler than ever, but seeing me out of dry, steady eyes.

"I do not know if I want her back," she said. "That Lukassa." Then Nyateneri had pushed the door open with her foot and was inside with her arms full of bottles of Dragon's Daughter. She was smiling savagely—I half-expected to see bits of Karsh's habitual dirty smock stuck between her teeth. She said, "A simple misunderstanding. I knew it would turn out so, once I explained the situation."

Perhaps it was the effects of exhaustion, reaction to her fight for life, or perhaps I am simply as vain as I've always suspected, but Nyateneri had a weaker head than I that night. No more wincing, no grimaces: she drank straight from the bottle like any common soldier, and it took distinctly less than one bottle before she began to tell us about the convent she had fled. I was right about *that*, after all, if about precious little else.

"It's deep in the west country," she said. "No, you don't know it, Lal, it's not anywhere near any place you could know, as much journeying as you've done. The closest town is Sumildene, and it's not close at all, and no one goes there who doesn't have to." Which is true enough, as I know, having been once to Sumildene, but there was no reason to go into that. Nyateneri said, "West and south of Sumildene, the land turns boggy, no good for anything but *tilgit* farmers, and not many of those." She grinned at our stares. "*Tilgit*? It's a kind of marshweed: you dry it out and pound it forever and it makes a perfectly disgusting porridge that seems to keep people alive until they'd rather die than eat any more of the stuff. Oh, we did look forward to fast-days at the convent. I'd have run away for that reason alone."

"What is it called," I asked, "that place?" Nyateneri spread her hands and smiled apologetically. I asked then, "How long did you live there?"

"Twenty-one years," Nyateneri said quietly. "From the time I was nine years old." She answered my next question before I voiced it. "Eleven years. I have been fleeing them for eleven years."

Lukassa sipped her wine, wrinkling her nose and mouth into a dainty sneeze. She said, "I don't understand. What kind of a convent could that be?"

Nyateneri did not answer. I said, "A convent that forbids its sisters ever to break their vows. There are such." The fox had come down from the table and curled in a corner, bright eyes glittering under drowsy lids. I continued: "But I have never heard of a convent that would pursue a recusant for eleven years, let alone set assassins after her." When Nyateneri opened a second bottle without looking at me, a mischief took me to add, "I must say, I don't think much of trackers who take that long a time to run down their quarry. I'd have found you in two years, at most, and I know those who would have done it within one."

It was purest bait, of course, and Nyateneri must have known it for bait immediately. In any event, she took a great soldier's swig, set the bottle down so that the wine jumped from the neck, and said to the walls, "The first ones caught me in less time than that. The convent breeds none but the best."

That left me breathless and speechless, I confess it. Nyateneri was well into the second bottle before I was able to ask, "The first ones? There were—there have been others?"

Nyateneri's smile this time, made her look old. "Two

other teams. They hunt in teams, and there is no losing them. You have to kill them." The smile clenched on me, exactly as I had imagined it gripping fat Karsh. Nyateneri said, "By and by, more swiftly than you'd think, the word gets back to the convent, and then a new team comes after you. I am the first ever to survive three such hunts. They will be displeased."

It took Lukassa to speak again, after a long silence, to ask the question that I was too profoundly bewildered to ask. She said, "Why? Why must they kill everyone who leaves them? They wouldn't do that if they knew what it was to be dead." There was an unpitying gentleness about her voice that was strangely terrible to hear. I can hear it still.

Nyateneri put her unhurt hand on Lukassa's hand. She did not squeeze at all, or stroke it; only left it there for a little moment. "I rather think they do know," she said, "more than most, anyway. They have too much knowledge at that place, too many secrets, and that is what may not leave." Lukassa drew breath for another question, but Nyateneri forestalled it, laughing and mimicking her, not unkindly, in a child's eager voice. " '*What* secrets, what knowledge?' Oh, they are grand and foul secrets, Lukassa, dreadful secrets, secrets of kings, queens, priests, generals, judges, ministers: secrets that would shake down temples here, an empire there, start this war, end that, compel *her* to flee her crown, *him* to slay himself, *them* to destroy a nation in order to keep one pitiful truth hidden. Stupid secrets, stupid secrets."

She slapped the other hand down on the table: not hard, but hard enough so that her lips flattened and her face lost a half-shade of color. I said, "Let me see that," but she held the hand out away from me and went on talking, her voice not less but more even than before. "The convent is very old. I do not know how old. The people there are of all kinds, some old, some quite young, as I was. The one thing they have in common is that they all bring their secrets with them. You must, everyone must have at least one secret to tell, or you cannot be admitted."

"You were nine years old," I said. I held her eyes with mine while I reached for her hand again. The back and the beginning of the wrist felt cushiony with heat, but my fingertips could find nothing broken. Nyateneri closed her eyes. "I had secrets enough for them. They were happy to take me in, and I—I was content there, I was, for a long time. I grew strong there. I learned a great deal. Pour me some more wine or give me my hand back. What garden spell are you working now?"

"No magic—only something I've seen done in the South Islands to fool pain. At times I can do it. They taught you much about pain in the convent, didn't they?"

Nyateneri emptied her mug in two gulps. She said, "I knew somewhat already," and then nothing for a long time while she drank and I drank, and I worked on her hand. Lukassa sat on the bed and watched us both, slipping some of her wine to the fox when she thought I wasn't looking. The tree hisses at the window; outside on the landing, slow feet tramp by, a heavy voice grumbles a sea-song—the sailor on his way to bed. Further off, next room but one, the holy man and woman are chanting in quiet antiphony. I know the prayer, a little.

"Why did you leave?" Her hand was beginning to respond—I have no idea why that island trick works as it does, and I am never comfortable with the sense of near-scalding water pumping through my own flesh, even though I know it to be illusion. But it does work.

Nyateneri shrugged. "I was invited to become a force in the convent, and beyond it. They had been training me for this since my childhood, and the time had now come for me to take my place with them, a superior being among superior beings. I was honored in a way, even grateful, and I still am. If they had not offered me the chance of power, I might never have been certain—as I was, on the instant—that power was not what I wanted. To spend the rest of my life as a sort of ringmaster of secrets, to be trapped forever in the dreary hidey-holes of the great with old unspeakable histories hanging head-down from the roof of my mouth, like sleeping bats—no, no, that bony little northern girl never agreed to *that.*" Nyateneri struck the table again, with her wine-mug this time; but then she looked away and spoke very softly, not at all to us but to the fox, no doubt of it. "She agreed to many things that she had no objection to, and to some others as well, but she never agreed to that."

The fox looked straight back at her and yawned very deliberately, as he had on the night of our meeting. *They know each other like lovers,* I thought, *past love itself, past hatred, past questions, past trust or betrayal.* I wondered how they had met, and how long ago, and how long foxes live. Nyateneri went on, "You cannot say no to such an offer. It is not allowed. So I said yes. I said, yes, thank you, I am not worthy."

"And you ran away that same night." Lukassa, leaning forward, brown eyes living Nyateneri's tale exactly as they lived any legend I ever told her. Nyateneri's thin, short smile. "I knew they would guard my door that night. I was gone within an hour. I have been running ever since."

Now some of the drovers crash past the door, yelling, laughing, spitting, stumbling into each other—Efranis, westerners far from home, by their curses. Karsh's sudden voice, quieting them—*not* a growl, but the sound that a large animal makes before the real growl. That fat man knows how to run an inn, whatever else he chooses not to know. The holy couple keep to their chanting, as we to our grim drinking. *This is all so long ago.*

"Well," I said. "Perhaps when this news gets back, the convent will grow tired of sending out killers to be killed." Nyateneri drew a very long breath, plainly about to reply. Then, instead, she stood up and walked to the window, looking out at dark leaves and a few stars. I said, "Perhaps there will be no more teams after this one."

How long did it take her to turn and look at me? A

long time, I think, but drink slows much down for me, so that I cannot be sure. It seemed a long time. Perhaps she never turned at all—I only remember her words, and the sound of her voice, whispering, "I have not told you everything," and bringing me instantly to my feet, wine or no wine, saying, "No, of course not, you never do." Did I shout it? I think I shouted. I really think I knew what was coming.

"There are always three of them," she said. "Always." Did we hear the first quiet steps on the stairs then, or just after, after I had begun screaming at her again? Nyateneri said, "Lal, be still, I am telling you the truth. The third moves apart from the other two; he watches, but he is not with them. He is always the cleverest, they make sure of that. He is never far away. Be still, be *quiet*, Lal." The knock came then, very gentle; you almost had to be listening for it.

NYATENERI

I was praying that it would be anyone but him. Anyone. I would have welcomed that third assassin, right then, sword hand no good and the rest of me feeling in much the same shape as those two stiffening underground. *Just not him, not now, if it please any interested deity. I am exhausted and afraid, and I cannot tell what will happen. I am afraid to see him now.*

Lal rose to open the door. I said, "Don't," not meaning to say it. Lal looked at me. I stood up myself then.

LAL

When I stood, the room pulsed in and out around me, and I had to close my eyes because the blurry throb of the candles made me dizzy. For that moment I could not even see Nyateneri clearly as she moved to the door. But my mind was knife-cold. I braced myself with the back of the chair, and I thought, *Stupid, stupid, I should not have touched the wine again, not after the bathhouse. Whoever is on the other side of that door, killer or drover or pot-boy, could slaughter the stupid three of us as we stand. What is happening, what have I let myself come to?* I put Lukassa behind me. My hands were sweating so that the swordcane slipped and slipped between them, and would not come open.

THE FOX

Yesyesyesyes, I smell him. I smell them all. Pigeons, too.

ROSSETH

The actors came in late and quarrelsome, but they didn't wake Tikat. They didn't wake me, either, for I hadn't even tried to sleep. I was sitting up in the loft, watching the moon start down and Tikat trying to claw his way through the straw pallet I had fixed for him. Lisonje, the one I always liked, climbed the ladder and popped her bewigged head through the trapdoor to ask me, "How fares our sylvan swain?"

"Well enough, so't please you, madam," I answered, "in the body." Every time the troupe came to stay with us—two or three weeks of every summer I could remember—I would be talking like them by the time they left again, and Karsh would spend the next week at least growling and grinding it out of me. I told Lisonje what had happened when Lukassa returned—no more than that—and she leaned on her elbows and regarded Tikat for a while without saying anything. She was still in her paint and costume as the wicked Lord Hassidanya's mistress, and she looked like a child who has been up very late with grown people.

"Once," she said finally, "and not too long ago, either, I would have shooed you down this ladder and lain down in that straw with him, for comfort's sake. And I might even now, if he were someone else and would not hate me and himself so stupidly afterward." She thought about it a moment longer, then shook her head briskly and said, "No, not even then, no, I wouldn't. I'm done with comforting, must remember that." Patting my hand, she started back down, but she put her head in again to say, "Rosseth, be watchful with him. I've seen that kind of heartbreak sleep before. If I were you, I'd wake him every so often. He doesn't want ever to wake again."

She slept quickly, as did the others. I did not move until I could identify every snore from every stall, from old Dardis' whinnying blasts to Lisonje's dainty chirpings. Then, as she had bid me, I shook Tikat by the shoulder until he blinked at me, whispering to him, "Something worrying the hogs, I must see to them. Go back to sleep." He cursed me clearly and healthily, and was asleep again before he had turned over in the straw.

I had no choice. I know perfectly well that most people who say that mean only that they have no excuse for the choice, and more than likely I was no different. But I was truly anxious about Nyateneri—where else might she be bloodlessly wounded besides her sword hand?—and it seemed to me that it would do no harm to ask whether I could be of any further aid. As for what Lal had said to me, where had Lal been when Nyateneri and I were at grips with those laughing little men in the bathhouse? We had shared a battle and a kiss, we had faced death together—not shoulder to shoulder, perhaps, but together—and I was entitled, obliged, to see to my comrade's comfort. Such reasoning it was that took me barefoot down the ladder, all the way to the inn and up the stairs to that room without waking so much as an actor, a hog, or Karsh snoring in the empty taproom, cheek pillowed in the crook of his elbow.

And yes, of course, so many years gone, of course I can say now that I stole up there for one reason alone, and that the old, blind, stamping one that's had you chuckling so dryly and knowingly to yourself all this time. *What else could it have been, eh, at his age?* Yet there was more, it was more than only that, even at my age, if not at yours. Let it be. Her mouth and her round brown breasts—let it be that, for now.

NYATENERI

If there is one thing in this world that I was raised and trained to know, it is that there is only so much you may ask of the gods. Victory in battle is their lightest gift; a quiet heart is your own concern. Even before I opened the door, I was already lowering my eyes to the point where they would meet his eyes. I think I may already have said his name.

"I was worried," he said, so low that I could hardly hear him. He said, "Your hand. Is your hand better? I was worried." There was straw chaff in his hair.

I did not invite him in. That I will swear until my last day. Whatever I may have mumbled, as thick-voiced as he, it was bloody drunken Lal who called behind me, "Welcome, Rosseth—welcome, come and join us, come meet the Dragon's Daughter." Bloody Lal, not me. I swear I would have sent him away.

LAL

What does it matter? From the moment we saw him on the threshold, we all knew what was going to happen. Well, no, not everything—at least *I* didn't. If I *had* known? I can't say. Whether or not it was I invited him in, the real choice was Nyateneri's. Nyateneri knows that.

Yes, I was drunk—though not nearly drunk enough, by my reckoning—and yes, I was adrift between old, old aches and furies, as I had not been for a very long time. But I do not love out of pain, and I do not desire out of need or fear, no matter how far off my course I am. What went to my heart about Rosseth that midnight—short, square, tangle-headed Rosseth the stable boy—was the way he looked at Nyateneri, somehow seeing her real injury through all the innocently selfish dreams that clouded his eyes. No one has ever looked at me like that; no one ever will; nor do I want to be seen so now, truly, it's far too late. But just then, just then.

I hope I was the one. I hope it was I who said it: *"Oh, come in, Rosseth, come in and welcome."* But I honestly don't remember.

Rosseth

No one invited me, not in words. Nyateneri and I looked at each other, and I babbled out whatever I babbled, and then she stepped back from the door and I walked into the room.

This is how it was. They were all standing—Lal behind the table, Lukassa between the bed and the window. The room smelled strongly of wine, of course, and there were empty bottles rolling everywhere; but the three of them were not drunk, not as I understood it then. Drunkenness to me was dragging Gatti Jinni up to his sad garret once a month, or watching Karsh wearily facing down some grinning bargeman with a meat-knife in one hand and a broken bottleneck in the other, with two farmers bleeding and vomiting on the floor. For myself, I rarely got a chance at anything but red ale in those days, and almost never enough of that even to feel drowsy. I never saw Karsh himself drunk, by the way. Karsh only drinks alone.

Yes, naturally I noticed certain things, even I. Nyateneri remained pale and taut as I had left her, but her changing eyes had gone a deep gray with no blue in them whatever, and they were very bright, as exhaustion will make eyes look sometimes. Lal was smiling—not at me, I thought even then, but at something just behind and above me—but the smile seemed to keep wandering from her mouth to her own golden eyes, and then back by way of the warm dark of her cheeks and brow. And Lukassa—Lukassa was the one who looked straight at me in that first moment, with high color in her face and a look of laughter barely held in. I had never seen her look at all like that, and *oh, Tikat* went through me like a slash of ice. I could not help it.

What did I feel, in that little room with those three women I loved, and the door creeping shut behind me of its own slow weight? What do you think I felt? I was hot and cold by turns: lips and ears afire one minute, stomach frozen solid the next. Lal's vagrant smile had me trembling until I could hardly stand, while Lukassa's flushed cheekbones turned me rigid as one of those enchanted idiots in the players' shows. And Nyateneri? I took her left hand as gently as I could—it seemed to cry out in my grasp, like a trapped animal—and I kissed it, and then I raised up on my toes (only slightly, mind you) and I kissed her on the mouth, saying as loudly as I could, "I love you." And I had never said that before in my life, although I *had* been with a woman, more or less.

Nyateneri sighed into my mouth. I can still taste that sigh today, all wine and surrender—more to herself than to me, certainly, but what did I care then? She said something against my lips—I don't know what it was she said. Over her shoulder I could see the fox in the corner, eyes shut tight, ears and body stiff with attention, red tongue smoothing his whiskers, left, right.

No, I did not sweep her up on the instant and carry her across the room to the bed (so few strides for so great a journey!). In the first place, I would likely enough have injured myself, being new at this, too; in the second, my first step had a wine bottle under it, and Nyateneri herself had to catch me up; and in the third place—well, in the third place there stood Lal and Lukassa. And whatever else you choose to believe of me, and of my story, believe that I was a modest boy. Lustful, certainly; ignorant and fearful, without question; but not vain. Vanity came a stride or two later.

LAL

What happened to me that night has never happened again.

Before, yes—I could see my omission in your face—yes, it had happened, if by *it* you mean my being in a bed with more than one other person. But I had no choice in that situation, and no pleasure in it, and I do not care to speak of it further to you. I am talking about choice, and about something more than choice, more than honest desire—something that I had truly never known, for all my old acquaintance with my own blood. When Nyateneri sighed and took Rosseth fully into her arms, then I had to have him, too. The madness was that sudden, that simple, that complete.

Too much wine, too deep a weeping? Like enough. It certainly had nothing to do with jealousy, with Nyateneri—I hardly *saw* Nyateneri in that moment, hardly heard anything but my voice saying nearby, "Not without us. Not tonight."

Why did I say it? And why on earth did I speak for Lukassa, concerned as I surely was just then with nothing on earth but myself? All I can offer for answer is that I must have seen Nyateneri in some way after all, must in some way have read the look she gave me then which was not one of anger, but of terror, pleading, desperation. The boy stood back gaping, poor child, but Lukassa—Lukassa laughed aloud, and the sound was as sweet as the sound that ice-covered twigs make in the spring, chiming and cracking together. I said, "Rosseth is ours. He is our knight, our pure and valiant lover, serving each of us three without favor or demand." My body was shaking—I could not hold it still—but my voice was calm and slow. It is another trick, one of my oldest, dearly learned. It always works.

"You have well earned your reward," I said to Rosseth. I walked up to him and I put my hands on his hot face and pulled him down to me. How many jokes and songs there are about kissing the slack-jawed lout from the stables, with manure on his boots and under his nails, mares and stallions his only visions of loving. Rosseth's mouth was soft and strong at once, and tasted like the first small breeze of a summer's dawn. His hands on me, when they came, were so tender that I felt myself about to weep all over again, or to scream with laughter, or run out of the room. If he had not held me then, I would have fallen.

It is fortunate that I have had very few chances to learn with what terrible ease gentleness finds my heart. I give thanks for my good fortune every day. Oh yes, I do.

THE FOX

Pigeons. Lift up my nose, no ceiling, no rafters between us. Close my eyes and see rumblysoft pigeon dark, juicy wing-beats filling the air with dust and grain, fluffy little under-feathers drift down. Much talking, much shifty-shuffly on their nests, restless with me. Close their pretty eyes like drops of blood, they see me, too.

Down here, hoho, down here all *sorts* of shifty-shuffly going on. Very crowded room, so many people trying to take other people's clothes off. Boy backs toward the bed, one hand holding Nyateneri's hand, other trying to open Lal's shirt. Lal helps him, breaks fingernail, swears. Boy's legs tangle all up with bed legs, he sits down. Lukassa kneels on bed behind him, laughing. Nyateneri turns, looks at me. We talk.

Do not. Do not.

Must.

Will not hold. Cannot hold.

I know. Must. Help me.

Window open almost wide enough. Tree goes *crick-sish,* one thin branch points up to pigeons' nice little bedroom. Nyateneri. *Help me.* Lal reaches out, draws her down.

Rosseth

Lal has dimples in both shoulders. Lal's collarbones are as proud and velvety as the spring antlers of a young *sintu*. The back of Lal's neck makes me cry as she bends her head down to me.

Lukassa smells of fresh, fresh melons and peppers and spice-apples on market stalls. Her breasts are softer and more pointed than Nyateneri's breasts, and the insides of her forearms are transparent, truly—I can almost see little blue fish sculling serenely in and out between her veins. Putting her hand on me, she finds Lal's hand there already. She turns her head and smiles, so simply.

Nyateneri. I cannot see Nyateneri. Her hands move on me, too, and she bites my mouth until blood comes, but I cannot see her face.

NYATENERI

No. No. I cannot let this happen, cannot. For everyone's sake, all sakes, no.

But such sweetness—such *friendliness*. When was the last time anyone kissed you as that boy does—kissed *you*, not your bow or your dagger, the things you can do, the things you know? When did hands caress you as wisely as Lal's hands, or with such welcome as Lukassa's? And you are so tired, and so lonely, and everything has been so long.

I cannot be letting this happen. It will not hold—*he* knows. I try to push Rosseth from me—but it is not Rosseth, it is Lukassa catching my aching hand and drawing it into herself, over herself, over Lal as though she were dressing her in my touch. The river-surge of Lal's belly against my mouth; the dear clumsiness of Lukassa's knee bumping me somewhere, Lal's broken fingernail scratching my hip. *No, no, it will not hold*. Lukassa. Lukassa's hair on me. *No.*

Lal

Someone's hands are under me, someone's mouth is on each breast. My eyes are wide open, but all I can see is someone's hair. Rosseth breathes my name; Lukassa whimpers, *oh, oh, oh, oh,* each soft cry a burning blessing against the scar on the inside of my thigh. I start to tell her who put it there, but someone else is murmuring, "*Lal*" into my mouth, kissing the old agony to oblivion. I put my arms around everyone I can reach, throwing all my doors and windows wide to let the wild comfort enter.

The Fox

Almost wide enough—maybe wide enough? Maybe for a little, little fox with soft fur? Along the wall, hurry, front paws on the ledge—nose, whiskers, ears can fit through. Hello, pigeons.

One quick look back, no one sees me. Hard to see Nyateneri, all those legs. Crying, laughing, poor bed thumps and grunts, last bottle breaks on the floor. Too noisy for a fox, much more peaceful somewhere else. Squeeze down small, push very hard—one paw, two paws, *one* shoulder, now head, now *other* shoulder—and here's one whole fox on nice broad tree branch, laughing, so clever in the moonlight. There is a Fox in the moon.

If Nyateneri called me, *come back*. Might come back.

Moon-Fox: *Too late. Too late. Nothing holds. Go see pigeons.*

Nyateneri's voice: joy, pain, despair, who cares? Not for me, no call for me. I run up the moonlight to the roof, toward lovely fluffy window, lovely bloodrustle that wants me there.

ROSSETH

It must be Lukassa. I cannot see her face—the bedside candle has long since been kicked over to smother in tallow—but the smell is Lukassa's, and the hair in my mouth, and the small, sharp teeth set in my wrist. Not right, not right, it should be Nyateneri—Nyateneri's wounded hand guiding me *oh unbelievable,* Nyateneri's long legs folding me in, keeping me fast. But everything is moonshadow and wine bottles, except for *this,* and Nyateneri has slipped from me, though I can smell her so close, as though my head were still in her lap and a few feet away those two men, a few minutes dead. And I can hear Lal laughing, low and beautiful—if I reach one hand to my left, so, I can feel that laughter on my palm. Between this finger and that, Lal's whisper: "Rosseth, boy, so strong in me, so kind, so lovely in me. Rosseth, Rosseth, yes, like that, yes please, my dear, my dear." The name Karsh gave me, the name I have always hated, so beautiful, my name. If I could hide in the way she says my name and never come out again.

But I am not in her, not in any way, even in this dancing darkness. It is Lukassa welcoming me—Lukassa arching back to kiss me, who never speaks to me, giving me her breath for mine—Lukassa's buttocks searing my incredulous hands. Too stupid even to bumble my way into the woman I most desire, how can I possibly be joining and joying two others at once? There are legends about such men, but I am only Rosseth—no knight, but only Rosseth the stable boy, such wits as he had flown to the moon, leaving his imbecile body tossing in this bed like a toy boat on the wild Bay of Byrnarik, that I have never seen. *Someone was going to take me there, someone was going to take me to play all day on Byrnarik Bay bay bay, where Lukassa is taking me now. It was a song. There was a song.*

Someone's hand is on my back, my hip, caressing, insistent, pushing hard, then yielding as I yield, moving with me on Byrnarik Bay. Lal's voice, a sudden shrill whisper, the way her sword must sound springing from its cane lair. "Rosseth? *Rosseth*?"

NYATENERI

In the end, it was my hair that betrayed me, as I really might have expected. Rosseth's hair is all tight curls—mine is as coarse and shaggy as his, but fatally straight beyond any deception. Once Lal's fingers clenched in my hair, it would have been all over even if, by some chance, the magic had held together.

Which it did not. It is a most curious sensation to feel even the smallest enchantment leaving you. I do not mean to be insulting when I say that it is not like anything you can imagine. It is like nothing *I* can imagine, even now, and I have known it three times in my life. Poets and hedge-wizards mutter of the passing of great wings, of a sense of being abandoned by a god after having been used and exalted almost beyond bearing. This is nonsense. The way it is . . . do you know how it is when a bubble bursts on your wrist, leaving nothing behind but a little cold gasp, already gone out of the skin's memory by the time the slogging mind even begins to realize—yes? So. Nothing more.

Perhaps, then, you also understand that the person under a spell can only know it by the way it affects other people. For all the nine years that I was Nyateneri, daughter of Lomadis, daughter of Tyrrin, it was never once a woman who looked back at me from any shiny helmet or any muddy stock-pond. The breasts that tormented and emboldened Rosseth; the soft skin, the curved, supple mouth, the rounded grace of carriage—all that was always a trick, the only one I knew that might gull for a while those who meant to kill me. I was disguised—disguised well enough to travel and live with real women on terms of daily intimacy without arousing the slightest suspicion—but I was not transformed, neither in fact nor in my own sense of myself. There was never a moment in those eleven years when I believed that I was truly Nyateneri.

And even so. Even so, in that overburdened bed, with Lal all around me, with Lukassa's hand prowling between us and my hand at last finding Rosseth, with the greedy, glorious astonishment of their three bodies answering itself in mine—whose name was real, whose gender was forever? It was Rosseth's innocent desire that had brought mine growling out of a long, long winter sleep; who was it, then, who wanted his mouth no less because of Lal's rich mouth, his hands no less because of once-dead Lukassa's tremulous caresses? Was it I—a man, as we say—or Nyateneri, the woman who never existed? All I know is that I kissed them all, woke to their kisses, no more or less as Nyateneri than as the man who was not Rosseth when Lal cried out and buried her hands in his hair. There were no census-takers in that bed that night, no border patrols.

LAL

For one moment—no longer than the instant it takes for me to yank Nyateneri's head back by the hair, hard, and stare through the shivering dark into that strange, familiar face above me—for that moment I am Lal-Alone again, cold and empty and ready to kill. Not because the woman in bed with me has turned out to be a man, but because the man has deceived me, and I cannot, *cannot*, allow myself to be deceived—day or night, bed or back alley; it is the only sin I recognize. My sword-cane is propped in a corner—oh, naked, foolish Lal!—but my fingers have crooked and bunched themselves for a slash that will crumple Nyateneri's windpipe, when the soft cry comes: "*He* taught me, the Man Who Laughs!" And I let both hands drop, and Nyateneri laughs himself, herself, and kisses me like a blow and moves slowly in me. And I scream.

Something is happening in the dovecote overhead: vaguely protesting burbles, fretful noises as though the birds were jumping on and off their perches. What can the drovers, the sailor, the holy couple imagine must be going on in here? What would that sly fat man think if he crept up the stairs, flung open the door and saw us now, this minute, tumbling over each other like a moonlight circus, all naked rope-dancers and slippery beasts? What would I think, if Lukassa's mouth and throat were not a sweet curtain across my mind, if I were not suddenly, suddenly about to do my own dance, Lal's dance, up there, high up there in the night-blooming night, up there above the pigeons, Lal's dance on no rope at all, nothing under me but the love of three strangers, who will not let me fall?

THE FOX

Up there in the rafters, three left, what does he want? Three tricky pigeons, just out of reach, yes, make attics and attics full of pigeons—why such roaring, such waking of poor tired everybody? Fat innkeeper shouts, swears, bangs in and out of rooms, slams through cupboards, looks under floors, under beds—*in* beds, even. Dogs in the courtyard, the stable, on the stairs, sniffing and yelping, just like fat innkeeper. Boy Rosseth runs here, runs there, two and three places at once, looking guilty and happy. Boy Tikat helps—*that* is a worry, this one knows too much about too much. Should have let him starve, kind fox.

Days and days, all for a few bony little pigeons. Nyateneri, Lal, Lukassa, they go on riding out, riding back, never a thought for someone hiding all the hot day in the fields, shivering all night in a hollow log. No chance even to take man-shape, not with boy Tikat here. Northern Barrens is better than this. Convent is better, except for nasty food.

This one morning. All cloudy, a thin mist, cold gray sweat. I strike off toward the mountains, trotting only, looking for birds, rabbits, maybe a *kumbii*—big juicy red mole-thing, my size almost. No *kumbii*, nothing nice, nothing but the smell of a storm coming, and one stupid lizard, falls over its own feet when it sees me. Bad to eat lizards, poison your eyes, make your teeth fall out. I eat half.

My fur hisses. Storm is rolling up from the east, green and black, all squirming with lightning. Frogs growing restless in the little slow creeks—maybe a pretty frog for me? Two frogs, even? I go softly along creek bank, just to see. A dog howls.

No dog I know. Bays again, closer—big, running hard. And still no smell of him, no taste in my whiskers, no shiver in my blood that says *dog, dog*. Morning yet, but too misty now to see more than trees, stones, the ribs of a falling-down fence. But I hear his breath.

Up the bank and away then, straight through brambles, tickberries, handshake thorns, places where dogs will not go. This dog will. Bushes crash and crackle behind me—a whine for a thorn, another long bell for a poor little fox that never harmed him, and here he comes, here he comes with the first thunder baying on *his* heels. But I am already among the plowed fields, flying over cart-ruts, jinking this way, that way across terraces, grape arbors—ho*ho*, I run like what I eat, how not, only better. Nobody runs like me.

More thunder, closer than he is, but not loud enough. Under all the rattling and groaning, always his breath, wind in hard lost places. And now the rain. Thunder is nothing, but this rain smashes me down, rolls me in muddy smashed cornstalks—and always, heavier, colder than the rain, his gray breath over me, inside me. On my feet in one breath of my own, never fear, and gone for the deep trees off to the right. Never look back, what for? Rabbits never look back at me. Down beyond those trees an orchard, and beyond orchard the inn, where nice old twinkly grandsirs find shelter from storms under Marinesha's skirts. Catch me *there,* wicked dog with no smell, catch me *there.*

But something happens. Nothing happens. In and out

of wild trees, orchard flashes past, inn is no closer. How is this? I can see it, even through wind and rain and mist—see chimneys, courtyard, bathhouse, stable, even my nice tree, branches blowing against women's window. I run and I run, should be there three times over now, but no running to the moon, no reaching the inn. Dog bays on my left—I swing away toward the town, double back in a little. But each time I try, the inn is further away, dog a bit nearer, and my fur wetter, dragging at my legs. Nobody runs like me, but nobody runs forever.

Rabbits don't look back. People look back. Under a tall tree, I turn and take the man-shape at last—what dog would ever hunt man-shape like a poor fox? This dog. Out of the mist and rain, now I see him, all howling jaws, wet teeth, stupid long ears, coming through the storm like a fire on four feet. Yes, yes, and so much for human mastery. Two bounds, welcome back my own four feet, off again where he wants me to go, straight for the town. No catching me, no escaping him.

The storm blows by us, dog and me, as we run, back toward the bad country where Mildasis live. Mist thins, thunder mumbles itself away over the rooftops, last lightning is lost in noonday sun. I remember a stone culvert, small, small culvert, drains slops from the marketplace, too narrow for a great ugly dog like this dog—howl for me there all day and night, he can. Best speed now, no chance for him to head me away. Sweet me, best speed now.

But the culvert is running like a river, rainwater surging high up the sides. I see dark dead things spinning past—rats, birds, me if I jump down there. No time to think, *yes, no,* time only for one lovely sailing leap, so pretty, a fox-fish, swimming in the air. Down and gone then, and one bark later his clumsy feet booming behind me again. Nothing for it but the market—nothing but a basket, a heap of cabbages, a turned-over barrow, any earth for such a tired little fox with his muddy tail dragging on the ground.

Empty market, everyone still hiding from the storm. Dirty canvas over all the barrows, awnings sagging with rain. I look left, right, a fruitstall, ten strides and a scramble to a hamper half full of squashy green things. Almost through the scramble, and a hand clenches the back of my neck—hard, hard, hurting, nobody touches me like that, even Nyateneri. I turn in my skin, jaws snapping on nothing. Another hand clamps across my hips, both hands lift me high, holding me stretched out like a dead rabbit. But my teeth are alive, and this time they take a mouthful of wet sleeve and a bony wrist between them, my beautiful teeth. A voice without words speaks my name, and I am so still, nice teeth not closing, not even loosening a thread. I know this voice. I know this voice.

The hands turn me, one lets go. I hang in the air before his face, and I do not move. Nyateneri would not know him. Lal would not know him. He is gray, gray everywhere, all the way through—bones, blood, heart, all gray. Gray as rain, thin as rain, too, clothes so ragged and wet he might as well be wearing rain. They would never know him. But he is who he is all the same, somewhere in one place that is not yet gray, and I wait for him to tell me that I can move.

After a long time, he says my name again, in a human voice now. Nyateneri knows my name, but never speaks it, never. He says, "You put me to much trouble. You always did."

Dog. No dog anywhere—no feet thumping forever after me, no cold empty breath. I say, very small, "The dog with no smell. You."

He laughs then, tries to laugh, that way of his, but it comes out like blood. "No, no, no, you were always a flatterer, too. The storm, yes, I can still manage a bit of a storm for a bit, but no more shape-shifting, never again. No, the dog was just part of the storm, like the illusion of the inn, and all *that* was only to drive you here to me. A troublesome business, too, as I said. You have grown strong and clever, while I have been busy growing old."

Long ago, long ago, longer than Nyateneri knows, he never needed hands to hold me, phantoms to call me to his will. I say, "Flattery yourself. What do you want of me?"

I feel the trembling as he sets me down gently. He looks around, still no market folk returning, crouches before me. "Lal," he says. "Nyateneri. A few miles only, but I am too sick, too weary to go to them. Help me, take me there."

No command, a request only, a kindness to an old—what? friend? colleague? companion? I have none. "Why do you bother with me? You are a magician, you can call storms and storm-dogs to hound a poor fox to your feet. Call one now to carry you where you want to go. Call a *sheknath.*"

Rags already steaming in the sunlight, he is still shaking, holding himself. "That was the last of my strength, that show, and well you know it. Take your human form, little one, just for a while. I need an arm, a shoulder, nothing more."

"Walk," I say. "Fly. If I were a magician, I would fly everywhere." I sit back on my haunches, smile at him. Nothing nice like this for days, not since the pigeons.

Two children run through the market, stop to splash in the puddles. He sinks back behind a pile of boxes, lets his gray breath out. I think he could not get up if he had to. He says, "Please. What hounds *me* is real and near. It must not find me in this place. Only take me to Nyateneri, to my Lal. You know who is asking you."

Better and better. "And who am I to make an enemy of your enemy? A simple fox, corn in the mill between two great wizards? Not for me, thank you, my master." And I turn away, a fox in the sunlight, looking for a place to curl up sweetly and nibble the mud-clumps out of his tail.

O, never take your eyes off them, not while they breathe, never do that. No hand on me this time, but the terrible bite of a magician's will: *snap,* my poor neck again, *shake* almost to break my back, and *bang,* down among the boxes beside him, whining for breath. He leans over me, says in my head, "Make one sound, one miserable whimper. You know who is asking you." Voices now, wheels on stone, rattle of awnings as people begin opening their stalls. He huddles even lower, nothing but gray rags to look at him. "Take the form," he says. "As you are wise."

Who thinks of me? No one thinks of me. Save their manners, their honesty for others, strangers, never for me. I say to him, "You said your strength was gone. Liar. Ask a favor, then kill me for saying no. Old, hunted, alone, no wonder."

Again the red ghost of that laugh, making my fur rise and my ears flatten back. "And no wonder you are still a fox, still, after so long and long a time, so much subtle knowing. Don't you ever ponder on it, why you should still be a fox?" Footsteps, heavy, *this is my fruitstall,* same stamping as fat innkeeper's feet. "Now—take the form!" and man-shape stands up among the broken boxes, lifting a gray beggar in its arms. Just so he held me, a few moments before, but I am more gentle. As I must be.

Fruitstall man gapes, scratches his head. Wants to roar, but at what? Nice old blue-eyed uncle helping nice old smelly unfortunate? Stands there making funny small sounds as man-shape bears its helpless burden past. Man-shape smiles, nods, human to understanding human. Burden snatches a handful of dried apricots from a jar as we go by.

He makes man-shape carry him all the way through the marketplace, eyes closed, face hidden in rags. Much sympathy, ever so much fluttering, so many anxious questions for man-shape. "No, no, he will recover, only a little care and patience, as we all need. No, no, thank you, righteousness is never heavy. Gracious concern, decency, very kind, thank you, thank you." A few coins, even, pushed nobly into man-shape's fingers, coat pockets. Small coins.

On the road out of town now, and he says, "I can walk,

perhaps a little. Help me walk." An arm around man-shape's neck, full weight on the shoulder, easier carrying him. "You marvel at what has become of me. How I could have come to such a state." Sees me more interested in track of a *starik* at last on the damp ground, more curious about frogs in the ditches—same ditch, two frogs, one green and delicious, one red-brown, nasty taste, why is this? His smile, as torn as his clothing. "Well, you are a wise fox, and no mistake. I have ill-used and insulted you—forgive me if you can." I do *not* forgive, I do not speak to him, all the miles to the inn, but he has fainted by then, so he never knows.

TIKAT

Of course I knew him. With that red soldier's coat of his and that way he had of walking—two steps forward, the third just a bit to the side—the distance didn't matter, nor that his face was half-hidden by the ragged man in his arms. I dropped my basket at Rosseth's feet (we were gathering windfalls and acorns for the hogs) and set off running.

I met him in the courtyard. The dogs were all barking madly, swirling around his ankles, and Gatti Jinni was shouting at them from a window. As I drew near, he set the ragged man on his feet, holding him up with an arm around his waist. The man sagged over his arm, coughing. He was very old, far older than my redcoated friend, and the sound of those coughs told me that there was no strength left in him, none at all. I thought he was dying. Redcoat looked at me over his head and said in the quick, shrill bark I knew, "My horse-thieving colleague. How pleasant to see you again."

"The Mildasis didn't get you," I said. Lame, if you like, but what would *you* have said to a person who had last brought you your breakfast in his teeth? He showed them now, white as I remembered. "Would you be feeding and currying a little gray horse if they had? Look sharp, boy, here's a friend for the ladies." I went slowly to him, and he let the old man fall against me. When I lifted him the heaviness of him amazed me, and even frightened me somewhat, for he should have weighed nothing at all, as little flesh as covered his fragile bones. But my knees bent under those bones all the same, and I staggered a step forward, which made Redcoat laugh mightily. I would have fallen—I'll tell you straight—but he gripped my shoulders and set me upright again.

"More to him than there seems, aye? Well, the old surprise us betimes, fellow thief. This one, now, his bones are full of darkness and his blood's thick and cold with ancient wisdom, mysteries. Weighs a deal, that sort of thing—wears a man out just taking himself from place to place." So he buzzed and chuckled while I strained to carry the old man as far as the inn door, where Gatti Jinni stood blinking slack-mouthed. I was grateful when Rosseth came up and helped me, never saying a word.

Karsh came out then. He pushed Gatti Jinni aside and stood scowling as we danced the poor creature along like a cumbersome piece of furniture. Behind me, Redcoat was still laughing: the sound of it prickled in my palms. Karsh looked at Rosseth, not at me. He never looked straight at me.

"Another one," he said. As sad for myself as I woke and worked and slept each day then, for that moment I pitied Rosseth with my whole heart, to be hearing that slow, offended voice every day of his life. Yet one thing I also realized was that in his own heart Rosseth did not hear Karsh at all. He heard the voice, the orders; he was always respectful, always responsible, quick and keen to jump to any task—but there was a way in which he always eluded his master, just as the words to say how it was escape me. Karsh knew it, too—you could see that he knew, and that he didn't like it. I do not believe that Rosseth knew that.

Now he only shook his head and answered cheerfully, "Not one of mine this time, sir, but a visitor to see Mistress Lal and Mistress Nyateneri. We'll take him to their room and let him rest there till they return." He nodded to me, and we began dragging and pushing the half-conscious old man toward the inn once again.

Karsh grunted and spat. He made no move to interfere, but stared hard at us with his pale eyes as we struggled by him. We had reached the threshold when he said, not loudly but very clearly, "A visitor, is it? More likely another body for the tickberry patch." I did not understand what he meant, but the color came up in Rosseth's neck. He called for Gatti Jinni to come and help us, but Gatti Jinni had faded away into one of the musty places he knew. So we got the old man up the stairs by ourselves.

I had thought I could go in. I knew that the room would smell of her, and that it might be hard to look at the bed where she slept and wonder if someone who had been dead could ever dream of someone living. But I had no more than lifted the latch and pushed the door an arm's-length open when I saw the velvet sash hanging across the back of a chair. It was the sash I had traded my first real woven cloth for at Limsatty Fair; it was the sash she was wearing when she drowned. I shut the door and turned away.

Rosseth meant to be gentle. He said, "Tikat, they left by moonlight, they'll be gone all day. She—Lukassa—she isn't in there." I remember that he flushed again when he said her name. Trying so hard to spare others' feelings must be very embarrassing, I suppose.

"I'll send Marinesha up," I said. "I am sorry." Then I ran back down the stairs as though all the beasts out of my walking nightmares in the Northern Barrens were after me together, so fast that I stumbled and fell to my knees in the courtyard. If Karsh had been there still, he would have split his fat belly with laughing, and well enough I would have deserved it. But I had suddenly come to the end of my tracking at that door. I had followed Lukassa through deserts, forests, across rivers and mountains, tracing out every least shadow of a memory of her passage that all these had kept for me—but into that room I would not follow, not if my one love stood beckoning in the doorway, no more, no. "Let her come to me if she will," I said to the dusty chickens clucking and scattering all around. "She must come to me."

And a foolish vow *that* was, as you will see—aye, and unkind as well, for all the while I yet believed her to be under a spell that kept her from knowing me. But I was very weary—I'll say that much for myself—and very angry, and full of despair; and just then, there on my knees, I did not love anyone, and I never had.

MARINESHA

If it hadn't been for Tikat, I would have gotten through that entire week without breaking a single plate. Oh, that may sound very silly to you, but you might not feel like that if Karsh were always after *you* about accidents and clumsiness and all kinds of things you couldn't possibly help. And I'd managed, in spite of his nagging and his sneaking up on me and *shouting*—I mean, if *that* wouldn't make you drop something—I'd managed not even to chip so much as a teacup or a panikin all week, even with all the hullabaloo that was going on about those stupid pigeons; and then here comes Tikat calling for me when I'm not in the least expecting it, in that nice rough country voice of his that never got my name quite right, and of *course* I dropped the porringer, who *wouldn't*? And of course I turned right around and slapped him—he understood that. Tikat was a gentleman, I don't care where he came from.

"I'm sorry, Marinesha," he said. "I didn't mean to frighten you. I just came to say Rosseth wants you upstairs."

"Oh, does he indeed?" I said. Because I didn't want him to think that I was someone who jumped whenever Rosseth snapped his fingers. "Well," I said, "you can go tell the Lord Rosseth that the Princess Marinesha will be there in good enough time to suit herself, and if that doesn't suit *him,* there's a delightful man in the kitchen who wants him *downstairs* this minute." Because Shadry absolutely hated Rosseth; it was dreadful what he used to put that boy through. I was sorry after I'd said that about Shadry. I said to Tikat, "I'll be up when I can, I just have to clean away these pieces and hope Karsh doesn't notice." But I knew he would.

Tikat had the prettiest eyelashes I've ever seen. You wouldn't imagine a village boy like him having such long, thick eyelashes, the color of warm afternoon sun on the courtyard dust when it's getting late. And he was tall, *much* taller than Rosseth, and there was that voice; and if he'd only paid a little attention to his hair, it would have looked like—I don't know. Like a beautiful bird or an animal, all by itself. Not that I ever gave him more than "good morning" or "good evening," I'm sure, but he was always *very* courteous to me, so that shows you.

But this time he was different. I can't tell you *how* different he was—if I said he was pale as this or shaking like that, then you'd think that was the difference, that thing, and it wasn't. Only that I hadn't seen him like that before. He said, "Marinesha, you will have to tell him yourself. I can't go back up there."

"What is it?" I said. "What's the matter with you?" His voice was so low. I mean, it isn't as though I didn't *know* what the trouble was. There probably wasn't even a *guest* who didn't know that he'd come all this terrible journey to find his girl, and then that pale, whispering little—well, I'll just say that little *thing*—just turned away and pretended she didn't even know him. I thought it was shameful, and I thought the other two put her up to it, the showy, arrogant pair of them, and *I* wasn't the least bit shy about saying so. Which took the wind out of a certain stable boy, I can tell you, but what did I care for that? Tikat had *manners,* and if there is one thing in this world I respect, there you have it. Manners.

But all he said was, "I can't—I am a coward—I cannot," and he was past me and gone, almost knocking Shadry over as he came through, which made me laugh—I couldn't stop myself. So after that there was nothing to do but smooth down Shadry, hide the bits of the broken porringer, and go up to Rosseth. He had just finished settling the oldest man I ever saw onto a straw mattress on the floor. The old man's eyes were closed, and he was the color of old snow. I was servant to a hedge-doctor once—hardly more than a baby, I was—and I have seen dead people, many of them. I would have thought *he* was dead, except that Rosseth was talking to him. He was saying, "There you are, sir, as comfortable as anyone at The Gaff and Slasher. I'm sure your friends will be returning by this evening. If there's anything more I can do for you." But the old man said never a word.

"The only thing you can do for *that* one," I said from the doorway, "is to ask him where he wants his body sent, and what sort of priests should meet the coach." Rosseth spun around and glared at me, but I just smiled. Rosseth always hated it when I did that, just smiled at him in that way. I said, "And the best thing you can do for *yourself* is pray that Karsh doesn't miss that spare mattress. He'd turn out your insides to stuff a new one."

Rosseth gave that long, long, patient sigh that was always *his* way of annoying *me*. He said, "This gentleman has only come to see his friends. He won't be staying the night."

"He won't *last* the night," I said. Rosseth put a finger to his lips, but I certainly didn't pay that any mind. I said, "Those three sluts will come back to find a dead man waiting for them." Which suited *me* well enough, and I laughed right there, just thinking about it. "Poor things. The only kind of man they won't be able to get any use out of. I don't *suppose*."

Oh, wasn't Rosseth furious at me, though? I did it on purpose, I don't mind telling you that. Because ever since those women came to the inn, Rosseth had been growing more and more impossible, especially in the last week or two. We'd been used to having our nice restful chats, when Karsh wasn't around, and sometimes our little walks in the woods or even an afternoon in Corcorua—but now he couldn't talk about *anything* except Lal's beautiful hands or Nyateneri's elegant ways, or how charming and friendly that Lukassa was, once you got to know her. So tedious, so *tiresome*. I'm afraid I'd just run out of patience with his daydreaming, that's all.

"Marinesha," he said to me—like that, through his teeth—"Marinesha, come here and sit down." He sat down himself by the mattress and beckoned me over. I stood where I was, thank you very much, until he said, "Please," really rather nicely. Then I went and sat across from him, on the other side of the old man, and I said, "Well?" Just that, you see.

Rosseth said, "You know something about healing. More than I do, unless it's a horse. Tell me what to do."

"I've told you already," I said. "Ask him where he wants to be buried. He hasn't eaten for days, by the look of him, and he must have gotten caught in that squall that came up over town this morning. And he's very old. That's all that's wrong with him, but there's nothing you can do about it."

Well, Rosseth looked so stricken at that that I really felt sorry for him. Some people look nicer when they're sad, and Rosseth was one of those. I asked, "Why should a stranger trouble you so? I'm sure he's a good old man, but he's no uncle of yours. Or is he?" I added that last because Rosseth is an orphan—I mean, I am, too, which gave us anyway *that* much in common—but at least I'd always known my parents' names and where they came from, and poor Rosseth didn't even know where he was born. So the man *could* have been a relative of his, you see, like anyone.

Rosseth said, "Look at him. He's somebody, he's important." At that I got angry all over again, and I said, "Why? Because he's a friend of *theirs*? That's what it is, that's why you're going on like this, isn't it?" But Rosseth just shook his head.

"Look at him, Marinesha," he kept saying. "Look at him." So finally I took my first real look at that old man's face—I mean, past the smudgy, gappy old mouth, past the lines and wrinkles and scratches, and the dirt ground into them all, past the awful grayness, past *everything*, past the features themselves, if you understand me. And I don't know—I don't know—looking at him just started to make me happy, in a funny way. It made me want to cry, too, but it was the same thing. I don't know, I just stared and stared, and Rosseth did too, and we didn't talk any more.

By and by we heard Karsh shouting downstairs for Rosseth. I said, "You go on. I'll just bide with him for a little." So Rosseth looked at me a moment, and then he smiled and touched my shoulder, and he said, "Thank you," and went out. And I sat there by the mattress, watching that old man, and presently I went and got a cloth to clean his face with a bit. Because there was no reason he *ought* to be dirty, even if he was old and sick and maybe dying. And while I was doing it, he opened his eyes.

"Oh," he said. "Marinesha." Just as though we'd known each other forever, and he was surprised to see me, but pleased, too. He had a thoughtful sort of voice, with just the least bit of an accent. He said, "My, I feel rather like a kitten getting its face washed by its mother. A refreshing way to wake up, I must say." When he smiled, it didn't matter that there were teeth gone.

I was very shy with him, all of a sudden. I couldn't help wishing that he'd gone on sleeping, just a while longer. I stood up quickly, and I said, "Sir, are you feeling better? What can I do for you?" Just like Rosseth, after all.

He laughed then. I don't know how to tell you about his laugh. A shaky little gasp of a laugh it was, this side of a cough, really, but you wanted to hear it again. He said, "Well, you could go on standing there in the sunlight—I wouldn't ask for more than that—but I think my friends are on the stairs. I know you don't much care for them, and I'd not want to shame you after such kindness."

And the next thing, there they *were*, the three of them, banging the door open and filling the room with their clatter and swagger. They stood there with their mouths open and their eyes popping, exactly like a row of fish in the market, and then the black one stammered out, "Rosseth *told* us—" and Miss Nyateneri swung her shoulders and demanded, "Where have you *been*?" like the boldface she was. As for that other one, she went straight to him and dropped on her knees beside the mattress. She put her hands between his, showing off that great vulgar emerald she always wore. He touched it, and he smiled and said something like, "So, it finds its way home again," which I didn't understand. But she was crying, of all things, and then he said, "Be still, be still. You are where you should be. Be still now."

Nobody gave *me* any more of a glance than they would a dish of dog scraps, of course, not when I opened the door and not when I closed it behind me. But I stood on the landing for a moment, *not* eavesdropping, just getting myself ready for what was waiting downstairs—dirt and smoke and food smells, Karsh and Shadry yelling, Gatti Jinni waiting his chance to get me in a corner, farmers and soldiers already laughing-drunk in the taproom, guests badgering me to do forty different tasks for them at once, and my own chores going on till midnight, longer if I wasn't lucky. What I had to do, you see, was make myself forget how nice it was just being alone with that old man—at least until I could get off with it by myself somewhere. I mean, otherwise who'd ever go downstairs?

LAL

Of course we were jealous, both of us—how could we not have been jealous? Here we were, Nyateneri and I, having journeyed at great risk and labor to a far country to aid our dearest master, having searched for weeks longer after that, day on dreary day, just for some sign of his presence in the world—and then having to stand and watch while he ignored us to greet a stranger, Lukassa, as though she were his long-lost daughter. Yet how could it have been different? He always went where the need was greatest, immediately, without having to be told. My life is witness to this, as is Nyateneri's.

Nevertheless, if he had called her *chamata* while all the soothing and comforting was going on, I think I might have hit him. That is *my* name, even if I don't know what it means. (I did hit him once, by the way, very long ago, when I was flailing mad with fear, and so young that I truly expected him to kill me for it.) But he spoke another name entirely, looking at Nyateneri and me over Lukassa's head, which was bowed in the hollow of his thin shoulder. He said, "His name is Arshadin."

He loves to do that, to sail from one of your unasked questions to another, like a monkey somersaulting through the high branches. He never lies—never—but you must climb right after him if you want to keep up at all. It is exactly as maddening as he intends it to be, and at times the urge to make him scramble a bit himself is overwhelming. I nodded towards Nyateneri and replied, "*His* name is Soukyan. I don't like it much."

The smile was unchanged, as tender and secret as ever. "In that case, I should go on calling him Nyateneri. Unless he objects very strongly." He looked solemnly back and forth from one to the other of us, as though he were settling a nursery dispute.

Nyateneri and I looked directly at each other, I think for the first time since that night we must all remember by different names. In the week since he and Rosseth and Lukassa and I had stumbled out of that battered, tipsy bed, we had trudged on about our everlasting search without saying more than we had to, communicating mostly by swift sidelong glances. Yet nothing much seemed to have changed, except that Nyateneri—his woman's guise reassumed, largely for the sake of Karsh's sanity—had taken over the tiny room next door, and that poor Rosseth could neither stay away from us nor speak to us. For Lukassa, as far as I could tell, the events of that night might have been no more than a sweet, lingering dream; for myself, they represented an annoying complication. I make love only with very old friends, of whom I have very few, and with whom there is no danger of falling in love, no chance of being distracted from the task or the journey at hand, and no need to guard my back. I do not sleep with recent acquaintances, traveling companions, professional associates, or people who are too much like me, and Nyateneri/Soukyan was all of these, as well as the most profound deceiver I had ever known in a life spent among liars. Whatever else might be between us—and I was not such a priggish fool as to imagine that there was nothing—there could never possibly be trust, not for a man who had tricked me so shamingly, and so dangerously. Injured pride, certainly; but there was regret in it, too, which is even rarer than trust, in my life.

Nyateneri said stiffly, "I am used to the name. I will answer to it." Then he went and knelt by the mattress, and *my friend* rested a hand on his head. I stood still, almost swaying with joy and relief, and irritated with everyone in the world. Even when *my friend* beckoned to me, I stood where I was.

"There's my Lal," he said without mockery. "My Lal, who must see everything, must think of everything, must be responsible for everything. *Chamata,* I teach those who come to me only what I am certain will be useful to them one day. I knew that you would always live close enough to Uncle Death to nod to him in the street, so I taught you a small trick of picking his pocket as you pass him by. As for your comrade here, he came flying from such hounds as even you have not yet known—hounds that will run on his track as long as he lives." Nyateneri looked at no one, showed nothing. *My friend*'s voice went on, quavering with fatigue, and a little also with his old laughter. "Hounds can smell wonderfully well, but they see quite poorly. You might say that I taught Nyateneri a way of confusing their vision, at least for a while." The last words bent upwards toward a question.

"For a while," Nyateneri said. "The last ones hunted by scent. The third still runs loose."

My friend nodded, unsurprised. "Ah, there's the difficulty in depending on tricks—they never work all the time, even the best of them. And when you have used them all, there is truly nothing left, nothing of yourself before the tricks, or beyond them. He taught me that, Arshadin."

The room was very still. I had to say something. I said, "Arshadin. The boy who came not long after I did, with the hill accent and the funny ears." And almost at the same time, Nyateneri said, "I remember. Short, southern, kept a *chikchi* flute in his shirt all the time." But *my friend* turned his head slowly from one side to the other, being too tired and weak even to shake it properly.

"You do not know Arshadin," he said. "Neither of you. Nor did I." He closed his eyes and was silent for a time, while Lukassa fussed about with pillows and Nyateneri and I stared at each other: wordlessly, grudgingly walking side by side through days and nights no less shared for falling years apart. *Oh, you never could hurry him, never get anything out of him but in his own way. Do you remember, do you remember how he used to, over and over, did he ever say to you, I remember, yes, and didn't that always drive you mad?* I heard a fly buzz in a corner of the window as we stood there, and Rosseth's pet donkey braying creakily for winter apples.

The pale, exhausted eyes, that had been so joyously green, came abruptly open. "I missed you after you were gone, *chamata*." His voice was even and ruminative. "I was not prepared for that, missing someone, not at my age. As well start cutting new teeth or singing under young girls' windows. It was"—he hesitated briefly—"it was disconcerting."

I blinked speechlessly at him, recalling that he had neither embraced me nor so much as waited to watch me go, that day when I set out alone again into the world because he said it was time. I was still young, and he was all I had then, and I cried for him many a night, huddled in my blanket under dripping trees, no more than their branches between me and the wind. But it would never have occurred to me to wonder whether *he* felt at all lessened or lonely without *me*, and the idea seemed nearly as unnatural to me even now as it must have done to him. Nyateneri smiled slightly, without malice. It annoyed me anyway.

"Disconcerting," *my friend* went on. "Either I am more sentimental than I knew, or else my vanity starves without someone to rescue and protect and teach. However that may be, Arshadin appeared at my door when I was, if you like, at a low ebb, a bit at loose ends. An ordinary-looking boy, without your fierce charm, Lal, without Nyateneri's presence. Nor was he a fugitive of any sort, but a farmer's second son, well-fed, moderately educated, and most calmly certain about what he meant to do with his life." He paused, absently stroking Lukassa's hair and looking with great deliberation from one to the other of us. I am the Inbarati of Khaidun, if I never see Khaidun again—and I never will—raised from infancy to tell tales, but I learned as much of the storyteller's sly art from that man as I did from my mother and grandmother and all my aunts. I never told him that.

My friend said, "Arshadin's simple, single ambition was to be the greatest magician who ever walked the earth. He achieved it."

Rosseth's donkey brayed again just at that moment, which set us all laughing too loudly. *My friend* fell silent again for a moment, and then resumed, speaking almost to himself. "You always wonder about it, you know, if you are one of those who cannot resist the enticement of teaching. *What will happen when I meet someone with a greater gift than my own? It is easy enough to be kind and helpful to those who do not threaten me—but how will it be with one who is my master and does not yet realize it? How will I be in that day?*"

Nyateneri and I began speaking at once, but he stilled me with a gesture that was no less commanding for being so frail and miniature. "If you don't mind, we can leave out the part where you both assure me loudly that I could never have to face such a decision. We all meet our masters, all of us—why do you think we are in this world?—and I am telling you that I met mine one overcast afternoon when I went to the door with my mouth still full of tea-cake. I knew him on the instant—as you will know a greater swordsman one day, Lal, with the first salute of your blades. And I invited him in for tea."

Nyateneri regarded him with a grave mock-frown. "That must indeed have been centuries ago. You insisted that I learn to make proper tea, just so, but you never would drink it. I nearly went mad trying to make tea that was at last fit for you."

"By that time I had given up other things besides tea," *my friend* replied very quietly. "By the time you came, I had long been occupied in making my *lamisetha*." We gaped at him dumbly, and he smiled. "It is an old word, a wizards' word. It means, more or less, 'road of departure.' If you are a wizard, nothing in your life is more important than how you die. Do you know why that is so? Nyateneri?" He might have been our teacher again, prodding and provoking us with riddles that seemed to have only one answer, and that one always wrong. "You used to be curious about that sort of thing, more than Lal ever was." But Nyateneri shook his head silently.

My friend said, "A magician *must* die in peace. I am not talking about temporal peace with his neighbors or the local ruler, or of what most people call spiritual peace, meaning that he has performed all the proper observances of whatever gods he may have served. What I speak of is truly of the spirit—a drawing-in, a particular sitting still that requires great preparation and that a magician can only attain by means of a long, motionless journey. That is the *lamisetha*. As I said, it translates poorly."

A knock sounded then, and I went to answer. I expected to see Karsh, but it was only Gatti Jinni, who had already begun backing away before I opened the door. He was notably afraid of both Lukassa and me, though he looked for excuses to attend loweringly on Nyateneri. He muttered, "Karsh. If the old man stays the night, more money."

"He stays the night," I said, "and longer, and in a better room than this. I will arrange it with Karsh. Meanwhile, send up bread and soup and wine for him, and not Dragon's Daughter, either." But Gatti Jinni had already scuttled off down the corridor. I turned back as Nyateneri was saying, "And yet you took me in. No holy calmness after that, certainly, but no question about it, not ever."

My friend's mouth twitched wryly. "Yes, well. It seems

that I am easily distracted—you were hardly the first to beguile me from the arranging of my soul. But I determined at the time that you would definitely be the last; that this old lure, this old trap would have no further hold on me after you were gone on your way in the world. And it did not, and it does not now. I have kept my word to myself, as far as that goes."

"Arshadin," I said. The word seemed to squirm free of me, like a live thing.

"Arshadin." When he spoke it, the name came out a sigh through cold, broken branches. "Arshadin became my son. Not of the body, but of the search, the voyage. Of the vanity, too, I am afraid. We do not fear death in the way that others do, we wizards, perhaps because we know transience rather better than most. And perhaps for that reason we hunger even more deeply to leave behind us some small suggestion of our passage. For some that may mean such achievements as appear to be commandings and shapings of the very earth itself, but for the rest of us it is nothing more than a handing on of knowledge to someone who at least understands how painfully it was come by and can be trusted not to let it slip away into darkness with us. But Arshadin. Arshadin."

He stopped speaking and was silent for so long that, although his eyes were still open, I began to think that he had fallen asleep. He could do that when he chose, most often in the middle of conversations that were becoming more intense or revealing than he cared to deal with at the moment. Or it may have been pure devilment—I was never certain. And he was truly old at last now, terribly old, and terribly tired. Looking at him, just for that moment, I wished that I could sleep like that, sleep my way out of seeing him so. He promptly grinned at me, holding his ruined mouth up like a banner, or a flower, and went on as precisely as though he had never paused.

"I deserved Arshadin," he said. "In every sense of the word. I was the greatest magician I ever knew—and mind you, I was prentice to Nikos and studied long with Am-

Nemil, and later with Kirısinja herself. I asked less notice from the world than any of these, but I always knew that I deserved a true heir, that it was my right to be father to one wiser and mightier than I—one as different in kind from me as a bird is from the shards of its broken eggshell. And so I did, and so it came about, and I was given exactly what my pride and my foolishness deserved. I have no complaints."

Nyateneri began, "I mean no disrespect—"

"Of course you do," *my friend* said placidly. "You always did. Lal was a wild animal, but before that she had been raised to honor bards and poets and even the crankiest of old magicians. But you were always mannerly, even in complete despair, and yet there was never any decent respect in you. I attribute this to a lack of education and a youthful diet containing far too much *tilgit*." But he took hold of Nyateneri's left hand, where the bruise and the swelling hardly showed at all now, and held it briefly to his breast.

"Meaning no disrespect," Nyateneri repeated, "all this praise of this Arshadin puzzles me somewhat. Neither Lal nor I have ever heard his name before now"—he glanced at me for confirmation and corrected himself—"rather, before Lukassa called it out of the air in that idiotic candyfloss tower of yours. And even there, he may have been the wizard who summoned—whatever he summoned—yet he was slain, and you survive. So how that makes Arshadin your master and the greatest of all magicians, neither of us can quite make out."

My friend sighed. Nyateneri and I looked across him again, and this time neither of us was able to keep from smiling. We knew that particular rasping, hopeless sigh as we knew the reproachful murmur of our own blood in our eardrums: *another thoughtless minute gone, another tick like the tock before—how many, how many, how many of those do you suppose you have?* He always sighed like that to inform his students that their answers to his last question had shortened his life by a measurable degree and filled his few remaining days with quiet despair. It always worked on me, even after I knew better.

"Lukassa," he said to her, "what happened to you when you died?" She looked back at him without fear, but with the sort of adoring transparent puzzlement that would have gotten *our* ears boxed even then, weak as he was. But now, he only petted her and asked, even more gently, "What happened to *you*, to Lukassa inside? Did you sleep? Did you sleep, as people say we do?"

He was nodding even before she shook her head. "Of course not. Wide awake and screaming, you were, just not breathing. Well, imagine—and I say this to you because you at least do not think you know everything about magic, unlike some—imagine what becomes of a magician in death. Most people are wide awake only now and then—on special occasions, as you might say. But a magician is wide awake all the time, on call for everything, which is why most people call him a magician. And he is never more so than at the moment of his own death." He deigned to look around at Nyateneri and me now, that theatrical old fiend. "If his dying is unquiet, if he has not been allowed to make his *lamisetha*, oh, then his wide-awakeness may become something truly dreadful. There is a word for it, and words to command it."

I cannot say that the room became as dramatically still as he would have preferred. A couple of carters were shouting at each other down in the courtyard; dogs were barking, chickens carrying on, and I could hear that particular *sheknath*-in-heat bellow that Karsh uses to restore order. But between the four of us, a separate quietness sifted down coldly. *My friend* said, "There were words that I did not want Arshadin to learn. He learned them anyway. There were things that I would not teach him. Others would. He went to those others. No hard feelings—never, never any quarrels or hard feelings with Arshadin. He even offered to shake hands when he left me."

Quite suddenly, and without a sound, he began to cry. I am not going to tell you about that.

When Nyateneri and I could look at him again—Lukassa never looked away, but stroked his face and dried his eyes as we would never have dared—he said, "I loved him as myself. That was the mistake. There was no Arshadin to love. There is no Arshadin, only a wondrous gift and a glorious desire. I thought that I could make a real Arshadin grow around those things. That was the vanity—the stupid, awful vanity. Thank you, dear, that will do." Lukassa was trying to help him blow his nose.

Nyateneri spoke gruffly, which startled me, I remember. It was the first time I had really heard his voice as a man's voice. "So. He went off to those who would teach him what you would not, and you went back to organizing a proper wizard's funeral. And in time I came along to distract you again, and what with one thing and another, you forgot all about Arshadin. Except now and then."

"Except now and then," *my friend* agreed softly. "Until the sendings began. They were not so bad, those very first ones—a few nightmares, a bad memory or two made visible, a few rather tremulous midnight scratchings at the door. Nothing you might not take as ordinary, nothing you might recognize as a sending. But I did, and I summoned Arshadin to me. I could do that then." He sighed, deliberately comical, even rolling his tired eyes. "And he came, and he sat in my house, just as he did at teatime that first day, looking no different, and he told me how truly unhappy he was that it was going to be necessary to destroy me. If there were any other way, but there wasn't, nothing personal, honestly. And the worst of it was that I believed him."

The food and wine I had sent for arrived then, brought, not by Marinesha, as I had expected, but by Rosseth. Karsh must have ordered him to do it. He was horrendously ill at ease, stepping around us all with his eyes lowered, once bumping into Nyateneri, once almost tripping over the mattress as he set the trencher down. I felt sorry for him, and irritable as well. I wanted him gone, this clumsy servant, this kind boy who had kissed me and found out my heart, Rosseth. Telling it now, so long after, I still want to ask him to forgive me.

My friend touched his arm and thanked him, waiting until he had stumbled from the room before he spoke again. "What Arshadin wanted to learn did not come cheaply or simply. There were powers to be supplicated, principalities to be appeased, there were certain unpleasant advance payments to be endured. But he felt that it was all well worth the price, and who am I, even now, to deny that? I have paid my own fees in my time, negotiated across fire with faces I would rather not have seen, voices that I still hear. Magic has no color, only uses."

How often had I heard him say that, whenever I or another of his ragbag of student-children voiced a question about the inherent nature of wizardry? Some of us, I know, left him convinced that he had no sense of morality whatever, and perhaps they were right. He said, "But then again, I have never before been a payment myself. It makes a difference."

He ignored the meal, but gestured for me to pour him a little wine, which I did according to the old ritual he taught us, in which the student sips from the cup before the master. The wine was better than Dragon's Daughter, but not much better. He took the cup from me and passed it on to Lukassa, smiling at me as he did so. He was accepting her as a student before she ever asked to be received, as he had done with me. I smiled back, trembling with remembrance.

"The true price of Arshadin's education is my *lamisetha,*" he said. There was no expression at all in his voice. "Arshadin is to make certain that I die, when I die, such a troubled, peaceless death that I become a *griga'ath.* What is that, Nyateneri—a *griga'ath*?"

The shock of the question—no, of that word—actually made Nyateneri grunt softly and take a step backward. He answered after a time, his voice gone as pallid as his face. "A wandering spirit of malice and wickedness, without a home, without a body, without rest or ending." I had never seen him look as he looked then, and I never did again, except once. He said, a bit more boldly, "But there is a charm against the *griga'ath*. You taught it to me."

"So I did," *my friend* said, suddenly cheerful, "but it doesn't work. I only made it up for you because you were always so frightened of those bloody creatures. Not that you had ever seen one, nor could I imagine that you ever would." He paused, and then added in a very different voice, "But I have, and you yet may."

Nyateneri could not speak. I knelt down by the mattress. I said, "It will not happen. We will not let it happen."

He touched me then, drew his finger lightly down my forehead and across my cheek, for the first time since he bade me farewell and closed the door, all that world ago. "There's my Lal," he said again. "My *chamata*, who trusts only her will, whose true sword is her stubbornness. What is a *griga'ath*, after all, but one more enemy captain, one more desert in which to survive, one more nightmare to fight off until morning? Only a little extra determination, another snarl of refusal—*Lal will not allow this! Lal exists, and Lal will not have it so!* What's a *griga'ath* to that?"

The words were mocking, but the light, dry touch on my cheek was love. I answered him, saying, "I have seen one of them, a long time past. It was very terrible, but here I am." I was lying, and he knew it, but Nyateneri did not, and it seemed to help. *My friend* said, "A rogue *griga'ath* is one thing; that fate sometimes befalls a poor soul who has died with no one to think kindly of him in this world or to call to him from another. But far worse than that is a *griga'ath* under the control of a powerful wizard—I saw that tried once." He fell silent, staring away past us, seeing it again in a dusty corner of the room. Or was that storytelling, too? I think not, but I do not know.

"And the most dreadful of all would be a *griga'ath* that

had been a magician itself during its life. There would be nothing, *nothing* that such a spirit could not do, and no defense against it, whether it came to the call of an Arshadin or those whom Arshadin imagines he is using." He gave an odd, papery giggle, a sound he never used to make before. "My poor Arshadin, he has absolutely no sense of irony. It is his only weakness, poor Arshadin."

Something at the door. Not a footstep, not a scratch, not the least rustle of breath or murmur of clothing—just something crouching at the door. Nyateneri looked at me. I stood up very slowly, turning the handle of my sword-cane until I felt the lock slip open. It is a well-made cane. The lock made no more sound than whoever was out there in the corridor.

TIKAT

I do not know why she did not see me. Perhaps it was simply that she knew the doorways on this floor are all too shallow even to conceal a child. Anyone but a desperate weaver caught completely by surprise would certainly have gone to earth in the alcove under the stairway. She looked only briefly to either side, then advanced very slowly toward the stair, her swordcane no more than a glint out of its case. I will never like her, and I still despise her condescending kindness to me in front of Lukassa; but I never felt more the bumpkin I am than when I watched her moving across the corridor. I had no business in the same world with people who moved like that, nor did my love. I pressed myself back against someone's door, held my breath, and tried not to think of anything at all. Thoughts cast shadows and make noises, in that world.

Having assured herself that no one was hiding in the alcove or the stairwell, she backed away into her own doorway, one silent, careful step at a time. The sword was out now, needle-thin, the least bit curved toward the tip, in the same way that her neck and shoulders were bending very slightly forward. One last long stare—not to her left, where I huddled only a few feet away, but to the right and the stair again, plainly expecting to see someone approaching, not escaping. Whoever she was waiting for, it was not me, not dungbooted riverbank Tikat. The needle-sword flicked this way, that way, like a snake's tongue, and there was honest fear in the wide golden eyes. Then the door closed.

I stayed where I was a little longer; then crept from my doorway to listen again, as I had been when my breathing or my heartbeat alerted them inside. The old man was saying, "He knew me so well—he took advantage of my arrogance as no one ever has. I warded off his absurd little sendings as I cooked my dinner, his annoying night visitations without bothering to awaken. To my own old sense of loss there was added a great sadness for him—for my true son—never to know the true depths of his gift before he betrayed it so foolishly. There was nothing I could do for him now, but I did try not to humiliate him any further."

He laughed then, and for a moment I heard nothing else, because it sounded so like the laughter of my little brother, who died in the plague-wind. When I could listen to words again, they were in the brusque voice of Nyateneri, the tall one. "But they got worse, the sendings, a little at a time?"

"A little at a time," the old man whispered. "He was so patient, so patient. Not for years—not until the night when I found myself at last at bay in evil dreams and unable to awaken, did I understand how he had used me to ensnare myself. He *knew* me, he knew what my body and mind love most and what my spirit fears in its deepest places. Neither of you, nor anyone else, ever came near that knowledge. Only Arshadin."

"And bloody good use he made of it, too." Nyateneri again, a snort like an angry horse. "What happened then? He came to you again?"

I had to press my ear hard against the door to hear the answer. "I went to him. It took the best part of my strength, but I went to him in his own house. He did not expect me. We came to no agreement, and he tried to prevent my leaving. I left all the same." Lukassa must have been close on the other side, for I could smell her new-bread sweetness as I knelt there. The old man mumbled on. "I fled back to the red tower and reinforced it against him as best I knew how. He followed, first in the spirit, with sendings that now strode through my counterspells like wind through spiderwebs—then in the body." I lost some words when a sudden coughing fit took him, and only made out, "The rest you know. Or Lukassa knows."

I must have caught something of the black woman's taut wariness: anyway, I found myself turning often to look over my shoulder for whoever she had been so certain of seeing on the stair. I heard her voice, plainly angry herself now, saying, "At least *we* knew you well enough to follow a trail of nightmares that had you trapped howling in the arms of burning lovers, falling forever through razory emptiness, running and running from striding flowers that cried after you like babies. Were those the dreams he sent you, your son?"

Right back at her he came—no more coughing or muttering, but quick and clear as a slash of lightning. "They were not dreams. They are not dreams. Have you not understood that yet? What woke you, what brought you here—it has all happened to me, exactly as you saw it. And those were the least of them." A small, sudden chuckle. "Do you imagine that a few indigestible dreams did *this* to me?"

A rustle of blankets, cloth, something. A woman cried out. I knew it was Lukassa—it was the sound she would have made if the river had given her time to call my name. I know this. I jumped up to hammer on the door, never mind what I had sworn to myself not an hour before. Something touched my shoulder, very lightly, and I turned to see what it was.

NYATENERI

And having shown us exactly what had been done to him in those dreams of ours, he decided that he was hungry after all, and bent his energies loudly to the bread and soup. After a time, I heard the scrape of my own voice. "Lukassa told us about the Others."

"Then I have no need to," he answered with his mouth full, indistinct but scornful. "Arshadin made the mistake of not trusting his own power. He took his mind off me just long enough to call for the help he thought he needed. That will not happen again." He gave that new faraway chuckle that sounded like something small and frightened stirring in dry grass.

I said, "Lukassa says that the Others killed Arshadin, and that he came back to life again. Isn't that what you told us, Lukassa?"

She looked up at him, gone mute and useless, hardly hearing me at all. He wiped his mouth and shrugged. "Since I took that one moment of his inattention to escape, it is hard for me to say what did or did not happen. There was a good deal of confusion." He met my eyes guilelessly, knowing that I'd not give him the lie with an army at my back. "What I can tell you is that I have been fleeing him ever since, never going to ground anywhere, nor daring to contact you for fear of betraying my presence to him. As I will, sooner or later, if I have not already done so by summoning your fox friend, Nyateneri. But I was very weary."

I had to speak briskly, to keep from thinking about what we had seen beneath the rags of his shirt. I said, "Tell us where his castle lies. We will set out in the morning, Lal and I."

If he had been as dead as we had feared for so long, I think he would have risen at my words. He sat up so violently that the last of the soup spilled down his front. "You will do nothing of the kind! I forbid it utterly! Do you understand? Answer me, both of you—I want to hear you swear it. Answer me!"

Behind me, Lal burst out laughing. A moment of absolute astonishment—she treats that man as though he were made of moonlight, and there she was, doubling over herself until she had to sit down on the floor—and then there was nothing in the world for me to do but lean against the wall and pound on it to make the room shake. I imagine that must be part of that song about poor Karsh—"the ceiling shook and the plaster flew." Poor Karsh. I certainly never said that before.

The old man took no notice of our impudence, nor of Lukassa trying to clean up the soup with the last of the bread, but kept shouting at us, "This is not for you! Arshadin is no river pirate, no two-horse, forty-acre baron with a stone barn full of staggering louts to do his bidding while the drink holds out. He lives alone in a house so plain you'd pass it by for a woodcutter's hutch, and fifty like you could no more break into it than you could leave this room if I chose to keep you here, shadow and candle-end that I am. Understand me, Soukyan!" and he actually seized my arm—not lightly, either. "This is wizards' business, and none of yours! You cannot help me, not in that way. Leave Arshadin to me. Do you hear me?"

Lal was still giggling. I sat down by him, crowding him until he shifted on the mattress to make room. I said,

"This is like one of those rhyming puzzles you used to set me—Lal, too, I suppose—and then forbid me to come back to you without the answer. Like learning to make the tea you wouldn't drink. I thought those were all special magic exercises, just as important as archery practice, meant to show me the sinews of the universe in a drop of water. In time I came to realize that you gave them to me, not to widen my understanding, not to teach me a single thing, but only when you wanted a little time to yourself, and for no other reason. So what I learned from those riddles was not always to pay attention to you. It was a most practical lesson. I have never forgotten it."

For the first and only time since I have known him, my Man Who Laughs could do nothing but splutter, briefly but totally speechless with outrage. I patted his leg. "There," I said. "We are not the children you knew, and we were never fools. And we know something anyway about dealing with wizards. Tell us where Arshadin lives."

He sulked. There is no other word for it. He folded his arms and sank back against the pillows, staring somewhere past us. Once again, Lal and I began speaking at the same time. Lal concerned herself with assuring him that we would track down Arshadin with his help or without it, but that it would be a good thing to find him before he found us. I had a number of things to say about stubborn, arrogant, ungrateful old men, and I said them all. Neither approach made the slightest difference, as both of us could have predicted. He simply closed his eyes.

Then Lukassa spoke. Since we came into the room, she had done nothing but make over him, uttering no sounds—once she stopped weeping—distinguishable from the sigh of blankets or the soothing murmur of soup. Even I had almost forgotten she was there, and I was usually very much aware of Lukassa, silent or not. Now she said quite clearly, in that south-country baby-bird voice of hers, "White teeth—white, white teeth. The white teeth of the river."

From Lal's expression I knew that, like me, she thought Lukassa must mean the river from which Lal had raised her drowned body. The Man Who Laughs tried out a soft snore, but no one was deceived. Lal said, "That was long ago, Lukassa. There is no river where we are now."

"In the mountains," Lukassa said. Her voice was stronger, as fiercely insistent as it had been in the cold, empty tower. "In the mountains he gives the river fine presents to make it sing. The *dharises* nest on his windows, and the great *sheknath* fish along the banks below, and the river sings *hungry, hungry, please more, please.*" She was breathing hard and roughly, as though she had been running.

When we looked back at the Man Who Laughs, his eyes were wide open, still drained pale but bright enough for all of that. I said, "There are things she knows."

"Obviously," he said, forcing a yawn. "As I know that outside this door, one of the boys who helped me up the stairs is lying hurt. Not the one who brought the food, my dear Lal"—for she was already across the room—"the other one. Bring him in and see to him, and then we will perhaps talk a bit more about Arshadin. Perhaps."

Rosseth

It was well before dawn when they came for their horses, but I was ready and waiting outside the stable, rehearsing once more the logical reasons why they should take me with them wherever they were going. I was certain that Nyateneri would refuse, no matter how well I pleaded, but I did think that I might have some chance with Lal.

As it happened, Lal never let me get my first speech out of my mouth: she took one look at me, perched up between two weeks' worth of stolen food and several really quite sharp gardening tools on the warm swayback of Tunzi, Karsh's old horse-of-all-work, and said, "No, Rosseth." I will always bless her for not laughing, nor even looking startled; but her tone was quietly final, and somehow left no opening for much but spluttering and arm-waving. It was Nyateneri who said mildly, "You did name him our faithful squire, after all. A temporary appointment only?"

I saw the warmth flood from Lal's throat all the way to her forehead, but she ignored Nyateneri altogether, saying to me, "Rosseth, unpack that poor animal and go back to bed. I have already told you that you cannot come with us. You must stay home."

"I but obey your orders," I answered. "Where you are, I am home." Bold words, but barely audible, as I recall. Lal neither smiled nor frowned to hear them. She said, "Look at me, Rosseth. No, look straight at me, and at Nyateneri, too. Rosseth."

I did look directly into her eyes, which was effort enough, but it was more than I could manage to meet Nyateneri's calm glance. It shames me still, a little, to remember how ashamed I was, not of what had happened between us, but of my worshipful dreams of the woman I had taken him to be. I was sixteen, and chuckling little assassins were easier to face than confusion, in that time.

Lal said, "I will tell you where we are bound, and why you cannot come with us. We are on our way up into the mountains to seek out a wizard named Arshadin, who plagues our master with terrible hauntings and visions. When we have explained to him that this is an uncivil way to behave, we will return. In the meanwhile—"

"I can help you," I broke in on her. "You will need someone to find water in the mountains, to search for paths where the horses can go, to carry packs when the beasts must be rested." Each argument sounded weaker than the one before, but I plunged ahead anyway. "Someone to make your camp and keep it clean—someone who will wait forever where you tell him to wait. I know how to do these things. I have done them all my life."

"Yes," Lal said gently. "But we need you to do them at the inn. Listen to me, Rosseth," for I had immediately started to protest again. "At this moment, Arshadin is hunting for our master. He is sitting in silence, closing his eyes and hunting for him, do you understand me? Our hope, if we cannot reason with him, is not to fight him—for he is a far greater wizard than we are warriors—but perhaps to divert him, to make him hunt us for a bit, while our master regains his own strength." She paused, and then added, with a very small smile, "We do not yet know how we will do this."

"Oh, we certainly do not," Nyateneri mimicked her. "It

took all our wit merely to persuade our master to let us go with his blessing—there was none left over for anything like a plan of action. Find mountain, find river, find wizard, do *something*." He sighed and shook his head in mock despair. "It lacks a certain precision."

Lal ignored him, taking my wrists in her hands. She said, "We need you to guard him while we are gone. It will help us greatly to know that he is safe and warm and not alone." She would have said more, but I interrupted her, pulling my hands away.

"A nursemaid," I said. "Be honest with me—I have that much claim on you. A nursemaid to a sick old man, that is all you need." I am telling you what I said.

Nyateneri's horse pushed past Lal's, and Nyateneri gripped me between shoulder and neck with the same hand that had caressed me just there, after I had saved his life and my nose was bleeding. I stood up in my stirrups, prying at his fingers. He said very softly, "Boy. There is a world you do not know. In that world there are wizards and mages who could spread you and me on their morning toast before their eyes were quite open, and truly never realize that we weren't last year's ice-flower preserve. And among those vast beings, there is not one who would not cast aside every preoccupation, every pride, every loyalty, on the slightest chance of being allowed to sit by that sick old man's bed. Think carefully about this, Rosseth, as you change his linen."

Lal made him let go of my shoulder. I think he was so angry that he had forgotten he was holding me. But I was angry, too—I could not believe the rage that took me over then. As I have said, in those days a show of anger was the greatest luxury I dared imagine allowing myself, and at sixteen, the actual emotion seemed already as rare and unnatural in me as the display. I tried to keep from shaking with it as I answered Nyateneri. I said, "There is Lukassa, who refuses to let your master out of her sight. There is Tikat, who is never so far from Lukassa that he could not hear her call him, if she ever would. There is

Marinesha, who knows more about sickness than all three of us put together. What can I do for the old man that they cannot?"

"I said it was a guard we needed," Lal replied. "In the first place, you must keep Karsh from bothering him. We have paid in advance for the extra room, and for the extra cost of Marinesha bringing him his meals. Karsh has no reason to be anywhere near him. Can you see to that, Rosseth?"

I was slow to answer her, not because what she asked would require any special new skill of me—what had my life been so far but learning to manage Karsh?—but because I was still feeling deeply slighted, and particularly furious at Nyateneri, who seemed to take no notice of what he must have known. He said, "In the second place, Arshadin will certainly find our master here, and sooner rather than later. Whenever it happens, there will be danger to follow, such as your Gaff and Slasher has never known. Given the choice"—he paused—"given the choice, we would rather leave someone on watch whose courage and wit and resourcefulness we have observed for ourselves. No one can help us now as you can, if you will."

To me then, it was the rawest, most contemptible flattery: surely as much an embarrassment to him as to me. I feel differently now. When I still said nothing, Lal took her turn again. "Rosseth, you must know this, too. Those men Nyateneri killed—there is a third. We think it was he who overcame Tikat outside our door. Without doubt, he will follow us into the mountains and trouble the inn not at all, but you must look out for him even so, as much as for any sign or sendings of Arshadin." She took hold of my hand, but there was no cozening in her touch or her glance. She was not smiling when she asked, "Do you still believe that we are offering you nursemaid's duty?"

At the inn, the kitchen door slammed loudly, heedless of sleeping guests. I knew that slam, and I knew that Karsh had come out into the cool mist to stand with his hands on his hips and peer around for me. It would be a moment yet before he started bawling my name. I looked back and forth from one to the other of them, these beautiful strangers who knew they could do what they wanted with me, having so quickly overturned and disjointed my life at The Gaff and Slasher that it might as well have been as much a dream as the song about Byrnarik Bay, where someone was going to take me once. There is no finding a dream again; good or bad, there's no returning to a dream. I said to them, more carefully than I had ever said anything, "What I believe makes as much difference to you as whoever has my throat in his hands makes to me." Then I got down from Tunzi's back and walked him into the stable to unsaddle him. I did not turn, and I did not look up when I heard them finally riding away.

The Innkeeper

I watched him come toward me, exactly as I had watched him walk away that night when there were dead men all over the bathhouse. Sounds carry far and long on damp mornings here, and I could still hear the hoofbeats even after they had reached the main road. I said, "Wouldn't take you along, heh?"

He answered nothing at all to that but, "I had to see to Tikat. I am sorry to be late. It was a bad night."

"There's naught in the least amiss with Tikat, and well you both know it," I said. "Nothing wrong with anybody who can turn an addled gape and a tiny bruise on the neck into two full days' eating at my expense. As for those women—ah, well, cheer up, keep at it. Bound to be a slave caravan or a bandit gang through here sometime soon, and you can run off with *them*. Steal a younger horse than Tunzi, though—he'd not make it past Hrakimakka's orchard, if he got that far." By this time, I was hitting him, or trying to: half-asleep, he was still all shrugs and sidesteps, catching blows on every part of his body that could possibly hurt me and not him. I don't believe I ever landed one solid clout on that boy after he turned eight or so. I really don't.

He kept mumbling, "I was not running away, I was

not," but I paid that no more attention than you'd have done. Who wouldn't run from fat old Karsh and The Gaff and Slasher to follow two beautiful women adventurers away to the golden horizon? I hit him for thinking I'd believe anything different, and for not having the wit and the courtesy to imagine that I might have done the same myself. As well as he imagined he knew me.

"Shadry needs wood and water in the kitchen," I said. "When he's done with you, I want those drainage ditches below the stable cleaned out. They're fouled again—I can smell them from here. Tikat's to help you, if he plans to spend another night under any roof of mine. As for *your* plans"—and I bounced one off the point of his elbow that left my hand sore all that day—"next time, don't let them hang on someone else's yes or no. Next time, you'd best keep running as straight and far as you can go, for I'll pulp every last drop of cider out of you if you try sneaking back. Do you understand what I am telling you, boy?"

He didn't, not then. He gave me one dark, puzzled blink, and then ducked past me toward the woodshed. I shouted after him, "Stay away from the old man, do you hear me? And the girl, too—I don't want you speaking a bloody word to that mad girl." When I turned, because I felt someone watching me, it was the fox, grinning between the withes of a berry basket. He was gone, vanished, while my shout for Gatti Jinni was still echoing, but I know I saw him. I saw him, all right.

NYATENERI

Lal said, "I'm sorry you don't like my singing. I don't care, but I am sorry."

We were walking the horses by then, letting the little Mildasi black lead, packhorse or not, because he understood this country: hardly a stone spurted backward under his feet, while our poor larger beasts flailed their way up the path like men floundering through a snowstorm. I said, "I never complained about your voice; it's what you sing that I can't abide. No tune, no shape, no end—just an everlasting melancholy whine quavering in my skull day after day. Meaning no mockery, this is truly what your folk call music?"

My horse flung back his head and balked, having winded the rock-*targ* I smelled a moment later. There's no high range without them, not north of the Corun Beg, anyway. I spent the next few minutes reassuring him that it was dead scent from a last-year's lair, which I certainly hoped was true. Lal waited for me a little way ahead. "So they do," she answered me, "and history, too, and poetry and genealogy, for the matter of that. Ride on ahead if it troubles you to hear. Or sing something yourself—*there* would be an interesting change. Even Lukassa sings now and then, and I've often heard Rosseth humming about his chores, only the gods know why. Never you."

"The air is thin here," I said. "I save my breath for breathing." We were four days out and up among the mountains above Corcorua, on a road that tacked constantly back and forth, as Lal said, like a boat trying to find the wind, at times veering three and four and five miles sidewise to climb less than one. For all that, we had scrambled high enough already to look down on the backs of coasting snowhawks, high enough that the foothills among which we had first sought our master looked as flat and pale as the farmlands they surveyed. The air was indeed thin, and chill, too, full summer or no, with a curious tang about it, rather like fruit about to go bad. Above us, the icy peaks leaned together, breathing grayness.

"To me, singing *is* breathing," Lal said over her shoulder as we started on. "I don't understand people who don't sing." She had been in a sideways quarrelsome mood since we set out—longer, really—never giving her disquiet proper voice, but neither allowing us a truly easy moment, even in silence. There are many who find deep contentment in such a situation, but Lal was not of them—I have known no one less comfortable with the common subtleties. Anger she could enjoy well enough; deviousness, never. I halted my horse a second time and stood where I was until she turned, hearing no one trudging behind.

"Are we no more to be companions, then?" I asked her. "Because of what occurred between weary and lonely friends who had endured much together, is there to be no friendship ever again between you and me?" My life has not led me easily to ask such questions, nor Lal's taught her to answer them, and she did not. She said only, so low that I could barely hear her, "We must reach Simburi Pass by sunset." This time she did not look back to see if I were following.

We did reach Simburi Pass—substantial name for what amounts to a goatherd's trail up to summer grazing, hardly wider than the stream where we made our camp. We spoke little until the horses were seen to, and then we sat down and faced each other across a shallow pit in which a hundred or a thousand generations of goatherds must have built their cooking fires. Lal said presently, "Where do you think he picked up our track?"

"Trodai," I said. "That place like a bit of lichen on a bit of stone, where we asked too many people if they knew of a river in these mountains. He caught up at Trodai."

Lal shook her head. "You do yourself an injustice. No one's taken that overgrown old path out of Corcorua in centuries, I'm sure of it. You gave us a day's start with that, maybe two. He found us no earlier than last night or this morning."

"What difference? Either way, at least we can have a fire. I'm tired of sleeping cold and going without my tea for his benefit. I'll gather some wood—you see if there might not be a few fish in that stream."

I started to rise, but Lal seized my arm and pulled me back, crying, "Fool, get down! Even Rosseth wouldn't stand like that against the sunset!" The Mildasi horse, reacting to the furious panic in her tone, made a strange low sound in its throat, less a nicker than a questioning growl.

My laughter plainly offended Lal, but I couldn't help that. "If he were within bowshot, and I think he is, he could have picked us off long ago. I told you, they never use weapons of any sort—it's one-third religion, two-thirds a question of pride. Now that he is alone, he might strike from ambush, but I doubt it." I stood up, deliberately raising my voice. "The one trouble with knowing that an armed warrior facing your bare hands is overmatched is that it leads to a certain vanity, a certain carelessness. That is exactly why his friends are dead. That is why he will join them in a while."

I took Lal's hands and she came up in a single motion, as I have seen her flow out of a sound sleep, swordcane half-drawn before her eyes were fully open. Now they were wary, probing: suspicious, but not altogether untrusting. My life has hung often on knowing that particular difference. I said, "I will find the wood. If we die tonight, it won't be on salt meat and stale bread."

There were fish, small but plentiful, and very tasty. Lal lay flat and scooped them out of the water as the *sheknath* do, and I cooked them crisp in oil and a bit of our precious flour. We had *darit*-root still, which keeps well and clears the mouth, and there was even a winter apple we had forgotten about. Lal made the tea, just as my Man Who Laughs had taught me to make it, as he surely taught every student he ever had. It is not a common blend; sometimes I fancy that I've surely left as plain a spoor of tea-leaves across two continents as any following killer could wish, and one far less escapable than my sex. Nothing much to be done about it now.

With those mountains toppling over us, we finished our supper in darkness. Our small fire was warm enough, but it threw its light no further than the horses' glinting eyes. There was no scent of rock-*targ* now, and no sound but the soft jingle of the stream. I said, "First watch to me."

"We should set out the *bima* sticks. They'd give us some warning, anyway."

"No, they wouldn't. Believe me." Lal met my eyes, nodded, and shrugged. I said, "He has no interest in you. I am all he's after."

"And suppose he gets me by mistake, what then? It's chance and stupidity that keep *me* awake, not any fanatical assassins. I really fear a stupid death." It is often hard to tell when Lal is joking.

"If he should kill you, it will be entirely intentional. That I can safely promise you."

"Thank you," Lal said. "That does ease my mind. Now, according to the folk of Trodai, we should reach the River Susathi by the day after tomorrow, assuming we reach it at all. From that point, it sounds very much to me like a good two weeks' journey at least to where Arshadin lives. Didn't it sound so to you?"

It was my turn to shrug, busying myself with the fire.

"No more than that—perhaps even a day or so less. They disagreed among themselves, you remember."

Lal said quietly, "I don't think we have the time."

Beyond the firelight there was a sudden rustle and a miniature scream: something very small catching something smaller in the dark. I said, "He escaped Arshadin, sick and feeble, and has eluded him ever since. Why fear he'll be any easier to take with his strength returned?"

Lal sat crosslegged, slowly tapping her left palm with her right forefinger. "First, because I know a lot of old tales about sorcerers dying and being resurrected, and I've noticed that they always seem to come back even stronger and meaner than they were. Second, because *my friend*—*our* friend's true power has *not* returned, and may well never return again. Yes, he can still protect himself better than we can guard him—yes, even now he can still work magics for which lesser wizards would give all that Arshadin has already given. But he is a gutted man."

The last words came out so harshly that for a moment I did not recognize them. I said, more hesitantly than I am used to speaking, "I would not call him that. Gutted."

Lal smiled at me for the first time in a long while. She said, "This is one place anyway where there can be no misunderstanding between us. We have had the same dreams, each knows what the other knows. What he suffered at Arshadin's hands took his belly, his"—she hesitated, stumbled, and finally used a word that must have been in her own tongue. "What's left is skill, wisdom, cunning, desperation. Let Arshadin close on him again, and none of these will avail him any more than they would you or me. We dare not give away so much as an extra day, let alone two weeks. Not to Arshadin"—she turned away from the fire and spoke loudly—"and certainly not to whoever hears us now."

A night bird chirred softly from its nest; a *nishoru* sang far away. Not far enough for me, but they have to be really hungry before they'll charge a fire.

"Sailor Lal," I said, "I see where this is going." Lal smiled smugly. I said, "I don't like it."

Lal's expression grew even more self-satisfied. She said simply, "You have not sailed with me."

"True enough. Something else I have yet to do is see a river running west to east. So I won't believe in this Susathi until I've washed my feet in it. And since we don't know exactly where we may strike it, how can we know if Arshadin's home lies upstream or down?"

"Think about what Lukassa told us. She spoke of the white teeth of the river—she said that it sang of its hunger. Do you remember?"

"A rapids," I said. "The house overlooks a rapids, which could be upstream as easily as not. Wonderful."

Lal began placidly to unroll her bedding and embark on her nightly search for the perfect twig to clean her teeth with. I have known it to take an hour. She said, demure as a temple novice, "Not everyone who can handle a boat is called *sailor*. There are other considerations involved." And after that she wouldn't do anything but mumble to herself and compare twigs.

I spent the night with my back against a boulder and the bow across my knees. I wondered what mischief the fox was most likely to be up to by now, and about the possible nature of Arshadin's Others, and I thought often of Rosseth. Both Lal's watches and mine passed without event; but he was very near, that third one, and he knew I knew it. Once, just before I woke Lal, a *tharakki* scuttled through the firelight and was gone again—it was the two-legged variety, you don't find the other sort this high—and at that moment I could have thrown a stone into the dark and hit him. You have to work to startle a *tharakki* from its hole, night-blind as they are, but he must have thought the joke was worth the effort. There would be no attack, not with Lal at hand; time enough for that after we came to the river. He was only saying hello.

We found the Susathi a day and a half later, flowing serenely through a steep slice in the mountains that took us utterly by surprise. As I've told you, our progress had been far less dramatic than tedious and serpentine: we never hung from crumbling ledges by our fingernails or coaxed our horses to leap snowy chasms, but mostly plodded off to the left one more time to toil up another sky-filling field of rattling, tumbling stones. No descents to catch our breath in, none at all: only one or two passes where the way was more or less level—keyholes between the mountains, half-choked by ancient ice-boulders and scree, harder to traverse than the slopes themselves. Then we trudged single-file around a bulging shoulder of stone and saw it, not that far below, a river as straight as a sword-cut, twinkling away, west to east, in the noonday sun.

Lal and I stood looking at each other, while the horses nudged our necks and stepped on our feet, smelling the water down there. I smelled it myself, a cool dance in my nostrils. Lal sighed presently and said, "Well. So much for the easy part."

"No rapids that I can see," I said. Her face took on that look again, so full of the knowledge of its own secret knowledge that she could hardly endure it herself. I felt much the same. She lowered one eyelid very slowly, let it float up again, then swung into her saddle and started down the trail. I mounted, caught the Mildasi horse's reins, and followed. Once I looked back, but of course there was nothing behind us but stone and old, old snow. I wished I had not laid rough hands on Rosseth.

TIKAT

It took me longer to recover from the bare-hand touch of a man I never saw than it did from my journey through the Northern Barrens. Days afterward, no mark on me, and I was still coming over dazey and faint and trembling without warning, unable to trust my body anywhere. Rosseth, uncomplainingly doing half my work as well as his own, told me about those three men who had followed Nyateneri for years and finally caught up with her at The Gaff and Slasher. He said there was no shame in my falling without a fight, like a market animal, and that I should be proud of myself simply for having survived the encounter. I took his word for it.

He never once asked what I had been doing at that door, which was as kind in its way as the other, the work. In spite of the fact that I am not easy speaking of myself, while he seemed to be always clacking along like a little windmill, somehow he ended up knowing nearly as much about my life as I did about his. I don't mean Lukassa and me—no hide-buyer or corn-merchant staying the night but knew *that* much by now—but about our village with its two priests and its one whore; about the blacksmith, whom everyone feared except Lukassa, and about my aunt and uncle and the weaver-woman who was teaching me her trade. I cannot say to this day how I came to tell him such things—even the story of my theft of *dirigari* fruit from my teacher's orchard, which shames me still. He was only a boy, after all, Rosseth, two years younger than I, innocent as one of Shadry's potboys—more innocent—and all the time thinking himself as knowing as an old bargeman. I do not know why I talked to him as I did.

"Tell me about your parents again," he would urge me; and when I stumbled, forgetting my father's favorite dish or the turn of a joke my mother liked to make, then an odd look would come into his eyes, almost reproachful, as though if he had known *his* parents he would have remembered everything; and perhaps he would have. His own first clear memory was of Karsh carrying him somewhere by the back of his neck—before that, there were only bits and shadows that might have been dreams, though you could tell Rosseth didn't think so all the time. When I asked him how he came to be at The Gaff and Slasher, he told me that Karsh had taken him from a traveling Creeshi peddler, "in trade for three gamecocks and a bag of Limsatty onions. He complains about it to this day—says two of those birds were champions, and sweet Limsatties have never been as good since. Gatti Jinni says one cock was blind, but I don't know."

He talked of Lal and Nyateneri hardly at all now, which suited me well. He made up for that, though, with his endless stream of chatter about Lukassa. She was surely not herself, he kept reassuring me—clearly she had endured a great deal, and many times such suffering changes people so that they cannot even recognize those who love them best. But patience and endurance on my part would triumph at last, he was certain of it; every day he could see her gentling toward me, see her expression changing bit by bit when she looked at me. It was all so well-meant that I could never tell him—as I would have anyone else, the first time it happened—that he was not to speak of this. But neither could I bear to listen to him;

so there was nothing for me to do but move away, if we were working together, or find some solitary chore that would keep me well out of earshot for hours. That is how I began to be so often with the old man.

He never told me his name. I called him first *sir,* and later on *tafiya,* which is what people in my village sometimes choose to call someone—man or woman, old or not so old—who is seen to have a certain kind of power, dignity, stature, whatever you want to call it. Hard to explain: my teacher is called *tafiya,* for instance, while the blacksmith is not and the one whore is not, but her mother is. One priest, not the other; two or three farmers and the brewer, but not the headman, not the doctor, not the schoolmaster. I cannot put it any better than that. I called him *tafiya,* and he knew the word and seemed pleased.

He was very weak at first: not so much in the body, though there was that, too, since he could keep down nothing but the thin soup with bread in it, and now and then some milk or wine. But the real frailness was elsewhere, and I cannot explain that any better than I can the real meaning of *tafiya.* Let it be a wind that puts your fire out, and often you can nurse it back to life, if you are patient enough and feed it and blow on it just so. But let it be a splash of rain, and you will build a new fire in a dry place or go without. I think the old man was waiting to learn, those early days, whether it was wind or rain in his heart, or in his spirit, as you will. I think that was what it was.

The women had paid for his room and care, and Karsh kept his word to them, so far as it went. Marinesha was supposed to be the only one looking after him—Karsh did his best to keep Rosseth too busy to go anywhere near that room—but she twisted her ankle slipping away from a pair of rope-dealers in the taproom. So, until she could climb stairs twenty times a day again, I was often told off to bring my *tafiya* his meals, arrange his new bedding, and empty out his chamberpot. I neither enjoyed the task nor minded doing it. It was all one to me then.

No, that is not true. I did mind doing it, very much, and I feared it as well, and of course he knew. I had not been attending him for more than three days when he said to me, as I was helping him into a nightshirt that Shadry thought was in a chest under his own bed, "I rather wish I smelled worse than I do. Perhaps then it would be harder for you to smell Lukassa when you come into this room."

I could not answer him. With the other women gone, I knew that she spent the best part of her time in his company, but I saw her on occasion walking the roads and meadows near the inn, or even chatting a little with Marinesha in the courtyard. That same day she had come on me carrying a load of firewood too high for her to see my face. When I stood before her, demanding once again, "Lukassa, Lukassa, it is Tikat, how can you not know me?" she screamed and ran away, as she had done before. I started after her, shouting her name, but the logs tumbled loose around my feet and I fell with them. Gatti Jinni and Shadry, who saw it all, were still laughing that evening, and my feet were still hurting.

When I did not speak, the old man touched my hand and said, "No. Well, I can at least assure you that you will never encounter Lukassa here, and that if you would prefer to come somewhat less often yourself, I will manage quite well, and never mind your orders. That much I can do for you, even in my present condition."

Did he see then how angry his kindness made me? Do *you* see it now, even a little? I have never been able to bear pity—it enrages me as nothing else in this world does. I suppose it goes back to my parents' death, with everyone who had survived the plague-wind weeping over me, feeding me, petting me. I wanted to kill them, the whole wretched understanding lot of them. The only person who ever knew that I wanted to kill them was Lukassa. Or maybe I have been this way since I was born.

I said, "There is no need," and went on adjusting the night-shirt. He was beginning to gain a little weight, but all his bones stood up like bruises under his skin. He watched me silently, eyes half-shut, until I had settled him in bed and begun gathering his day's cups and dishes. Then he said abruptly, "Tikat. She will not ever remember."

I did not dare let myself look at him. I went to the door, careful to hold the dishes safely while I fumbled for the latch. They would never chip or break if you dropped them, those dishes, but always shattered beyond repairing. Behind me, he said, "If you want her, you must go where she is. She cannot come back to you." I closed the door and took the dishes down to the scullery.

But in the middle of the night I went back. The inn was shuttered and locked, of course, and the dogs roaming, but they knew me now, and Rosseth had shown me a way to get in through a loose window-sash in the root cellar. No one awake except a journeying Mazarite priest and his body-servant: they aren't supposed to do anything at all with their hands, those Mazarites, not so much as comb their beards or scratch an itch, but I could have led a regiment past *that* door, instead of creeping all the way to the other one, as I did.

His eyes were open, glinting in the moonlight, but I had already seen him sleeping like that. I stood in the doorway, unable to speak to him, unable to turn away. He said, "Come in, Tikat."

So I took a three-legged stool from the corner and sat down by his bed. It was hard for me to talk, but I said, "I want to know what you meant. About Lukassa, about me going to her. I have already followed her beyond death, across deserts and mountains to this place which is—" I could not find words—"which is so much not our place that I think as long as we are here she cannot know me. But if she were to come home, to come home with me—"

"It would be no different." His voice was gentle and

merciless, comforting. "I told you that you would have to go where she is now, and that place is neither here nor there. It is a country where Lal and Nyateneri have always been her older sisters, where I am, if you will, her grandfather, and where you never existed. Do you understand me, Tikat? No long, long river afternoons, no dreaming in the willows; no tall, sweet boy who played boats with her, and told her stories, and kept the other boys from teasing her. It never happened, Tikat, none of it—she never rescued you from the wild pigs, nor put the cool leaves on your back when your uncle beat you for drinking his featherberry wine. You cannot go back to a world and a life that never was."

How did he know what he knew? How do *I* know? He was my *tafiya*. I did not weep—no one but Lukassa has ever seen me weep—but there seemed to be a very long time before I could speak as I wanted. I said at last, "What must I do to be with her?"

He rolled his eyes, mimicking me brutally. " 'What must I do, O master? Advise me, direct me, think for me, greatest, wisest of wizards.' Whose wisdom got you this far, yours or mine? Who loves that child best, you or me?" He slapped his hands down so violently on the blankets that the gesture shot him upright, glaring at me in utter disgust. "The older I become, the more I wish I had a reputation for total, transcendent idiocy. Perhaps that would mean even a few less idiots whining for my magical counsel. Get out of my sight—there is a particular kind of intelligent stupidity that I cannot abide, and you embody it absolutely. Get out of my sight!"

If it was a real rage or not, I could not tell, but I paid it no heed at all, because I am far more stubborn than I am either foolish or clever. When I did not move from the stool, he grew calm almost as suddenly as he had become furious with me. "Never ask me what you must do, Tikat. Tell me what you will do—then at least we can argue properly. Tell me now."

I said slowly, "If I am to begin as a stranger—if I am

to begin all over, everything, with no history between Lukassa and me, no childhood, no love from the moment we crawled into each other's vision—why, then so be it, so be it. I will go to her tomorrow and speak to her as gently as I would any stranger, assuming nothing, hoping for nothing but to assure her that I am a friend and no madman. This is what I will do tomorrow—beyond tomorrow, who knows? And so be it."

I did not look at him as I spoke, but at my cupped hands; it was all I could do at the last not to ask, "Is that well? Is that the right way for us to begin the rest of our lives? Will you help me now?" But I did not—not that it would have been any use just then, for he had fallen quite asleep. I sat beside him almost until dawn, when I slipped off back to the stable so that Rosseth could rouse me to begin our day's work. In all that time he never stirred, but snored away sweetly and politely, even when I dabbed a bit of dried soup from a corner of his mouth. I said aloud, "I am becoming Lukassa, finicking over you so," but he did not awaken.

Above the woodlot there is a little shrubby slope where Karsh has built a shrine, as innkeepers are required to do, for the use of all such holy wanderers as that Mazarite priest. Just for a moment, as I was going into the stable, I thought I saw Redcoat squatting by a thornbush halfway up the hillside. He was smiling with his mouth closed and his eyes almost shut, and Lukassa's locket glinting between his dreaming fingers. I stopped for a better look, but if he was really there I lost him in the dazzle of the morning rising behind him, pale blue, palest silver.

LAL

Downstream."

"How can you know?"

I bent my head a second time to the river water cupped in my hands. I made a bit of a spectacle out of it, more than a bit, letting the water trickle over my lips and throat and smiling lingeringly as I sipped it. Finally I said, "Human life leaves a taste. In the air, in the water, in the ground. One house—not a village, only a single house, with a few people, an animal or two, coming and going, fishing, eating, using the river—it changes the flavor. It just does." I sampled the water once more and nodded. "There's no one living anywhere upstream. Try it, you can tell."

Nyateneri said thoughtfully, "How nice to hear the most ridiculous statement of my entire life while I am still young enough to appreciate it." He crouched beside me, scooped up a few drops, licked at them impatiently and stood up at once, looking abruptly angry and embarrassed. Only when we were well into the mountains had he let his woman's form dissolve again, showing himself lean and gray; heavy-boned, yet more graceful than he should be for his size, the hair as ragged as ever (he chopped it periodically into the same scorched-earth monastery cut, for no reason that he would ever tell), and the eyes still as slowly changeable as twilight skies. A gentle mouth still, in a hard, tired face.

"This is stupid," he said. "I know all the stories, I am quite ready to believe that Lal-Alone can give a lizard two weeks' start and track it across any desert you like, blindfolded if you like. But one fisherman pissing out of a skiff—no, no, I am sorry, I spent my youth in a cloister, my trustfulness is not what it should be. No."

Well, it served me right for making such a grand show of my skills. "No rapids further up, either—no taste of white water at all." Nyateneri snorted. I wiped my hands on my breeks and pointed to the sky as I stood up myself. "Very well, consider our friends there. Name them for me. If you like."

Nyateneri gave the black-and-white birds circling just upstream of us a brief glance, and answered, "*Vrajis.* In the south we call them priest-catchers. Why?"

I said, "Because even in your country it is surely known that these birds do not nest where men are. If there were a settlement within fifty miles, you wouldn't see a *vraji* here until the village had been ashes for fifty years. Tell me I am mistaken."

No chance of that, anyway—there must be jokes and proverbs in a hundred tongues about the *vrajis'* antipathy to human beings. One of my own folk's nastier religions is based upon it. Nyateneri sighed, rubbed his neck, stared at the birds, walked away from me, walked back, rubbed his neck again and said, "So. Not one house." It was not exactly an agreement, but it was not a question either.

"You really can tell by the taste," I said. "It doesn't take as much practice as you might think." Nyateneri had wandered off again, morosely studying the stony, sloping quarter-moon of shore where we stood, and the dark trees beyond. I raised my voice slightly. "The real question is not where Arshadin's house is, but how distant it is, and how we plan to get there. Having completely exhausted my legendary woodcraft, I would welcome any suggestions."

When Nyateneri finally turned to me and spoke, my blood stopped moving for a moment, because he spoke in Dirvic. That tongue has been dead for five centuries, which is not nearly long enough. I have met three people who knew Dirvic, including the one who taught it to me, and each came to an uncommonly evil end. How Nyateneri learned it, and how he guessed that I knew it, I still do not want to discover. He said, "My first suggestion would be that we speak this terrible language from now on. Can you bear it?"

The sudden kindness of the question made my eyes sting, which angered me. "I will bear it," I said. Dirvic hurts the mouth and coats the throat with a thick bitterness. It was never meant for ordinary conversation. Nyateneri said, "There was one man at the monastery who spoke it, but he died. I am betting our lives that there are no others. Now. Since you have obviously been nursing a plan of attack since we set out, it is pointlessly polite of you to ask for my own ideas. Tell me how you propose to build the boat."

"A raft would be more like it," I said. Even putting that simple a sentence together in Dirvic, meaning seemed to slough away from the words like burned skin. I went on, "I am no boatwright, even if we had the time and the tools. But I have made rafts out of less than this, and sailed them, too." I gestured at the trees—a type of thin-barked conifer I had never encountered before—and at the luxuriant blue vines enlacing most of them. "You and I could have a serviceable raft together by sundown. We might even manage a keel, the way they do in the O'anenue Islands. I've seen that done, long ago."

But Nyateneri was shaking his head slowly. "Not with these trees." His expression was more gentle than mocking, even a bit sad. "There is no reason for you to know them, but in the north country where I was born we call them *jaranas*—jokers, joker-trees. They look like softwoods, but they're so dense that they'll drag the teeth out of any saw but the best Camlann work. And a raft made of joker-tree logs would sink before you had time to get aboard. I could have told you, if you had let me know your plan."

There was no triumph in his face, but in Dirvic everything sounds like a whining sneer. My turn now to look away, to pace silently back and forth, chewing one side of my tongue (a childhood habit) and feeling like an imbecile. It is true, what *my friend* said—I hate not knowing everything, even when it is not possible. More important, I had left myself with no back door, nothing in reserve in case it proved that I didn't know everything. Even a ground-hare, a *kumbii,* knows better than that—in his world, just as in mine, carelessness is another name for Uncle Death, and I had been calling that name far too often lately. So I walked in circles and stared up at those useless trees until Nyateneri spoke again.

Dirvic affects the voice in strange ways: it made me sound as young as Lukassa, and brought Nyateneri's tone and pitch back almost to what it had been when I had thought of him as a woman. He said, "You are forgetting our faithful companion."

"Likely that's the only thing I haven't forgotten," I said sharply. "Why else would we be fouling our mouths with this vile talk but for him in the shadows? What about him, then?"

Nyateneri said, "I think he should help us with our boat. It seems only fair, when you think about it."

I looked at him so long that he finally began to smile, trying earnestly to smother it, I suppose to keep the man watching us from suspecting anything he didn't suspect already. "Lal, I do not expect him to make one for us, no more than we could ourselves. He is no wizard, only a carefully trained murderer, but the heart of that training has to do with being very well prepared for the unexpected. And if the unexpected should include a journey by water, he will be ready." He put a hand on my shoulder, and once again I almost jumped and snapped at the kindness of it. He said, "It is an old intimacy." Dirvic has no such word; I had to guess at his meaning. "I know these men as you know your dreams."

I stared at him a moment longer, and then burst out in loud laughter, gesturing my derisive rejection of his suggestion as broadly as I could. Pushing his hand from me and turning away, I said over my shoulder, "We will have to make him believe that we have set off downriver. That will not be easy."

Nyateneri shook his fist, shouting after me, "No, it will not be. Go sulk over there and think about it for a while."

So I did that. I walked off down the riverbank until I came to a low flat boulder, and there I sat with my knees drawn up to my chin, and I brooded as visibly as I could manage. And back in the middle of the quarter-moon, where we had tethered our horses and dropped our dwindling supplies, Nyateneri did the same thing, now and then shouting bits of classical northern poetry in impromptu Dirvic translation at me, accompanied by particularly threatening grimaces, which I did not deign to acknowledge. However the man may end, he was born to travel with a troupe of players, such as those sleeping in Karsh's stable when we first arrived at The Gaff and Slasher. I have mentioned it to him since.

We kept this up for some two hours, while the matronly Susathi slid by us, making no sound, and barely a ripple to blink in the sunlight. It was a dangerously peaceful place: no matter how urgently I set about the problem of getting away from it, no matter how furiously I bent my senses to catching the least rustle of breath or blood or footstep, the instant I allowed myself a breath for myself, then the soft, humming warmth had me again. I did not doze, exactly; but just once, when a fish jumped in midstream, I found myself on my feet, sword fully drawn, crying something in that language I no longer speak. I think I was calling to Bismaya.

Toward evening, we began to move slowly and sullenly

together, not shouting now, but speaking in a grumbling manner which Dirvic made suitably menacing. Almost simultaneously, almost in the same words, we said, "First of all, it must seem to be one of us, not both." We could not help laughing truly then, but that was all right, because of what laughter sounds like in Dirvic. Nyateneri said, "The question is whether we fight or merely separate. I do think a fight would be nice."

"If you and I fought, someone would die. Quite probably the two of us. He knows that."

"Not a proper fight, just a sort of scuffle. Harsh words, cuffs, pushes—lovers irked beyond endurance. That's what he thinks we are, after all."

He *was* mocking me now: that was clear enough, even through the impersonal malevolence of the language. I did not answer, but regarded him levelly up and down, making it plain in my turn that I was remembering the taste of his skin, and the rake of his nails down my sides, and the flowering leap of him inside me. Remembering everything, without regret and without longing. I said, "I will have to strike off upstream, leaving you here. You must appear to be building a raft alone."

"It will have to be a trash raft—driftwood, dead branches, whatever litter I can find. That's the part that worries me, making the thing look like something that such a wily fugitive as Soukyan might sensibly try to ride downriver—let alone take over a rapids. Intimacy again, you see."

The deliberate use of his true name jarred me silent for a moment. I had only spoken it once since learning it, and I made quite sure never to think of him as anything but Nyateneri. "Wait until twilight, and stay well clear of the trees. How near can he possibly come without your seeing him?" Nyateneri gave me a tolerant glance which would have enraged Queen Vakalshakva the Unspeakably Good, who—as the tales have it—was of so benevolent a temper that savage rock-*targs* and *nishori* left their lairs to make pilgrimage to her court, lie at her feet, and ask blessing. They soiled the carpets and ate the servants—who, if not as saintly as she, were at least tasty—but Vakalshakva patiently replaced both and never rebuked them. I know eight songs about her, none written by either rock-*targs* or servants.

I nodded slightly to a coil of tawny water-weed spinning slowly in a little eddy near the bank. "Gather as much of those dead-man's-ringlets as you can. The stalks end in clumps of air-bladders, and you could very well be fixing them under the raft for buoyancy. They might even work."

"So they might," Nyateneri said in a vicious Dirvic snarl, not looking in that direction. "Thank you, that's a clever idea." The words came out sounding like a blood insult, and he punched my shoulder abruptly, knocking me backward into a crackling tangle of brush, then laughing uproariously as I struggled to pick myself up. I said, "I'll leave your pack with all the rope in it," and hit him in the mouth.

"Leave the empty water-bottles as well," he reminded me, shaking me until my teeth clicked together. "Anything that floats. Circle back after dark, without the horses."

So we agreed on details, such as they were, all the while slapping and knocking each other up and down the shore. Our beasts looked on, nickering unconcernedly, and fish continued jumping after insects; and somewhere close among the joker-trees Nyateneri's tireless enemy waited for nightfall. When all was as settled between us as it could be, I spat in his eye and stormed away, pausing only to shout back at him, "I'm very sorry that I didn't tell you my plan about building a raft. I am still Lal-Alone, and confiding even in a partner is hard for me. I am sorry."

Nyateneri bared his teeth and lifted a threatening hand. "I understand. I should tell you, incidentally, that I cannot swim." I almost ended our charade right there, gaping at him in deepening alarm, but he growled, "Confidence for confidence. On your way, and remember that you have never in your life met anyone as dangerous as our little friend. Go now!"

I stalked back to the horses and began furiously loading them, making a point of throwing Nyateneri's pack to the ground when I hitched his horse to the Mildasi black. Then I mounted and set off, heading upstream, due west, not a backward glance until we were rounding the upper horn of the quarter-moon. Nyateneri looked small and distant already, bending to pick up an armload of the thick, rubbery dead-man's-ringlets. I called, "Be careful!" trusting that evil language to make the warning into a parting curse. Nyateneri never raised his head. I spat again, this time, to rid my mouth of the shame of Dirvic, and rode on along the river shore.

The Fox

Man into fox—fox into man—which?" Boy Tikat asks me that when we meet, only I stop his silly mouth with food, best way then. But truth—truth is not one on top, not the other underneath. Fox and man-shape side by side, never enough room, and below, oh, below! Below is *nothing*, such an old, old nothing, long ago it turns into a *something*. True. Even nothing *wants*, sometimes even nothing grows hungry to hear voices, songs, smell morning earth, drink water, munch up a pigeon. Me? A finger of nothing, a toe—but me even so, doing what I want. Nyateneri wants this, man-shape wants that, I do what I want. But when old nothing calls, I go.

And old nothing is stirring—cold, heavy, sleepy nothing *feels* him, tricky magician at the inn, alone in a little place, gone to earth like a fox—yesyes, and that other, it feels *that* one too, reaching, searching, almost knowing, almost sure. Over the inn, all around, power gropes for power—dogs know it, chickens know it, even weather knows it. Bright, hot sun, not a cloud, day after day, and always the smell of rain, but no rain. Old nothing says in me, "Find out. Find out."

So. Nyateneri is far away, and man-shape sits all rosy in

the taproom again, tells long stupid stories, asks, listens, watches. Inn is swarming like a dead log full of grubs—always pilgrims, peddlers, canal bargemen, soldiers on leave, once or twice a *sheknath* hunter with his razor-silk net, his double lances. Rosseth too sad to talk, Marinesha too busy, never liked man-shape anyway. Gatti Jinni will talk all day, keep the red ale coming, but what does little angry-face know? Same for Shadry, the cook, stupid as the potboys he beats. Boy Tikat keeps all away from man-shape, never even looks across the taproom. Fat innkeeper lumbers in and out and in, fetches and serves, shouts at soldiers when they pinch Marinesha. He looks hard at man-shape every time—nice smile back, every time, why not? No pigeon feathers on *this* smile.

"The girl," says old nothing. "The girl." But she spends most times with wicked magician, only goes back to her room at night. If a soft, so soft fox slips under her arm, nuzzles close, then she whispers, "There you are," and bends her head to me. "Small one, where is Lal, where is Nyateneri, do you know? The *tafiya*—"that is her name for him—"the *tafiya* says they are fools, and will be eaten by rock-*targs* and fall in a river and drown, and not to worry about them. But I do. Tell me where my friends are, small one." Over and over until she falls asleep holding me too hard.

No use to old nothing in that, but what to do about it? Humans talk one way to a bedtime toy, another way to another human. Take the man-shape in her bed? Say, "Hello, only me, we have slept like this nights on nights." Wake Lal and Nyateneri, that scream would, wherever they sleep now. Best to wait until very early morning, first twilight, sometimes she walks a little by herself. Best to wait, I tell old nothing.

But the sky is pulling tight. Every day, one horizon to the other, sky and air creaking as power gropes for power. Wind grinds, aches; water comes apart—you can taste, see it in the least little dog-puddle, hear it in stone floor of the taproom, hear it in voices. At the inn, peddlers struggle to lift packs, sit down and cry. Soldiers drink and nothing happens, pilgrims forget prayer words, fight each other—bargemen, everyone sick, stumble into doorposts, say Shadry poisons them. And all of it the working of him upstairs, all of it. I know. Hide, keep hiding, yes, pull the air tight, tight over him, that other must not find him. Oh, never mind foxes, people, no matter pilgrims even—no matter if everything *tears,* splits down the middle like a water beetle hatching itself into a thunderwing, and what then? What hatchling comes then, do they wonder, those two? Nono, never mind that, never mind. Magicians.

Old nothing: "The girl." So outside with man-shape, out into dusty twilight, museful stroll in the courtyard, contemplate *naril* tree, a turn through the orchard, a turn back. Now she comes—little sharp steps, quick turn to look here, there, every moment afraid of meeting boy Tikat. See her, sad round ordinary face, and behind it the white fire—but not *her* fire, nothing to do with her, poor thing—see her coming just so, so many paces this way, so many that way, an invisible cage, real enough to throw a shadow. Sorry for a human? Not possible, not for me, not. And still.

Forward Grandfather man-shape: dim, gentle smile, peaceful movements, not to frighten in the dusk. Beautiful evening, sweet birds singing (truth: hardly a one, not these nights), how good to find even more loveliness abroad. Such a fortunate old gentleman. Walk with, a little?—perhaps toward the highway and back? Even politeness happily accepted, this age.

No word, no nod, but she takes man-shape's arm and we walk. Prattle, mumble, pat her hand sometimes, first time walking so in twenty years, imagine. But where are her companions? The tall brown woman, elegant as rain? The black one with her long, graceful eyelids like ships' sails? Man-shape will say anything. She is shivering, not in the flesh but all the way down, beyond bones. "In danger." Other words, too, but so low I hear only those.

Old nothing: "What danger?" What danger?—caught between stupid magicians, what else? But no care for that, old nothing needs more. Never says what it needs—feels, feels, hungers, always sure about that, but never the *words*. Very hard on a poor fox, all this living sideways through three worlds. I say, "Indeed, these mountains can be most perilous. There are bandits, there are *nishori*, rock-*targs*—"

Shakes her head—"Not those, none of those. My friends—they have gone to fight a wizard, and there is no fighting him. I know this, I know this!" Trembling in the body now, brown eyes full of tears, but none fall. "He cannot be killed—I know!"

There, old nothing? Is that it, what you want? Man-shape chuckles, much hand-patting, says, "Take heart, my dear, there never was a wizard who could not die. All the stories about bargains with Uncle Death, about elixirs, hearts hidden in golden caskets or hollow trees or the moon—all stories, child, and you may believe me." And a comfort to me, as much as the girl—an immortal magician, the thought of it, the *injustice*. Old nothing would never permit, surely.

But she is not comforted, never even lets me finish, but pulls her arm away, crying, "No, no—I told them, I did tell them, but they would not understand. He cannot be killed!" Staring at me, pale face pleading, wanting so much for nice white mustache to understand. Me? Oh, I look up, down, away toward the highway, away toward the inn. Well-pump squealing, a few drunken drovers singing, no one in sight. But something watches. I know what *I* know.

Her voice, low, quiet, but tearing too, like the sky. "I was dead once. I drowned in a river. Lal found me." Every night, the same whisper into bedtime fox's fur, telling herself the same story again, maybe this time it comes out differently? She says, "Lal promises me and promises me that I am alive now. But all I understand is death." No Uncle Death—always supposed to call him "Uncle

Death," even foxes. Lukassa says, "Everything I knew before the river has been taken from me. In that emptiness, death sits and talks to me and tells me things. Lal and Nyateneri cannot ever defeat Arshadin, cannot ever kill him. He is just like me—there is no one to kill."

"*Ah*," sighs old nothing, a long, long breath across all my lives. "Ah." Very good for old nothing, but man-shape still has to make words. Man-shape pulls mustache, rumples side-whiskers, rounds kindly blue eyes. "Well, child, if your friends have gone off to do battle with a dead wizard, the worst that can happen to them will be a long walk back. Dead is dead, whoever you are, and you may believe me."

But now she is the one looking away, not hearing at all. Turn, quickly, and there he is, stumping along, big pale hands shut tight, big bald head down, dirty apron slipping off his waist—who but fat innkeeper himself? Lukassa's hand slides through man-shape's hand like snow. Not another word, not a glance, straight past innkeeper, proud as princesses she has never seen, walking back to her invisible cage. And in me, of me, old nothing: "*Ah*." All slow and dozy again, got whatever it wanted, time to sleep now—good, let it sleep, sleep, turn, grumble, sleep more, stop playing with fingers and toes. Time to leave poor foxes alone for a while.

Innkeeper looks after Lukassa, rubs his head, slow look at man-shape. Oh, too much not to laugh, too much to ask! Quick-quick, squeeze it into rumbly old chuckle, a greeting to fat fool who tumbles his own house upside down, every room to pieces, every guest out of bed, all for such a few, few pigeons. Always stares at man-shape, never speaks, never serves. Imagine if I tell *him*, "Hello, new foxhound is no good, waste of money. More birds in soon?" Instead a deep bow, one gentleman to another, a smile, a compliment on beautiful evenings always served at his inn. Man-shape will say anything.

Grunt. "None of my doing." Grunt. "You see my stable boy anywhere?" In the stable, surely? Grunt. "Looked there." Rubs head again, yanks off dangling apron. "Bloody boy, never where he's supposed to be these days." Not angry, not quite sad—not quite anything, only tired. Interesting.

"Ah, well," says man-shape, "on a night like this, it would be a shame if your boy isn't out singing foolish songs under some little girl's window. Don't be hard on him when he returns, mine host—leave him the one bit of his childhood, yes?"

Not listening at all—nobody listens to Grandfather man-shape lately—but the last words, ah, those catch him. Scowls heavily, angry enough now. "What do you know about it? What do you know about it, heh? The idiot brat wouldn't have *had* a bloody childhood, if not for me. Worst day's work I ever did in my life, but I did it, what else should I have done, heh? No bloody choice." White, lumpy face redder and redder, even through the dusk, little pale eyes squinting and burning. "What does anybody know of it? And what did I ever get out of it but aggravation and a bellyache and"—stops himself then, hard to do, skids along just a bit further—"and plain bloody inconvenience? Heh?"

My. Even man-shape looks around for answers, not that mine host bothers to wait. Another scowl, another nice grunt, and away back toward the inn, bawling for stable boy. "Rosseth! Rosseth, damn your miserable skin, Rosseth!" How pretty, evening song of one fat innkeeper, leave man-shape to listen. Something tasty rustles beside pathway, hurrying home. Never gets there.

LAL

I never sensed him behind me, not once, but the Mildasi horse did. As long as those shaggy black ears stayed back and those scarlet nostrils kept flaring and rumbling, I kept moving upriver in the dying light.

The trap we were laying was so childishly obvious that we could only count on our pursuer's dismissing it out of hand as a blind to cover our true deadfall. We had expected him to track me some distance, against the off chance that I really might double back to ambush him. But it would seem far more likely—or so we hoped—that I might be trying to lure him away from Nyateneri, and he could never afford the greater risk of his quarry actually escaping on some lashed-together heap of floating debris. He would turn back before I dared and reach Nyateneri well before me. Exactly how well was my responsibility.

When the black's behavior finally told me that we were no longer being trailed, it was past sunset and I had lost sight of the Susathi. I had held to its course as closely as I could, but the further I traveled, the more impassable the bank became for a rider, and I was forced steadily away into brambles and sword-grass, and so into the trees. I could not even smell the river now.

I dismounted, unsaddled and unburdened the horses, and loaded myself with whatever would not slow me. Then I took the beasts' heads between my hands, each in turn, saying certain words, and told them that they were free to follow me back down the river or not, as they chose, and that the Mildasi black would be their leader and bring them safely to kindness and good grazing. *My friend* taught me always to do this when forced to abandon horses. What use it may be to them, I cannot say, but I have always done it, just so.

Hard going it was at first in the wild old tree-dark, on a path that only my three horses had trodden before me. There were mossy roots to stumble over, thorny creepers to snatch at my legs, and a sickly weight in the air that sometimes forced me to stand still for too long, my heart pounding absurdly and my mind unfamiliar. In those moments, nothing would stay in focus, not even Nyateneri's peril, which became infinitely less real than the dimmest of my old dreams. I did not then know what was happening to me, and that frightened me as nothing waiting in the woods or on the river shore could ever have done. Madness is my enemy, not wizards or assassins.

I lost the path twice, and nearly my swordcane as well—a vine twitched it neatly out of my belt, leaving me to scrabble wildly through brush and leaf-mold in the dark—but I did find my way back to the Susathi at last. No moon yet, but better than the moon is the long summer twilight of the north that turns clouds to a pale gold-violet that exists nowhere else, and riverbank reeds to glowing shadows. Compared to the woods, it was brightest noon, and I slung my boots around my neck and settled down to running with great relief.

I am a good runner. There are many faster, but not so many for whom it has been as necessary to learn to become nothing but flight. Even with boots and saddlebags bouncing heavily over my shoulders, I covered the same ground in less time than I had on horseback with two other horses to mind. No other sound but my breath and the river, much louder now in the evening stillness: a blue-black carpet with its nap ruffled the wrong way to show the pink and pale gold beneath. Sometimes I walked over rough ground, and twice waded carefully through shallow streams with soft, hungry beds. But for the most of it I *became* my own running; and had I thought of anything at all, it might have been of another woman on another night path, and of what was behind her then. But running cannot think.

Running cannot think. It was plain chance that I recognized the sharp bend in the shoreline beyond which I had left Nyateneri. I stopped and waited for a few moments, letting myself return a little slowly to myself and listening for any least noise from that quarter-moon of stones and swordgrass. But I heard only the creaky piping of a long-legged *skira* stalking through the reeds. I shrugged my burdens silently to the ground, and I put my boots on and went forward.

No one was there. The late moon was rising, almost full, too full to hide from. I walked down to the water's edge and squatted on my heels to read what I could. Most of the driftwood and all the heaps of dead-man's-ringlets were gone—so Nyateneri had managed to build his mock-raft—and a few scrapes in the pebbly mud indicated that he must actually have launched it, though I saw no darkness of the right size or shape anywhere on the river. But the moonlight did show me two men's jumbled footprints, one set booted, Nyateneri's; the others those of a smaller man, barefoot. The prints skidded across each other, trampled and blurred each others' outlines. I found no dried blood, no sure sign of a leg crippled or a body dragged. There was nothing to tell Lal the Great Tracker how it had been when Nyateneri turned in the twilight to meet the man coming out of the trees.

I stood up slowly, with no idea of where to turn myself—not even which way to look, let alone what to hope for, what to do next. The *skira* kept calling, and the moon grew smaller and colder as I watched, and so did I. My stomach hurt with my fear for Nyateṇeri; and then I grew furious at him for being someone I was frightened for, and for having the bloody nerve to be lost and dead in the night. It did not once occur to me to be angry with his killer until the little river wind shifted and I smelled him.

The two men in the bathhouse had smelled only of sudden death, which wipes out the natural odor instantly and forever. This was a nearly familiar smell, too sharp to be sweet, but not at all acrid; not the scent of a wild hunter, but of wild weather coming. My sword was already clear, though I did not remember having drawn it. I never do. I said, "I see you. I see you there."

The chuckle just behind me was pleasant kin to the smell: warm, sleepy lightning, stirring in its nest. "Do you so?" I was facing him before the last word was out, but I should have been dead by then. In a way I did die, right there, all that time ago, and this is a ghost who has been telling you stories and drinking your wine. You don't understand. Never mind.

He was small, like the other two, smaller than I—a long-faced, crook-necked, thin-built man in loose dark clothing, strolling toward me out of a particular clump of reeds where there had been no one when I scanned it a minute before. I stepped backward, with the sword steady on his heart. "Stand," I said. "Stand. I don't want to kill you yet. Stand."

He kept walking, more slowly now. In the last of the twilight his eyes were so pale as to be almost white, and the teeth in his long wry mouth were the color of the river where it broke over a hidden snag. His hair was very short, hardly more than a shadow on his skull. Holding up his empty hands, he said pleasantly, "Well, of course you don't want to kill me, Lal-after-dark. You don't even want to be under the same moon with me."

Rosseth had told me that the men Nyateneri fought had questioned him in strange voices, both having a cold, questioning lift to every phrase. This one spoke with the flat accent of this mountain country, touched only slightly by the sideways glide of the south—more than a bit like Nyateneri's voice, in fact. He said now, "For myself, I've no quarrel at all with you. My work is completed. Let me pass."

My stomach stopped hurting, strangely or not, and both fear and anger went from me. I answered him, "Not until you say what you have done with my companion, and likely not then. *Stand.*"

He smiled. I backed and backed again, making certain that I stayed on open ground and requesting of gods whose names I had nearly forgotten that I not stumble. He walked patiently after me, barely beyond the sword's point, thin hands swinging loose at the ends of his thin arms. "He's dead as dinner," he said, "and well you know it. Unless you suppose that he fled me one more time, and what indeed would I be doing here in that case? Down sword, colleague, and let me by."

"Thank you, not I," I said, and went on retreating. "Where is the body, then? We buried your two consorts, but that's not your way, is it? What have you done with Nyateneri's body?"

He did stand still for that moment, and had I chosen, I almost think I might have had him, though perhaps not. Perhaps not. He waited, eyes moon-white in the moon; not the first man who ever savored his power over me. He said lightly, "Why, I bundled it aboard that poor pile of sticks, and set all adrift and alight. And a fitting end, surely, for such a one, wouldn't you say? As much of a Goro as he was."

The Goro are a brave and cunning people, once cousins to my folk, who live on a double handful of islands in the low Q'nrak Seas. They raid their neighbors and one another; they sail everywhere in the world, fearing nothing in it; and when one of them dies, the body—or what is left of it, following certain rituals—is placed on a richly draped barge and sent out with the tide, after being set afire. I said, speaking very carefully, "I think there is no raft out there on the river. I know there is no funeral pyre."

Oh, how he clapped his hands at that! And, oh, how he laughed, like carrion birds mating, bent almost double with his hands on his thighs and went on laughing himself to soundless wheezing because I could not strike, did not dare to chance his lie. In time he managed a cackling whisper: "Ah, you don't know our way nearly so thoroughly, after all. Watch a bit with me, I beg you, watch but a little, little more—" he was dissolving into merriment again"—and see what it is to be on good terms with fire."

I did strike then, a thrust you would not have seen. That is a fact, nothing more. Wrist and forearm only, no lunge, no wasted motion—which means no thought—then clear and away while Uncle Death is yet groping for his bedside slippers. But the small man with the moon-white eyes was not there. He was almost there, mind you—the point scored his tunic—but not quite, and not quite laughing anymore, either, but making a sort of purring, private sound. "Oh, well done. They spoke truly of Swordcane Lal. This will be an honor for me."

Listen now. In the moment it took him to speak those few words, I had struck at him three more times. I tell you this not out of vanity, but to make you see what *he* was. Not even Nyateneri knows that I not only missed with each blow, but missed badly, never even grazing him again. The best I can say for myself is that his counterstroke—which I never saw—came when I was extended and off-balance, and I was still able to leap aside and slip his second stroke as I landed. Then I backed out of range as fast as I could, while he followed, purring. "This *is* nice, this is very nice. Your friend now, he turned out a bit of a disappointment. I hope it doesn't offend you, my saying that?"

I answered with a shoulder feint and pass that had nearly cost me my life to learn, and did cost me four years to learn right. He seemed hardly to notice it, but drifted after me, all amiable amusement. "To be fair, he didn't see me soon enough. It might have taken longer if he had. Still, I must say that I'd expected something rather more from a man who eluded us for almost eleven years. The record will never be equaled, I am sure of it. Ah, you see it now, the fire."

I did what he wanted. I looked past him, over his shoulder, only for an instant, one instinct already wrenching my head back as the other turned it toward the river. I saw no floating fire, not until he hit me. The left side it was, and why it cracked no more than one rib I do not know. There was no pain, not then; there was no feeling at all in half my chest. Somehow I kept hold of my sword-cane, even while I was tumbling clear across the quarter-moon shore to bring up hard against a fallen log. He was on me before my vision had fully returned, but I kicked out and stabbed and rolled all at once, and that time he did not touch me. In the reeds, the *skira* gave the bubbling little murmur which means that it has taken prey.

I came up spitting and sneering, because that is what you do, even when there isn't enough air in your body to make the contempt entirely convincing. "That was your death-blow? That was *it*?" But another such would have killed me, and he knew. He did not laugh, but that purring sound deepened and took on new colors, and he came lazily on, saying, "Oh, you really are so good, you are unbelievable." The words and the voice were those of a lover, and I think that was the worst thing of all.

For a time, little or long, I did nothing but fight to get my lungs working again, and to keep him a sword's length away from me. My side was beginning to hurt very badly, which did not trouble me in itself—I have been taught to set pain aside, to be dealt with later, as some put off doing the household accounts—but I knew that it must slow me down, and I knew certainly now that nothing but speed could save me. I spun, sprang, twisted and flipped in midair, somersaulted away when he tried to pin me against a tree or a boulder; cracked him with a knee, an elbow—once even the top of my head—when I missed with the swordcane, which was always. Nyateneri's dagger at least marked his two accomplices here and there, before Rosseth's wit blinded them; all I could have claimed as my proper signature would be a bruise or two in fairly pointless places. But I stayed alive.

The long dusk was fading at last—perhaps to my natural advantage, perhaps not, since the moonlight flattened out the sheltering shadows. He halted abruptly, deliberately allowing me an instant to stand still myself and breathe, and understand how badly I was injured. He said, "Swordcane Lal, you make me regret that I will never have children and grandchildren to tell of you. I can only promise that the eternal annals of my strange home, where nothing is forgotten, will forever be telling more great ones than you know how valiantly you died." He sighed elaborately, blinked away a single real tear, and added, "That lovely weapon of yours will never be soiled—I'll snatch it from the air before you hit the ground. You have my word on that."

It pleases me to remember that I was at him before he had finished speaking. Back down the shore we went, and this time he was the one doing the dancing, having to leap this way and that, to duck and roll and spring away out of corner after corner. No, I touched him no more than I had; but for all that, I heard his breath mewing thinly in his chest this time, and in those white eyes at last I saw the same distant curiosity that he must have seen in mine. *Is it you, really? Is it to be you?* I do like to remember that.

But by then it was over. Not because of the rib—I have been worse hurt, far worse, and fought better—nor because I was past my best, although I had known that for some while. Younger, I would have struck four times, not three, when he was praising me, and missed as surely then as now. *My friend* was right: a master knows his master very quickly indeed, and this one would have been my master on the finest day I ever knew. I still had to kill him.

"The raft is burning," he purred, over and over. "The raft is burning, you can see the flames in the water." But I never took my eyes from his again—what use to Nyateneri in that?—and the result, inevitably, was that a piece of driftwood turned under my heel and I fell. I was up on the instant, scrambling away in the direction he least expected, but he caught me with both bare feet, high on the right thigh and again on the right shoulder. I went down.

Sometimes, in the sea, when a great wave smashes over you, you can find yourself swimming *down,* into the cold blackness, too dazed to realize that life is the other way. It was so now with me. When I clawed myself up to one knee, he was standing calmly, arms folded, marveling at me all over again. "And even so, even fallen witless, yet you brandish that swordcane high and clear. Your heart may touch the common earth, but not that blade. Truly it must have a mighty meaning for you, O Lal of the legends."

At the time I took it for a cruel taunt; today I know that he meant to be complimentary. What mattered was that one word, *legend,* recalling me to a breeding and a heritage beside which all this nonsense with swords became less than children's stick-battles. I said, "The same meaning it has had for many before me. It was forged in my country five hundred and ninety years ago for the poet ak'Shaban-dariyal. I am his descendant."

Eternal annals, was it? Nyateneri had once implied that these folk were, in their way, as much in bondage to memory as my own, who would interrupt a wedding, abandon a harvest, or simply forget to die in order to hear another tale about something that once happened to somebody when. My man, at least, with every opportunity to finish me off, had dallied on the casual chance that there might be a story to my swordcane. I could barely stand erect to face him, and my body was ice on the right side and howling mush on the left, but there would certainly be a story.

"Father to son, son to daughter, and so on," he said, politely enough. "The same everywhere. A pity such an inheritance must end here." I did not dare so much as a step back now, but bent all my remaining strength to keeping his eyes on my eyes, hoping always to read the next few seconds there and praying that he could not do the same. Then I took a long breath and handed my swordcane to him.

"Actually, the custom is a bit different in my family," I said. "The sword is not handed on, generation to generation—it must be stolen. Look at the blade."

He lifted it between us, squinting in the moonlight at the engraved words few had ever had the time even to notice. His hands, as well as his eyes, seemed occupied then, but I knew enough to let the opportunity pass. "*Steal me, marry me,*" he read aloud. "A curious warning. If it *is* a warning."

I laughed, although it hurt my chest. "You could say so. That swordcane has been a thieves' magnet since the day it was made. Why, the smith himself tried to steal it back from my ancestor within a week of presenting it to him, and from then on the poor poet never slept a night through for the constant racket of burglars falling off his roof, digging under his house, fighting and yowling when they bumped into each other in his closet. Old and young, man, woman, and little scoundrelly children, they came from every corner of the country to try their slyness at relieving him of that same sword you hold now. Even his closest friends were not to be trusted—let alone his gentle, doddering old parents. It all became quite wearying. Soon enough, my ancestor was ready to hand the swordcane personally to the very next housebreaker he found hiding in his pantry, or the next bandit who tried to lure him down an alley behind the marketplace. I assure you, it's the truth."

"Ah, but naturally he didn't give it away, or where

would we be?" Still not looking at me, he took a step or two back, in order to make the moonlight shudder along the thin blade as he tilted it up and down. "And how did the good man resolve his difficulty?"

"As it happens, my ancestor was not a good man at all," I said, "but he was a clever one. After much consideration, he had those words you see etched on the swordcane, and when a particularly bold and cunning young thief actually did manage to lift it from him—in broadest daylight, if you will—he ran the man to earth himself and offered him a daring proposition. He might keep the swordcane and welcome, if he would marry my ancestor's eldest daughter and become a part of his family. The thief agreed on the spot—as did the daughter, for he was apparently a pleasing youth. And so began our most ancient tradition."

Up, down, tip it toward the moon, tip it into darkness. "A fascinating tale." And he *was* fascinated, though careful not to show it; so much so that he paid no heed when I let myself move at last, the slightest shuffle, more to the side than backward. "Even if the thief's only other choice was death. Meaning no disrespect to your ancestor's daughter."

"Ah, but that wasn't the case at all." And with that I had him. He forgot to play with the swordcane and stared at me; and for the first time he looked like a human being, round-eyed (though he narrowed them quickly) with blessed human puzzlement and my dear, dear, precious, beloved human hunger to know what happened next. Hurt, exhausted, and frightened for my life as I was, that look is, at the very last, my home.

I said, "The young man could have gone free and unharmed, nevermore to see the beautiful sword. He was happy to obey the graven command, *steal me, marry me,* and he turned out to be a faithful husband to both his wives. And since he knew so much better than my ancestor all the ways of thieves, not one ever again came within sight of the swordcane, no one but those whose last sight it was. The only difficulty was that he never could bring himself to leave his treasure to any of his own descendants, even on his deathbed. Myself, I think that he would have ordered it to be buried with him, if a quick-fingered serving wench hadn't made away with it at the very last—which meant, of course, that his eldest son had to track her down and marry her in his turn in order to keep both the sword and such skill in the family. And so it has gone ever since, except for Grandmother. Always excepting Grandmother."

Even then I could not be sure that he had taken the right bait, for all that he kept blinking from the swordcane to me and back again. "Keep the blood moving, that's the way," he purred, almost to himself. "Much as we do, imagine." But he had to know, you see, and what's a foot more or less of distance between one person and another when you have to know how a story comes out? "Your grandmother," he said slowly; and *I* said, entirely to myself, *You are mine.*

"Ah, Grandmother," I sighed. "The most magical figure of my childhood." So she was indeed, bless her wicked, utterly shameless heart. "Grandmother was Great-Grandfather's daughter, so therefore she was not eligible to steal the swordcane and marry to keep it. This struck her as a great injustice, and my grandmother never could abide injustice. She was small, like me, and easily ignored then, but from the age of twelve or thereabouts, she did little else but stand watch over the weapon and learn its use—that, at least, was permitted her. She studied every morning, before he had started drinking, with the old Kirianese master L'kl'yara "—I saw my listener's eyes go even wider than they already were"—until she knew everything he knew and could invent her own variations on his guards and counters, his legendary traps and responses, for hours on end. She became very nearly unbeatable, my quiet little grandmother who sang nursery songs to me every night, even when I was really too old for them. And when she understood that she was unbeatable—then one day, after her regular practice, she simply took the swordcane and vanished."

"Vanished?" I was half-singing myself now, as completely fallen into the manner of storytelling that I was taught almost with my name as he was into the tale itself. But I have learned other things since my name, and I knew that I must slow everything down, *everything*—not merely my movement away from him, but my breathing as well, my pain and my banging blood, and even my thoughts—slow all down to the rhythm of the cold, quiet moon. Off to the right, under a scrubby bush, a shapeless blue shadow that must be his pack.

"Actually, she went to her room," I said. "It was much the same thing, however, since for three whole years she only emerged to push out the body of the swordcane's latest midnight claimant and pop back inside. No one saw her but her victims and the servants who brought her food—oh, her mother and father came almost every day to plead with her to behave sensibly, give the swordcane back, and marry whomever should steal it from them properly after that. But all their beseechments were in vain. Grandmother wrote them affectionate notes, asked after the health of her brothers, apologized for the condition of the last thief, and went on standing off all sieges. In the third year, I think it was, Great-grandfather, utterly exasperated, sent soldiers to break down her door. When she was finished with them, she never replaced the door, but deliberately left the room wide open from then on. Not a soul ever dared so much as a peep across the threshold—not until my one-eyed grandfather came prowling along. But that is another story altogether."

Is that his pack, then? It *must* be, but what could it contain, what can these people travel with? Nyateneri had said that he would have come prepared for water, but what sort of boat but a toy would fit into a bundle that small? Fool, don't look at it, for your life—keep those white, entranced eyes on yours, hold him, *hold him*—pick your spot now, half a step, *so*, let your right leg shiver and buckle just a bit, as it's crying to do—I wonder if there's a rib gone on that side, too, don't let there be—and under all that a very different trembling, deeper than any of it. *I can still do this, what I was made to do, it has not left me. I can still tell a story.*

"And that was the woman who taught you to fight as you do?" His voice startled me strangely: in planning so totally to kill him I had almost forgotten about him himself, if you understand. He still wanted to know the ending before he killed me.

"No," I said, "no, not exactly," and let the leg go all the way this time, stumbling aside and down with a whimper that was quite real, breaking the fall with my left hand while my right was in and out of my boot in the same motion, and I was the one to catch the sword-cane, after all, before either it or he had fallen. The tiny dagger had sunk so deep into his throat that only the hilt was visible, jerking and bobbing with his breath as he stared at me. I got up slowly and walked over to him.

"My grandmother never touched so much as a carving knife in her life," I said. "I bought that thing off a peddler's cart in Fors na'Shachim, and I've no more notion than you of what that inscription means. And the person who taught me the sword was a vicious, drunken old soldier who would tell me before each lesson what his payment would be this time, and let me think about it as we fought. The dagger is his."

That much I am certain he understood, but the white eyes were fading when I added, "I apologize for cheating you. You were too good for me to defeat honestly. Sunlight on your road." We say that also at parting. I do not know if he heard.

NYATENERI

At first I did not understand that I was moving. That may sound strange, but I was feeling very strange and sick, and the only thing that registered during those first few moments was that I was blind in one eye. There was a red darkness to my left side different from the cool, moony river dark around me on the right. Between that and the throbbing bewilderment in my head, it was some little while before I realized that I was not after all lying motionless while sky and river flowed courteously, distantly over me. My right foot was actually trailing in water, and the vague discomfort in my back turned out to be a knobbly bit of driftwood that floated away when I sat up. I was impossibly aboard the trash raft I had never intended to launch, and it was gently dissolving beneath me, and I was half-blind and could not swim. And if I did not scream my lungs out for Lal, the only reason is that I was even more dazed just then than I was frightened. That state of things changed quite rapidly.

I did not dare to stand, but spent what seemed like the next two weeks wriggling up to a kneeling position. The last thing I remembered had been knotting strands of water-weed to make my driftwood look—at least in a bad light—as though it might possibly hold together if anyone were fool enough to launch it. That had been well over an hour ago, to judge by the moon, and most of the raft was, remarkably, still with me, but fraying. I could feel logs shifting and slipping as the dead branches I had jammed between them to make them fit tightly worked free one by one. Dead-man's-ringlets are supple and easy to splice into cables, but they have one serious failing. They stretch. I gave the good ship *Soukvan's Coffin* a conservative ten minutes, and myself an optimistic five.

What I hated, even more than the thought of drowning, was the idea of dying without ever knowing what had happened to me. Plainly I had been the one ambushed, taken offguard as easily as Rosseth or Tikat would have been, not so much as glimpsing my attacker. For all the pains and numbnesses in my head and body, I could not recall being struck one time. My left eye was one of the few parts of me that did not hurt, no more than it did anything else. It might as well not have been there.

I stayed on my knees, afraid that the slightest movement might hasten the raft's unraveling. The dreaming river of the afternoon now seemed to lunge under me more hugely with every minute, hurtling me between black banks, faster and faster, on my way to a humiliatingly helpless death, a death not to my liking. Another branch slid free of the dead-man's-ringlets, and a log I was gripping turned over in my hand. Idiotically, I imagined the Man Who Laughs settling down comfortably to discuss with me the exact moment when the fact of a raft must cease to exist and become only the fact of a passing agreement of sticks. It was just the kind of thing he would have debated all day, jumping to my side from time to time when he got bored with his own arguments and impatient with mine. The fact of water began to dance up through the gap where the branch had been, splashing over my legs.

My left eye seemed to be beginning to distinguish between shapes and shadows, but I could not tell how far

I was from either bank, as though it would have made the least difference. Still kneeling, I groped as far as I could reach in every direction, hoping idiotically to find a broken board, something to paddle with, some way of angling the raft toward a shore I could not see. One hand came up against something that felt like a little gilt-paper tube, like the paper whistles they blow in the west country to celebrate Thieves' Day. It took me the longest instant of my life to understand what it was, but then I understood, and I dropped my arm back until my knuckles rasped on bark, and I threw the tiny thing as far away from me as I could. Still in the air, it melted soundlessly into fire, turning a quarter of the sky to dawn, a white dawn raked bloody from one horizon to another. In that terrible light, in that impossible silence, I saw the tumbling river and the trees on its banks, and the birds asleep on their branches, all blanched and dry of color. I saw night insects burning all around me, thousands of them, flaring up and gone, one filigreed second apiece. And I saw Lal.

Only for that moment; then the little device that a wheezing man at the monastery used to make by the dozen, as needed, fell into the water and went out. The darkness returned and Lal was lost to my one eye, like the sleeping birds. But I could see her still, as I do now, flying down the river after me, sitting crosslegged in the stern of a boat smaller than my raft, a tapered chip of wood with a sail and a rudder, and looking for all the world as though she were clucking calmly to it, shaking the lines a bit to urge it along like a fat old horse. When she saw me, she waved to me.

I would have waved back, but by that time I was using both hands, and my feet as well, in a hopeless, ridiculous attempt to hold what was left of the raft together. It was all drifting to pieces swiftly now, having held together so much longer than it was ever meant to do: all my debris sliding loosely through the water-weeds' slackening grip. I heard Lal calling to me to abandon the raft and cling to any log until she reached me. Easy for *her*, born on the water—I would have been calmer in a burning tower, and jumped from it far more lightheartedly than I gave up on the idea of that raft. Absurdly, perhaps, I dallied to find my bow, but while I fumbled in the darkness, the last few remaining logs skidded away beneath my feet and I went straight down, tearing at the river, biting and kicking it, dancing in it as I sank like a hanged man in air. A humorous picture, I do agree with you. Smile again and I will push your face as deep into your soup bowl as will improve your understanding of what I felt then. I promise to hold you under no longer than I was.

Lal says that I was indeed draped over a log when she fished me out, holding on so tightly that I went round and round with the log as it spun and rolled over in the water. I know nothing of this. I came to myself a second time sprawled face down across the deck of Lal's toy boat, coughing and puking, while she went on hauling on the lines, at the same time drumming briskly on my back with both feet to make me vomit some more. That much I remember. Lal's feet are small but memorable, especially the heels.

When I could speak, I said, "This is *his* boat." It didn't deserve an answer, and it didn't get one. I sat up very slowly, dizzy and shivering, wiping my mouth. Even by moonlight, with only one eye working properly, I saw the way she was sitting, the way she held her body, the cold pallor under the black skin. I asked, "How badly are you hurt?"

"Rib," she said softly, indicating her left side. "Maybe two." I could hardly hear her above the noise of the river. The coolly invulnerable Sailor Lal had vanished completely—now that I was safely aboard, she was at last permitting herself her own pain. Her wide eyes had stopped seeing me; in another moment she would surely collapse where she sat, leaving this unlikely craft to the equally dubious charge of Captain Soukyan, who had just recently gone down with his own ship. I took gentle hold of her shoulders and leaned close, asking, "How do you stop this thing? Make it go to land, I mean."

I had to repeat the question several times before she shook her head violently, as though to clear it, and put my left hand hard on the tiller. "Push," she whispered; then pressed the lines controlling the little sail into my right hand, managed to mouth the word "Pull," and sagged into me, so completely unconscious that her dead weight almost took us both into the water. I caught hold of the mast to hold us back.

Even in the river darkness, her lips were blue. Her heartbeat was too quick, her breathing too slow and torn; though I rejoiced, as much as I had time for it, to hear no sound suggesting a punctured lung. I braced her against the base of the mast as well as I could, while the damnable boat chased its tail and the thing whose name I always forget—the boom it is, and well-named—kept swinging across, trying to kill me, because I could not attend to Lal and do all that pushing and pulling as well. I hate boats. I know somewhat more about them today than I did that night, and I hate them exactly that much more.

Once I was able to sit down to sailing, however, it became plain that Lal had given me the shortest possible course of lessons in making one of the things go where you want it to go. You shove the tiller over one way—hard left, in my case, so that the boat veered toward the right bank of the river—and then you pull the lines in the other direction, which *should* make the sail fill and the boat move properly forward. Of course, if you do not have a strong wind behind you, and don't know how to make the best of what wind you have—both being true for me—then the sail flaps and sulks, while the boom thing comes around and breaks your head. Nevertheless, I pushed and jiggled and coaxed and cursed and ducked, and the boat wandered diffidently toward the bank, eventually stopping when it wedged its pointed prow into a tangle of overhanging tree roots. I tied it there and carried Lal ashore.

She never stirred as I undressed her to learn the extent of her injuries. I could feel the broken rib immediately—only one, thank the gods—but she appeared to be hurt nowhere else. I knew better, of course, but the strange and terrifying thing was that there were almost no marks on her body; nor on mine, for that matter. All her right side was hot to my hand, and when I touched her she twitched away and moaned, but did not wake.

Our provisions were not on the boat. I am fairly adept with herbs and simples, but not at night in a strange country. There was a spare sail tucked away in a compartment under the prow. I cut part of it into strips and set and bandaged her rib as well as I could. Then I forced some water between her lips, took off my own soaked clothes, and lay down beside her, drawing the remainder of the sail over us both. I held her all night to keep her warm, and myself as well. I had not expected to sleep, but I did, and deeply, nor did I dream at all.

Lal had hardly moved when I woke. Her breathing seemed more regular, but her skin was still too cold, and the blue tinge had spread to her face and throat as well. The vision in my left eye was only a little hazed now: one of the blows I never saw must have numbed a nerve. I still ached in many other places, but that would pass. I stood up in the thin, red mountain dawn and took in our situation. In front of me, the Susathi—not white-toothed yet, but not the placid creature of yesterday, either—in all other directions, nothing but stones and pale stubble and a scattering of the joker-trees. Unpromising, certainly, but nothing with a river in it is ever hopeless. I covered Lal with the sail again and limped naked down to the water to see about breakfast.

Fish in these mountain rivers generally stay well away from the shores, because of prowling *sheknath*. The way to call them in is to snap your fingers underwater—if you do it right, using the second joint, *not* the first, for some reason the vibration is irresistible—and then to tickle their bellies very slowly, until they practically fall asleep in your hand. My sister taught me that trick.

Coaxing up two fish of a proper size took time—time well-spent, as it turned out—but Lal was still asleep when I returned to her. Having lost my own knife, I used her swordcane to clean the fish and cooked them on sticks over a scanty driftwood fire as fragile and transparent as a baby bird. The good smell did not waken Lal for some while, but as I was beginning to grow truly alarmed, she opened her eyes and muttered, "Lost the yellow pepper. Sorry." She was in too much pain even to sit up, let alone move to the fire. I fed her the little she would take, waking her when she dozed off, and gave her more water afterward. When she was asleep again, I banked the fire, borrowed her swordcane once more and went back to the riverbank. There, a few feet from where the boat was tied up, I had noticed several rocks blotched with smeary patches of a gray lichen that made them look as though they were rotting from the inside. This is called *fasska* in the north—*crin,* I think, in the eastern hills—and it grows only in high countries, and never plentifully. When I had scraped off what there was, I could have closed it all easily in one fist, except that you must not ever crush *fasska* so, else you destroy its virtue. If it smells at all bearable, you've already ruined it.

I carried it back to my fire very carefully, wrapped it in my shirt—which was beginning to dry, the sun having finally escaped the mountain peaks—and set about finding something in which to heat water. Our cooking gear was with our packs, wherever *they* were; in the end I was lucky to find a broken *tharakki* egg, almost a good half, the size of my cupped hands. I rigged an absurd arrangement of sticks to hold it properly over the fire, then filled it partway with water, which I prayed would boil at this height. Lal woke a couple of times and stared silently at me out of eyes that were too large and shone too dryly.

I talked to her while I worked, whether her eyes were open or closed. "Did *he* ever feed you this disgusting swill? It tastes like the dirt under your nails, but it's useful when the spirit has taken the same beating as the body and they have to heal together or not at all. He made it for me the same day I came to him, and it's a wonder I didn't run off as soon as I could stand. One other time, too—you've seen that scar that runs halfway around my back? A rock-*targ* bit me half in two, and had a good start on the second half when I managed to shove an arrow into it. But by then I had screamed and prayed and wet myself and fouled myself with such fear that sewing me up was meaningless by itself. If he hadn't poured enough *fasska* down my throat to wash away Corcorua market, I might still be staring at his ceiling. It's that good, this muck, if you can only keep it down."

Lal said nothing. My eggshell of water did finally come to a boil, and I dumped the lichen scrapings into it and covered them with a broad leaf to hold in the heat. You have to steep *fasska* forever, or at least until you truly cannot endure the smell an instant more. The best thing then is to add two dried *kirrichan* leaves while it cools; somehow they tend to make the drink, which always remains silver-gray as a slug trail, a bit more palatable—but we were as short of those as of everything else but fish. Lal would have to take her healing raw, no help for it.

Strangely, frighteningly, she put up absolutely no resistance when I made her sit up and began tipping the stuff into her mouth. I expected her to spit it back out—to the side, if my luck held. I expected snarls, curses, kicks in the shins with those horn-hard feet. What I got was a Lal who swallowed the *fasska* obediently, with no more protest than an occasional cough; beyond the slightest flinching of her lips, she might have been drinking ice-vine tea or red ale. When it was gone, she closed her eyes again and lay back silently, and did not stir for the rest of the day.

I bathed and cleaned her as was necessary, washed myself in the river, slept a little, fished again, and spent most of the time in studying our one remaining possession. I had never seen such a boat before; indeed, it seemed more kite than boat to me. It cannot have been longer than twelve feet, and in its broadest section hardly as wide as I am tall; and finally it was nothing more than round and flat sticks fitted so tightly together that you could scarcely see the grooves between. Some of the sticks—the mast, for example—were actually a sort of hollow reed, and many must have telescoped to allow them to fit in a traveler's pack. The wood itself was far lighter than any wood I knew; the sails were like silk, but not silk. Two people could have lifted the entire affair out of the water, but it was plainly made to carry one deadly passenger alone. I could not imagine how Lal had assembled it unaided, nor how we should manage the rest of our journey downriver—and just how far was that to be?—on a miniature that marvelously delicate. The sun slipped back down behind the mountains while I brooded on this, and the small breeze sharpened. Night comes early in the high country.

I have said that Lal did not move all day, unless I moved her, neither before drinking the *fasska* nor after. When I lay down by her that second night, she was unchanged: heart steady, breath even enough, but her body distinctly colder than before. The firm pulse lied—she was slowing, she herself, in a way that I could do absolutely nothing about, if the drink could not. Her skin felt terribly dry, like the husk of an insect, and there was a sweet, faraway fragrance to it that alarmed me even more than the coldness. Someone's childhood may perhaps smell like that, in memory, or someone's dreams of an afterlife. Lal-Alone, Sailor Lal, does not.

But in the night, sometime after midnight, she began to turn fitfully, waking me, and to mutter words in the language of her long private songs. Her voice grew louder, sounding frightened at first and then increasingly angry, and she struggled in my arms with her eyes staring. I held her as strongly and as carefully as I could, fearful that she would do one of us an injury if I let her go. For all that, she scratched my face more than once and bit her mouth bloody, crying out to someone whose name I did not know. That was nothing at all; what made it difficult to hold on was that the strange new scent of her body had become as unbearably sweet as the *fasska*'s smell was vile.

Then the sweat came. Between one moment and the next, the cold dry fever had broken, and she was running with ordinary human sweat, soaking, sluicing with it, gasping and crying like a newborn, her head thrown back as though she were bathing under a waterfall. The drink had done its work—her smell was her own again, spicy and tart, almost bitter, her own, and there was Lal, slipping through my damp grip to sit up and announce shakily, "My swordcane smells of fish guts."

I had set it beside her, like a familiar toy, in case she woke. Now I gaped at her as she sniffed the thing a second time, made a face, and tried the blade against her thumb. Instantly she rounded on me—naked, shivering, barely able to hold herself erect—demanding fiercely, "What have you been *doing* with it? You've bloody ruined it, do you know that? Damn you, Soukyan, you've ruined my sword!"

I took it out of her hand—already feeling her strength returning as she resisted me—and wrapped the entire sail around her to keep her from a chill. She struggled and swore, but I made her lie back down and sat by her, saying, "I needed an edge. Your sword was all we had."

"Edge? Edge? Do you know how long it took me to *put* that edge on that blade? I'll never be able to get it decently sharp again! What possessed you, what were you using it for, chopping stove logs?" Weak as she yet was—once she was down, she could barely lift her head to rail at me, and from time to time her voice cracked into inaudibility—she was also angrier than I had ever seen her. "Marinesha would have known better—*Shadry* would have known better!"

"Shadry and Marinesha didn't have to feed you and

physic you," I said. "I did, and I used what there was. If you hadn't left our packs behind—"

"*I* had to kill a man, build a boat, and save your stupid, pointless life! That stupid raft was about to catch fire, sink, I didn't know when—I didn't know if you were alive or dead, I wasn't going to waste time hauling those bloody packs to the boat! He kept saying, *'It's burning, it's burning.'* " Her voice did not break then, nor were there tears in her eyes, but I felt as strange and uncertain as I had when she called me by my true name. She was so angry at me, and she looked eleven years old.

I told her what had happened since she pulled me out of the river. She listened very quietly, never taking her eyes from my face. The sweat had stopped running—even her hair was drenched and her small ears dripping—and I realized for the first time how much weight she had lost in only two days. When I finished, she looked at me for a moment longer, then shook her head and blew her breath out softly. "Well," she said. "Well. Thank you."

"You remember nothing of this?" I asked. "Not even the *fasska*? I can't imagine that anyone could ever forget having drunk *fasska*."

"I remember nothing," Lal said flatly. "I don't like that." She was silent again for a time before she smiled, and now she looked easily fifteen. She said, "But whatever you gave me, it was the right thing. I don't know whether it saved my life, but it brought me back from"—she faltered briefly"—I think from a place where a gardener's rhyme would not have reached me. Thank you, Soukyan."

"Thank you, Lalkhamsin-khamsolal," I said. "Sleep now."

I dried her face and body with my shirt, and she was asleep before I finished, or seemed so. But as I lay down once more, settling my arm over her waist just as though we were veteran bedfellows, comfortable old campaigners, she mumbled drowsily, "Tomorrow we will be off downriver."

"No, we certainly will not," I said into her ear. "You wouldn't get as far as the boat." My answer was a snore as delicate as lace. I lay awake for a little, listening to the water and watching stars disappear behind Lal's shoulder.

We had words before we had breakfast. She was entirely serious about taking up our journey immediately, and I nearly had to wrestle her down to persuade her even to listen to any contrary proposal. Which would have been difficult, incidentally: I have never known anyone, man or woman, with Lal's recuperative powers. One rib cracked, the muscles beneath another badly bruised; left arm all but useless, right thigh too tender to touch, the rest of her body clearly shrieking in sympathy—all that, and she was on her feet before I was, inspecting the boat and trying to resharpen her swordcane against different sorts of rocks. We had words about that, too.

Eventually we came to a compromise, aided perhaps by a brief dizzy spell on Lal's part. We would be on our way on the following morning, come wind, come weather, and in addition she would continue to wear the sail-bandage around her battered ribs. For myself, I swore to treat her with no more consideration than I had since we left Corcorua, and never, *never*, to ask how she was feeling. On that understanding, we fished, dozed and talked through the day, discussing with some chagrin that third assassin who had so humiliated us both, and making what plans we could for our utterly futile assault on Arshadin's home.

I want to make that very clear to you. Between us, Lal and I have a good deal more experience than most of strange combats in stranger places. But neither of us had ever had the least illusion that we were about to overcome a wizard powerful enough to make a desperate fugitive of our master. As I had told Rosseth, we were a diversion at very best, nothing more, and we could only hope that my Man Who Laughs would be able to make good use of whatever breath we might buy him. Assuming, of course, that Arshadin ever bothered to notice that he was under attack. Part of our experience has to do with knowing when you have attracted the attention of such things as wizards, and I had no sense at all that we were being observed as we bathed in the river, dried ourselves in the afternoon sun, and spoke of the days to come. Which shows you exactly what experience is worth.

"I have never pretended to be a sailor," I said, "but I will never trust any boat that fits in somebody's pack. Even I know that's wrong."

"It's beautiful," Lal said. "An absolutely beautiful design. I wish you knew more about boats, or about your old religious colleagues, either would do. I became so fascinated, trying to learn how it went together, I almost forgot that I was hurt and you were in danger. Anyway, I promise you that it won't sink under us. I really don't think it can. Amazing."

She was as delighted with that wretched boat as though we had already completed our mission and destroyed Arshadin. I felt at once guilty at having to remind her of reality and angry at her for making me feel guilty. I said, "It had better be amazing. It had better be able to shoot a bow, climb a wall, fight off rock-*targs*, *nishori*, and magicians, sew clothes, forage for game, and practice medicine. Because all our stores and all our weapons are back there up the river, with a dead man to guard them. All we can hope for, as far as I can see, is that Arshadin may laugh so hard at us that he hurts himself. I am told it happens."

I expected Lal to flare out at me again when I spoke so, but she remained placid for once, even seeming a bit amused. "All we need do is annoy him," she answered, "and if you and I cannot make ourselves thoroughly disagreeable with nothing but our fingernails, then we should retire and help old Karsh to run The Gaff and Slasher. Now help me take this sail down, I want to try a different rigging." As we worked, she began singing to herself in her usual tuneless, monotonous manner. I was almost glad to hear her.

That night, when I thought she was asleep, she turned

suddenly and pressed herself against me, holding me as hard as one working arm would allow. Even at the inn, that one evening, she had not embraced me in that way. I stroked her hair awkwardly, and tucked the sail closer around her shoulders. I said, "What is it? Are you feeling ill?" Then I remembered that I had promised not to ask that question, and I said, "I never meant to alarm you about our chances. We will deal with Arshadin as we deal with him." But *that* sounded as foolish and condescending as it was, and I did not finish saying it. Lal made no answer, but held onto me a moment longer, and then rolled away from me in one abrupt, violent movement and was instantly asleep. I could feel her arm around my back for a long time afterward.

At least we had no trouble loading our pocket boat in the morning. There was nothing on deck but the pair of us, one dulled swordcane, and as much fish as Lal had managed to smoke in the last two days. Now she ran up the sail while I pushed the boat away from the bank and scrambled hastily aboard, clinging to the mast and her undamaged ankle. Waist-deep is as far as I go voluntarily.

As you might imagine, I never became comfortable on that tiny, slippery deck, not in the three days that it was all my existence. I dreaded standing up, clung frantically to the mast when I did, and most often moved from one place to another by sliding along on my rump, like a baby. When we tied up and camped on shore, my dreams were an unending procession of nightmares about drowning. The smoked fish was not only dry and tasteless, but gave me gas, so that when I was not merely terrified I was embarrassed, angry, and constantly hungry. Being useless baggage was a new experience for me, very nearly as bewildering and maddening as being on a boat. And still I remember those three days with a wondering affection.

Idyllic? Hardly. Whenever my arms were around Lal during that time, it was to keep myself from falling into the Susathi, or to retie her bandage after washing it. If our intimacy was total, it was also enforcedly discreet. We afforded each other such privacy as two people isolated on a twelve-foot bit of driftwood have to give, turning our backs without being asked, somehow making place for solitude. One day passed almost wordlessly, I recall, except when it came my turn to replace Lal at the tiller. (*There* was a dainty procedure, by the way, invariably unnerving for me, since the rear of the boat was too narrow for us to trade places in safety. It quickly became simpler for Lal to slip into the water to let me by, and then ease herself back aboard, or sometimes hold onto a rope and trail behind for a while, testing her injuries against the river.) Apart from our few words then, the only sounds were birdsong and sometimes a wind ruffling the water. Our boat, built for silence, moved downstream like the shadow of those little sharp winds.

Yet that same night Lal woke gasping and shouting out of one of her nightmares, which had not happened since we left The Gaff and Slasher. She calmed herself very quickly, but she did not want to go back to sleep, so we talked until nearly dawn, lying close together beside a fire too small to be easily noticed and far too small to warm us.

What did we talk about: two scarred, skilled, and decidedly aging wanderers in the dark? The past, more than anything, and our childhoods most of all. Lal has two brothers, older and younger, whom she has not seen since she was taken from her home at the age of twelve. I had an older sister, whom I loved very much, more than anyone, and who died because the man she loved was a stupid, careless man who loved no one. He was the first man I ever killed. I was also twelve at the time.

Lal spoke of friends and playmates, all of whom she remembered perfectly, down to the way they dressed and the games they favored. I had no such companions, except my sister, but once I knew a woodcutter. He must have been middle-aged then: a south-country peasant, illiterate, superstitious, completely honest, completely ruled by petrified fears and customs. Yet he always shared his meals with me when we chanced to meet in the forest, and he told me long, long stories about trees and animals; and when the family of the man I killed hunted me to his door, he took me in and hid me and lied to them, though they would have burned us both in the house if they had known. I fled on the next day, not to endanger him further, and I never saw him again. But every morning when I wake, I say his name.

Out on the river we could hear the *leeltis* coming up to feed in the moonlight. They are sleek black fish with webby forelegs, and they splash the water to stir up insects—sometimes they even startle a fledgling out of its nest. Lal said, "Tell me about your parents."

"They sold my sister," I said. Lal put her arm over me. After a while I said, "I will hate them until I die. That must seem terrible to you."

Lal did not speak for a long time, but she did not take her arm away. At last she said, "I will say something to you that I have never said aloud, even to myself. When I was sold and stolen, I was desperately frightened, truly almost out of my mind. All I had to cling to was my absolute sureness that my parents would come and find me; that while these—things—were happening to me, my wonderful mother and father were hours, minutes away, following, following, that they would never again rest until I was safe and home and avenged. Perhaps it kept me sane, believing that. I used to think so."

I could barely hear the last words. I said, "But they never found you."

"They never found me," Lal whispered against my side. "Damn them, damn them, they never found me."

Her eyelids were so hot to my lips. "They were looking for you all that time," I said. "They hunted for you everywhere. I know they did."

"They could have tried harder!" She turned her face away and muffled the one long howl in the sail, grinding her jaws on the fabric like a trapped beast madly determined to bite itself free of its own foot. Indeed, she bit me hard

when I kissed her, so that her mouth tasted of dust and tears and my blood, and of the two of us sleeping under that sail for five nights. Yet we made love very gently, as we had to do, because Lal's body could not bear my weight, nor her arms and legs hold me as she desired. It went on for a long, teasing, murmurous time, for that reason; and when it was over she said, "Bad water tomorrow," and fell asleep on top of me with her nose in my left ear. And that was how I slept, too.

Three miles downriver, rather late the next morning, and the bad water began. I noticed the wind first: it became steadily stronger and harshly constant, not playful as it had been—Lal had less work to capture it and more to keep the boat in hand. It even smelled a little like a sea wind. The Susathi had been narrowing since the day before, the mountains on both sides closing over us as the canyon deepened. We had to look straight up now to see the sky. There were no rocks ahead yet, and no white water, except in the shadows; but the boat was beginning to pitch, and when I gripped the mast I could feel it straining under my hands. I asked Lal, "How did you know?"

"By the fish," Lal said. I blinked at her. "The fish we ate last night. Fish that swim in rough water taste differently from what we've been eating. I don't know why that should be, but it is."

I went on staring at her until she began to smile. She said, "That's not true, Soukyan. The truth is that last night I was very happy with you. Happiness like that is rare for me, and I do not ever want to get used to it, because right behind it there comes trouble, always. So I said what I said about the river for luck, in a way. Do you understand me?"

"I was happy, too," I said. There was more I wanted to say, but just then the front of the boat went up while the water dropped away under it and a wave thumped into us from behind, so that the front went down and down. I flattened myself out on the deck and closed my eyes. Lal said, "Ah. Now it gets interesting." She sounded quite happy to me.

It did get interesting, very quickly. The little boat rocked and pitched ceaselessly; with my eyes shut, we seemed to be blowing over the water in every direction, completely out of control. Whenever I managed to look around for a moment, I realized that we were still somehow heading downriver, almost as straight as ever, only much faster; and that the waves were actually quite small for the power with which they slammed and pounded the boat. But they were all white now, white as ice-flowers, raw white as *sangarti* blubber when the great *sheknath* rip them open. And there were the rocks, black, ragged, there and there and everywhere, flying by so close that I could see the green and red mosses on their sides, waving dreamily in the rushing water. It was like racing forever down a long, foaming gullet, and I tried not to think to the belly at the end of the run.

"It's an old river," Lal called to me once, "and full of tricks. Deep old bed, any number of sly little sideways currents. We're lucky it's not in flood." They are true, those stories about Sailor Lal. Crosslegged as always, drenched with bitterly stinging spray, her neck and shoulders so bruised yet that she could only look ahead, she eased our boat through that wildness like a needle through folds of silk. Sometimes she would sit absolutely still, neither hand moving at all on the tiller or the lines; again, she might lean back slightly or twitch her fingers as though coaxing a pet, and the boat would lilt this way and fall off that way and wriggle between two green-gummed rocks: a jaunty morsel eluding the teeth of the river one more time. Most often the bow was completely under water, and me with it—up and down, down and up, like the little prayer rags that boatmen in the west tie to their oarblades. Yet I will tell you that for once in my life I was shocked by my own excitement, and that I can understand better now why there are those who love to sail the bad water. I have never told Lal this.

For all that my Man Who Laughs had told us about Arshadin's house being no castle but as plain as a shepherd's hutch, we came very near to missing it altogether. In fact, the only reason that we did notice it was that we both saw the *dharises*, as Lukassa had seen them before us: there, circling near the windows of a reed-thatched cottage, a full dozen or more, where the sight of one in twenty years can have an entire village abandoned—fields, houses, and all—by nightfall that same day. They are smallish blue-gray birds, fish-eaters, rather plain except for the deep blue slash across the chest; and why, rare as they are, they should signify ill luck, disaster, and horror in every land I know, I cannot say. But there they were, crowding each other to roost on Arshadin's sills, and I felt my face grow cold. When I looked back at Lal I saw her making a sign in the air with her left hand that I know now is meant to ward off evil. I would have done the same.

Lal threw the tiller hard left and shouted, "Hold it there," as the boat veered against the wind and the current, laboring toward shore. I hung onto the tiller as she wrestled with the sail, but suddenly it bellied out hugely, unnaturally, and tore the lines from her hands. The boom swung around, caught my shoulder as I ducked, and smashed me overboard. I heard Lal cry out as I fell, but her voice was lost in the cold piping of the *dharises* as they came wheeling and fluttering above us. An instant later, the boat went over—the mast came down beside my head even before I had started sinking, and the hollow sections that fitted so perfectly together came all apart and whipped away past me. Poor little boat. I swear I remember thinking that.

What I also thought was, *Well, Lal won't be able to save you this time.* Because there was no chance of her finding me in that boiling gullet; I hoped she had at least enough strength left to save herself. The river was slamming me into one downstream rock after another, and I was trying to catch hold of each one and not succeeding—the moss was too slippery, the current too strong. I asked—I do not pray—I asked to drown before I was beaten to death. I tried to say certain things that I was taught to say before dying, but the river dashed them back down my throat, and I went under again. After a while it stopped hurting. I felt as though I were falling asleep, moving slowly away from myself toward rest.

Then my feet struck the bottom.

If you want to hear anything more, be quiet and try to imagine what it is like to be certain that your body is lying when it tells you that you are alive. I tell you, standing there on firm ground, looking down to watch the water dropping to my chest, my waist, my knees, I *knew* beyond any question that I had died. At the monastery, we were absolutely forbidden to speculate on the afterlife (it was enforced, too, that prohibition), but when I turned and saw Lal a hundred yards upstream on a growing island of muddy riverbed, with nothing between us but a strip of water a baby could have splashed through—well, what could I think but *this is how it is, after all, walking away with your friends into a world made new and new again with every step you take*? And maybe that is exactly the way it will be. Like you, I hope never to find out.

The river had not parted for us, as in the old stories: rather, like a pet scolded by its master for bringing its bloody, wriggling prey indoors, it had recoiled, dropping us and shrinking away against the opposite bank, pretending it had never been interested in us in the first place. Listen to me—I know very well that rivers cannot behave like that, that no wizard you ever knew of could ever make a river do such a thing. I am *agreeing* with you, man—you have no idea how much I agree with you. I am telling you what happened.

Very well, then. I waded through the mud to Lal, and we stood together looking back toward the farther shore where the river cowered in less than half its bed as far as we could see. I think it was not even flowing; sunlight glints and bounces off moving water, but what Lal and I beheld was a silent, lifeless greeny-brown mass that might have been earth as easily as water. I was not frightened when I thought I was going to drown—I was frightened, terrified, of this, of the *wrongness*. Lal and I stood there: soaked, shivering, exhausted, up to our ankles in stony ooze, holding hands like children without knowing it. Neither of us dared to turn toward that wattle-and-daub cottage that we could feel looming behind us as high as a castle now, not even when the laughter began.

LAL

Laughter does not always mean to me what it does to others. I have heard too many madmen laughing in my life: men, and women too, who were not too mad to realize that they had the power to do anything they wanted. Yet I am alive, having heard them. I have even heard the laughter of the red *sjarik* at noon, and I am alive, and not many can say that. But this was the worst of all, this sound over those naked stones. There was no quickness of any kind to it, good or evil: no proper chaos, no surgingly joyous cruelty—no *smile,* even in its triumph. I will remember the dreadful smallness of that laughter when I have forgotten what it is to see a river stop flowing.

"Turn," he said behind us. "Come to me." We did neither. He laughed again. He said, "Easy to see whose students *you* are. As you will, then," and he let the river go. We saw it flash into life, heard its great blinding cry of freedom as it sprang toward us, roaring back across its bed faster than any beast could have run. Any beast but us: we scrambled up the bank, wet and half-naked as we were, so frantically that I actually bumped into Arshadin and fell at his feet. Nyateneri had charged on past him, but he wheeled back instantly to help me rise. And that is how we first encountered the wizard Arshadin.

He was between us in height: a thickly-made man in a plain brown tunic, with a pale, bald, wide-jawed face. I say bald, not because he had no beard or mustache, but because—how can I make you see? Yes, the hair was graying; yes, there were folds around the mouth and creases framing the eyes—even a tiny old scar under his chin—yet none of that added up to an *expression.* Life gives us lines and pouches and the rest, everyone, even wizards, who live longer than most and always look younger than they are. But only our confusions give us expression, and Arshadin's face was so bland of those that it appeared painted on, wrinkles and features alike. I have once or twice seen infants born far too soon to breathe more than a few minutes in this world: they have a cold transparency about them, and a terrible softness. Arshadin was like that.

"Welcome," he said to us now. "Lalkhamsinkhamsolal—Soukyan, who calls himself Nyateneri." His eyes were a strange hazy blue, seeming to focus on nothing at all, and his voice could have been a woman's voice or a man's.

Miraculously, my swordcane had somehow remained thrust into my belt. Edge or no bloody edge, it would still go through even a thick wizard. It embarrasses me to talk about what happened next—who should know better that because a wizard is not looking at you doesn't mean he isn't watching? But this man's presence somehow filled my head with smoke, putting slow clouds between me and all my bitterly won skills and understandings. I lunged—quite prettily for a limping near-cripple—watched from far away as the point sank into his belly, and still had time to take him in the chest as he sagged toward me. Except that he did not sag, and that my blade came out with no burst of blood following it into the sunlight. No sag, no wound, no blood. Not a drop, even on the swordcane—only a wisp of something like bright smoke, and then not even that. He did not laugh now, but regarded me as though I had interrupted him while he was talking.

"Stop that," he said, tonelessly irritated. "I have watched and touched every step of your journey. I can command rivers and *dharises*—do you suppose I am for your nursery sword, or that carpet-tack in your boot?" He clenched his left hand and opened it again, and Nyateneri—who had imperceptibly shifted his weight onto one leg, bracing himself for a certain spinning kick—doubled over, his face without color. If he made a sound, it was lost in the jubilation of the river.

Arshadin never looked at him. He repeated the gesture, and all my muscles turned to ice, holding me where I stood. He said, "Whatever your plans, they have failed. You cannot harm me, and you cannot help your master. Do you wish proof of that? So, then," and he sketched a wide circle on the ground with one foot and spat into it, closing his eyes. Instantly a grayness shivered heavily within the circle, and within it stood *my friend*. This was no bodiless image, such as he had sent to me in the Northern Barrens: wherever he, and that grayness, truly existed, it was the man himself, snatched from bed in The Gaff and Slasher, blinking mildly at the three of us, whom he plainly saw and knew. He was still in his nightgown, but even so the sight of him made me feel as dizzyingly, immediately safe as it had one morning on the Lameddin wharf when my stinking, sheltering fish basket was suddenly lifted away and there he was, blinking. There he was.

"Well," he said, looking vaguely around him. "This is a bit sudden even for you, Arshadin." He did not bother to greet Nyateneri and me, but gazed up the slope at the thatched cottage with earnest interest. "A very nice job you made of rebuilding, I must say. No one would dream what it looked like, the last time I left here."

"You destroyed my home," Arshadin's empty voice said. "I have not forgotten."

"You have apparently forgotten that when I asked you to let me leave, flames leaped from the walls and great fanged pits opened in the floor. I regarded that as childish and ungracious, in addition to doing your woodwork no good at all. I said so at the time."

Arshadin said, "What shall I do with your servants? What is their return worth to you?"

"Who? Them? Worth to me?" *My friend* stared a moment longer, and then he threw back his head and laughed in *his* way—as though no one in the world had ever even dreamed of making such a prodigious noise before—so that neither of us could forbear to laugh with him, wretched as we were and humiliated to have him view our helplessness. "Worth to me? Arshadin, you brought me all this way to ask me *that*? How often have I warned you about that sort of wasted power—it's really not inexhaustible, you know. A simple letter would have done just as well."

Arshadin had not yet looked at him directly. "Power is never wasted. Strength grows only with use. So, apparently, does frivolity. I will ask you again—what shall I do with these two?" His voice was flat and distant, hardly inflected even on the question.

My friend laughed briefly again. "Do? Do whatever you will, why should that be my affair? I told them not to meddle with you. I told them to stick to bandits and pirates—that in you they were dealing with a force beyond their imaginations, let alone their abilities. But they would challenge you, and now they must take what comes. I cannot forever be rescuing them from the consequences of their own folly."

Does that sound heartless to you? To us it was music and miracles; it was food, clothing, home all in one. Riddle and berate us as he might, he would never abandon us—we trusted that as we could afford to trust nothing else in our separate lives. Nor am I even now ashamed of our dependence on him for our lives: he was depending on our wit, our attention, for more than that.

Heads lowered in feigned despair, we awaited the tiniest signal, while Arshadin watched us with his hazy pupilless eyes.

"As for myself"—*my friend* went on more briskly now—"if I were you, I would send me back to my bed as quickly as possible. You cannot get at me where I stand, and it is costing you energy—energy you can no longer spare—merely to hold me here. I am giving you good advice, Arshadin."

He looked even more fragile than we had left him—I was amazed to see him on his feet. Nevertheless, his eyes showed a trace of the sea-greenness that had been gone for so long, and—most important to me—there were two bright pink ribbons twined through his bristly gray beard. I had last seen them in Marinesha's hair. Arshadin answered him, saying, "Yes you always gave me good advice, and nothing more. I think it would be instructive for you to remain and see me dispose of your friends, or whatever they are. You might learn more of what you should know from that than ever I learned from you."

His voice remained sexless and rigidly ordinary, but with the last words his face changed. If I had been frightened before of a face that gave witness to a lifetime of showing nothing, I was more frightened now of what happened to his eyes when he finally turned them on *my friend*. The bitter rage and loss in them made his heavy, shovel-shaped face seem strangely delicate, almost transparent, like a burning house just before it collapses on itself. His mouth was slightly open, the lips twisted slightly up at one corner, down at the other. I remember even now a fleck of cracked skin in the down corner. He said, "Afterward it will be time to meet those who are waiting."

My friend was silent for a moment, then rubbed a hand across his own mouth, as I remembered him doing very long ago, when I would somehow come too close to winning an argument. "As you please. But if you are considering doing to them what I think you are, I must drearily warn you again—you cannot do it and still hold me in this place. You probably have the strength, yes"—oh, the gentle contempt in that *probably* would have maddened *me*, never mind an Arshadin—"but you have nothing like the mature precision that is necessary. If you did, I could never have escaped you, and if you had gained it since, I could not have remained out of your reach, as I will remain. Free yourself of me, have that much sense, and then—" He looked full at us and shrugged. "A nasty, messy little parlor trick, I always thought it—but there, your tastes are your own affair, quite right. Who am I, after all, to plague you with counsel? Quite right. Quite right."

His voice had fallen into a sleepy singsong drone, which instantly alerted Nyateneri and me: that was the way he always sounded when he was about to set you a particularly exasperating riddle or challenge. He nattered on, buzzing away, turning slowly one way and another within the grayness like a fat fly against a windowpane. Arshadin's deathly heed was all on him: he watched him with a completeness that—for that moment—left no room for us. We realized so suddenly that we could move that it was shockingly painful not to. I still remember that strange pain of stillness.

Nyateneri sprang first—I lost an instant in getting my sword clear, because of my bad arm. I heard *my friend* shout furiously, "Fools! *No!*" Arshadin turned the vermillion-striped face of a rock-*targ* on us, all bony frills and great dripping mouth horribly topping the same squat human body. Nyateneri never faltered, but lunged in under the neck-plates, bare hands reaching for the still-human throat, trusting me to follow with my blade. So I did, but the *dharises* swooped screeching at my eyes, hurling themselves against my face and head until all I could do was to flail at them with the swordcane, helpless to aid Nyateneri as he clung desperately to Arshadin's constantly changing form—rock-*targ* to bellowing *sheknath* to eight-foot-high, axe-beaked *nishoru* to something that I would, quite simply, kill myself to keep from seeing again. Nyateneri held on and held on, sometimes with only one hand, riding barely out of reach between hairy shoulders or razor-feathered wings like some baby animal perched high on its mother's back. He was laughing, his lips stretched grotesquely back from his teeth like any rock-*targ*'s, and his eyes straining wide in the same way. So Rosseth must have seen him when he killed those two in the bathhouse. Everything seemed to be happening very slowly, as it always seems at such times. In fact, of course, everything is happening so fast that your mind trudges along far in the rear, dusty and lame. I remember at some point glimpsing Nyateneri through that battering cloud of *dharises* and thinking quite seriously, *Well, he certainly does enjoy this more than sailing.*

My friend, for his part, was jumping wildly up and down in his foggy prison, kicking and pounding at silent gray walls. All dignity seemed forgotten, even that of a caged animal; he was only a mad old man in a nightgown, yelling till his voice cracked in frustration. "Stop that! Lal, Nyateneri—idiots, idiots, *stop* that! To me, you imbeciles—here, to me! You cannot kill him!" Arshadin had taken the *nishoru* form—more or less—a second time; now he spread those stubby, scabby, glittering wings and finally shook Nyateneri loose, hurling him ten yards away, back toward the riverbank. He landed rolling, but brought up hard against a rock. I could hear the wind retch out of his lungs even from that distance.

Arshadin was already turning, himself again, ignoring me as I ran past him toward Nyateneri. With his rightful shape, his ghastly blank calmness returned; he glanced briefly toward *my friend,* dancing and swearing futilely, then let his breath out in a long, barely audible sigh that became a bolt of black lightning and made exactly the same sound slashing into the grayness that a blade makes in flesh.

The grayness did not vanish or blow apart, but hissed and darkened like meat over a fire; in a moment I could not see *my friend* at all. Nyateneri was on his feet, swaying—I clutched his wrist and dragged him forward, while Arshadin shouted boulders and *dharises* after us. The rocks came careening down the cliffside out of nowhere, gouging real tracks in the dirt and bringing real trees and stones ripping and skidding down with them. I lost hold of Nyateneri and screamed for him until grayness came down over me like a heavy, smothering cloth over a birdcage, and an irritable voice announced, "*Chamata,* a little less bustle, if you don't mind. This wretched thing is difficult enough to manage at the best of times."

Close as he was, I could barely see him, let alone distinguish him from Nyateneri. He was sitting straight up, as though in a high-backed chair, slightly above my head. His eyes were closed. The river gorge, the house, and Arshadin were gone, as were earth, sky, and everything but the grayness, which had no dimension and no ending, but only dwindled off into a further grayness, in which, at the very end of my eyesight, I thought I saw darker shapes appearing and vanishing again. I asked loudly, "Where are we? What has happened? *When* are we?"

I have dealt with magicians before. There isn't one of them, even the best—even *my friend*—who could ever resist the least excuse to play with time. I think it must be the first thing they are all warned never to do. True or not, it *is* the first thing they turn to in a crisis, as others turn to red ale. I dread it and want no part of it, ever, and I always know when it is happening again.

Without opening his eyes, *my friend* said, "Sit down somewhere and be quiet, Lal." Nyateneri touched my arm and drew me away. The air had become bitterly thin and cold; no matter how fiercely you drank it in, there was never quite enough breath in your lungs. That was the only sound: our shallow, too-rapid breathing. There was no wind, no flicker in the grayness, no slightest sense that we were moving, except for the distant come-and-go shapes that might have been nothing but eyestrain. I hugged myself for warmth and huddled beside Nyateneri.

"We are in a far place," *my friend* said presently, "neither where nor when, but what you might call *elsewhen.* This"—and he gestured blindly at the freezing mist around us—"this is not a fairy coach, not a magic carpet sweeping us away to safety; it is a bubble of time—but it is not *our* time. Do either of you understand me?"

Nyateneri said simply, "I don't want to understand you. Why do you have your eyes shut like that?"

"Because I am not entirely sure what would happen if I opened them. You might cease to exist—*I* might cease to exist. Or existence itself might—no, let that go, it makes even me a bit seasick. Like as not, we would merely end up back with Arshadin. Which would amount to the same thing."

For all the familiar and comforting testiness, there was an undertone to his voice that I had never heard before. It was not a note of fear or anxiety or plain uncertainty—it fell between all such words, such sounds. But *I* was frightened, and literally uncertain even of what was under my feet; and cold as well, rattling with it. I demanded, "What happened there, back with Arshadin? Where are we going now? And why, in the name of"—but I could find no god quite equal to the situation—"why are you sitting in the air?"

My friend laughed, but for once it did not comfort me to hear him. "Am I? I hadn't noticed. Where are we going? Why, back to the inn, if I should be permitted to manage it without undue distraction. I have never liked this particular method of travel, and I don't think I have a natural knack for it. Arshadin, now—Arshadin has the knack. He used to scurry about like this all the time, no matter what I said to him. Had it fetch his lunch sometimes."

He was silent for a moment, his eyes squeezing a bit more tightly shut. He said, "It betrayed him this time, that knack. There was no way I could resist him when he used the time-bubble to bring me here; but it drains so much strength merely to hold such a thing in this world, let alone make it work for you, that I knew he could not possibly keep it and me and you two all under control at once. I have told him so often—all energy has its natural limits: all, even his. I did tell him." The last words were spoken in a near-whisper, and not to us. "And then you two caused your diversion—clumsily, if I may say so, but quite effectively—and he tried to kill me in the bubble, believing that I was manipulating you, which shows a certain touching faith in his old teacher, even now." His half-laugh held more rue than triumph.

Nyateneri said, "He spoke of *those who are waiting*. Are they waiting for you?"

"They are indeed," *my friend* replied with surprising cheerfulness. "But they may have to wait a little longer yet. Now, if nobody asks me any more questions, I think—I am very nearly sure—that I will be able to bring this unseemly anomaly to rest at Karsh's dining table. Whether it will be the *right* Karsh, of course, or the *right* Karsh's table—well, well, in any case we should all find it an instructive experience, especially Karsh. Lal, if you close your eyes, too, you will not shiver so much. Do as I say."

He was right—the murderous cold receded once I could no longer see the grayness, as though the sight of it had been what was truly invading my bones—but I could not keep from stealing small glances around me, though nothing was visible except the tiny dark figures that never drew nearer and never quite disappeared. I said, "Those. Who are they?"

"The people whose time we are using," he replied shortly. "Close your eyes, Lal."

I shut them. I said, "Arshadin does not bleed. My sword went almost through him, and there was no blood."

"Because there is no blood in him," *my friend* answered. "Lukassa is quite right—he gave his life to the Others, that night in the red tower, and they gave him back a kind of aliveness for which blood is not necessary. I know of such bargains, very long ago, but I never thought to see one struck in my time. My poor Arshadin. My poor Arshadin." And after that quiet, toneless wail, he said nothing at all.

How much more time passed—ours or someone else's—I cannot say. I heard *my friend* humming to himself: a maddeningly repetitious up-and-down five-note pattern that came, after a while, to seem like the drone of a great engine under us, tireless and strangely soothing. I think I slept a little.

No, I know I slept, because I remember jolting painfully awake at the tensing of Nyateneri's arm around me. He was saying very quietly, close to my ear, "Lal. Something is happening." Even through the grayness I could see how stiff and pale his face was.

"What is it?" I asked. Nothing seemed to have changed: we were still motionless in freezing nowhere, and *my friend* was still sitting in the air, humming the same notes over and over. The only difference, if it was a difference, was that the little shapes at the edge of my vision had finally vanished. Nyateneri's hand tightened on my left arm, the bad one, and I did not notice at all; not until later, when I saw the new bruise. *"Look,"* he said.

The grayness was thinning slowly, down from mist to dirty bathwater, and there were people appearing through it, and they were us. How much more plainly, or more madly, can I say it? I saw the three of us—perfect duplicates, down to the ribbons in *my friend*'s beard and the river mud caked on Nyateneri's feet—but they, the figures, they didn't see us. They went on about their business, which was not here, and were followed by others—some of them were us again, but more were being Karsh and Marinesha, and there seemed to be more Tikats than anyone else. No two were identical: there were versions of *my friend* that had neither ribbons nor beard nor nightgown, and variations on Nyateneri that I might not have recognized but for the height and the changing eyes. As for me, it made me giddy and a little sick, seeing so many copies of myself obliviously passing two feet away. There were small differences enough between them, as well, in dress and mannerism; but to my mind they were all twins, and all too short, too wide-mouthed and pointy-chinned—the old goblin face I have learned to tolerate in the glass, but not in bloody *dozens*!—and every one of them walking with the same awful swaggering roll. Do I walk like that? I still cannot believe I really walk like that.

There were others, too, crowding around and past them, coming and going in the dissipating grayness. I recognized Rosseth—looking wide-eyed and kind in every translation, and stronger than any of them knew—and other servants or guests at The Gaff and Slasher; beyond those were countless faces I had never seen, or anyway could not remember having seen. They were opaque but not solid: they passed through one another as they did through the mist, without taking notice. What *I* noticed, gaping and shaking my head, was that not one of them was Lukassa.

Beside me Nyateneri said, quite loudly, "Master"—and then he pronounced what I had always believed to be *my friend*'s name—"enough mystification is enough. What are we seeing, and who are these?"

My friend's eyes were still so grimly shut that the corners of his mouth squeezed up with them when he turned toward us, but in that instant his face was very terrible. I did not know that face at all, and I was frightened of it—of him—then. He said in a slow, light, almost dreaming voice, "We will now all proceed to be extremely glad that I have at least maintained sense enough never to tell either of you my true name. If you had spoken it here, now, the three of us would have been spread through time—no, *across* time, smeared over it like so much butter. Do you have the least notion of what I am telling you?"

Before that blind face and that even more terrifying voice, I cowered as silently as I had when he first found me; but it was worse now, because I was older and could almost conceive of what he meant. Nyateneri tried for a moment to face him down, then crouched humbly before him. The voice said, "No, of course not, what possessed me to ask you that? If you ever came anywhere near understanding what I just told you, that understanding would drive you mad. At present, I think I could endure that well enough, but sooner or later I would probably start to feel bad about it. Probably. Are all that lot gone yet?"

Almost all of the duplicates had passed out of sight, save for a couple of the Tikats and one Karsh. I told him so, and he nodded and sat up straighter in the chair we could not see. His hands were shaping something equally invisible that seemed to be leaping and struggling between them, and growing as well. "When those go," he said, "those last, tell me. Immediately."

The Tikats vanished together, and there was just Karsh left—a younger, brown-eyed Karsh, wearing the embroidered vest and leather leggings of a prosperous south-coast farmer. It did not surprise me that he was the only one of all those figures who stood still even for a moment, peering briefly but very intently into the grayness all around him. Wherever he really was, he knew that something to do with him was happening somewhere. I said, "He's going away now. He's gone."

"So, then," *my friend* said softly, like Arshadin. He spoke several words that did not even sound like a language: from another room, I would have thought he was snoring or clearing his throat. The unseen thing growing between his hands seemed first to surge into him, and then to explode out of his grasp with a violence that rocked him backward, almost knocking him off his perch in the air. The grayness turned to night, but not any sort of night I knew. The air was too clear, as though its skin had somehow been ripped away, and the stars were too big. I never breathed that air, but held my breath for an hour or an instant, until *my friend* suddenly opened his eyes, and we were all three sitting quietly, like picnickers, on the stubbly little hill where Karsh has his travelers' shrine. It was late afternoon, with a gray quarter-moon already rising in the west, behind the inn. We could hear the hogs snuffling in their pen, and Gatti Jinni shouting across the courtyard.

The moon over our little boat's masthead last night had been full and golden, dripping ripe into the river. Nyateneri and I looked at each other. Someone began whistling in the stable.

The Innkeeper

They paid me handsomely for the horses—I will say that—and did me the honor of offering no explanations as to what had become of them. When you are my age, you'll have long given up expecting the truth from anybody, but you will appreciate not being lied to all the more for it. As for where they had been and, more important, how they got back in only seven days from a journey that had left the black one limping badly and a good ten pounds thinner, while Miss Kiss-my-ring Nyateneri looked as many years older . . . well, what could they have told me that I'd have believed, then or even now? I took the money, told the boy to tell Marinesha to bring dinner to their room, and bloody let it go.

The old man was starting to have me more nervous than the women by then, anyway. I knew him for a wizard, of course—had from the first day; you can't miss them, it's almost a smell—which made no matter by itself. I don't like wizards—show me someone who does—but they're usually mannerly guests, generous to the help, and a good bit more careful than most about keeping the landlord sweet. But I also knew from Marinesha that this one was frail, sick, practically dying, hadn't stirred out of his room since Rosseth and Tikat carried him there. And here he was now, on his feet at any rate, and plainly up to his neck in whatever those women had been at since they left the inn. No simple woods wizard, either, curing colicky animals and promising sunshine for the harvest—oh no, thank you, this one was turning out to be just the sort that trouble delights in following home like a stray dog, never mind whose home it may be, nor who's to feed the beast. I'd no idea what breed of trouble it was likely to be, but I could smell that, too, as you smell rain, or a cartload of manure coming around the next bend. Unmistakable. About that, at least, I am never wrong.

Turn him out? Turn him out? Oh, aye—Karsh, who hadn't the stomach to order three women out of The Gaff and Slasher, Karsh is now to tell a wizard to take his custom somewhere else. Well, I have no shame in telling *you* that I smiled and nodded at him whenever I saw him, asked him if his room was comfortable enough, and sent him up better wine than Miss I've-killed-men-over-a-bad-vintage Lal ever wrinkled her nose at. He appreciated it, too—said so in her royal presence more than once. Even innkeepers have their moments.

Yet nothing seemed to happen—nothing you could call happening, anyway, smells or no smells. The summer days creaked by, travelers came and went—Shadry's wife ran off with one of them, the way she does most summers, just for the vacation from Shadry—horses got looked after, meals got cooked, dishes went on being washed, rooms were more or less swept out, carters lugged casks of red ale and Dragon's Daughter into the taproom, and a family of Narsai tinkers left in the night without paying their score. My fault for not charging them in advance—my father was half-Narsai, and I know better than that.

The three women behaved almost like ordinary guests, taking the sun and buying trinkets and antiquities at Corcorua Market; though why they stayed on, except to nurse their wizard friend, I couldn't fathom. Tikat seemed to have given up running after that daft white one, Lukassa—hardly looked at her these days, except to move out of the way when she passed by, more like a little wandering ghost than ever, with those eyes eating up her face. I'd have kicked *him* out, just to be kicking someone, but he was more than earning his keep between the stable, the house, and the kitchen garden. A silent, grum-faced lad, with a south-country brogue to curdle beer, but a good worker, I'll say that.

In honesty, the only real complaint I could have mustered during that time had to do with the boy. And I couldn't have put it in words, either, as well as I know him and myself. He was happy as bedamned to see those women back, of course—took on to unsettle your dinner, and was forever slipping off to see if any little chore of theirs wanted doing. Nothing new about that, certainly: no, what niggled at me was an idea that something was niggling at him, and growing worse by the day. Not that he said a word about it—not to me anyway, of course, he'd die first—but Gatti Jinni could have read that face, and that anxious way he was developing of looking quickly around him at odd moments, just as though he were sneaking off to bother Marinesha and heard me shouting for him. I thought it was the wizard then. I thought he'd taken to hanging after him, as he did with those women. It gave me a bit of a queer feeling.

ROSSETH

Part of it was the heat, surely. That part of the country, high as it is, turns hot as a forge in late summer. I grew up used to the weather, of course—I miss it now, to tell you the truth—but after the wizard arrived, every day felt stretched tight over a bed of white coals, as the people there scrape *sheknath* hides. The nights are usually a relief, because of the mountain breezes, but that summer they never came. Dogs and chickens lay in the dust and gasped; the horses hadn't the energy to swish away flies; the guests sprawled in the taproom, keeping their gullets cool at any rate; and even Karsh stamped and roared a little less than usual, and had a few less orders for Tikat and me. Myself, I woke up sweat-soaked in the hayloft every smoldering dawn, already exhausted, with a head full of cinders. Nearly twenty years it's been, and I can still recall exactly the strange, hopeless taste of those wakings.

Because it wasn't really the weather—not that *taste,* not that sense of being under a glass: a lens that was focusing the heat of someone's attention on The Gaff and Slasher. It got even worse when Lal and Nyateneri returned: there was rarely a moment, asleep or awake, when I couldn't feel myself watched more and more intensely by a cold considering that had nothing to do with me—*me,* Rosseth, or whoever I am—nor with anything I understood or loved in this world. Sometimes it seemed far away; at others, close enough to share my bed-straw and finger over my dreams. In either case, there was no avoiding it, and no fighting off the evil dreariness that always attended it, that kept me constantly frightened in a vague, dull way, and truly tired to death. *Sad* to death, I suppose you could say.

If Tikat was suffering from the same complaint, I saw no sign of it. Not that I saw much of Tikat in those days: he had quietly taken over the nursing and guarding duties with which I had been entrusted, and now spent most of his free time with the old man upstairs, whom he called *tafiya.* I missed him sharply—until he came I'd never had a friend of almost my own age to work and talk with, mucking out stalls or lying awake in the loft—and I envied him terribly as well. Mainly, of course, because his closeness to the wizard brought him close to Lal, Nyateneri, and Lukassa every day; but I was jealous, too, that somebody valued his presence and asked for him often, which is different from being sent for. I could have gone on my own, I know that, but I didn't, and there it is. I was very young.

The women kept even more to themselves than they had done before, whether they rode out or stayed shut in their room, or in the old man's room. When I saw them at all, I always saw them together, which wasn't what I wanted. Most particularly I wished to tell Soukyan—who still looked and moved and smelled like Nyateneri—that I liked him no less for the deception, and that I was not avoiding him out of anger or shame. I wanted to ask Lal why and how they had returned so soon, and to tell her that I had looked after her wizard as well as I was permitted. (The third assassin never turned up, by the way—to this day I don't know what became of him.) And I wanted to say to Lukassa that every time Tikat heard her voice or saw her in the stair or crossing the courtyard, his heart cracked in one more place. Oh, I had a speech ready for Lukassa, I certainly did. I used to practice it aloud on the horses.

But none of all that ever happened, somehow: it was almost as though the three of them had never come riding around that bend beyond the spring, as though I had dreamed the trembling dimples in Lal's shoulders, dreamed that I watched Nyateneri kill two killers singlehanded. All that was real was a loneliness I had never given name to before they came—that and the heat, and the fear.

Once I asked Marinesha how the wizard was faring, because I would not ask Tikat. She answered, not in her usual starling chatter, but in a subdued, hesitant mumble, "Well enough, I suppose." When I pressed her further, she bridled at first, and then began to weep—not in mim silence, like a lady, as she always tried to shed her tears, but with great honks and sniffs, wringing my best nose-rag to shreds. What I made out of her misery was that she had hardly seen the old man since Lal and Nyateneri's return—"but I hear him every night, Rosseth, all night every night, marching up and down the room till dawn, talking and chanting and singing to himself. He can't be sleeping at *all*. . . ."

I petted and quieted her as well as I could, saying, "Well then, he must sleep by day, that's what it is. And he's a wizard, Marinesha—wizards don't need things like sleep and food and such, not the way we do." But she pulled free of me and looked into my face, and there was a desperate sorrow in her eyes that I had never imagined they could show.

"There are *others*," she whispered. "Sometimes there are *others*, and they answer him. They sound like little children." She ran away then, back to the inn, still crying, taking my nose-rag with her.

Tikat knew nothing of any voices, and I believed him when he said so. I don't think that gods, spirits, demons, monsters, or any of that lot will ever put in an appearance in Tikat's presence. They'll just wait patiently, as long as they have to, until he goes away. Karsh isn't like that. You'd think he would be, if anyone would, but he isn't. I will say that about Karsh—the monsters haven't always waited for him to leave.

It was a day or two after I spoke with Marinesha that he came looking for me in the kitchen. Tikat was patching the rotting horse trough once again, and our most recent potboy had disappeared—Shadry beats and bullies his way through a dozen in a year; the best you can say is that they often run away without even stopping to collect their wages. After cursing Shadry for at least five minutes without once repeating himself, Karsh suddenly looked up as though noticing me by chance, as he always does, and grunted, "Outside. Wait."

I stood outside and waited for another five minutes before he came out, purple in the face and wiping his mouth—you'd have thought he had just eaten Shadry with a couple of side dishes. He stood there for a while, not looking at me, muttering to himself, "Bloody stupid, bloody stonefingered, dungmouthed imbecile, whoever gave him the goatfucking notion he was a bloody cook?" Presently, when it suited him, he said, "Rosseth." I think of that often—the way Lal said my name, and the way he did. I can't help it, I still do.

"You told me to wait," I said. Karsh nodded. He said, "Thank you."

I'll not stand here and swear that that was the very first time Karsh ever said *thank you* to me. It may not have been. I can't even be sure that I really heard it, strangled as he sounded. I'll just tell you that it shocked me, as much as if he had begun to jig and spin in a circle with his finger on the top of his head. I stared at him. That made him angry, and he shouted, "What are you gawping for now? What's the matter with you? Always gawping at everything, I never knew anybody like you for gawping, since the first day, first time I ever saw you."

He stopped there, coughing and spitting, but not taking

his eyes off me. I waited, wondering whether he wanted to berate me about the drains again, or warn me to stop upsetting Marinesha. But he shook his head furiously, wiped his mouth, drew in a long breath, and said, "Rosseth. How are you?"

I sputtered a bit myself, getting the words out. "How am I? I am well enough." Karsh nodded several times, as solemnly as though I had just given him the answer to some riddle that had been itching him all his life. He muttered, "Good, that's good," and then, looking just past me, "Rosseth, been meaning to tell you something. A long time now."

I waited. Karsh said, "You were a . . . you weren't a bad child. Didn't cry much, didn't get underfoot. You were a *nice* little boy."

The last words cost him so much effort that he had to roar them out, daring me to give him the lie. He stood there glaring at me, actually panting, his eyes that strange blue-black they go when he's really furious. A moment only of that—then he turned and tramped back inside, yelling more insults at Shadry before he even had the door open. I stood where I was, under that scraped white sky, shaking numbly with wonderment and weariness and fear, and wishing I knew my own name.

THE FOX

Too hot. Too hot. Poor little fox, slipping and turning inside nasty draggly bag of wet fur. Man-shape has no fur, but Nyateneri threatens a dozen times death if she sees. So no man-shape, no nice red ale in the taproom, nothing but hot wind in the hot weeds under the tree where chickens sleep. Like eating old brooms. Poor fox.

Day, night, on and on. Nothing to do but sleep. I can sleep a hundred years, if I want—eat nothing, drink nothing, wake if you think about me. But once I look up and there she is, looking down, Lukassa. Eyes so old in that face—as old as I am, almost. She says, "Fox, fox," so softly. Bends down, picks me up, like the first night, tucks me against her shoulder, against her neck. I lick sweet salt, only a little little.

"My fox," she says. "Help him."

Him? Lukassa feels me growl, holds fast. "Oh, fox, he is kind man, he is kind to people." Not to foxes. Lukassa: "And he is in such danger." Good. Let that other one take *him* by scruff and tail, see how he likes it. I lick her throat again. Take man-shape now? But she squeezes me till I squeak, says, "You know them, the ones who come at night. I know you know them. You can make them go away."

Make magician go away, nicer. Lukassa: "He needs to die. It is his time, he *needs* to die." I curl up in her arms, close eyes. Lukassa says, "But if he dies now—sick, sleepless, raging—then he will become like them, only worse, much worse. There is a word, but I forget."

Griga'ath, yes, too bad, who cares? Lukassa lifts my head, waits long for me to look back. "Fox, fox, I know there is nothing you can do to help me—but please, for him. I am asking you because we are friends."

Kisses nose, sets me down. "Go to him." And stands there, all trust, all believing, waiting for me to trot right away, off to save wicked magician from night visitors. I lie down where I am, let my tongue hang out. Lukassa's eyes bright with sadness. "Fox." Waits, turns away. I yawn in the dust—any chickens having bad dreams, slipping off branches? No. *My* sadness. One eye awake for Nyateneri, one ear up for fat innkeeper, then back to sleep—no trouble in stupid *griga'aths,* not for foxes. Trouble is magicians.

But, but. No sooner wriggled some comfort out of crackly weeds, here comes old nothing at me again. "Find out, find out. Too much restless, what is moving?" *I* know what is moving—stupid magicians, snatching at each other across the sky. Stupid, stupid magicians, no more, no less—but old nothing says, "Find out," and there, no more sleeping for poor fox. So here I am after all, trotting right off to Lukassa's wizard, hello, and is it bad voices keeping you awake, kind friend? How nice, some justice yet. Perhaps a fox can add a few words.

Deep, hot dark. Inn door all locked and barred, but mice know a rotted board in the kitchen, and what mice know fox knows. Scrape, wriggle, shake, and here we are under Shadry's great oven—still warm, too, fire snuggled down into ashes for the night, like the dirty small boy asleep on a couple of chairs in a corner. Not a sound, only my claws clicking across the stones.

Up the stairs with the draft, down the hall with frightened beetles. Candlelight squirming under door of magician's room, trying to get out of there, and no wonder. Oh yesyes, I do know those voices, I know smells. Smell like lightning, they do, smell like drains under bathhouse, like bloody snow where *sheknath* have been eating. For a moment my fur shivers for poor old magician, but it passes. Too many magicians in the world, no one knows like me.

Outside the room, and as soon stay outside. No fear, but I do not like to be near them. Voices hurt my teeth. Old nothing: "In, fox." Man-shape or this, which? Think about it, take the man-shape—why, who knows? Better to walk in on two legs, maybe. Easier to look through the keyhole.

The room is full of them, maggots heaving in a dead thing, making it seem to breathe. Some with faces, some without, some with glass, fire, pulsing flowery guts where face should be. Some with no shape, no body—only a little shadow, little dark bending in the air. Some pretty as pigeons, rabbits—others, eyes refuse them, those others, even my eyes. They crouch on bedposts, sprawl on windowsill, scuttle this way, that way along the rafters. Never saw so many in one place. Most times, you have to look a special slanty way, close one eye, to see them at all. Other side of mirrors, they come from.

Magician sees them. Ho*ho,* magician sees them. He walks back and forth, back and forth, never looks at them, never sits down on bed. Must not stand still, must not rest, not with them. Gray once, white now he is—ash-white, burned white, like Lukassa. Lines raked down his face, clawmarks without blood. Back and forth he goes, head up, feet stamping, singing a bad song, a soldiers' song:

"Captain asks the corporal,
brother, how's your mum?
Corporal says to captain,
you can kiss my ruddy bum.
And it's left-right, one more mile,

> left-right, stop awhile,
> put down your packs and tell the
> captain, kiss my bum . . ."

Over and over, wheezing it out in his burned voice, even Nyateneri doesn't know *that* one. So many verses, too. If he stops, even once, they will be on him—oh, not with claws and teeth, though you'd think so to see them, but with eyes, voices, sweet slithering laughter, on him with old shames, old betrayals, old rotting secrets. Twist your memories, they can, wrench good dreams into shapes too wrong to bear, too real to bear. Have your soul hanging in ribbons that fast, I know.

Magicians never lock their doors. I push it open, walk in, leaving just a crack in case of accidents. Hot everywhere else, [illegible]l as knives here. Jolly Grandfather man-shape gazes around, thumps magician's shoulder, booms out, "Ah there, scoundrel, why didn't you tell anyone you were having a party?" Eyes as big as coach wheels, eyes in dark wet bunches, eyes on the tips of tails and tentacles—all turn toward man-shape. Shouldn't be there, shouldn't be able to see them, bright-eyed Grandfather. Only magician never looks up, but trudges on, up and down the room, croaking away:

> "Captain asks the corporal,
> what'll we do for tea?
> Corporal says to captain,
> piss in your hat and see.
> And it's left-right, one more mile . . ."

Tired, tired, tired he is, man-shape's slap almost knocked him over. Lukassa would weep. Not me. I say to old nothing, *This is what it is, what is moving, no more than that. Goodbye, thank you, fox can go now.* But you never know with old nothing. "Stay. Watch. Too much power here, wild, wrong. Stay and see."

And *there's* fair for you, *there's* justice—nothing better for a fox to do than wait among nasty figments until morning comes or magician dies, either. Push in with them on the bed, on windowsill, must I, listen all night long to captain and corporal, all because old nothing thinks one magician is different from another? Nonono, not this time, not this fox, no fear. Too many chickens expecting me elsewhere.

But what, then? Man-shape cannot simply walk out, old nothing would never permit. Very well, sendings must leave, just as Lukassa begs, because it suits me—*me,* no one else. Think, fox. Man-shape slaps magician on shoulder again, keeps him company in the chorus:

> "And it's left-right, one more mile,
> left-right, stop awhile,
> put down your packs and tell the
> captain, kiss my bum . . ."

A good song. Magician keeps stamping and singing, eyes down always—won't even look at nice old Grandfather man-shape, no more than at sendings. But Grandfather looks at everything, eyes bright as my teeth. Grandfather shouts out to sendings, greeting them by their names, names like night in the mouth, like broken glass, names like burning oil, dead water, like wind. Wind in bad places.

They don't like it, being called by their names. Don't scream and scatter, don't turn to stone, but they don't like it. Interesting. Couldn't harm them if I cared to—or they me—but interesting still. Grandfather man-shape shouts louder, makes stupid jokes of names, even puts them into marching magician's song. Hissing and mumbling now, angrier at me than ever at him. Brighter and brighter they grow, all seething with the same black fire, mark of the power that set them on old magician. Room surges with their hurtful little voices, they drown *left-right,* even drown man-shape's bellowing. Magician buckles, stumbles to knees, hands over ears, over face, no more song.

On him in a moment now, the lot of them, laughing, mocking, gnawing, he'll not rise again as what he was. Too bad, Lukassa—enough for you, old nothing? One less magician—one more *griga'ath,* and who cares? Not this fox.

But then this magician turns, still on his knees, eyes wide, blazing green as the sky just after sunset. He throws out one hand, says three words, dry grass rattling—and *gone,* all of them, all at once, gone, blown-out candles, slamming doors, dew-bugs in a *starik*'s mouth. Nothing remains—not an echo, not a twist of smoke, only a cold narrow room left huge by its emptiness. This magician stands up, slowly, smiles very slowly.

"Thank you," he says, as Grandfather man-shape blinks and shrivels into a red fox sitting on the bed. "That was becoming quite exhausting."

"No thanks wanted," I tell him. I am puzzled, hate that, hate puzzled. I say, "It was not to help you."

Smile widens and widens, teeth or no teeth. "I know that, but I am still just as grateful. It was most clever of you to realize that their own names hurt their ears as much as they do ours. There will be others here, very soon, but at least I will rest a little and perhaps think of a new song to keep them at bay. The captain and the corporal are beginning to lose their charm."

Brushes me off the bed like dust, lies down sighing. My nice teeth grind together, but too many stories about foxes who bite magicians. "Snap your fingers, mumble words, send them off," I say. "Why bother with songs?"

Half-asleep already, he looks smaller with every breath. "Too tired," he whispers. "Have to face them, hear them, too tired, they'd have me. Too tired for anything but singing. Thank you, old friend."

Last word is a snore. I stand looking at him for a long time, not wanting to. Friend of his, this fox, friend of any magician? He knows better, wicked old tired man. Yet I have gone to him, not wanting to—helped him, not meaning to, meaning only to help this fox. Just as Lukassa begs, kissing nose. I hate this. Magician snores on, ends of mustache fluttering in the wind. Some other is here, watching with me—*not* old nothing, but a deadness, a dead place, window-high, just beyond bed, no bigger than my front paws together. Where it is, no air. Not for foxes, this room. Good Grandfather man-shape, to leave the door a little open.

So back down the hall, *clickclick, clickclick,* past more snoring, past sighs, whimpers, a fox indoors, swimming through currents of human noises, human smells. I hear magician muttering in his sleep, same as always:

"And it's left-right, one more mile,
left-right, stop awhile . . ."

My feet pick up the rhythm, not wanting to.

TIKAT

Of course I knew that he was ill. I was usually the first to see him in the mornings—before the women, even—and I know the air of a sickroom as well as any. But sickness to me is the plague-wind, is childbed fever, is colic, black blood, bone-rot, and all the village complaints that we treat exactly as we do the ailments of farm animals. My *tafiya* slept poorly, plain enough; he lost weight by the day, his color grew steadily worse, and his voice was most often a rasping whisper, as painful to me, listening, as it must have been to him. Yet when I would have slept in his room, he forbade it at the top of that tattered voice, as he forbade me ever to visit him again after dark. How should I have realized that he was being galloped to madness and halfway back between every sundown and every cockcrow? That is no air I know.

Tending him drew Lukassa and me together in a strange way, as though I were again slipping up on the Rabbit, my Mildasi horse, step by step, praying not to alarm him by any smallest thought of capture. We spoke rarely; what mattered was that she did not seem to fear being in the same room with me, although how it would have been without him there I cannot say. Our duties were silently self-appointed: she bathed and shaved him, whether he would or no, and changed his sweated linen daily. I never learned where she got the clean sheets, those being one of Karsh's chief economies. Once or twice she asked me for help in turning his mattress, and several times I took the chamberpot from her hands and emptied it myself. She thanked me politely each time, but she never spoke my name.

For my part, I brought his meals, swept the floor, took away yesterday's platters, and listened when the mood to talk was on him. It never happened when Lukassa was in the room—or the other two either, when I think about it. They loved him, you see, and I did not. You don't have to love a *tafiya;* you can even hate him, as you might anyone else. I thought he was the wisest person I had ever met, except for my teacher at home, but it was a wisdom too playful for my comfort, and the play was too quickly apt to turn edged and pointed. Yet he had a liking for me, I knew that—perhaps because I owed him nothing and did not care so much for his good opinion. It may have been just so, contrary as he was.

Sometimes he spoke of his life, which had been a very long one. I never knew how old he was; but if even half of what he told me is true—half the journeys in quest of hidden learning, half the tests and terrors and magical encounters—it would surely have taken two ordinary mortal lifetimes to crowd them all in. Wizards must lie like other people—only better—but in fact he mumbled quickly over the adventurous parts and kept returning again and again to the plainest human sorrows and defeats. "There was a woman," he said once. "We traveled together, many, many years. Then she died." I saw no tears in his pale greenish eyes, but I don't think you can tell with a wizard.

"I am sorry," I said. The eyes had turned away from me; now they swung back with an impact I could feel in my flesh. "Why? Imagining that moping and pining for

Lukassa fits you for understanding someone else's loss? There is no comparison. You understand nothing." And he spoke no further for the rest of that day.

Yet another time he asked me, very suddenly, in the middle of a complaint about Shadry's bread, "Is there anything you fear, Tikat?" The words came lightly, but his voice was like thatch tearing in the wind. "Tell me what you fear."

I had no need to think longer than it took me to draw breath. "Nothing. Before . . . *before,* I was afraid of everything in the world, everything that had the least chance of parting Lukassa and me. Now the worst that could have happened has happened, and there is nothing left for me to fear." I stopped for a moment, as he began to smile, and then I added, "I truly wish there were. I don't think it can be right, to fear nothing at all."

The smile widened, exposing his withered gums and stumpy teeth. I thought that I would never let myself fall to ruin like that, not if I could mend such things with a snap of my fingers. He said softly, almost dreamily, "No, it is not, but I envy you all the same. You see, the thing you are most afraid of is always the thing that happens—always." The last word seared the air between us. "We make it happen, we all do, wizard and weaver alike, though I could never tell you how. Yet here you are—here you sit by me, and your worst fear has come true, it's done with, and you did not die. Indeed I do envy you, Tikat."

I thought he was mocking me. I said, "I survived. I do not know if that is the same as not dying."

"A dainty distinction for a village boy," and this time there was no missing the ravaged amusement in that voice. "Now I recall that I have feared many, many things myself, in different times, but I seem to have outlived them all, just as I have outlived loving and hating as well. The irony of it is that in all these years I have never feared death, being what I am and knowing what I know. Now I do. As much as you dreaded living without Lukassa, so

I live in absolute horror of dying. It is a great humiliation for a magician."

All mockery, whether of me or of himself, was gone from his voice. He reached up to grip my shoulder, and I could feel how thin and tremulous his fingers had become. "Tikat, I dare not die, I must not, not yet. Do not let me die."

Panic and bewilderment spilled through me then, as though from his fingers on my arm. I said, "Why turn to me? What can I do to help you?"

But he was looking beyond me as I spoke, toward the one window. He said loudly, "Ah, there you are. I was beginning to think you had forsaken me."

There was no one else in the room. He was talking to a dance of sunlight just below the windowsill. "No, no, certainly not, I trust I know you better than that." The voice held a bantering tone, close almost to laughter.

I left then, before I could begin hearing the sunlight answer him. In the corridor, sweeping, Marinesha looked up too quickly and then away. I knew that she had been listening at the door—Marinesha is a bad liar, even wordlessly. I said, "He is no worse. No better than yesterday, but no worse."

I would have gone on by, but she came and stood before me, closer than was usual for her. If I have not said that Marinesha is quite pretty, with large dark-gray eyes, a generous mouth, and skin that should have been coarsened by her work and has not been at all, it is because her appearance meant nothing to me, one way or the other. She talked too much, but she always treated me gently enough, while giving Rosseth the raw side of her tongue on any pretext. She said now, anxious but hesitant, "Tikat—Tikat, did he speak to—to *another* in the room?"

"Aye," I said, "an old acquaintance who just happens to look like a wall. For all I know, wizards have many such friends." In truth, I was concerned to be away, to puzzle over my *tafiya*'s words by myself. But Marinesha did not move from my path. She bit her lip and looked somewhere else again, and said, very low, "Tikat, Lukassa is not the only woman in the world."

I could hardly hear her. She was blushing so deeply that even her yellow-brown hair seemed to darken with blood. I said, with a harshness that was starting to come too easily, "And if she were, I would not have her, nor any other in her place. I want no one, Marinesha. No more of that for me, never."

Marinesha put her hand timidly against my cheek. I took hold of her wrist and shook my head, saying nothing. I think I was not rough, but when I looked back she had pushed the wrist hard against her lips, as though I had bruised her. It plagues me to this day, that sight of her. There was no need to hurt Marinesha.

The days strained toward autumn without seeming to grow any shorter or cooler. I felt that I had been all my life drudging at that inn, like Rosseth, and wondered often why I should stay on another hour. There were some still who might be missing me at home; and the Barrens, killing in spring, would be impassable when the snow came. There was nothing for me in this place; there never had been. It was all a waste, all of it, and time to say so and be done. And still I drudged on.

One afternoon Karsh ordered Rosseth and me to replace several rotted roof beams in the smokehouse. This would have been weary work in any weather; now it was both exhausting and dangerous, since the timbers slipped constantly through our sweating fingers and twice came near crushing our legs. We finally rigged a serviceable hoist, and I was standing underneath, guiding a beam up to Rosseth on the roof, when I saw Nyateneri in the doorway. The fox sat on his haunches beside her.

We got the beam properly set in, and Rosseth began hammering hard and wildly, never looking at Nyateneri. She was a handsome woman, in a soldierly way, as tall as I, with changing eyes and short, thick gray-brown hair. Not at all beautiful, nor suddenly, unexpectedly pretty like Marinesha—but even in my village you would stare when she strode past, and remember her long after the beautiful ones. I had never seen her and the fox together. He looked straight at me, putting one ear back and laughing out of his bright yellow eyes.

Nyateneri said, "I need to speak to you both. Come down, Rosseth." She did not raise her voice, but he looked up, hesitated for a moment, and then dropped lightly from the roof to land in the straw beside me. "Soukyan," he said, almost whispering. I did not know what the word meant then.

"He is dying," Nyateneri said. "There is nothing we can do." Her brown face showed no emotion, but her voice was slow in that way I know myself, when each word seems to be dragged back into your throat by despair. She said, "It will be tomorrow night."

"How do you know?" Rosseth had hold of my hand, a child's blind clutch, which I still felt long after he had let go. "He's strong, you don't know. I never thought he'd last out the first night he came, but he did, he did, and he'll last through this one too. You don't *know*." He was blinking very fast.

Nyateneri looked at him with more softness than I had ever supposed in that swaggering woman. "He does, Rosseth. He knows." Rosseth stared at her for a long time before he nodded very slowly. Nyateneri said, "He wants us there. You, me, Lal, Lukassa—Tikat." She paused just enough to let me know whose idea *I* was. "He wants us all there."

"Why tomorrow night?" Rosseth's dark eyes were dry and stubbornly angry now, the way he gets. "How can he—why tomorrow night?"

"Because of the new moon." Nyateneri seemed genuinely surprised. "Wizards can only die on new-moon nights." Plainly she had thought that even louts like us must have known so simple a thing, and was annoyed with herself for the assumption. She turned away without another word, but the fox sat where he was, yellow gaze never leaving me. I heard him in my head, no mistaking that grating, derisive bark: *Well, boy, well now, fellow horsethief, and aren't you a longer way from home than anyone in the world?* I could not move from where I stood until he stretched himself lingeringly, fore and aft, like any dog or cat, then sauntered off after Nyateneri. A dust-draggled little bird flew up almost under his nose, and he pounced stifflegged at it but missed.

Rosseth was looking at me as I had looked at the fox. He said, "You have another new friend."

"Not likely," I said. "I leave a few tidbits out now and then, to persuade him to spare Karsh's chickens. He knows my smell by now, I suppose."

"When did you ever care about Karsh's chickens?" Rosseth's voice was tight and thin. I shrugged and reached for the last beam remaining, but Rosseth caught my hand again, crying out, "Tikat, no one tells me what is happening. Why is the wizard really dying? How can he be certain that he will go with the new moon tomorrow night? Something terrible is happening, and no one will tell me what it is. Guests fight in their rooms—horses kick down their stall doors and go at each other like demons, for no reason, even poor old Tunzi. Marinesha says that Shadry wakes everyone every night, screaming that he is being buried alive. Why did Gatti Jinni throw a wine bottle at that street-singer yesterday? Why does the well water smell filthy-sweet as gangrene, and why won't the wind ever, ever stop? What is Karsh trying so hard to say to me—and why now, why now?—why do you have secrets with a fox? And Tikat, Tikat, what is *watching*? What is watching us all out of the wind and the well and the horses' eyes?"

I put my arm around his shoulders. He looked as surprised by the gesture as I felt. Rosseth always called a—a something, a *wishfulness*—from me that no one else has ever summoned, except Lukassa. It frightened me each time, but each time a bit less. I said, "I don't know. I was sure it must be my imagining."

Rosseth shook his head violently. "No, it is all real. Tikat, talk to me, let us put what knowledge we do have side by side. I will tell you what I almost see—you tell me what you think you imagine. I'll tell you what I begin to guess—you'll say what you—"

"—what I fear," I said, thinking of the wizard. Rosseth blinked in puzzlement. I said, "Never mind. Go on, Rosseth. Let's talk, then."

So we talked for a long time, longer than we ever had before, while spiking the last beam in place and plastering a mix of straw and horse dung over the roof to seal the cracks. We do it just so at home. I spoke of the fox being also Redcoat, and of my drowned Lukassa having been drawn up from the riverbed by Lal's song. Rosseth drew breath both times to give me the lie, but did not; no more than I when he told me about Nyateneri being no woman but a man named Soukyan, who had left two other men—fell, dire men—dead in the bathhouse. (Was it one such who touched me and left me unconscious in the corridor outside the wizard's room? I never knew.) He flushed and stammered over much of that, but I understood enough to pat his shoulder and nod slightly. In my village, one of our priests says that love between men is a great sin—the other argues that nothing at all is sinful except weak ale, overdone meat, and building a fire in any way but his. As for me, my notions in such matters are my notions.

"So what do we know, when all's said?" I asked at last. "We know that Lal and Soukyan came here in search of their friend, their master, and that they found him the prey of a wizard named Arshadin, more powerful than he. Agreed so far?"

Rosseth objected. "We don't know that Arshadin is the greater wizard. If this one were in his proper health, rested and strong, it might well be another story." Rosseth is very loyal.

"That's as may be," I said, "but it's Arshadin who keeps him from resting, who sends voices and visitations to plague him by night, if Marinesha's to be believed. So that makes Arshadin *his* master, by my count." Rosseth chewed his lower lip and looked stubborn. I said, "And if this Arshadin can do such wicked wonders, then he's like enough to be at the bottom of all else that's been bedeviling The Gaff and Slasher all summer." I realized that I had never spoken the inn's name since the day I arrived there, and suddenly I longed more than I can say for the world in which I had never known it.

Rosseth was nodding eagerly, beginning to speak, but I cut him off as coldly as I could. "Not that any of this is any of my concern. This midden-heap is your home, not mine, and there's my one great joy in life just now. Whatever happens or does not happen, whatever becomes of your squabbling little wizards, I'll be off where I belong, and never know." I stood up. "We're done—I am supposed to help Gatti Jinni in the storerooms."

Rosseth let me get to the door before he said, "Lukassa will be here." I began to answer, but he interrupted me as harshly as I had done to him. "And so will I be, and Marinesha, who has been kind to you. Will you truly never want to know what became of us, Tikat?"

Two years younger than I, and already going for the belly like a starving *sheknath*. We stared silently at each other until I looked down first. I said, "I will not leave until she is in a safe place, if there can be such a place for her. Afterward—why, afterward the Rabbit and I may as well go home as anywhere." Rosseth said nothing. I went on. "The rest of you must look after yourselves. I have no skill at loving more than one person at a time, and that is hard enough. Now I'm going to the storerooms."

I was already outside the smokehouse, closing my eyes against the onslaught of light, when he called to me. "Tikat? I have lived here all my life and never once called it home, not once. But you are right—it is my home, after all, and I will defend it as well as I can, and my friends, too. Thank you, Tikat, for teaching me." I did not turn, but kept walking toward the inn, uphill in the pounding sunlight.

The Potboy

That was the best time there ever was at that place, because Shadry used to fall asleep by noon, sprawled across his big chopping block like one of his own thick, slubbery sides of meat. Once he began snoring, he'd never stir until it was time to prepare the evening meal, if anyone had the strength to eat. Even so, none of the others ever dared to sneak out of the kitchen with me, not for so much as a quick squint at the guests, or to pet Rosseth's old donkey. They all curled themselves away in the darkest corners they could find and slept through the day like our master. Snoring exactly like him, too, some of them.

Not me. Each day, the moment Shadry's wet, squirmy mouth sagged open on his wrist, I was across the scullery and through the side door, already opening my own mouth to gasp even before the full morning hit me. I have never known heat like that: barely past sunrise and you'd feel the sweat begin to sizzle on your skin, like fat meat in the pan. I never saw such a sky, either—first white as bone, then white as ashes in the afternoon. At night, late, it turned a sort of white-streaky lavender, but that was as dark as it ever got; and day or night, indoors or out, we all went on turning and turning in the pan. Everything was the pan.

The scullery would have been cooler—the scullery was the nicest shelter of all, except for the wine cellar where fat Karsh napped out the worst part of the days. But I wouldn't have passed a single free second in that kitchen, not for anything in the world; and none of us except Shadry was allowed to go anywhere else in The Gaff and Slasher. So I usually stole off first to the stables and helped Rosseth with the horses.

Rosseth was my friend. He was years older, of course, grown up, and often he had too much work to do, or something on his mind, and then we couldn't talk about things the way we liked to. But he never got angry at me, and two times he let me hide in the hayloft and lied to Shadry when he came hissing after me, swinging his long arms. Rosseth never was afraid of Shadry, no matter what he did. I was always safe with Rosseth.

That day the horses lay in their straw and would not even stand up to be curried or have their feet seen to. Rosseth did what he could with them, and I carried water in and pushed fresh hay down from the loft. Then we rested in an empty stall, where we couldn't be seen from the door, and we talked for a while. I remember, I asked why it was so hot all the time, even at night, and Rosseth told me that it was because two great wizards were fighting in the sky. He made a whole story out of it for me, but I fell asleep in the middle, with my head on his arm.

I didn't get to sleep very long, because Tikat came in and woke me—he woke up Rosseth, too, I think—saying that heat or no heat, Karsh wanted a cart of market vegetables unloaded. I never liked Tikat. Not that he ever did me any harm—I just didn't like him. Sometimes I couldn't understand what he was saying, because of the southern way he talked, and when I could he was telling me to get back from there, get out of everybody's way. But he did point at his lunch—a winter apple and two whole *heshtis*, all crusty-brown with cheese—as he and Rosseth left, meaning for me to eat it. So he wasn't so bad, I suppose, for a southerner.

For the rest of that day, I dodged everywhere around The Gaff and Slasher, slipping back into the kitchen now and then to make sure that Shadry was still asleep. I hid in the smokehouse, the buttery, the bathhouse—even in the smelly little shrine place on the hillside—trying to follow the shadows as the sun moved. But after a while it seemed to me that the sun was hardly moving at all. I watched and watched it, looking through my fingers, and it didn't stir as much as the length of my thumbnail. From high noon it hung up above the stable, growing riper and heavier every minute, and brighter too, until it was almost white on the outside, white as daisies. But on the inside it was dark—all hard, swollen dark, like a yolk gone bad in the egg. I stopped looking at it when it went like that, but then I began to hear it *beating*, thumping like an iron heart—you could feel that slow clang everywhere, all the time, in your bones, in your eyes. And it never moved, that clanging sun.

I didn't know what to do. I wanted to find Rosseth, to show him what was wrong with the sun, but he was still busy with Tikat somewhere. Gatti Milk-Eye came out, and I talked with him a little, because he hates Shadry and wouldn't ever tell him about me running off from the kitchen. But all he could say, over and over, was how frightened he was of the new moon that night. Over and over, rolling his white eye—"I don't *like* it when there is no moon, no, I don't like it. There should always be a moon, just a little piece, so you can find your way between things. Not good to see the night without a moon." So it wasn't any comfort to be with him.

Then the old man in the red coat came, and that *was* a comfort. He came in the afternoon, late—on any other day, it would have been already twilight. That was his usual hour to walk out from Corcorua, where his grandson lived, and sit a while chatting and drinking in the taproom. I know that because Rosseth told me—I was only once in the taproom, to clean up after a fight—and because that old man talked with everybody, he knew everybody, even potboys. He had a funny voice that really hurt to listen to, as though it kept hitting some kind of crazy-bone inside your head. But everybody liked him, except fat Karsh.

When the old man saw me hanging about in the big shadows of the courtyard trees, he called my name, saying, "Little one, what are you doing so far from your kettles and cauldrons? Do you realize that the sun is refusing to set because it is so astonished to see you out in its light?" He gave me a dusty boiled sweet out of his coat pocket.

"No, it's not," I said. He didn't seem to mind the awful heat at all—it might have been any other evening, except that I'd have been in the kitchen, running and fetching, stirring and scouring, trying to keep one jump ahead of Shadry's long swinging arms. I said, "I don't know what's the matter with the sun or the weather or the people, but it's nothing to do with me. I just want it to stop."

He picked me up and swung me around in the air. He was very strong for somebody with white hair and thin old hands. He said, "Why, I can stop it, child, if that is what you wish. Shall I do that? Shall I argue with the sun and tell it to go to bed, so that *you* can get to your rest? Say the word and it shall be done." I nodded, and he said, "Well, then," and set me down, both of us laughing.

I went off a few steps and turned around again. I don't know why. He was already stumping toward the inn door—not the one to the taproom, but the big carved one for the paying guests. When I called to him, to remind him of his promise, he just kept walking. He didn't knock on the door, either, but pushed it open and went inside, bold as Karsh himself. The door slammed shut behind him, hard, without making a sound. I saw it.

Then right away the sky began to darken, and the sun stopped its awful slow clanging. Birds started making their night noises all at once. If I had turned my head, I know I would have seen the sun skidding down the sky, butter in the pan now, but I didn't turn. I just stood there with my eyes closed, and felt the stars coming out.

LAL

It was absurd. I was never so ashamed of myself. Here we were—Soukyan, Lukassa, Rosseth, and I—crowded together around *my friend*'s bed, just as though he were about to read us his testament before folding his hands on his chest and wafting politely off into the next world. In fact, we were five friends doing the best we could to say a hopeless, terrifying farewell; but what I remember best is the pain in my still-tender ribs from containing a torrent of schoolgirl giggles. No excuse, absolutely no excuse. I *think* only Soukyan noticed anything, but if they all had it would serve me right.

He had been gone from us all that day and the night before: not dead, not wandering in his mind, but far away on a frontier we could not begin to imagine, fighting back the new moon. There was never a chance of that, of course, not even for him. But he fought on anyway—unconscious, drooling, wasted to a new moon of a man himself, he lay on a mattress in a tiny, shabby room and fought for daylight, and lost.

The instant the sun passed from sight, he gave a small, quick gasp and opened his eyes. As though he had only been interrupted by a cough or a witless question, he said, "Now this is what you will need to do about the *gri-*

ga'ath." Of all that happened so soon afterward, of all that has happened to me since, nothing has ever been as frightening as those few words in that calm, rasping voice.

My friend said, "We have only a moment, so pay attention for once. There is no defeating or destroying a *griga'ath*—you are hearing me, aren't you, Lal? It is possible, however, to divert it briefly, and perhaps escape, if you all do exactly as I tell you." He looked around the darkening room. "Where is Tikat?"

Rosseth answered, his voice cracking hoarsely. "He is surely on his way—Karsh had him cleaning the sacrifice stones at the shrine. He will be here in a minute, I promise."

My friend reached out and put his trembling hand over Rosseth's hand. He said gently, "The *griga'ath* will destroy this place and everyone in it. You may be able to save a few people, I don't know. I will not be able to help you."

Soukyan was crying, not making a sound, standing with his shoulders back and one single tear at a time wandering down one side or the other of his nose. Lukassa's face, for a wonder, was pulsing with color, and her mouth was drawn tight and hard as *my friend* went on. "There are beings, as you know, who can only travel in a straight line—the simplest screen will head the worst of them off—and there are others who cannot cross running water. *Griga'aths* have no such weaknesses." He nodded toward a vase of silvery sweet-regrets on the table. "Fetch those to me, Lukassa. Quickly."

Marinesha had set them there that morning, wilted and dry before she ever picked them, but a find for all that, so deep in that evil summer. Along with the sweet-regrets (in the south they grow taller and darker, and are called windshadows), she had also placed two or three *shuli* flowers in the vase. *Shuli* are always the exact shade of the sky above them; these were completely colorless, warm to the touch even in water. *My friend* took the vase from Lukassa, though he seemed barely able to hold it upright. The flowers stirred feebly between his hands.

"These will not save you," he said. "The *griga'ath* will not recoil from them, shivering in a corner. But for perhaps an instant it may remember flowers. It may remember that it was human once."

He never gave us a chance to break down. I think none of us dared to look at one another—I certainly did not—and for my part I felt as though all the blood in my body had turned to tears. He said, "It will look like me. You *must* understand that, for your lives' sake. It will look exactly like me, and it will be hungry. Listen now. Throw the flowers in its path, vase and all—that had better be you, Soukyan—then turn and run. Do not look back, not even to aid each other. Do not meet the *griga'ath*'s eyes. Have you understood me?"

None of us could speak. I heard his impatient little sigh—familiar to me as my own breath, and as dear—and again I was oddly struck by the dry-eyed anger and resolve in Lukassa's face. *My friend* said, "You must not weep when I go—there will not be time," and at that moment the door opened and the old man in the red coat came sauntering in.

I know now about the fox. I know what he was, and I know how he and Soukyan met, and what they meant and did not mean to each other. But at that time I made no connection between him and courtly, over-jolly old Redcoat, and I was astonished to see Soukyan whirl on him furiously, shouting in a sibilant tongue that I should have recognized from hearing him speaking to the fox, that very first night. Redcoat paid him no mind at all, but beamed benignly on us all and started toward the bed. I barred his way, without knowing why.

"Let me pass, foolish woman," he ordered me, in a voice that started out as Redcoat's fox-bark and became something else, something I had also heard before. Behind me, *my friend* said softly, "Let him pass, Lal." Then I knew who it was, and I stepped aside.

He did not shift shape until he was standing close beside the bed, looking down at *my friend* out of the fox's yellow eyes. They were the first to change, turning the unfocused, pupilless blue that I remembered. The rest of the metamorphosis seemed to happen slowly—hideously, languorously slowly—yet when it was over, it was impossible to believe that anyone but Arshadin had ever been there, saying in his own flat, arid voice, "I told you long ago we would meet like this at the last. You cannot say I never told you."

My friend answered him, infuriatingly calm as ever. "Do not preen yourself quite yet, Arshadin. Great as you are, and weak as I am, still it took you long and long to pry the sun from my grasp and force it down into darkness. And even now you cannot kill me, but must await the new moon. I would have brought a book, or a bit of needlework, if I were you."

But there was no baiting Arshadin, not this time. Bleakly placid, he replied, "I can wait. You know better than any how I can wait. It is the others who cannot."

"Then they will have to learn," *my friend* retorted. "I am better acquainted than you with those *others* of yours, and there's not one would dare try conclusions with me as I lie here. Come, draw up a chair, let's talk a little last while. Indulge an old pedant," he added, and I caught my breath, thinking, *he has a plan, oh he has, I must be ready.* Even then I would have believed that he knew something Uncle Death did not know.

There was a stool, but Arshadin never looked at it, nor at anyone else in the room. He remained standing, blank and heavy and damp as so much cheese; but his attention was such a physical reality that it seemed a visible beast, crouching red-jawed over *my friend* on the bed. He said stolidly, "What have we to talk about, you and I? I know what you know, and you must finally understand what I have been trying to tell you since the first day I was your student." The word broke free of his taut, flat lips with such force that *my friend* put up a hand as though to ward it off. "Your student," Arshadin said again. "Your disciple, your apprentice, your anointed crown prince, your inheritor. I would have sold myself gladly to the vilest west-country slaver to be rid of those wondrous birthrights forever. Do you hear me now, now, at last, my master? Do you hear me now?"

My friend did not answer. Soukyan growled very softly and took a step toward Arshadin. I caught his arm. Rosseth kept glancing at the door, plainly needing Tikat to come through it. As for Lukassa, she never took her eyes off Arshadin: their expression was so rapt that she might have been gazing at her lover, if you ignored the set of her mouth. She looked far older than she was.

Arshadin did not notice her. Beyond the window, the last stains of twilight had already bled away into a strange, pale dark: not the transparent summer night of the north, but a watery false dawn, gray and evasive as quicksilver. There was a light bent through it, faintly brightening the room though no candle had been lit. Rosseth's body was utterly rigid, his eyes too wide and still. I put my arm around him, so that he could let himself tremble against me.

On the bed, *my friend* mumbled, "I had very little to teach you, Arshadin, but that little will cost you dear when you learn it at last, at other hands." His voice was fraying, his words beginning to blear into each other. He said, "You were never my student—that was the mistake. I should have mocked and browbeaten you, riddled you without letup, insulted you, challenged you morning to night, just as I treated Lal and Soukyan and all the others. But *they* were students—*you* were my equal, from that first day, and I let you know it. That was the mistake." He had no strength even to shake his head, but barely managed to turn it from this side to that. "Yet what else should one do with an equal? I had no practice at it—perhaps you will deal more wisely in your turn." The last words might have been drops of rain in dry leaves.

I thought he might be dead then, but Arshadin knew better. He leaned down over him and shouted at his closed eyes, "If you thought me your equal, why did you never trust me with those things I needed to know? Why were you so sure that I would use them for ill? I was young, and there were choices yet before me—there were other ways, other journeys, there *were*!" Once again, for an instant, I saw his thick, empty face turn almost incandescent with old pain, almost beautiful with bitterness. Then he caught himself and went on stiffly, "Much could have been different. We were not doomed to end here."

My friend opened his eyes. When he spoke this time, his voice was different: weary beyond telling, but calm and clear and strangely young, as the nearness of death often makes voices sound. He said, "Oh, yes, yes, we were, Arshadin. There was never but the one road for you, being who you are. Being who I am, I loved you because of what you are. So we were doomed to this, you see, it did indeed have to happen so." He reached up and took sudden frail hold of Arshadin's right hand. He said, "And yet, knowing, I did love you."

Arshadin snatched his hand away as if the old man's touch had seared it through. "Who ever cared about that?" he demanded. "Your love was your own affair, but I had a right to your faith. Deny it and you'll die lying." He was screaming now, more human in his fury and pettishness than I could have imagined him. "By every filthy god and demon, I had a right to your faith!"

"Yes," *my friend* answered him softly, "yes, you did. Yes. I am sorry." I had never heard him say such a thing before. "But I must tell you even so, you were a fool to trade your heart's blood for your heart's desire. It is an old bargain, and a bad one. I expected you to make a better deal."

Arshadin made no reply. *My friend* beckoned Soukyan and me closer, and we came, standing together across the bed from Arshadin. I could smell Soukyan's hair and the unmistakable cold fragrance of *my friend*'s dying. Arshadin was sweating heavily, but there was no smell to it at all.

My friend looked toward the window and nodded,

greeting the new moon. To Soukyan he said only, "Remember about the flowers," and to me, more sharply, "*Chamata*, whatever you may be plotting, give it up right now." Lukassa and Rosseth pushed in between us, clutching blindly for his hands. He used the last of his earthly strength to push them away, whispering, "No, no, no, don't come near me, no." We moved back from his bedside, even Arshadin, and he said a name I did not know, and died.

I recall certain things very clearly from that moment. I recall that the four of us immediately stared, not at his body, but at Arshadin, as though—logically enough—he were the one bound to change into a demon. He looked strangely startled and uncertain himself at first, but then he sketched a couple of hasty signs over the bed, and gabbled some words that made my skin prickle and my ears ache down inside, the way such things always seem to do. Rosseth put his hands to his own ears, poor child. I pushed him further behind me.

Over Arshadin's shoulder, out of that pallid night, eyes began to glitter at the window: first two, then four, then many on many, like frost forming on the glass. Not one pair was like another, except in the shining malice of their gaze. Arshadin turned and spoke to them—to them, and to something else, something surging deep below and beyond them, the great wave that was dashing these wicked sparklings at the window. He cried out, "Behold, he is yours, he is in your power for all time! I have done as I pledged, and our covenant is ended. Give me back my blood, as you promised!" If there was an answer, I never heard it, because it was then that *my friend*, who was dead, stirred and muttered and slowly opened his eyes.

We looked away instantly, as we had been warned. I cannot speak for the others, but I looked back just as quickly, sideways, because I had to. He—no, *it*, I have trouble saying that even now—stood up on the bed and stretched itself, making a soft, thoughtful sound. It might have been a child in a nightgown waking to a new day.

Then it stepped to the floor and walked toward Arshadin. It was smiling just a little, just enough for me to see the fire behind its black teeth.

Arshadin looked a bit flustered, but not frightened—I will give him that, and admire him for it. If he had expected whatever moved beyond those eyes at the window to materialize, thank him graciously and relieve him of his fearful creation, he showed no sign of any alarm. He spoke haughtily to the *griga'ath*—this time in the language wizards speak together, which I can follow somewhat—bidding it to know him and do him honor. Even in such plain speech, his words shook the room, as though the walls themselves were trying to obey.

Walls heed wizards. *Griga'aths* do not. It kept coming, shuffling on through one sky-splitting spell after another as the wizard backed and backed away. It still looked like the man we had known: it did not grow an inch taller or more massive, nor did it sprout rows of extra heads and arms, as demons are always drawn in my country. But it smiled flames, and burning, stinking yellow tears spilled out of its eyes, and it reached out both beckoning hands, and it walked silently toward Arshadin.

And even then he faced it, calling down power to make the poor old Gaff and Slasher rock to its wine cellars—we could hear beams cracking above us, windows exploding in other rooms, doors slamming and slamming themselves in pieces. Courage must have nothing to do with having blood, or a soul, because Arshadin was a terribly brave man. But he might have been ten times more brave and a hundred times the wizard he was, and it would have meant nothing to the thing that had been *my friend*. It kept walking toward him.

And we four? Soukyan never looked once at the vase of wildflowers, and I neither fled nor even thought to harry Rosseth and Lukassa into flight. A wizard had wasted his desperate dying counsel on us: we were separated from one another as though by miles and centuries, each alone forever in a lonely place with the *griga'ath*. For my part, there was no room anywhere in me for anything but the impossible truth of the being that stalked Arshadin, its faint smile flickering over the shuddering walls. So I know only that I gaped and gasped and stood petrified where I was; more than this I cannot tell you.

Arshadin was a proud man, as well as brave, for he did not call again for aid until the *griga'ath* had brought him to bay against the window. Then he wheeled, turning his back on it, on us, on everything but the night, and he shouted, still in the formal tongue of wizards, "Will you dare use me and abandon me so? Nay, but I've my own employment for such a creature. Give me back my blood, or I'll find such occupation for him as may make you wish you had kept faith with me. And so be advised, my lords."

Bravado? Perhaps. He would not turn from the window, even with the *griga'ath*'s hands almost on him. I think that it did touch him, but I will never know. The night stepped into the room, not only at the smashed window, but spilling through every crack, separation, and nail-hole in the walls, through the exhausted pores of the wood. As it must have done when Arshadin summoned it in the tower, it puddled together in a corner, slowly forming a shape that was round at the top and broken into jagged, twisted shadows below, the whole barely as high as Rosseth's chin. As in the tower, it had become a passage to somewhere else, a dark archway that drew my vision in and would not let it go again. A wind began to stir under the arch: a wind from somewhere else, smelling of burning blood.

The darkness spoke to us. What it said—not in words, but singing in the roots of my hair, writing with broken glass on the underside of my skin—*"Come to me. Be with me. Be me."* I obeyed immediately, without a moment's hesitation, without any sense of having a choice, or wanting one. Soukyan was beside me on my left, and Rosseth took my right hand. Lukassa cried out, but the sound seemed to come from very far away. We were marching straight into that black court, and in that instant I saw, or felt, or knew what was on the other side. It is not what you think, that place.

But that is not to be talked about here, for the darkness did keep its word to Arshadin, after all. What the darkness had come for was not any of us but *my friend,* in this form that it could swing like a hammer against the foundations of the world. It lost interest in us and stopped calling. Do you know what that was like? It was like being rescued from drowning just as you have begun to feel so sleepily peaceful; it was like being snatched back from a high place just as the whisper has finally convinced you that it is bound to happen anyway, so you might as well let go now. One more moment and I, at least, would have been truly lost. I am grateful. I know I should be more grateful than I am.

The darkness was calling to the *griga'ath* now: *"Be with me, be me, be me."* It turned swiftly from Arshadin, making a sound I could feel but not hear, like the deep whine of the air that comes before an earthquake. Soukyan and Lukassa and Rosseth averted their faces, but this time I did not. This had nothing to do with courage or defiance—I simply froze, too dazed and confused not to look into the eyes of the *griga'ath.*

They were not his eyes. They were green, yes, but it was the green of the deepest northern seas, the icy, oozy green of the weeds that come up with your anchor from those unhealed places that have never seen the sun since the world began. They were hunting the sun, those eyes, they meant to eat the sun; but infinitely more terrifying was the fact that nothing else of him had changed. *"It will look like me,"* he had warned us, and so it did—exactly like him, only more so, in the way that trusted faces so often become hugely, monstrously familiar when my dreams turn nightmare. Perhaps we are all, even wizards, no more than faded sketches of the good we contain, the evil we might have done: if that is so, what faced me now was the original of *my friend,* the sum of his nature. He was all himself, all his possible self, and he was nothing, nothing but destruction. No, I did not turn to stone seeing him, as people do in the old tales; but neither did I escape whole. And the rest is my business.

The *griga'ath* paid no attention to me. It moved past me, still wearing the face and form—and even the smell, like an old boat in the sun—of someone I loved. Fire was just beginning to leak through the body now, twinkling coyly between the ribs and under the arms. *Griga'aths* blaze without burning, eternally; in time they become exactly like stars cloaked in human skin, shattering and swallowing what they come near. It halted a step before the darkness, turning *my friend*'s body this way and that: strangely uncertain, even looking back once. I hid my face from it, like the others.

Someone was pounding furiously on the real door of the real room. As though the noise had suddenly tipped the balance, the *griga'ath* took a single stride forward and passed from this world. I could still see it for what seemed a very long time, glowing steadily brighter as it grew smaller, spinning slowly away down the black archway that runs between what we know and what we cannot bear to know. I think I cried after it; if I did, the sound was lost when the door gave way and Karsh lunged into the room. Tikat was just behind him.

The Innkeeper

I suppose I should give thanks that the bottles hit the Kinariki wagoner and not me when they toppled from the taproom shelves. The Kinariki was paying his score at the time: his hand pulled across mine—courteously leaving his change behind—as he widened his eyes and sank to the floor without a sound. Do the gods expect my gratitude for that? Very well. I give thanks.

And that is all the gods get from me for the rest of my life, and you may tell them so if you're much in the habit of chatting them up. Between one minute and the next, The Gaff and Slasher, my home for thirty years, came crashing to ruination around me, as I knew would happen the day I let those three women cross my threshold. The bottles were followed by every mug and wine glass I owned, and then by the hanging lamps. I thought *javak* at first, though we haven't had one of those corkscrew storms since Rosseth was small. But when the two windows blew out—not in, out—as though they'd never been there, and the shelves behind the bar started pulling loose with a long squeal of old nails in old planks, I knew that this was no *javak*. The beer pumps were groaning and bucking under my hand, trying to plunge free of their sockets; the few rusty tag-ends of armor I had anchored to the walls to keep people from stealing them shot across the room like crossbow bolts. A hide-factor from Devarati got hit that time, but I think he recovered.

Earthquake? *Earthquake?* There wasn't so much as a twitch out of that floor—my customers, the conscious ones, were down flat, clinging to it with their fingernails, like lizards to a wall, while benches and broken glass and overturned tables hurtled past them. Within thirty seconds, I was the one object still standing in the taproom, supported by nothing but outrage. For I never doubted the source of this catastrophe for one instant. Storms and volcanoes and family spats of the gods be damned—the cause, the bloody *cause,* was only a few bloody inches above my head, and I was already on my way up there even though I may not have seemed to be moving at all. I was just waiting for my feet to catch up with my fury.

Tikat staggered through the outside door just then, crouching low to stay on his own feet. When I came out from behind the bar to meet him, I felt like a very small boat pushing off from shore into a howling rapids. Tikat was yapping something at me and pointing upwards. I couldn't hear him in the confusion, but I knew he must be asking about his mad white Lukassa. I shook my head and shouted back, "Where's the boy? Have you seen the damned boy?"

He never bothered to answer, but only reeled on by me, treading on customers and armor bits alike, slipping in the puddles of mingled ale and wine, heading for the stair. I scrambled after him, pushing him out of the way well before we reached the landing. No one was going to break down *that* door but me.

TIKAT

Down in the taproom it was bad enough. Even with the windows gone, the pressure around me was so great that it was like being under water when I dived and dived for Lukassa. I found myself holding my breath for fear of drowning, and pushing the air away with my spread arms as I struggled forward. But on the stair there was a hot, stinking wind blowing straight down, battering Karsh and me from wall to railing while the steps themselves flew apart under our feet. We seemed to be making no headway at all: now we were birds beating against a storm, flying slowly backward, counting it progress to lose only a little ground. How long this went on, I cannot tell you.

I think today—I say I *think*—that I might well have given up then, but for Karsh. Not that he spared me even a glance after he thrust me aside, let alone any encouragement; indeed, he missed his footing once and lurched full into me, and would have had the two of us bouncing all the way down those splintering steps if I had not been able to catch hold of him and brace myself in time. But he never lost heart or looked back, that fat, roaring man. He bent his fleshy neck and bowed his shoulders, and lumbered ahead, heaving and cursing, hacking out a way through the wind. I followed, gratefully riding his wake, unable to imagine what could be driving him on so savagely. Because it was Karsh, you see. If it had been anyone else, surely I would have understood, but it was Karsh.

On the landing he paused for a moment, shaking himself heavily, and I saw his face, huge with that pale rage that takes him over when nothing is going as he would have it. The blue eyes were darkening as I watched, turning almost lavender; his teeth were set savagely in his lower lip, which was bleeding. Then he was off again, charging along a corridor choked with falling plaster and roiling dust and shrieking half-clad guests trampling each other to reach the stairs. I was knocked down myself, almost immediately, but managed to roll aside and get to my feet by climbing up and over someone in a purple night-robe. The hallway was booming and rippling, like the metal sheets those actors used to use for thunder. I stumbled along, arms across my face, toward the *tafiya*'s room.

Karsh was already there, hammering on the door, rattling the knob, pounding again, then beginning to heave his whole body against it: one slow, muffled thump after another. For once there was no breath in him for bellowing—I could hear it wheeze out each time he smashed himself into the thick old wood. I was not quite up with him when the door finally burst open and we fell through.

At the far end of the room there was nothing. There was an emptiness. No, listen, don't interrupt, listen to me. The emptiness was a mouth: you could see its edges writhing and folding like lips, beginning to close, and the foul wind seethed between them. Far away, or far in, or far down, a bright, bright spark tumbling forever, blazing bravely in the void. I knew what it was.

Lukassa was standing with her back to me, near the empty bed. There were others in the room, but I only saw her. She did not turn at the noise when Karsh and I broke in, but began to walk toward that black mouth that was closing more quickly now. Her steps were as light as they had always been when she came to meet me, never quite running, but running in her heart and her eyes. She was gone into the emptiness before I could call; and before I could reach it myself, it had snapped shut and vanished, leaving nothing behind but a sagging, crumbling wall in a little wrecked room full of the sound of her name.

LUKASSA

I am not Lukassa.

I am no one.

No one can pass the gates of death twice. I am no one. I walked through, and they waited for me. They do not want to wait, but I will make them.

Cold, cold, cold, like the river. Someone was calling, is calling me, far behind on the edge of Lukassa. But I was not Lukassa then. I am a drawing that has been scratched out, scrawled over, erased again. Far ahead, a star, singing, promising to tell me my name if I can catch it in time. Is that why I am here, was here? I should hurry. Did I hurry?

Death is a nowhere lined with lightning. I remember. There is cold nowhere under my feet, but I walked swiftly, because I remember the way. There are faces now, there were faces before, flowing by in the dark, between me and the star. When I die the first time, I will see those same faces.

Down here in the riverbed, it is quiet as quiet. Above me, on the surface, the water snarls and tears, as it will tear me when I fall to its jaws. But in the riverbed, I looked up through stillness and watch the faces flowing past, so many heavy, weary village faces that should not smile at me with such tender knowledge. They should not do that. I am no one.

Beyond them, my star. I brush the faces away and climb over the water, over the beanfields and thatched roofs, and I follow the singing of the star. If I walk without tiring, without thinking, without expectation, so very gradually the star draws nearer. I remember.

This is different. Why is this different? Death is death, but something is different, the darkness. I can see great yellow claws smashing through from the other side, ripping down and down, and a greenish glow beyond. The claws withdraw, strike again, they leave simmering weals across the darkness, like the ones on his back when his uncle will beat him for stealing fruit. Beat whom? The faces begin to snap their jaws as they hiss by. There were so many, sometimes they hide the star.

Why must I still hear him? It is noisy here, not like the riverbed, with the faces coming at me like lances now, with the thing on the other side of the dark chuckling to itself as it strikes and strikes, and the darkness growling in pain, louder each time the yellow claws slash down. And even so I heard him calling from far away, farther away than anything, calling that name he will call me. That name that is not, was never, mine, me.

I must listen to the star, nothing else. The star had a woman's voice, a low voice, city-rough, with a foreign lilt. I lose the star often, because the darkness is thrashing and convulsing all around me, but I could always hear it singing, clear as morning wind. One day I will catch up with it, if it keeps singing, and then it will tell me my name.

This time it was very different, being dead. This time death is seething, bustling with so much movement and color and earthly to-do. It might almost be another marketplace, except for who was tending the stalls, and what might be for sale there. There will not be words or thoughts for such beings, such things, but that makes no matter, because they were not real. The riverbed is real.

As I pass they will come after me, those beasts of fire

and filth who jabber and coo and tear at my shadow, because they have none themselves. No matter. This death is all shadow; this death was like the hand pictures that someone used to make for whom? Thin twisting fingers sending smoky monsters stalking across what smudgy plaster wall with the long crack near the broom closet? This death is a false, shabby country, peeling back, peeling away, layer on layer, under the yellow claws. And even the thing outside is nothing but loud shadow when I will face it at last in the rubble of the darkness. The claws are soft and puckered like gone-bad vegetables, the blood-wet chuckle a senile cough. No matter, pass on.

Is the star nothing but shadow, too? With the darkness raked to shreds, a low, thick sky remained, the color of the claws. The star seems larger, nearer, moving sluggishly, fighting against the stickiness of the sky. It was a man, the star, not a woman. He burns so brightly, no wonder that I will see him clearly from so far away, singing and demanding. What must I do when I reach him? I could not remember, but I know.

Something is here. Something is here that is not shadow. Behind all the foolish racket and show, there was a waiting, a something that quickly drops its puppets and slips away when I come near. Did I ever find it? It wanted the star, it is moving toward the star, like me. Real as the riverbed, it sidles toward the star.

"Show yourself," I said, but it will not. I say, "Show yourself, why be afraid? This is your play, not mine." But it lets me just so close, shuffling through the crackly wrack of lath and plaster universes, before I can feel it slinking off after the star again. This made me angry, because although it never caught the star, it will drive it forever out of my reach. I have forever, but the star does not. How can I know that?

The riverbed will be a better place than here. Worlds underfoot like children's toys, and nothing true in any one of them except the star and me, and that sly, sliding other just ahead of me. And *he* still calls so loudly, constantly braying that name that I am not across endless counterfeit heavens and hells. Ashy creatures made of dead wet leaves roused at the noise; gold and scarlet butterflies with long thin fish-teeth will swirl and snuffle around my face; things like shambling hillsides move in silently behind me. Things like men and women made all of twilight come twining about me and dancing on, looking back and weeping when I will not follow. Smothering tides of stagnant fog hide them then, barring my way. But the star summons me, and I pass on.

Pass on to what? and where? and has all this already been? The star drifts backward toward me so slowly, and that other prowls sideways off to the side, unseen, breathing. Suddenly there will be no faces, no more carnival ogres, no more painted scenery: every color but absence has run away like rain, leaving a little waxen starlight over a ribbon of nowhere, and me between. In this last emptiness, three small sounds: the angry singing ahead, the calling so far behind, and the soft rough breath matching my pace. A thousand years, ten thousand, ten thousand thousand.

How can he keep calling so; how can I hear him? I lay back down in the riverbed, just for a moment, to see the other faces again, but they were gone, too. Even so, it will be hard for me to rise and walk on after the star, although I cannot grow tired. I think I wish I could be tired, could be hot or cold or angry or afraid. How good to be afraid. But I had something to do, and only the star can tell me what it is. *Why did he keep calling that name?*

Was I singing? Have I been the one singing, all these centuries, trudging behind my own song?

"Some say *yes*,
and some say *no*,
and that is how it was meant to go.
Some say *no*,
and some say *yes*,
and that's the way the gods do bless.

Some have more, and some have less,
and some say *no,* and some say *yes,*
days without end, world without cess . . ."

It was a children's rhyme, but what children? Cousins, someone's silly cousins, they used to chant that sort of nonsense. But the star? Was the star never singing, never? Was it always me, singing him back toward me, as what someone will sing me up out of the riverbed? *Vegetables. She sang vegetables.*

So close now that I can see that there is no star, but only the man, an old man, falling across this old, old sky. He will smile and hold up his hands, showing me the flames oozing from under his fingernails. The flames see me, too—they beckon, laughing, reaching for my hands. The man has a beautiful face, wise and eager. He spoke to me, but I can never hear his words, because the fire under his tongue gets in the way. But I did not need to hear him. I know my task now.

When I touch his hand, he will be free of the sky and the fire as well, free of whatever this pale place wants from him. We go back together then, back to the riverbed. It is quiet there, and the water will heal his burning. I stand on tiptoe to touch his flaming hand.

And then. There.

It stands between the old man and me, and its voice, its voice is all there ever was. It says, *Mine.*

I cannot see, I cannot think. *Mine.* My eyes must be bleeding, my ears, there is blood running inside my head. The voice pierced me here, here, here—*Mine. Mine. Mine. Mine*—until I crumble down, covering myself, trying to scream, "Yours, yes, yes, he is yours, I am yours!" But the words refused to come out of me. I have something to do, and the words know it. *Mine, mine,* but I cannot give in, I was not permitted. I stand up.

This is what I will see.

It looks almost human at first. It is tall, naked, hollow-chested, with big bony shoulders that tip up at the ends.

Thin smears of no-color hair. Huge eyes in a head too small for the too-thick neck: beautiful shapeless eyes like flowers, like splashes of pond water in the sun. Long three-fingered hands; no ears, none. Maggot-white skin, drawn tight and twitching around a wet blue mouth. The mouth is full of tiny raspy teeth, swirling all the way back into the throat, blue and green. Even the lips are jeweled with them, even the mildewy tongue. It cannot make words, that round brilliant mouth, yet one came slicing at me, over and over, days without end, world without cess. *Mine. Mine.*

I put my hands over my ears, though it will not help. I say, "No."

Mine. A hot needle in the marrow of my bones, but I did not fall again. My bones answer, "No. He belongs to me." No one belongs to me, because I am no one, but that is what my bones will say. "You cannot have him. I have come to take him back to his own place. Stand aside, you."

Again I reach out toward the burning old man—again he offers me his fire-nailed hand—and again that word flays my mind as though that tongue had licked across it. *Mine!* But for a moment the voice itself will be somehow different—almost puzzled, almost uncertain, the demand almost a question. Another word then, a new scream in my bones. *Bargain.*

Someone answered. "*He* made no bargain. You have no claim on him." My own voice, shivering naked at the end of everything. I reach once more to take the old man's hand. I can hear a greedy watching in my head, but no more words, not yet.

The hand burns fiercely in mine without burning me. Pale black smoke goes up where they join, but I felt only something alive moving softly between our palms. The old man will look at our two hands together and bend his head, solemn-swift, to kiss mine. *That* burns, and I try to snatch my hand away, but he comes with it, part of me, grinning. He is not what I thought, not what I thought at all. Yet I still had something to do, something for him, with him—but if it is not to find the quiet riverbed again, what can it be?

I must act as though I knew. I must move. There is no left or right, up or down here—I might have spun in a circle, stood on my head, and not known it—but any road away from nothing must be the right one. Keeping a firm grip on that hand, feeling the fire beating like a bird's heart behind the papery skin, I turned to start back the long way I came.

Fiery fingers will close on my wrist, still without hurting, but pulling me to a stop. The old man kept grinning, mocking me, waiting. Behind him, *it*, waiting, the round blue mouth pulsing like another kind of heart, in and out, in and out. When I look straight at it, I will feel my own heart slowing, my blood drifting backwards. They mean me fear, but I am no one, I am dead—who are they to make me afraid? I pull back on the old man's arm, hard.

"You are to come home now," I said, just as though he were a straying animal—or whose gentle drunken father? I say, "We are for the riverbed, you and I."

He came quietly along with me for a few steps—while *it* watches, not moving—and then he will wheel on me and spread his arms wide, putting my hands aside like a child's hands. One more smile, rustling and crawling with flame, and he explodes out of any human size, steepling up into the haze above us so fast and so high that it can barely keep him in, no more than my eyes can. He spills out, spills over, filling the night with himself, with a silent, rushing howl that swallowed me like the river. I tumble as helplessly through his unending rage as he through the pale old sky.

But he cannot harm me. I have been twice through the gates of death, once of my own choice, and whatever can harm me is not here. So I will stretch up again for his bonfire hand, and I will shout up to ears like sunset clouds, "You are to come with me. I will take you home."

A year later, or a month later, or a few minutes, he is

back at a proper human size, seeing me for the first time out of curious, terrible eyes, green as the air before a great storm. He made a queer sound, a low hiss, hoarse and warning and sad. I say, "You do not belong here, and no more do I. You know this."

And now *it* will move. Now *it* came gliding on long bird legs that bend backward as well as forward, straddling our way, the blue mouth in the twitchy white face pushing out, alive by itself, nuzzling toward me until I want to hide from it behind the burning old man. But I remember that I held my ground, only shrinking inside. You have to do that, or the children will be cruel. I will say again, "You have no claim. Let us pass."

Bargain. Our bargain. Every word brands itself into the bones of my skull, never to heal. My own words answer, "Our bargain? Speak of that with him, the other one—there was your bargain." I do not understand them, the words, but the old man will look at me and laugh redly and soundlessly. He strides by *it* without giving it another glance, without waiting for me.

A three-fingered hand reaches out and down, groping for my shoulder. I could not let it touch me, not that hand, not seeing what I see slow and sticky on the long white palm. I flinch away, but the hand pointed past me, pointed ahead where there should be a horizon but is only a little colorless roiling where nothing meets nowhere. *It* means us to go. I thought that. I look back once and follow the old man.

They will appear all at once, all together, rising into the dark like star-pictures. Not one was like another, nor any like *it*, and yet they are the same, all different bits of the same nature. One was no bigger than I, human-shaped, blind, fringed with tiny human arms and legs like an insect. One is like a great rearing thundercloud down to the middle, and all throbbing red slime below; and there will be one as beautiful as a beautiful fish, in its way, but so thin and transparent that I can see the busy little shadows skipping inside it. Another like a heap of jewels, with glinting eyes scattered among the stones; another was nothing more than a bright tracery in the air, a star-picture done with goldleaf and blood. Another then, and another, and another, and no way around them for the old man and me. They are here, and they wait in the riverbed, too, and in my bones, forever. *Our bargain. Our bargain.*

The strange part is that the terrible crying is no worse for me when they are together than when they are only *it* alone. One nature, one desire, it must be. For the rest, all I knew was that they desire evil—though I cannot know what evil means anymore, nor if they know themselves—and that they are real, whether I see them truly or not. And that they must have the burning old man.

"Well," I will say to him. "We have a long journey to go, and they are in our way."

This time he was the one who took my hand. We walk toward them, and they thicken to meet us, without moving, as frightened creatures can make themselves look bigger. Beside me, the old man raised his other hand, leveling all five fingers at them. The fire under his nails spreads out around us, blue and green; the flames have the raging heads of animals—*sheknaths, nishori,* rock-*targs*—and they grow larger with every step we take. Those waiting will not take even one step backward, but they were afraid all the same. *It* is afraid of him.

The old man smiles for them, letting the doors of his furnace face swing apart just a little, to show what lies beyond. I said, "By your leave," as someone will be taught to say politely, and they part, too, just enough to let us into their midst. Then they closed around us, towering together out of sight, talking hotly together in my bones. But the fire-animals surround us, too, and they talk their own talk, they hiss and snarl their own by-your-leaves; and where we will walk there was always just room for us to pass.

Suddenly it has all been too much for someone dead. Too strange, too lonely, too mad. If not for the old man, I think I might lie down, here on the other side of never, lie down here among the bright-eyed stones and the whispering pairs of insect legs and the tips of folded wings and let *it* do as it will do with me. But *it* wanted only the old man—why I do not know, nor why this is not to be allowed. Only that it is not to be allowed. I hold onto his hand, fluttery with fire, and he looked down at me and smiles his ravaging smile, and so we will pass on.

Bargain, bargain. Our bargain. Evil *it* may be, but evil can suffer injustice, too. The wail of wrong follows me still, long after *it* has stopped following, long after we were through and past and on our way back to the riverbed. Or did we go back to the gates of death themselves, or even beyond them, where the calling has at last ended, too? Where is the old man supposed to be, besides not with *it*? Where does he want to be? Each time I look sideways at him, he will be looking at me, and though his face was solemn each time, the fire behind his skin is laughing. It sounds like paper, someone wrapping presents. How do I know this? Who wraps presents for no one?

On the road back—or was it forward? was it to or from?—we will follow no songs, meet no hungry shadows, journey through no beast-markets that turn out to be worlds that turn out to be all sawdust and broken pots. Only the two of us, traveling silently in darkness forever, and I did not have forever anymore. Now I am tired, as I could not be before, and the longer we walk the less I knew where we are going. I did not know before, but then I will have the singing to follow, and the star. Now I almost wish that someone were still bellowing my name, which is not my name. I could follow that, wherever it leads, and then the old man would follow me. But the dark is drawing in and in—I can feel it nudging at my shoulders—and it is laughing, too, and now I will begin to be afraid. As though I were alive.

When he turns I was ready, even so. I said, "No. We are for the riverbed. No. You need my help if you mean to find peace." But he will rear up over me, fire racing from one hand to another to soar out behind him in a blue-white mantle, while he opens his mouth to chuckle flaming venom straight into my eyes. I put my hands up vainly in front of me, and I cried out for someone, because I am at the end of endless night and the end of myself. But who comes when no one calls?

THE FOX

*M*an-shape! He stole the man-shape!

Felt it go, *felt* it go—a cold whisper, knife slipping out of a wound. Never, never, never before, no one dares such tampering, such thieving. Beautiful Grandfather man-shape, beautiful white mustache, red soldier's coat, such smiling cheeks, such bright listening eyes, beautiful freedom to stand, sit, talk, laugh, sing, drink red ale—all gone, all scooped away, and insides with it. Rap on my belly, hear the echo, that was Grandfather man-shape. Gone, gone.

The other. Not wicked old magician, that other, his master, the one who held him prisoner. Snatches the sun first, now the man-shape, *hoho, what can a poor fox do against such power?* Hoho, more than he likes, foolish magician. Not even old nothing ever touches man-shape, not once in so much coming and going on its errands in this world. Oh foolish, careless, vain magician, this is no fox to trouble so lightly.

But this is a fox to sit under Marinesha's *naril* tree and think very fast in a very little moment. Sundown at last, still hot as one fox's plundered heart, no wind at all, not under the tree. I sit watching until the inn's windows come drifting out at me, bright and hard as snowflakes.

Chimney dribbles down roof, roof ripples sweetly—sad, sad for nice warm pigeons—eaves wriggle like eyebrows. Crashes, shatterings, screamings inside, fat innkeeper roaring like *sheknath* looking for lady *sheknath.* Lightnings raking down the sky straight for magician's room—it is all in there, in that room, wind and fire and darkness, yesyesyes. Man-shape, too.

So, fox—fox forever now, unless so quick and so clever—back to that room? Yes, and yet. No time, no time for *and yet*—but what is this? The little white mad burning one. Lukassa. Away in the wind, beyond the wind, far beyond friends, innkeepers, pet foxes, Lukassa where humans are not to go. Away there in that place, and after a *griga'ath* that was wicked old magician. Lukassa.

No concern of mine, no more than magicians' wars. My business is all with man-shape, all. Let them spit their spells at each other, let them smash each other's playthings, conjure each other back and forth across this world, that—only let them keep magic hands off what belongs to old nothing and me. Old nothing says, "Find him. Find the thief. Explain to him." So. Lukassa is Lukassa's business now.

And yet.

Old nothing and I, we have no friends. Agreements, yes—conveniences, yes—friends, no, not possible. Hard enough telling humans apart, never mind feelings, wonderings. Nyateneri, Lukassa—a nice saddlebag, nice warm arms at night, no more. Kiss nose as much as they like, who cares? Not possible.

"Find," says old nothing. More crashes, more shrieks, more windows turn to snow. Fat innkeeper's inn twists and grinds in the earth. People shaken, spilled out into the courtyard, running, fighting, falling down. Up in magician's room, backed against empty, splintered windowframe. Him, that other. Face says *I win, I win,* shoulders not so sure. Old nothing: "There. Now."

Lukassa is Lukassa's business.

Help her, help wicked magician. Never.

Care for a human, one human, no end to it. Not possible. I am who I am.

Old nothing: "You are my little finger, my baby toe, my whisker, my wart. Bring me to him, now, quickly. This is he, this is the one whose hunger disturbs my sleep. You shall have back the man-shape, I will lap up his power along with it. I will make him my left hand."

Rotten board behind oven again? Stroll in the front way, like a guest, bite Gatti Jinni's bottom, walk between fat innkeeper's legs, pause a moment to wet his shoes—who would notice tonight? I start toward the inn. I stop. Old nothing: "What now?" I do not answer.

"What now, fingernail? Whisker?" So soft old nothing's voice in me, it might be evening breeze barely stirring my fur. "Is a human more to you than the human shape? Choose then. This is interesting." Everything interests old nothing when it is awake—everything, and nothing at all.

At night, just before sleeping, she asks, always, *"Fox, fox, what is your name?"* I have no name, she has lost her own. Alike that way, a little. Old nothing: "Choose." I take two steps left, four steps straight up. Left again? Left, yesyes, four steps around a corner, one behind the other. And there. Magicians make such fuss of journeys.

Same darkness, why imagine any different? Same thin black road under my feet, same bad sky. Dull place, I always forget. I come here sometimes because old nothing never does. Cannot? No knowing. Hard to know things here, too sideways, too slithery. Sit still, fox, sit empty, listen. Never anything to see in this place, anyway. Listen for her.

I wind the *griga'ath* first. Smell cold, they do, not hot at all—under the fire, a sweet distant chill, smell of winter drawing near in summer. No mistaking. Ears go back, fur stands up, already on my feet unaware. No fear of *griga'aths,* never me, only the body. Then I hear Lukassa.

Different here, around this corner. Time has no meaning, end is just the same as beginning, space is not real. Lukassa and *griga'ath*—perhaps behind me, perhaps beside, anywhere, underneath even. I might be facing them, never know it. But I hear Lukassa, because I am listening. Where man-shape was, that place hears her.

One short, small cry—why more, with no help ever, and a *griga'ath* turning? I answer—fox-bark only, words gone with man-shape. A moment later, just above me in the dark, there, Lukassa, almost lost in the fire-shadow around her. *Griga'ath* wants to swallow her, make her a living part of its fire. They cannot all do that, but this one can, could devour pretty me if I look away once. So. Fox sits back, very carefully, barks again.

Lukassa turns. Brown eyes gone gray with haze of being here. Wrong for humans here, wrong as bones being on outside. Cannot see me, not those eyes, cannot see anything but *griga'ath.* Wicked bloody magician should have told her what happens. Too late, after all.

But Lukassa: "My fox!" and I do not want this, but two words go through me like cold iron. "My fox!" and she is away from *griga'ath* and to me, kneeling, reaching across all nowhere to hold me. A calamity, she is, a weeping, laughing confusion of fear, exhaustion, joy, madness, ignorance, love. For this sake I let man-shape go. A favor, pigeons. Come and eat me.

Griga'ath over us, a blazing white sky of his own. Put me down, idiot Lukassa, but no words, no more. Nothing to do but nip wrist, hard—yelps, lets go, looks hurt, too bad. Back away slowly. Does he know us least little, old magician in there? No. Cold green eyes seeping through flames, he reaches to pick us up, gulp us both down, feed his oven heart. He can do it. If I could still take man-shape, he could still do it.

One way left. One.

How long, then? Long, long, long, even wicked magician not yet born last time I walk in my own self. No need, no use, too much trouble, fox will do. And when fox will not do, man-shape will. Now, no help for it. Old nothing would not like this. Old nothing is not here. No help for it.

Lukassa's arms around me again, not caring if I snap or no. Trembling, shivering, holding too tight, trying to keep me from *griga'ath.* A calamity, that girl. I look in her eyes—let go, Lukassa, must not change in your arms, must not, believe me. Friend. My friend. Let me go.

And she does look straight back at me and let me go, as *griga-ath*'s hand closes on her. I reach down and in and down, shake my self awake, the deep that is no borrowing, no form, no part of old nothing even. Me. So sorry to disturb, nice nap, I hope. You are needed, me.

Never any notion of what I look like, but I see the change in Lukassa's eyes. No cry when *griga'ath* takes her, no struggle in its hand—but now such terror, such betrayal, almost it would pain, except not possible. So dreadful, Lukassa, truly? Not to see me? No leavings of your fox, even in ancient thing I am? I would know you.

Griga'ath's turn to back away, holding Lukassa up between us like a lantern. Deciding—fear, not fear? My turn to reach out, long gray arms and hands I have, a glittering edge to them, ridgy gray fingers bend the air. I say, "Put her down." My voice a gray crushing. Lukassa covers her ears, her face. I say, "Put her down."

A rising in me, a remembering. Water and sky, this world, when I came to be—water and sky and terrible trees and old nothing. Foxes, yes, plenty of foxes, but no humans, so no *griga'aths.* No magicians, not one, no magicians scuttling here, there, trying to be gods, demons, ordinaries, all together. Creatures like me, there were—other things, too, in the water, in the trees. Fox forgets, manshape forgets. I remember.

Griga'ath remembers something. Sets Lukassa down slowly, she looks back and forth, which is more terrible? I say, "Lukassa, to me," but she cannot bear my voice. I move toward her, reach out, she flitters away, behind me now, good. *Griga'ath* hisses, grins monsters at us, undecided yet. I speak to it in the First Tongue, fox and manshape never knew. I say to it, "Behold me and begone.

Dry stick, dead leaf, depart to whatever waits for you." And I turn my back.

And for me an end of it. No more but to bring Lukassa home to that other world, hers. A skin away from this one, less, a whisper, but no coming and going, only the dead, the mad, the fox. Lukassa is not mad. Old magician's doing, it would be—fool, fool, how could I not see? Lukassa. Poor one.

Look back a last time. *Griga'ath* crouches, not moving, will not attack again. A smaller fire now, under this liquid, shifting dark—instead of *griga'ath* consuming us, darkness is already drawing it in, drinking it down into itself. And serve you right, wicked magician, waking the dead to adore you. Even for a magician, shameful. What you have become, you always were. Justice for once to leave you here, a pleasure, too.

But Lukassa will not come.

Four steps right and around and down, that simple—but she will not. Afraid still, drive her ahead, use fear, no time and no choice. She eludes me, darts this way, that way, stupid-stubborn as a chicken, trying and trying to return to *griga'ath. This* is madness, what is this? I tell her to stop, come with me, but the voice makes her truly wild, she would hide behind *griga'ath* if she dared. She says, "I came for him."

Always. Always. Any concern with humans, any feeling at all, there you are, telling yourself you do not know what you know. Walk right through you right now, she would—you, *griga'ath,* no difference, all for one wicked, lost old man. Dead, alive, an idiot, to the bone. And serve *you* right, idiot fox. Foolish, I clutch at her, carry her off where she belongs, be done with it. She scrambles out of reach—"No, no, I came for him! Fox, where are you? Help me, fox!" Looking at me as she cries.

Squeeze back into fox-shape to quiet her? But by now I am as stupid as she. Humans do that to you. Once more, no help for it. I turn to *griga'ath,* speak to it slowly, carefully. "Come along, then. Come with us." Oh, never again, never again. Old nothing must be hurting itself with laughing.

"Come with us." *Griga'ath* takes a single step. Lukassa gasps her wonder—another step, another gasp. *Griga'ath* halts, looks at us, eyes like green cinders. Not knowing us, can it know who it is? Can it choose? this world, that? "Come, so, come." A blue-hot snarl, a step. Lukassa claps hands, sings hope. Never again. "Come, then."

Rosseth

There is a hole in my memory, just here. I can remember the wind, the tremendous, unbelievable noise, people shrieking in the halls, and The Gaff and Slasher shuddering violently all over, like a terrified horse. I remember holding Lal's hand, walking with her and Soukyan toward a blackness where a wall had been, a blackness that asked us in very sweetly. It showed us pictures, the blackness. I can't say now what it showed us, but I was going there gladly. I remember that as well as I remember the *griga'ath*.

Then nothing—no, not even nothing, not a hole but a hiccup. The next thing, without the slightest pause, is Karsh shaking me and shouting at the top of his voice. I recognize the words by themselves, but all together they make no sense. I flop back and forth in Karsh's grip like a dishrag, while beyond him Tikat is screaming, "Lukassa! Lukassa!" at a wall. The other wizard is there, too, watching him with a strange faraway smile widening on his lipless mouth. It is like a dream, and always seems to continue for a long time.

Soukyan stopped it. He put me behind him, holding Karsh back with one hand on his chest. I remember him saying, his voice so deep and hoarse that Karsh must surely see past any disguise to the truth of him, "Stay there, fat man, where you are." I understood his words. He said to me, "Rosseth. Are you all right?"

Before I could reply, if I could have, Karsh was bellowing, "Well, what in bloody hell do you think I've been asking him, fool woman?" It gave me a fit of the giggles, I couldn't help it. Not so much because of what I knew, as because I had never heard Karsh talk that way to a paying guest. Soukyan had to shake me a bit this time. I said, "Yes, all right, it's all right." I pulled away from Soukyan and turned to look about me.

The room was a ruin, window gone, and the door hanging by one hinge—Karsh's doing, though I didn't know then. Not that there's much you can do to ruin a grubby little box like that, kept up mostly for bargemen to sleep off drunks; but the walls were leaning in as though the room had been pinched between some gigantic thumb and forefinger. Half the floor was seared black, warped upward into a sharp ridge by the heat of the *griga'ath*'s passage. I saw Marinesha's wildflowers scattered in a far corner. They were unharmed, strangely, except that their vase was broken.

Lal was with Tikat, trying to calm his endless, heartbreaking calling. Out of the side of my eye, I could see Soukyan moving very slowly toward the wizard, Arshadin. There was death in his face. Arshadin went on smiling at no one, touching his own face and body in a kind of awful wonder. He seemed not to notice anything else at all, but it was Soukyan to whom I wanted to shout warning. But then Karsh was at me again, demanding in the same breath to know if I were truly all right and what the goat-fucking hell I was doing in the damn wizard's room in the bloody first place. His face was red and pale by turns, and he was trembling rather like a horse himself. I thought it was the inn, the devastation of the only thing in the world he loved. I felt sorry for him.

Soukyan took the last step before the spring, and I did cry out to him, but Arshadin had already turned. One thick white hand gestured vaguely in Soukyan's direction, and Soukyan fell to the floor. His mouth was open, but he could not breathe—you could see his eyes bulging, his chest straining, strangling there at Arshadin's feet. He rolled from side to side, hands tearing at his throat, crazily trying to rip it open to let the air in. Arshadin looked down at him, nodding thoughtfully.

I started for Arshadin, but Karsh grabbed my arms so hard that I carried black bruises for days. Lal flew across the room like a thrown dagger, golden eyes slitted and cold. Arshadin glanced sideways at her, and she stopped dead still, staring wildly in all directions, half-cowering, half-challenging, throwing up her arms to ward off attackers none of us could see. She plainly recognized no one, not even Soukyan writhing on the floor. This part also goes on forever, but it is not like a dream.

Arshadin spoke. "It is over," he said in that light, sexless, dreadfully placid voice. "There is a new master here." Soukyan interrupted him with a frantic convulsion, first kicking out at Arshadin with all his fading strength, then trying to tangle their legs and drag him down. Arshadin stepped aside, and Soukyan's effort trailed away into a feeble drumming of his heels, as mine had rattled on the wall when the blue-eyed assassin pinned me there by the throat. I couldn't stand it. I managed to get an elbow into Karsh's belly, and he grunted and let go of me. I went for Arshadin again.

He nodded to Lal, and she spun to intercept me, crouched and glaring. Arshadin pointed down, saying, "Take warning by *him*—" but he never finished, because it was just then that Lukassa and the *griga'ath* reappeared.

They came out of a fold in the air, a swift crumpling and smoothing that I glimpsed only for a moment as it parted for them. Lukassa was first, turning apparently to coax the *griga'ath* on through, and behind them . . . behind them in that moment was something I know I could not have seen. It was gray and big, and it saw me, too, and it could not have, and that is all I want to say. In my next breath, the gateway was shut and gone, and Soukyan's fox was leaping to the floor, where it sat coolly on its haunches and watched Arshadin turn different colors. He made sounds, too, but they weren't nearly as interesting.

What happened then happened so fast that I have to talk about it very carefully. Lukassa took two steps forward and collapsed, not into Tikat's waiting arms, but into mine. She knocked me down, and her head bumped hard against my mouth, cutting my lip and loosening a tooth. The *griga'ath* shook itself, sneezed, and was the old wizard again—and if you wonder how I could be sure, his first act was to snap two words at Soukyan, who drew in breath for what seemed to me the first time in a hundred years, tried another, and sat up slowly, immediately reaching out to Lal. She pulled him to his feet, and for an instant they held each other. Then they both turned to look for Arshadin.

He was mad, of course—anyone who must be master is mad—but does that mean that his courage was all madness? I don't think so, for my part. He faced the old wizard as boldly and contemptuously as ever, saying, "Here we are again, then. Where would you like me to send you next?" But his lips moved stiffly around the words, and his face looked like melting ice.

The old man looked immensely weary himself, but the smell of death and despair was gone from him. His green eyes were clearer than I had ever seen them, and bright as new leaves, and his laughter was spring water dancing up out of stone. He said, "Never mind about me, my poor Arshadin. Let us consider—and very quickly, too—a far enough place to ship you as you stand here. For nothing is ever over, and those whom you have failed do not understand failure." Under the laughter, the voice was hard and urgent.

Lukassa stirred against me. I handed her to Tikat as gently as I could. Our eyes met briefly; then he bent his head and touched her hair. I looked away. Arshadin retorted, "I kept my bargain. If they were too weak to hold *you*, what shall they do with me? Nothing has changed."

Behind me Karsh was muttering, "I'll kill him. Let me just get my hands on him, I'll kill him." I thought he meant Arshadin; that he had realized who was finally responsible for the destruction of The Gaff and Slasher. But he was glowering at the fox, who went on sitting up, observing everything with its tongue lolling and its expression serenely scornful. It turned at his words, and looked at me as it had from Soukyan's saddlebag that first day, with my true name glimmering and turning far down in its eyes.

The old man said, "Arshadin, there is no time. I will agree to anything you like, but we must get you gone from here this minute. Arshadin, listen to me. I am begging you."

Arshadin laughed. It was a surprising laugh, slow and suddenly real and deeply amused, and I hear it still and wonder. Did he laugh in the comfort of arrogance, in certainty that his dear-bought new power would shelter him from any revenge, human or other? Or was it the laughter of someone with nothing to lose and no possible escape to debate? I don't know, of course, but there are worse ways to remember a bad man.

"Nothing has changed," he repeated. "Only you could come back from where you have been still whining at me to behave." The air crumpled again, close beside him. A ripple appeared in it, exactly like the circles that spread out and out when you toss a stone into quiet water. This circle darkened, tightened, and became a blue mouth, its lips sparkling wetly with tiny red and blue teeth. Arshadin turned and struck at it, crying out words that sounded like trees snapping in a windstorm, one after another. The round mouth pushed forward, as though for a dreadful kiss. It puckered around him, drew him in, and was gone.

In the silence, I heard Tikat singing. He had never looked up, but was rocking Lukassa in his arms, his long light hair half-hiding her face, mingling with her own dark tangle, as he droned along so softly. I knew the song—it was the lullaby about Byrnarik Bay. He had the words all wrong; or perhaps I do.

TIKAT

She slept without stirring for not quite three days.

Without asking leave, I put her in the best upstairs room, the one that Rosseth says goes vacant all year sometimes, because Karsh insists on keeping it for the kind of people who rarely come to Corcorua. When Karsh grew noisy about it, the *tafiya* said to him, mildly enough, "Good Master Innkeeper, when Lukassa wakes in this bed, that day will I restore your establishment to its former condition, and get rid of the stink-beetles in your walls into the bargain. But if you say another word on the matter between now and then—" and he gestured around him at the wreck that the wizard Arshadin had made of The Gaff and Slasher—"I promise you that you will forever look back on *this* as the good old days." Karsh stormed off to check on the outbuildings, and the *tafiya* sighed and sat down to watch Lukassa through the night.

He did better than his pledge, in fact, for we all woke on the third morning to find the inn's roof back where it should be, whole windows set neatly into new frames in remade walls; the floors certainly as level as they ever were, the two stone chimneys as straight, the foundations probably more sound, and such things as beer pumps, cisterns, and water pipes working as though they'd never been wrenched up like weeds. The stink-beetles were indeed gone, and the sign over the front door had been freshly painted over, which strangely infuriated Karsh. He stamped around all that day mumbling that there had been nothing wrong with the sign the way it was, and that there never was a wizard who knew when to leave well alone. Which is true enough, as I can say now.

Lukassa did not wake until that evening. The fox was asleep on her bed, and the *tafiya* had fallen asleep himself; or I think he had—he was a deceitful old man in some ways, and enjoyed being so. She came awake all at once, her eyes too ready for terror. I put my hands lightly on her arms, chancing the terror, and said, "Lukassa."

I am not certain whether I could have borne it if she had not known me this time. But I saw that she did even before she spoke. She said, softly but clearly, "Tikat. There you are, Tikat."

"I'm here," I said, "and you're here with me, and so is *he*," and I nodded toward the *tafiya* snoring earnestly in his chair. I said, "You saved him. I think you saved us all."

She did not answer, but looked at me in silence for a long time. Her face was a stranger's face, which was as it should be. Love each other from the day we are born to the day we die, we are still strangers every minute, and nobody should forget that, even though we have to. Marinesha looked in at the bedroom door, smiled shyly, and went away again. Lukassa said, "When I was there, in that place, I heard you calling me."

My throat was raw with it still. I bowed my head over her hands. She went on, halting often. "Tikat, I don't remember you from—from before the river. *He* says I never will remember, not you, not myself, not anyone." There were tears in her eyes, but they did not fall. "But I do know that you are my friend and care truly for me. And that I have hurt you." One hand turned over in mine to close on my fingers.

"It was nothing you could help," I said. "No more than I could help calling after you. I never thought you would hear me."

"I did, though." She smiled for the first time, the smile she always tries to rein in, because if her happiness spreads past the left corner of her mouth a crooked tooth shows. "It was very annoying, until I needed it to find my way back. But then I couldn't hear it anymore."

"I couldn't call anymore," I said. Lukassa looked into my eyes and nodded. Her hand closed tighter on my hand. I said, "I couldn't, Lukassa." She nodded again. I turned my head to watch the fox: slanting eyes shut tight, fluffed-out tail across his muzzle, the black-tipped fur parting with his dainty snores. Lukassa stroked him with her free hand, and he wriggled against it without ever waking. "He was the man in the red coat, you know," I said. "I met him on the way here, when I was following you and Lal."

"There is something else he is," Lukassa whispered. "Something else, something not like anything." I could barely hear her, and she did not go on. We were silent for a while, just holding hands, looking at each other, looking away. All the questions I wanted to ask her sat on the bed with us: the mattress seemed to sag under their weight. At last Lukassa said, "I want to tell you about that place, about being there. I want to tell someone."

I began to say, "I have no right—" but she interrupted me. She said, "I want to tell you, but I cannot. The person who could have told you how it was is dead." I stared at her, not understanding at all. Lukassa said, "She never came back—she died on the other side of that black gate, as surely as the girl you knew died in the river. And here I am, here I am talking to you, and who am I? Tikat, am I dead or alive, can you tell me that? And if I am alive, who am I?" She tried to pull her hand from mine, but I held hard onto it, even when her emerald ring ground against my finger. The fox woke up and yawned elaborately, stretching his forepaws and watching us.

"You are as alive as I am," I said, "and you are yourself. If you are not the Lukassa I followed here, maybe there never was any such person. Myself, I cannot again be the Tikat I was, and I am well content with that, as long as you and I recognize each other." I opened my hand then, and she took hers away, but then brought it back so that our fingertips touched. I said, "What do we do now, Lukassa? I thought we could go home, back to those two other people, but we never can."

"No," she said very quietly. "Lal would take me along with her, if I asked her, but only because I asked. And Soukyan—" She spread her hands out, and I saw the scars I had been feeling, the two long cloudy blotches on the pale right palm, and the dark whiplash across the back, just below the ring. She said, "Soukyan would take me if Lal asked. So there we are." Her smile was not the one I knew.

I took her hand and kissed the scarred palm. She clenched it for a moment, then let it fall open again. I said, "I would take you anywhere, but I don't know a place to go." We were quiet for a little, and then I added, "We could always stay here and work at the inn. Grow old with Karsh."

It was said as a joke, but her face clouded and I realized that she had taken me seriously. I was just beginning to explain when the *tafiya* coughed politely behind us. He said, "If nobody would mind a suggestion?"

How long had he been awake and listening? We never knew. You never do know with him. We turned together, and there he sat, green eyes as mocking as the fox's yellow eyes. Very full of himself, he was, exactly like the fox.

"It seems that my *lamisetha* can wait a bit longer," he said. "I will take you with me." When he looked at Lukassa, his eyes changed. He said to her, "I have passed the gates of death myself, but I was worse than dead. I would have been worse than dead through all eternity, if not for you. So you have a claim on me that I will never outlive. Also—"

Lukassa shook her head fiercely. She said, "What I did, I did without choice, without any idea of what it all meant. I have no claim on anyone." Her voice was tired and flat.

"Don't interrupt," the old man said severely. "I turned Soukyan to stone once for ten minutes, for interrupting me one time too many." But he was smiling at Lukassa almost with admiration. He said, "Also. Apparently my need to be forever teaching somebody something has survived the black gate as well as I. If you have sense enough to come with me, I may be able—"

Lukassa broke in again, "I do not want to be a wizard. Not for me, not ever." She took hard hold of my hand again.

The old man sighed. "Is Lal a wizard? Is Soukyan a wizard? Be quiet and pay attention. If you come home with me, it is possible that I may in a while remember a way to let this Lukassa and *that* Lukassa—the one still there in the riverbed—visit each other, talk together, perhaps even live together. Then again, perhaps not—I promise nothing. But the roof doesn't leak, and the food is generally quite good, and the house is a restful one." He grinned then, a joyous, teasing, snaggle-mouthed grin, and I recalled Redcoat's words, the fox's words—*Bones full of darkness, blood thick and cold with ancient mysteries.* He added, "A little disquieting, just from time to time, but restful."

Lukassa said firmly, "Tikat has to come too. I will not come without him." The *tafiya* looked at me and raised his caterpillar eyebrows slightly. I said, "I can work, you know that. And what I can learn from being in your house, I will." It made me nervous, to be talking to him in this way, and I kept turning Lukassa's ring around and around on her finger, hardly aware that I was doing it.

The *tafiya* said nothing for a long time. He seemed to be looking, not at either of us, but at the fox, who presently yawned in his face, jumped down off the bed and trotted importantly away, tail high. Finally he said, and his tone was oddly melancholy, "You are as welcome as Lukassa, Tikat, but I would think carefully in your place, because you may find yourself learning more than you meant to learn. There are gifts and dreams and voices in you that may wake in my house, as they would nowhere else. So I would be very careful."

I did not know how to answer him. I kept toying with Lukassa's ring until it slipped over the knuckle and almost off her finger into my hand. She clutched at it immediately, saying, "Don't, don't do that, I must never take it off. Lal gave it to me when she raised me—if I lose it, I will die for good, fall to the dust I should have been so long ago." Her hands were damp and shaking, and her face was old with fear.

The *tafiya* gazed at her with such concern, such tenderness that for a moment his face became like hers—he *looked* like her, how else can I say it? Only for a moment, it was, but I will remember it when I have forgotten every feat of wizardry I ever saw him do. Very, very gently, he said to her, "Lukassa, it is not so. I gave Lal that ring, and I should know. It was made to comfort and quiet certain sorrows, nothing more. Your life is yours, not the ring's. Lukassa's heart and soul and spirit are what keep Lukassa alive, not a dead green stone in a piece of dead metal. Give me the ring, and I will prove it to you."

It took a long time for her to stop trembling and listen to him, and even then she would not take off the ring, for all his talk and mine. At first she said nothing but, "No," over and over, into her fists; but at last she turned to the old man and told him, "I will give it to Lal. When we leave here, Tikat and I, to go with you, then I will give it back to Lal, and she can return it to you if she chooses. Or not."

And from there she would not budge. The *tafiya* shook his head and blew through his beard and grumbled, "If we begin like this, teacher and student, how shall we end? You minded me better when I was a *griga'ath*." But he had to be content with her decision all the same, and I think he was, in his way.

The Innkeeper

It has never been right since, I don't care what he said or how great a wizard he was. Oh aye, everything *works,* if that's what you mean by rightness, and some things work even better—I'm not such a fool as to say they don't. But none of that is the same as being the way it was. Things can be replaced, fixed up perfectly, but they can't be put back. Repaired doesn't mean *right.*

Never mind, never mind—it isn't worth the trouble, and besides there's not much more to tell. The next two weeks were chaos, no more and no less. Marinesha and Rosseth had to run the inn—pity me, gods!—while I spent my time groveling and begging pardon before angry guests, injured guests (mercifully, a very few; as for the Kinariki wagoner, we never did find him again), and guests so terrified that some of them would not come back even for their belongings, not to mention settling their bills. Not only did I lose any number of valuable old customers, but of course the story got around everywhere, and I've been from that day to this building my clientele back to something like what it used to be. No wizard offered to help with *that,* I can assure you!

The woman Lal let me know that she and her companions would be leaving at last, as soon as the wizard and the little Lukassa were fit to travel. She also expressed her regrets—pointlessly but quite prettily, I will say—for all the troubles that had come with them to plague The Gaff and Slasher. "All the troubles"—as if she could have understood the half of what her lot had done to my life. But it was a change to have someone ask *my* pardon, so I told her we'd say no more about it, and let it go. Miss Nyateneri never bothered with any apology of her own, but that's as well. I couldn't have dealt with any more shocks just then.

Rosseth stayed out of my way to a remarkable degree during those days. It's not that he doesn't try to avoid me as much as he can, in the normal run of things; but in the normal run we don't go much more than a long afternoon without my having to shout at him about something. To be honest, I made no great effort to bump into him, either. I had charged up a collapsing stairway through a stampede of screaming idiots and broken down a perfectly good door, all because I couldn't endure the thought of having to train another stable boy. You never know how people take these things. It can be awkward afterwards, that's all.

I became certain that he was once again planning to run off with the women and the wizard, and didn't want to face me because he knew I'd read him first glance. I took council with myself one night, consulting in my room with two bottles of that fermented harness polish they make east of the mountains—*Sheknath*'s Kidneys, the locals call it. What all of us decided eventually was, if he wanted that much to leave, let him leave and be damned. I had headed him off a dozen times when he and I were both younger; he was sharp enough now to give me the slip tomorrow, the day after, if not today. Well, let him, then, and good riddance, the best riddance—but before he showed me his heels, I had a thing or two to show him.

Thinking about that made the night go too slowly, and the *Sheknath*'s Kidneys far too fast, and I was moving a bit gingerly when I sought him out the next morning. He was rubbing a vile-smelling ointment that he makes himself into the flanks of a bay gelding whose owner obviously enjoyed owning a pair of spurs. Rosseth was talking to the horse as he worked—not in words, just murmuring quietly, smoothing his voice into the raw places with the ointment. I waited, watching him until he felt somebody there and whipped around fast, the way those women do. He said, "I'm almost through with him. I'll get to the hog-pen right away."

Because there was a rail coming loose there, you see, and I'd been after him for a week to replace it. He finished with the gelding, forked some fresh hay into its manger, and then just leaned against it for a moment, the way horses will lean against each other, before he came out of the stall. We stood looking at each other, him braced for orders, keeping a careful eye on my hands; and me studying the size of his own stubby hands, and the two swirls of down on his upper lip. Won't ever be as big as I am, but he might turn out stronger.

"I want to talk to you," I said. Oh, that made his eyes go tight, flicking back and forth between me and the stable door. He said, "Well, the rail, the hogs might—" I nodded toward a bale of hay and said, "Sit."

He sat. I wanted to keep standing, but my head was clanging too much for that, so I turned over a pail and sat facing him. "If you want to go with that old wizard and the rest of them," I said, "you don't have to sneak away. Go. I won't beat you, and I won't try to stop you. Just take what's yours and go. Close your mouth," for his jaw was sagging like that hog-pen rail giving way. "You understand me?"

Rosseth nodded. I couldn't tell if he was joyous, relieved, angry, somehow disappointed—I can't always tell. I said, "But there is something you have to hear. The only condition I'm making is that you have to sit there and listen to this. All of it. Close your *mouth*—you don't have to *look* like an idiot! Do you hear me, Rosseth?"

"Yes," he said. Chatters endlessly when you don't want to hear one more word out of him, goes dumb as a fish when it really means something. My head got worse just meeting those blank, watchful eyes of his. Why did I bring up this whole damned business now? It could have waited. As long as it's waited already, what's another day, or another week, or the rest of my life? I said, "All right, then. A long time ago, I had to go to Cheth na'Deka, never mind why. It was a long journey there, and a worse one back. You know why?"

"Bandits?" Not much of a guess, considering that Cheth more or less *means* bandits, always has. "Bandits," I said. "Or maybe there was a war going on—not much difference down there, except for the clothes. I never did find out which gang it was that had been through that village."

Rosseth was listening. I got up, kicked the pail a bit to the right, walked around it, sat down again. "I was coming back alone and on foot, not by choice, but because I couldn't hire a coach or a guide for any money. You still can't, as far as I know. All I had for protection was a staff, my father's, the kind with a big chunk of iron at one end. I traveled at night, and I stayed off the main roads, and the third evening I saw smoke far away. Black smoke, the kind you get when it's houses burning."

He kept his eyes absolutely still, flat as a stock pond, but he was leaning forward a little, hands gripping the edge of the hay-bale. "I didn't go any further that night," I told him. "I heard horses, a lot of them, passing close enough for me to hear men laughing. It wasn't until noon the next day that I started on again, and I spent so much time hiding in the trees by the roadside that I didn't reach the village until mid-afternoon. Tiptoeing slows you down a good deal." I didn't want him getting any idea that I was trying to sound like a hero. It was going to be bad enough as it was.

"What was its name?" His voice was so low I couldn't

make him out the first time. "What was the village's name?"

"How should I know? There wasn't a soul alive to tell me. Just bodies up and down the one street, bodies lying in their own doorways, bodies shoved down the well, floating in the horse-trough, sprawled across tables in the square. There was one crammed into the baker's oven—his wife, his daughter, who knows? Split open like a sack of meal, like the rest of them." I said it all hard and fast and as tonelessly as I could, to get it done with. I left some things out.

"There wasn't anyone?" He cleared his throat. "There wasn't anyone left alive." It wasn't a question. We could have been in a temple, with the priest lining out the invocation and the worshippers chanting it all back to him dutifully. I said, "I didn't think so. Until I heard the baby."

Well, he saved me the least little bit of it, anyway. He whispered, "Me. That was me."

I got up again. I thought about really trying to tell him what it was like: the silence, the slow buzzing, the smell of blood and shit and burning, and the tiny, angry, hungry cry drifting upward with the last trails of smoke. Instead I stood with my back to him, hands in my apron pockets, staring at that mean little black horse of Tikat's and wishing I'd had the sense to bring whatever was left of the *Sheknath*'s Kidneys with me.

"I couldn't find the place right away," I said. "Get off the street and it was all just ruts and holes, break your ankle like that. It was a one-room cottage—clay walls and a peat thatch, the usual. There were a few sweet-regrets around the front step, I remember that. And a little bundle of *dika* thorns hanging on the door."

They do that to keep away evil, in that country. He didn't speak. I said, "The door was on the latch, and there was something jammed against it. I knocked and I pushed, and then I called out." I turned back around. "I did, Rosseth. I called four, five, six times." I don't know why I so much wanted him to believe that. What did it matter if he believed me or no? It seemed to matter then. "I called, 'Hello, is anyone there? Is anyone there? Can you hear me?' But there was no answer, none—nothing but the crying."

He tried to say, "Me" again, but it didn't come out—only his mouth shaping the word. I heard footsteps outside, and voices, and I waited, hoping to be interrupted, even by Shadry, even by the bloody fox. He hadn't shown his face at the inn since the night everything went to hell, but by now I saw him in every shadow and under every bush, and I'd have been happy to see him swaggering into the barn just then. But there was no one but me, and my head, and my throat getting drier, and my voice going on. And Rosseth's eyes.

"I went to the window," I said. "Forced the catch with my staff and climbed over the sill. It was dark inside there, Rosseth, because of being shut up so tight and me coming out of the sunlight. I could hear the baby—you—but I couldn't see you, or anything else. I just had to stand still until I got used to the darkness."

He knew what was coming now. Not the way I knew, but you could tell. He wouldn't look at me, but kept wetting his lips and staring down at the barn floor. My face and hands were cold. I said, "Somebody hit me. Hard, here, on the side of my head. I thought it was a sword. I went straight down, and they were all over me. Not a sound out of them—it felt like a dozen people hitting me everywhere at once, kicking, pounding me like mashing up a *tialy* root. A dozen people, killing me, I couldn't see even one of them. I swear, that's what it was like."

"But there were only two," Rosseth said. His face had gone as white as Lukassa's, and so small. He said, "There were only two."

"Well, I didn't know that, did I? They never said a word, I told you that. All I knew was, I was being fucking murdered." I didn't realize that I was shouting until a couple of the horses nickered in alarm. "Rosseth, I couldn't see for the blood, I thought they'd split my head. Look, right here, it's still tender after fifteen years. I thought I was dead as that thing in the oven, do you understand?"

He did not answer. He got up off the hay-bale and turned in a circle, arms hanging, eyes vague, still not looking at me. After a bit of that, he wandered back toward the horse he'd been doctoring, but then he turned again and just stood there. I said, "I had my staff. I got my legs under me somehow, and I just struck out, left, right, swinging blind in the dark, trying to keep them off. That's all I wanted to do, keep them off me."

I had to sit down again. I was dripping and reeking with sweat, and beginning to wheeze as though I'd been for another brisk stroll up those stairs. Rosseth stayed where he was, looking down at me. He said, "My mother and my father."

I nodded, waiting for the next question, the one I hear in my sleep most nights, even now. But he couldn't ask it, he could not make the words come out. Trust him, I had to say it all myself, and me with a load of mortar hardening in my chest. "I killed them," I said. "I never meant to. I didn't know."

In the dreams he usually comes for me, screaming, trying to tear me apart with his hands. I was ready for that, or for him crying, but he didn't do either. His knees folded slowly, and he dropped to the floor and stayed there, kneeling with his arms wrapped tight around himself and his head bowed. He was making a tiny dry sound. I'd never have heard it in that burned-out village.

"They must have thought I was one of the killers coming back," I said. "Soldiers, outlaws, whoever it was." I told him that I had buried his parents, that I didn't leave them to rot with the other murdered ones, and that I could take him right to the village and the grave, if he ever wanted to go there. Which is certainly the truth—I could find that terrible place again if the sea had rolled over it.

He was rocking back and forth on his knees, just a little. Without looking up he whispered, "And you took me with you. You buried them, and you took me with you."

"What else could I do? You were weaned, thank the gods. I bought a goat in the next town, and I used to dip bits of bread in her warm milk and feed you like that, all the way." I tried to make a joke, to get him to stop that rocking. I said, "Heavy as a little anvil you were, too. Lugging you along with one arm, dragging that goat with the other—I don't know how women do it. If you'd weighed an ounce more, I'd have had to leave you where I found you."

Well, that did get him off his knees, no question about that. Shoulders hunched and shaking, the whole face writhing back from his bared teeth, hands clawing up, not toward me but himself. "I wish you had! Oh, I wish you'd left me there with them and just gone on your miserable, stinking way, and never given any of us another thought ever again! Rot your fat guts, I wish you'd left me to die with my family, my family!"

There was more, fifteen years' worth of it. I let him go on as long as the supply lasted. He did hit me once, but he doesn't really know how, and my body soaks these things up. When he finally ran out of breath, wheezing like me, I said, "I'm sorry I killed them, your parents. That started the moment I stood up in that shattered house and mopped the blood out of my eyes. I've lived with what I saw every second since, waking or sleeping, a lot longer than you have. It's my business, and it will go on being my business until the day I die. But what I will not apologize for, not ever, to you or anybody, is that I brought you away from that house with me. Beyond a doubt it's the stupidest thing I've done in my life, but it might be the only good thing, too. One or two others, just maybe, but the chances are you'll be all I've got to show. When my time comes."

How long did we stand looking at each other? I can't say, but I'll swear I felt the sun rising and setting on the back of my neck, and seasons changing, and I know I saw Rosseth grow older before my eyes. Was it the same for him, I wonder, looking at me, seeing me, seeing his childhood march away? And what I mumbled, after so many years, so much fuss, was, "You're all I've got to show, and I could have done worse." And we stared at each other some more, and I said, "Much worse."

Rosseth said at last, "I am not going with Lal and Soukyan." His voice was quiet, with neither tears nor anger in it, nothing but its own clarity. "But I am leaving. Not today, but soon."

"When you please," I said. "In your own time. Now it's my time to go and kick Shadry and roar at Marinesha. An innkeeper's work is never done." He just blinked—he never knows when I'm joking, never has known. I turned and started away.

He stopped me at the stable door with a single word. "Karsh?" The shock of it was completely physical—not a sound at all, but a touch on your shoulder when you thought no one was there. I cannot remember when he last called me by my name. He said, "There was a song. Someone used to sing me a song. It was about going to Byrnarik Bay, going to play all day on Byrnarik Bay. That's all I remember of it. I was wondering, do you think—do you think they used to sing that song, my parents?"

There's a good reason I'm the size I am. Fat softens and soaks up other things besides blows. "Only parents would sing a song like that," I said. "Must have been them," and I got myself out of there and went on up the hill to the courtyard. He'll sing "Byrnarik Bay" to his own brats, soon enough, and always grow damp around the eyes and soft around the chin when he does, and welcome to it. The song's as idiotic as any of that sort, but it's the only one I know. I sang it to him all the way through that bandit country where I found him, over and over, all the way home to my country, to The Gaff and Slasher.

LAL

I said, "What? Excuse me? You are going to do *what*?"

"I have to go back," Soukyan repeated. "There really is no other choice."

We were alone in the travelers' shrine. Soukyan wanted to make a departure prayer, since we would be leaving tomorrow. Until now he had not spoken of his plans, and I had assumed that we might journey pleasantly together as far as Arakli, where many roads meet. Now, carefully fitting the greenish lumps of incense into the two tin burners, he said, "I am tired of running, Lal. I am also getting a bit old for it. If I am not to spend the last years of a short life trying to deal with new teams of assassins as they keep coming after me, then I must return to the place they all come from. The place I come from."

I said, "That is completely insane. You told me yourself—they don't forgive, and they won't rest until you're dead. You might as well commit suicide right here, where you're guaranteed a decent burial, and spare yourself the ride."

Soukyan shook his head slowly. "I don't want them to forgive me. I want them to stop following me." He made a quick gesture of blessing over the burners and lit the incense. "I want it done with, that's all, one way or the other."

"Oh, it will be done with," I said. "That it will. I fought one of those people, remember." Soukyan had his back to me, murmuring inaudibly into the thin fumes that smelled faintly like marsh water. I was furious. I said, "So you'll fight them all at once and get it done with indeed. A hero's death, no doubt of it. I would have let you drown if I'd known."

Soukyan laughed then. His laugh is a private laugh, even when shared: there is always something kept aside. "Did I say I was going to fight them all? Did I? I thought you knew me better than that, Lal." He turned to face me. "I have a plan. I even have an ally or two back there, and some old sleights and confidences to bargain with. Believe me, I will be as safe as I was with you on the river." He put his hands on my shoulders, adding quietly, "Though not as happy. Likely, never again."

"Stupidity," I said. "I cannot abide stupidity." I sounded like Karsh. I had never been so angry with him, not even when I discovered his deception, and I was angrier because I had no possible right to be angry. I said, "What plan? Let me hear this wonderful plan."

He shook his head again. "Later, maybe. It's far too long a story."

"Everything is a long story," I said. I felt very tired, suddenly not the slightest bit ready for any new adventures, any voyages anywhere. I put his hands away and moved restlessly around the little windowless room. It was designed and appointed more or less like any travelers' shrine in this half of the world: always white, always freshly painted (there is a law, and even Karsh apparently heeds it), always provided with the ritual cloths and candles and statues of a dozen major religions. They vary somewhat, depending on the region, but the one in which I was raised is never among them. Mostly I find that just as well, but not then.

Behind me Soukyan said, "Lal, it has nothing to do with you. This is my life, my past, my own small destiny. I am finished with waiting for it to bring me to bay one more time. I will go and meet it, for a change—and not in a bathhouse or on a river shore, but on a field of my choosing. There's really no more to be said."

Nor was there, for some while. He commenced a cumbersome process of passing his bow, sword, and dagger back and forth through the two tiny threads of incense, muttering to himself as he did so. I went outside and sat in the dry grass, chewing weeds viciously and watching a flock of *tourik* birds mob a snow-hawk that had ventured too close to their nests. Then I came back into the shrine, though you're not supposed to reenter after leaving a ceremony. Soukyan was kneeling, head bowed, weapons arranged just so before him. I said, "You can't cross the Barrens in winter."

Without looking up, he answered, "I know that. I will make for the coast and turn south at Leishai. A longer road, but a safer one, for some way at least." When the last of the incense had smoldered away, he rose stiffly to his feet, making a final obeisance to nothing. He said, "And you?"

I shrugged. "Arakli, I suppose. I have wintered there before." The marshy incense-smell still lingered in my nostrils, irritatingly heavy with memories that were not even mine. Soukyan said, "And after Arakli?" I did not answer him. He said, "Come, I've told you my destination. It would comfort me much to know where you are."

"I am Lal," I said. "That is where I am." Soukyan looked at me for a moment longer, then nodded and strode to the shrine door. When he opened it, we both heard Lukassa laughing nearby, a sound neither of us had ever imagined hearing: it went by us like a breeze in the grass. Soukyan held the door, but I said, "I will stay here for a little," and turned back toward the white chests full of other peoples' gods.

ROSSETH

I rode with them as far as the turning where I had first seen them, by Marinesha's bee tree. Not clinging behind Lal this time, but on Karsh's old white Tunzi, who clearly felt very important to be part of such a procession. The wizard led the way, mounted on a tall sorrel stallion that had simply appeared in the stables the night before, calmly munching oats and barley with the guests' beasts as though it had every right to be there. Tikat and Lukassa rode beside him on the two little goat-eyed Mildasi horses, and I rode in the rear between Lal and Soukyan. I must always remember it just as it was, because I never saw any of them again.

It was a cool, windy dawn, and leaves dead too soon were rattling across the path, hundreds at a gust. With the end of the terrible summer of the magicians, autumn seemed to be rushing in too fast, reaping the dry sticks in the fields, stripping the trees of the scabby brown lumps that the birds wouldn't eat. It saddened me to see it then, because I felt that my life was being stripped of companionship and excitement and dreams in the same way. Soukyan read it in my face, surely, for he leaned from his saddle to put his hand on my neck, as he had before. Once we had passed out of sight of the inn, he had let his woman's guise rise from him like mist, dissolving in the morning sun. His gray-brown hair was growing out, the harsh convent cut fading as well, but the twilight eyes and the reluctantly gentle mouth were still Nyateneri's.

"Nature always likes to clear away and start over," he said. "Mark me, next spring will be richer than anyone has seen for years. You'll never be able to tell that a couple of wizards fought a war here."

"No, I won't," I answered, "because I won't be here next spring." Lal put her arm around me, and I breathed in her smell of great distances and strange, warm stars. She said, "So many lovely things burned without having a chance to ripen. Be sure that this does not happen to you." Her hand brushed Soukyan's hand then, and she pulled it away sharply, covering the movement by ruffling my hair. She began to sing softly in that half-talking, rise-and-roll-and-fall way of hers. I inhaled that, too, as I did Soukyan's exasperated sigh and Tikat's quiet, almost invisible attentiveness to both the old man and Lukassa. I wanted to move up beside him and say a proper farewell, because we had been friends, but he was already gone from my world, as surely and finally as the wizard Arshadin was gone.

Oh, it was never so short a ride to the tree and the spring and the bend in the road as it was that day. Nothing I could do or say or think about could make it last any longer. All that was left was to concentrate on remembering everything: the blowing leaves, a scuttling *shukri* that hunched and spat at us by the roadside, the sudden cross-currents of cold air down from the mountains, the colors of the six ribbons in the old wizard's beard. Lal's song, the flickering loose end of Lukassa's white headscarf, Tunzi's constant farting which embarrassed me so. And I did remember it all, and I fall asleep to it still.

You can't see it until you round the turn, but just beyond the path divides, one fork skirting the mountains toward Arakli, the other slanting eastward to meet the main road that runs to Derridow, Leishai, and the sea. The wizard drew rein at the bee tree and wheeled his horse to face the rest of us. Fragile even now, to my view—I know Soukyan thought he would never be truly strong again—nevertheless he held himself as straight in the saddle as Tikat, and the green eyes were as eager as though everything, everything, good and bad, were waiting to happen for the first time. People of my age are supposed to feel like that, but I certainly didn't, not that morning. I felt as if everything were over.

"We part here," he announced. "We shall not meet again." Somehow he made it sound joyous—hopeful, even—but I could never explain it now. He said, "Tikat and Lukassa and I will travel west together. It seems to me that I have a house somewhere near Fors na'Shachim, or perhaps I mean Karakosk. Wizards' houses tend to move around as much as wizards, but I am sure we shall encounter it sooner or later, and it will know me if I have forgotten." He turned to Lal and Soukyan. "And you two, who have all the gratitude of a foolish, vain old man whom you have long outgrown? Where shall I think of you after today?"

Lal did not answer. Soukyan said, "I have a journey south to make. It will be hard, and I shall need your thoughts. As much as ever, I shall need them."

"Nonsense," the wizard said, but he looked pleased all the same. "Very well. But it will be more practical for you to mind your manners, stay off the Queen's Road after Bitava, and give up any notion of the secret stair. It is guarded since your time—they will not make that mistake again." Soukyan nodded. The wizard made a small gesture that might have been a blessing, or not. He said to Lal, "And you, *chamata*?"

When she spoke it was not to him but to Soukyan, low enough that she might have been talking to herself. She said, "If you are going by way of Leishai, I might ride that far with you. I have been too long away from ships—no wonder I cannot think clearly. I need to be on a ship."

Soukyan put his hand over hers. He said, "I will see you aboard." He had drawn breath to say something more, when the fox followed its black nose and glowing eyes out of his saddlebag, as it had done on that afternoon in early spring. Soukyan spoke to it, saying, "Ah, so you *have* chosen Lukassa. I thought you might." To Lukassa he said, "He is not mine to keep or to give you—he goes where he will, always." He stroked the fox's neck once, briefly, and said into a pointed ear, "Go, then, companion."

But Lukassa laughed and shook her head, riding close to look into the fox's eyes. "Come with me and the wizard as well? Not likely, is it? Not you." She took the sharp muzzle between her hands, bending down to whisper something I could not hear. Then she kissed it quickly, just below the mask, and the fox yelped indignantly and ducked down out of sight. Lukassa said quietly, "He only wanted to say goodbye."

And after that it is all goodbyes, happening all around me, happening too fast. Tikat shakes my hand, suddenly shy, mumbling something about the little brother he lost to the plague-wind. Lukassa kisses me as she did the fox, with a sweet clumsiness, and what she remembers or does not remember I will never know. Lal kisses me differently, saying, "Wherever you are, whatever happens to you, somebody loves you." Soukyan takes a silver medallion from his neck—this one, see—and puts it around mine. "It is worth very little and has absolutely no magical powers, but it will at least buy you a meal somewhere—or make you a friend, if someone should recognize it." The medallion has an eight-angled figure on one side, and raised lettering that I cannot read on the other.

When I protest, "But I have nothing to give you," Soukyan smiles and fetches something out of a pouch at his belt. It takes me a moment to understand—then I recognize the shabby cloth spattered with rust-brown stains. Soukyan says gently, "Do you think that many people have shed their blood in my defense? I treasure this as much as anything I own." And he kissed me, too, so there were my three.

As for the wizard, he said, almost absently, "Tell Marinesha that her kindness is not forgotten. Farewell, farewell." He was plainly anxious to be off, and had already turned his horse again when Lukassa remembered to give her emerald ring back to Lal. Lal hesitated, looking at the ring with some longing, and then handed it over to the wizard. He shoved it unceremoniously into a pocket and touched his heels to his horse's sides. The stallion leaped away immediately, and Tikat and Lukassa followed without a backward glance. But as they rounded the bend, the old man turned in his saddle and called loudly to me, "Your name is Vand! Remember us, Vand!"

So then there were only Lal and Soukyan and me, and my true name. Soukyan said, "A good thing he thought of it in time. His memory for such things is completely gone."

But Lal answered, "No, that's always been his way. Pure strolling player, to the last." And after that there was nothing left to say, and they bade me a last goodbye and trotted away, already arguing. Both of them looked back before they passed out of sight, but it was hard to see them clearly.

Tunzi did not at all want to return to the inn. He whinnied and surged under me trying to follow the others; when I tugged on the reins to bring his head around, he danced lumbering caracoles on the path, even rearing once, which was exhausting for both of us. He turned reluctantly, just the same, and slouched along home at a disgraceful pace—I could have done as well walking and leading him. But I was crying then, and it took longer than I had thought it would, so that was as well, I suppose.

Karsh met me at the crossroad, which was nearly as astonishing as Tunzi's insurrection. He was walking slowly when I saw him, but his voice sounded as though he had been running not long before. "I thought you might have gone with them, after all. Last-minute sort of thing."

"I will tell you when I go," I said. Karsh nodded and took hold of Tunzi's bridle, but the horse snorted and pulled away, still trying to turn back. I said, "But *he* would have gone, and gladly too. I've never seen him like this in my life."

"Well," Karsh said. He shrugged heavily and began leading Tunzi along the path to The Gaff and Slasher. "Even fat old white geldings have dreams. Surprising sometimes."

I dismounted after a little while, because it felt strange to be riding while Karsh walked beside me. We did not speak until we were close enough to the inn to hear cocks crowing, the outside pump squeaking, and Gatti Jinni wailing to heaven about something or other. I said, "My true name is Vand." Karsh tried it over once or twice, without expression. I said, "You can go on calling me Rosseth, if you like, until I leave. It doesn't make any difference."

Karsh shook his head. "It matters," he grunted. "Vand. If that's your name, that's your name. Vand." Tunzi smelled breakfast, and began to walk faster.